THE SINS OF

THE MOTHER

www.daniellesteel.com

DANIELLE STEEL

THE SINS OF THE MOTHER

CORGI BOOKS

TRANSWORLD PUBLISHERS
61–63 Uxbridge Road, London W5 5SA
A Random House Group Company
www.transworldbooks.co.uk

THE SINS OF THE MOTHER
A CORGI BOOK: 9780552159067
9780552159074

First published in Great Britain
in 2012 by Bantam Press
an imprint of Transworld Publishers
Corgi edition published 2013

MIX
Paper from
responsible sources
FSC® C016897

Typeset in 12/15.5pt AGaramond by Falcon Oast Graphic Art Ltd.
Printed and bound in Great Britain by Clays Ltd, St Ives plc

2 4 6 8 10 9 7 5 3 1

To my beloved children,
Beatrix, Trevor, Todd, Nick,
Sam, Victoria, Vanessa, Maxx, and Zara,

May you find jobs and careers that
excite you and reward you,

May you find partners who treat you
with love and respect and support you
in all your endeavors,
and enhance your lives,

May you make wise choices,

May you look on those you love
with tenderness, forgiveness (above all),
and compassion,
and may they do the same for you,

May your children delight and appreciate you,

May the best in life be yours,
And may you always be greatly loved,
as much as I love you.

                              with all my love,
                                   Mommy/d.s.

THE SINS OF
THE MOTHER

Chapter 1

Olivia Grayson sat in the chairman's seat at the board meeting, listening intently to the presentations, her intense blue eyes taking in each member of the board. Her eyes were quick and sharp. She was totally still, wearing a well-cut navy blue pantsuit, and a string of pearls around her neck. Her hair was a sleek bob, cut to the level of her jawbone just below her ears. It was the same snow-white color it had been since her early thirties. She was one of those striking women you would notice in any room. She was timeless, ageless, with high cheekbones and an angular face, and elegant hands as she held a pen poised above her notepad. She always took notes at the meetings, and had a flawless memory of what went on, in what order, and everything that was said. Her keen mind and sharp business sense had won her the reputation for being brilliant, but more than anything she was practical and had an innate, unfailing sense of what was right for her company. She had turned the profitable hardware store her mother had inherited years before into a model for international operations on a mammoth scale.

The Factory, as they had renamed it when it moved from its original storefront in a suburban locale outside Boston to an old empty factory building, was an astounding success, and Olivia Grayson along with it. She was the image of power as she presided over the board meeting. She was strong, innovative, and creative, and had started working at The Factory after school when she was twelve.

Her mother had been the daughter of a genteel family of Boston bankers who had lost everything during the Depression. Maribelle Whitman went to work as a secretary in a law firm, and married a young insurance salesman, who got drafted into the army after Pearl Harbor, and was sent to England in the summer of 1942, four weeks after their daughter, Olivia, was born. He was killed in a bombing raid when she was a year old. As a young widow, Maribelle moved to a modest suburb of Boston, and went to work for Ansel Morris at the hardware store, to support her daughter. For fourteen years, she helped him grow his business, had a discreet and loving affair with him, expected nothing from him, and brought up her daughter on the salary she made. And when she unexpectedly inherited his fortune, Maribelle wanted nothing more than to send Olivia to college, but Olivia had a thirst for business and no interest in college and academic pursuits. She had a passion and a love for commerce that drove her to take risks and make bold moves, and each decision she made catapulted the business forward to unexpected places and dizzying heights. Despite her youth, she made few mistakes, and had an instinct that proved her right every time. She had had the respect and admiration of her colleagues and competitors for years. Olivia was an icon in the business world.

And when Olivia went to work at The Factory full time, at eighteen, straight out of high school, three years after Ansel died, her visions had transformed the local hardware business into something her mother, and surely he, had never dreamed of. Her mother was running it then, Ansel was gone. And Olivia convinced her mother to add low-cost furniture with simple modern designs, not just the basic, ordinary items The Factory had sold until then. Olivia had added a fresh look and the excitement of youth. She brought a new design aspect, at low prices, to their merchandise. They bought bathroom fixtures from foreign suppliers, modern kitchen cabinetry, and appliances. Within a short time they were as well known for their innovative international designs as the reliability of their products, at astoundingly reasonable rates. Olivia used volume to their advantage, and kept their prices lower than anyone else's. Her mother had been worried about it at first, but time had proven Olivia right. Her instincts had been flawless.

Fifty-one years later, at sixty-nine, Olivia Grayson had created an empire that had reached around the world, and an industry that no one could compete with, although many tried. By the time she was twenty-five, Olivia had become a legend, and The Factory along with her, with its reputation for creative designs for anything for the home, from tools to kitchens and furniture, at rock-bottom cost. There was nothing for the home you couldn't buy at The Factory, and she traveled constantly to find new suppliers, products, and designs. Her empire was still growing, and her reputation along with it.

Remarkably, there was nothing harsh in her face as she sat in the familiar chair at the board meeting, flanked by her sons on either side. Both had joined the business, fresh out of business school in Phillip's case, and after getting a master of fine arts and graphic design in John's.

Olivia's mother had long since retired. The Factory was

a product of Olivia's genius, and the enormous fortune she had made from it was her legacy to her children. She had worked a lifetime for what she'd built. Olivia was the embodiment of the American dream.

Although she wielded enormous power and her eyes were sharp, there was something gentle about her face. She was a woman everyone took seriously, yet she was quick to laugh. A discreet woman, she knew when to speak. And she listened carefully to fresh ideas, which then spurred her on to new creations, and even now she was always seeking to stretch The Factory into additional places and to greater heights than it had ever been before. She didn't rest on her laurels, and her passion and main interest was continuing to make her business grow. She still had the same excitement about it she'd had in her youth.

There were six members of the board, in addition to Olivia and her two sons, Phillip and John. She was the chairman and CEO, and Phillip was the CFO. He had his father's steady head for finance and had come to the company from Harvard Business School after he earned his MBA with honors. He was a quiet person, more like his father than his mother. Each of her sons had inherited a facet of her abilities, but neither combined them as a whole. John, her third-born child, was head of creative and design. John was an artist and had studied fine arts at Yale. Painting was his first love, but devotion to his mother had driven him into the business at an early age. Olivia had always known that with his artistic sense and training in design, he had much to offer them. He was more gregarious than his older brother and resembled his mother in many ways, although the money side of the business was a mystery to him. He lived for aesthetics, and the beauty he saw in the world. And he still spent all his free time painting on weekends. He was an artist above all.

At forty-six, Phillip was as serious and solid as his father had been. Phillip's father, Joe, had been an accountant and had helped Olivia run the business, quietly from behind the scenes. Phillip had inherited his financial accuracy and reliability, and none of his mother's creative spirit and fire.

John had inherited Olivia's innate artistic sense for design, and at forty-one, as an artist, he constantly brought new life visually into what they offered the world. He had enormous talent that he had funneled into The Factory, while dreaming of painting full time. Both men were essential to the business, but its life force was still their mother, even at sixty-nine. The Factory was still a family-held business, although they had had frequent opportunities to sell it and go public over the years. Olivia wouldn't think of it, although Phillip had been sorely tempted by some of the offers they'd had in recent years. Olivia insisted that The Factory was theirs, with its many stores around the world, and she intended to keep it that way.

Their enterprise was booming and continuing to grow exponentially. And as long as she was alive, she intended to see to it that there were Graysons at its helm. Her two daughters had no interest in the business, but she knew that her two sons would run it one day, and she had prepared them well. Together, she felt certain, they would be able to maintain the empire she had built, and she was nowhere near ready to retire or step down. Olivia Grayson was still in full swing, running The Factory and traveling around the world, just as she had done for almost fifty-two years. She showed no sign of slowing down, her ideas were as astounding and innovative as ever, and she looked ten years younger than her age. She was a naturally beautiful woman, with a passion for life, and ten times the energy of people half her age.

With her usual quiet, orderly style, she brought the board meeting to a close shortly after noon. They had covered all the matters on their agenda, including Olivia's concerns about some of the factories they were using in

India and China. Phillip's main concern was their bottom line, which was healthier than ever. The products they sold at incredibly low prices were making them a fortune and were being distributed by The Factory around the world.

Olivia always wanted to know that their factories' practices were sound. And Phillip had assured them all again that morning that although they couldn't know everything about their Asian factories, they were using a reliable industrial investigative firm, and all appeared to be in good order. And the prices they were paying were leaving them the profit margins they had benefited from for years. Theirs was a model that their competitors envied and never succeeded in matching. Olivia had a magic touch.

John had also introduced a series of new designs that morning that they all knew would be snapped up by their customers in the coming months. The Factory was ahead of every trend, with sure instincts about what would sell and what their customers wanted, even before they knew it themselves. John had an unfailing sense for shape, design, and color. The combination they offered of low prices and high design, for items their clients were begging for, was unbeatable. They created a need and then filled it. The Factory leaped ahead financially every year.

The empire Olivia had founded was rock solid. And she knew her late husband, Joe, would have been proud of her, just as he had been in his lifetime. He had been the perfect mate for her. And he hadn't been surprised or critical when the business they grew together kept her from spending time with him or their children. They both knew it was inevitable that she'd be busy, especially when she was traveling, and even when she was at home. Joe had made up for it, with his more predictable schedule and less demanding financial duties in the firm. Trained as an accountant, he had been their chief financial officer until he died and Phillip stepped into his shoes. Olivia's mother, Maribelle, had retired from the business to take care of Olivia's children, shortly after Phillip was born, and that role suited her much better, and was less stressful for her. The business in Olivia and Joe's hands had long since outgrown her by then. Olivia had been the driving force of The Factory, and shouldered the responsibility with ease, despite the time it ultimately cost her with her children. She had tried to make it up to them as she got older, particularly in the last fourteen years since her husband's sudden death at sixty. He had died of a heart attack while she was away visiting new factories in the Philippines.

Joe's death had been a terrible blow to Olivia and their

children. Since then she had been more attentive to them, and made a point of taking her children and grandchildren on a vacation together every year. She loved them, and always had, and her husband, but she loved the business too. The Factory was her passion and her life. It was an all-consuming eternal flame that devoured her and sustained her. Joe had understood that and never minded, and her children also knew it, although some were more accepting of it than others.

Their senior house counsel, Peter Williams, had been at the board meeting that morning, to discuss some of the issues that Phillip had raised, about what the financial impact would be if they ever decided to shift from factories in Asia to different, more transparent ones in Europe. They all knew it could hit their bottom line unfavorably, and Phillip didn't recommend it. Olivia had wanted their senior lawyer at the meeting. And Peter had voiced his usual carefully measured and wisely weighed opinions. She sought his advice on many subjects, and he always counseled her sagely. He was conservative by nature, but always practical in his suggestions, and he was creative in helping them find solutions to sometimes dicey legal issues. And inevitably there were some, in an enterprise as vast as theirs. He had enormous respect for Olivia, and had devoted the lion's share of his time to The Factory for nearly twenty years. He never objected to the long hours he had to spend on it, the sacrifices he had to make, or its impact on his personal life. He had always been fascinated by the business, and the woman who ran it, and deeply impressed by her.

'What did you think of the meeting?' Olivia asked him as they waited at the elevator together. Phillip and John were still in the boardroom, and she had to get back to her office. Peter was heading back to his, a dozen blocks away. But as The Factory was his biggest client, he was at its main offices frequently. Olivia had moved the head-quarters to New York from the outskirts of Boston forty years before. Her children had grown up in New York. Once they had opened branches in New Jersey, Chicago, and Connecticut, and on Long Island, New York was a more reasonable location for them than a sleepy suburb outside Boston. When they added the South, Midwest, and the West Coast, and eventually expanded their inter-national operation, being based in New York made even more sense. Their offices filled an entire building on Park Avenue, and they had warehouses all across the country, and in Asia, South America, and Europe. Their stores had been international for thirty years. Olivia had been faith-ful to their old locations and maintained them but had added countless new ones. Worldwide, they now had close to a hundred stores, and every one of them was profitable and booming.

Olivia had made few mistakes over the years, and corrected them rapidly when she did.

'I thought Phillip brought up some valid points,' Peter answered her as they got in the elevator together, and she pressed the button for her office floor. Phillip and John's offices were on the same floor as hers. 'I think we're keeping a close eye on any potential trouble spots. That's all you can do for now,' Peter reassured her.

'I don't want to use factories with questionable practices.' She echoed what she had said in the meeting, which was a mantra for her. She had a powerful social conscience that was in operation at all times. She had a strong sense of morality, as well as a good head for business. She was an ethical woman, with a kind heart.

'I don't think there's anything to worry about, that we know of. And we're keeping our eyes and ears wide open,' Peter said firmly.

'Are you comfortable?' she asked Peter directly with her piercing blue eyes. Nothing escaped Olivia's notice – it was one of the many things he admired about her. And she never sacrificed her ethics for the bottom line.

'Yes, I am comfortable,' Peter said honestly.

'Good. You're my barometer, Peter,' she said with a small smile. 'When you're not comfortable about our factories, that's when I'll start to worry.' It was an impressive compliment coming from her.

'I'll let you know if anything changes. I believe that our sources are keeping us well informed. Do you have time for a quick lunch before we both go back to work?' She knew that he worked as hard as she did, and had as little idle time. They enjoyed talking business together and catching up on each other's news. Peter was sixty-three years old, married, with a grown son and daughter, and had had a rewarding career. They had fought many battles for The Factory side by side, and won.

'I can't,' she said regretfully. 'I have an interview with *The New York Times* at one-thirty, and a mountain on my desk to deal with before that.' She dreaded the day he would retire. She relied heavily on his advice and clear-headed analysis of situations, and valued his friendship. She trusted him more than anyone else. And fortunately, he was vital and in good health and had no plans to retire for now.

'I would tell you that you work too hard, but I'd be wasting my time,' he said with a rueful smile, and she laughed as the elevator stopped on her floor.

'Tell that to yourself,' she said with a wave, as she

got out, and the elevator doors stood open for a minute.

'When are you leaving on vacation?' he called after her, and she turned back as she answered.

'Not for another six weeks, in July.' He knew about the birthday trip she took with her children every year. Each time she chose a different spectacular venue to entice them and entertain them. It was a tradition she had started after her husband died, and she knew Joe would have approved. It was something she did to try and make up to them for the father they had lost, and the time she hadn't spent with them when they were young. She knew she couldn't make up for lost time, but the trips she arranged for them were wonderful for all of them, and she put a lot of thought and effort into it every year. She considered it a sacred time.

She waved to him and hurried back to her office just as the elevator doors closed. It was nearly twelve-thirty, and she had an hour before the reporter from *The New York Times* arrived. She had already asked her assistant to provide a salad for her at her desk. She didn't want to waste any time. She often did that or skipped lunch, which gave her the still-lithe, girlish figure other women envied and admired. It contributed to her looking younger than her age, along with her youthful, surprisingly unlined face. She never thought about her looks.

Peter had reminded her of something with his question about her trip, and she stopped to speak to her assistant, Margaret, on her way back to her office.

'Did the e-mails go out this morning about the trip?'

'I sent them at ten o'clock this morning. And your lunch is waiting on your desk, with your messages and your call list.' She was planning to have her own lunch at her desk as well. She knew how busy Olivia was on the days that they held board meetings. Olivia would spend the rest of the day trying to catch up, and probably work late that night. Margaret was prepared to do the same. She never begrudged Olivia the time, and arranged her personal life accordingly. Her dedication to Olivia came first. Olivia inspired those who worked for her to work as hard as she did herself. They found her energy exciting.

Olivia thanked her and walked into her large, elegantly appointed office. Everything in the room was light, airy, and beige. There were contemporary paintings on the walls, some of them by her son, and a handmade beige silk rug she'd had made in Italy. It was a pleasant place to work, and there were a couch and several chairs in one corner. It was where she would conduct the interview in an hour. It was for the business section of *The New York Times*. She was being interviewed by a young reporter she hadn't met before. Margaret had already given her a sheet with his credentials and his background. He sounded relatively harmless to Olivia, although a little green. But she had profound respect for youth, and always valued a fresh perspective and new ideas.

She loved talking to her grandchildren for that reason, and having them on the summer trip with her. It was a time she cherished with them every year, as much as she did with her own children. She hoped they'd all be excited by the trip she'd planned for them this year. It sounded like it was going to be one of their best. In her mind, it was an invitation, and in theirs it was a command performance. They knew she expected them to be there, and her invitations were always hard to resist.

The next hour flew by, as Olivia returned dozens of calls and responded to several e-mails herself. She didn't have time to touch her salad before Margaret called on the intercom to tell her the reporter from *The New York Times* had arrived. Olivia told her to bring him into her office, and she stood up to greet him and came around the desk, and led him to the comfortable couch and chairs.

The man who sat down with her and returned her gaze was somewhere in his mid-twenties and was wearing jeans, running shoes, and a T-shirt. His hair was long and wild, and he looked as though he hadn't shaved in several days. It was a familiar look for someone his age. He certainly hadn't dressed for the occasion, and Olivia didn't mind. She was used to earnest young reporters. Most of them looked awestruck or intimidated when they met Olivia, but this one didn't. He began firing questions at her immediately. Olivia was undismayed by his lack of preamble or manners, and answered his questions clearly and directly, with a pleasant expression, undaunted by his style and appearance.

The interview went well for nearly an hour, despite the unbridled frankness of his questions. He asked her some hard questions, and she enjoyed them and had ready answers. And then he broadsided her by touching on the topic of their meeting that morning. He was both alert and well informed, and obviously hoped to hit her Achilles' heel and surprise her. Nothing showed in her face, as she carefully answered him.

'Are you concerned about possible violations of child labor laws in the factories you've used in Asia?'

'We have no proof of that,' she said calmly, 'although we've done extensive research. That's always a subject that concerns me, in any aspect of our business.'

'Don't you think it's fair to assume that in those locations, and at the prices you're paying, there must be violations somewhere along the line?'

'I can't assume anything,' Olivia said quietly. 'We're continuing to explore that possibility on an ongoing basis. We have no evidence of abusive practices from any of our sources.'

'And if you do at some point, then what will you do?'

'Respond appropriately, and take action. We don't support human rights violations,' she assured him. 'Nor child labor law abuses. I have four children and three grandchildren. The plight of children has always been a subject of deep interest to me.'

'Enough to be willing to raise your prices, if you have to change factories? And start buying products at higher rates in Europe?'

'Absolutely,' she said without hesitation. 'The Factory does not support any kind of violation, of children or adults.' He moved off the subject then, satisfied for the moment, but she could tell that he was leery of her, and he had been very aggressive with her. He was skeptical of what she'd told him but had no proof otherwise. There was none to have. The Factory was clean and aboveboard in its dealings, which was a source of great pride to her.

She accorded the young reporter nearly an hour and a half, and then her assistant came in and rescued her, and reminded her of another meeting, which she actually didn't have. But an hour and a half seemed long enough for an interview. He would have stayed all afternoon if she allowed it. And Olivia's time was precious, she had work to do and an empire to run.

They shook hands, and the journalist sauntered out of her office looking as though he owned the world. She sensed that it was all posturing for her benefit, and as soon as the door closed behind him, she called Peter Williams to report to him on the meeting.

'He asked about the child labor law issues at the factories in Asia,' Olivia said, sounding concerned about it, but pleased that they were alert and had raised the issue at the board meeting.

'We have no proof of anything,' Peter reminded her. 'And we're keeping a very, very close watch,' he reassured her.

'You're still not worried?' she asked, checking the barometer again – no one else could advise her as well as he could on this issue. She trusted Peter's judgment completely.

'No, I'm not,' Peter said easily. 'We're clean, Olivia, no matter how hard he tries to scare you. It's a cheap shot. Don't buy into it. We're keeping a very careful eye on the entire situation.'

'We'll see what happens. I hope the article is decent.'

'It will be,' he said kindly. 'How could it be otherwise?'

She laughed at his comment. She knew better than that. The press wasn't always fair, and seldom kind, even to her.

'It could be otherwise, and we both know it,' Olivia reminded him. 'We're just lucky things are going smoothly for the moment. This would be a big headache if it ever went against us.'

'We'll take care of it, if it happens,' he said, sounding unruffled. And she knew he would. He had handled other difficult issues before, strikes in their factories, threatened lawsuits, and all manner of big and small aggravations, which was part of his job. 'Just forget about all this now. We have it all in control. And in six weeks, you'll be on vacation.'

'I can hardly wait,' she admitted to him. She'd worked hard for the past several months, just as she always did. She worked long days, and her travel schedule was brutal. She had a trip to Brazil planned, and another to New Zealand.

'You deserve the time off,' Peter said kindly. Sometimes he wondered how she juggled all that she did, and how she survived the constant stress of her responsibilities. So much was expected of her and rested on her shoulders. And she wore the heavy mantle of her position with patience, fortitude, and grace. He knew what a toll it took on her, but she rarely if ever complained, and the stress never showed on her. She always appeared to be completely in control of any situation. And a few minutes later Olivia went back to work and forgot the interview and the conversation with Peter. All was well. The concern they had about child labor violations in their factories appeared to be unfounded. That's all she needed to know, and if something changed, she'd be the first to react. And Peter Williams knew it as well. Olivia Grayson was a force to be reckoned with, like no other, and God help the person who thought they could put something over on her, and expect her not to respond. That day would never come, no matter what the cost to her. Olivia Grayson was an honorable woman. And for the rest of the afternoon, she worked like a demon at her desk, just as she did every day, and had for nearly fifty-two extra-ordinary years. It was everything she loved best in life. She thrived on hard work and always had. She knew that would never change.

Chapter 2

Olivia had been helping her mother run The Factory for four years, and was twenty-two years old, when Maribelle decided they should bring in a financial adviser to help them manage things. They were growing so rapidly with the changes Olivia had made that Maribelle could no longer handle the books herself. She had hired two more bookkeepers, but Olivia and her mother agreed they needed more than that. Maribelle put out feelers through their bank, and within a short time they recommended a young man from Vermont. Joe Grayson had a bachelor's degree in business and economics and after graduating had become a CPA. He was twenty-seven years old, and seemed far more mature than his age. He was a quiet, solid man, and had been working in the Boston area for a year, doing accounting work for small businesses. The bank manager introduced him to Maribelle, and a week later he was going over their books. And after studying them carefully for a week, he made several suggestions that made sense to her. She hired him immediately, and although he still did work for others, he rapidly became a fixture at The Factory, and was frequently in the offices at the store. He was a pleasant, easygoing young man, with a good head for figures and a practical mind. He was even-tempered and reliable, and Olivia began discussing some of her expansion plans with him, and he gave her good advice. He never just told her what she should be doing, but explained the reasons why, and she began to consult with him more and more.

What she didn't know, as she chatted with him whenever he came by, was that he was absolutely dazzled by her, and in awe of her advanced ideas. He could easily see that with a little careful guidance, she could turn The Factory into a major industry. He was enormously impressed by the soundness and feasibility of her plans, and he showed her how to do what she had in mind. He soon became a valuable member of their team, and Olivia had a deep respect for what he said. He added elements she knew nothing about and taught her a great deal.

And Maribelle noticed long before her daughter how taken Joe Grayson was with her. Maribelle invited him to dinner one night, in order to help things along, and after that he became a frequent guest, staying late at the office, and coming home with them at night for a simple meal. And because of his natural shyness, it took him six months to ask Olivia for a date, and she was startled when he did. She had never thought of him in that way, but only as a co-worker whose sensible suggestions she valued, and she valued his expertise with money. She discussed nearly everything with him by then, and he was always excited and astounded by her plans.

When he took her out to dinner, all they ever talked about was work, which made it even more amazing when he told her one night that he was in love with her. She had never considered that possibility at all, and looked up at him in amazement, but she had no objections to what he said. In fact, she liked the idea. They made an excellent working team, and she knew he cared about The Factory by then almost as much as she did, and they shared many of the same ideals. He was a man of sound morals and good values. He wasn't an exciting person, but she could tell that he was a kind man. He walked her home after dinner that night and kissed her for the first time.

Their courtship wasn't wild or exciting, he didn't sweep her off her feet, but she wouldn't have wanted him to. Olivia was a sensible woman herself, and she preferred the friendship they were building and the easy way they shared whatever was on their minds. Just as she trusted him to handle the money, he was certain that her creative concepts for The Factory were sound, even when they were things that had never been done before. He could see that she was building a model that could serve as a template for many, many stores. Everything she talked about made sense to him, even if it didn't to someone else. They understood each other perfectly, sometimes even without words.

And on Valentine's Day, three months after they had begun dating, he gave her a small diamond ring and asked her to marry him. He had no parents or living family, and all he wanted was to start a life with her. When they told her mother, Maribelle thought it was an excellent idea and she was pleased. Joe Grayson was the perfect man for her daughter. He gave her a solid foundation, and a base she could rely on, while she built her brave new world. Maribelle was thrilled. What Olivia felt for him at first wasn't girlish or romantic, but it was solid and sure, just like his growing love for her.

They were married in a small ceremony, six months

after they started dating, a year after they had met. He quit his other jobs and came to work at The Factory full time, and he laughed when Olivia turned their honeymoon into a buying trip for the store. He took her to Europe on his meager savings, and they went to England, France, and Italy, and spent the last two days in Denmark, to look at Scandinavian furniture designs. Olivia had placed several orders, and had found some remarkable things. But the most important thing she had found in her lifetime was her relationship with Joe. It was exactly what they needed and grounded them both. It gave Joe a warmth and affection he had never had, and Olivia a solid man she could rely on. Other than Ansel Morris, there had never been a male figure in her life. And she knew Joe was the right one for her.

Olivia came home from their honeymoon ecstatic about what they'd seen in Europe, and energized by her plans for the store. She was even more excited when the goods they'd ordered began arriving, and opened many of the crates herself. She and Joe went over the new inventory together at night. He was tireless in his desire to help her in every way he could. Things had been going so well that Olivia was dismayed when she began feeling sick. She had no idea what it was, but in a short time she was feeling seriously ill, and Joe was deeply concerned.

He consulted her mother, and thought Olivia should get to a doctor as soon as possible. He took her to a doctor a friend had recommended in Boston, and Olivia was even more upset when she found out what it was. She had gotten pregnant on their honeymoon, which had not been in her plans. Joe had talked longingly about having children, but they had both agreed that they wanted to wait several years, Olivia thought at least five, until she implemented everything she had in mind for The Factory's expansion, got the business firmly on its feet, and maybe opened one or two new stores. She had no time for a baby now and cried when she heard the news. She thought a baby would ruin everything. And in spite of his sympathy for her, Joe was utterly and totally thrilled. He couldn't think of anything more wonderful than having a child with her. Olivia was the woman of his dreams, and he promised to do everything he could to make it as easy as possible for her, and then Maribelle stepped in with an irresistible idea. She said she was ready to retire and leave the business in their hands. They were both far more knowledgeable than she was anyway, and she had contributed very little to the business in recent years. And Joe had the business end of it in full control. They no longer needed her, except to care for their child.

Maribelle offered to move in with them and take care

of the baby. Olivia was overjoyed at the idea. She knew the baby would be in good hands, and she and Joe could go on working full time. And Joe was insistent that he would do everything he could to help, so that Olivia would be free to work. It was the perfect solution and made having a baby sooner than they planned far less upsetting for her. And Maribelle was thrilled. Taking care of their baby seemed like much more fun to her than working at the store. She'd been doing that for years, and it had outgrown her by leaps and bounds, thanks to Olivia and Joe.

As far as Olivia was concerned, this was no time for her to stay home. The changes she wanted to implement were crucial to the business and couldn't wait.

She worked right up until the last day of her pregnancy, and she and Joe were going over accounts and inventory in the office late at night when her water broke. And for a moment, Olivia was scared. It was happening. It was real. He reassured her immediately, calmed her down, called her mother and the doctor, and drove her to the hospital. He hated to leave her, but they wouldn't let him attend the birth. Instead, he sat in the waiting room for twelve hours, while Maribelle came to see him from time to time, to let him know how things were going. She said that first babies were always slow, but Olivia was doing well. He was worried sick about her, and hoped it wouldn't be too hard for her. He was deeply in love with her by then, and excited about their firstborn.

And for Olivia, it was rougher than she'd planned or known it would be. She would have been even more frightened than she'd already been, if she had known how painful it would be. Phillip weighed just over nine pounds, and she looked exhausted and in pain when Joe saw her at last, moments after the birth. He had never loved her more, and their baby was the most beautiful sight he'd ever seen. They had both cried when they saw him and Joe held the baby for the first time. It seemed like a miracle to him, but to her, it was the hardest thing she'd ever done. But by the next day, she had begun recovering and thought the baby was very sweet. She nursed him for the first few days, and then they switched him to a bottle, so Maribelle would be able to feed him at night. Joe didn't want Olivia exhausted, and from what he could tell, she had been through enough of an ordeal, and he treated Olivia like hand-blown glass when he took her and the baby home after a week. She insisted that she was feeling fine by then. She was twenty-three years old, and both she and the baby were healthy and strong.

Maribelle got Phillip on a schedule immediately, never let him out of her arms, and fussed over him constantly.

And the moment she set him down, his doting father picked him up. Olivia had barely had time to bond with him when she went back to The Factory in another week. She worked half days until Phillip was a month old, and then she went back full time. Joe thought it was a little soon, and he wanted her to regain her strength, but he knew how anxious she was to be in the store, and he didn't have the heart to object. He shortened his own days to go home to their son, allegedly to give Maribelle a break, but in truth because he wanted to be with Phillip himself.

Phillip was a happy, easy baby, with a father and grand-mother who doted on him and catered to his every need and whim. And when Olivia came home at night, she took turns with them holding him. She still couldn't believe that she and Joe had a baby. He felt like someone else's to her, but by the time he was six months old, Phillip's face lit up every time he saw his mother, and sometimes Maribelle brought him to the store in the pram to visit his proud parents. Joe showed Phillip off to everyone. He had been born to be a parent, which wasn't true of Olivia, but she was a very loving mother, even if she wasn't around all the time. Her main focus was still the store. She was implementing all her plans, and had new ones every day. Joe could hardly keep up with her, and he couldn't tell who he loved more, his wife or their baby. He was a profoundly happy man. And their arrangement with Maribelle taking care of Phillip had worked out ideally for all three of them. Maribelle enjoyed caring for her grandson more than she had working at the store. She was only forty-eight years old, and thrilled to have retired, particularly for such a happy cause. And Joe was the perfect partner for Olivia, and the visions she had for the store.

He had suggested that she phase out basic hardware and tools by then, and that they concentrate on the items Olivia had selected that were selling well. He knew from their spreadsheets and constantly growing profits just how brilliant Olivia was. He knew genius when he saw it. And he was teaching her more and more about finance.

She was quick to learn. And Olivia had an ever-growing respect for his judgment, practical mind, and advice. And he was wonderful to her and their son. She couldn't have wished for more. Their marriage had been the best decision she'd made so far.

Shortly after Phillip's birth, Olivia decided to open a second store. Joe was worried about it at first and didn't want them to overextend themselves, and then as usual, he realized she was right. They launched it within six months, at a location on Long Island, and then a third store, in New Jersey, when Phillip was a year old. He had his first birthday at the inauguration of the new store. That night she told Joe she wanted to start a store in Chicago, and he knew there was no stopping her or slowing her down. She was on a roll, but he also knew she was right and this was their time. In each location she had found an old factory similar to the one they had near Boston, their flagship store.

And by the time the plans for the Chicago store were well under way and they had found the right location, Olivia was pregnant again. She wasn't as upset about it as she'd been before, since Maribelle said she'd be happy to take care of both children. It had worked out so well having her take care of Phillip, and Joe spent a great deal of time with him too, which was fortunate since Olivia was always running between the three stores they had. She had an instinctive sense for everything that went into the home, and a knack for finding reliable suppliers at rock-bottom prices, who were willing to follow her suggestions about design. They were growing by leaps and bounds, and so was she.

She was nine months pregnant when they opened in Chicago, and Joe was terrified she'd give birth at the opening or on the train, but she insisted she had to be there. It was the biggest store they had so far, and an overnight success. Business was already booming when they left the next day to go back to Boston, while Joe insisted she lie down the entire way and not move. He didn't want to have to deliver their baby on the train on their way home. He thought she was crazy to have come. But she was young and strong and excited about what they were doing. They had opened three new stores in two years, and they were making more money than Joe had ever dreamed they could. Olivia had made no mistakes so far, and he didn't think she would.

She went into labor the night they got home, and he got her to the hospital just in time. Liz was smaller than her brother had been, and was born two hours after they got to the hospital, and it was easier for Olivia than Phillip's birth. She was beaming, holding their baby girl, when Joe walked into the room. They named her Elizabeth for his late mother, whom Olivia had never met. And, two weeks later, Olivia was back at work full time. And Maribelle loved having a granddaughter to look after too, and a new baby in the house. It was a happy moment in all their lives. And it was almost as though motherhood had made Olivia more creative than ever. Joe could only marvel at what she'd done and was planning to do.

She began traveling more then, on buying trips for all

four stores, or in search of new designs. Joe missed her when she was gone, but the result of what she was doing showed up steadily on their balance sheets. Olivia never got to spend as much time with him and their children as she would have liked, but she kept telling him and herself that things would slow down to a dull roar soon, and a more manageable pace, but they never did. She was busier than ever, although she enjoyed being at home with him and the children whenever she could. But she was making millions, and Joe was investing it as fast as he could. Thanks to Olivia, their future, and that of their children, was assured. It was important to him as well as to her. She was building a fortune that would benefit all of them for many years. The Factory had become a legend, and Olivia Grayson along with it. His name was famous now too.

Olivia was never afraid to try something new or take risks, as long as Joe approved of what she did. She did nothing without his advice. And he even approved of her many trips. She never left town without consulting him, but he respected what she needed to do to maintain and improve on what they'd built. And if she wasn't able to be with the children as much as she would have liked, Maribelle and Joe covered the bases for her. As far as they could see, their system worked, and Phillip and Liz were happy children, thriving on the love of three people instead of two. And they never seemed unhappy when their mother was out of town or at work. When that was the case, Maribelle and Joe met all their needs. They were constantly being loved, pampered, or held, even if Olivia wasn't there to do it. It made her sad sometimes to miss important moments with them. She hadn't been there when Liz took her first steps, or for her first tooth, but she was doing something important for them too, assuring their life and well-being in the years ahead.

They had opened four more stores, and had eight in all, when John was born three years later. They barely made it to the hospital in time for him. Olivia had been watching them inventory new merchandise that she had designed herself, and she missed all the early signs of labor. Joe rushed her to the hospital when she suddenly doubled over, and John was born in the elevator on the way to the delivery room. Joe teased her about it later, as he held his second son.

'I don't know what you're better at, Olivia Grayson, having babies, or running a business. You're mighty good at both.' John had been a beautiful child and looked a lot like his mother. He was peaceful and lay in his father's arms with an angelic look. And when Joe handed him back to her, he nestled happily at her breast. Phillip was five by then, and Liz was three, and Maribelle was delighted to take care of all three of them, and did it with ease. Olivia and John hired a housekeeper to help her, and a cook, and Joe left work early to lend a hand whenever he could. Olivia never seemed to be able to get out of the store till dinnertime, but she was religious about getting home before they went to bed. And putting them to bed herself was a sacred ritual to her, except when she was traveling, which was happening more and more. She was responsible about both her family and her work.

Olivia opened their first store abroad in a suburb outside London, followed by a store in Paris, and Dublin opened after that. Two in Germany, and another near Milan. They expanded into Sweden then, at the same time they opened a store in Texas and two on the West Coast. Olivia had been on the covers of *Time*, *Business Week*, and *Fortune* by then. She had become one of the most important women in business in the United States. She wasn't arrogant or showy; she was smart, brave, and practical, and her visions for the future had no limits. She dreamed of setting up stores based on their successful model around the world. And she managed to keep their quality high, their designs appealing, and their prices on the cutting edge. Ansel Morris's hardware store, expanded into an old factory outside Boston, had become a world event.

Olivia's marriage to Joe remained uneventful and strong. He backed her in everything she did, ran the business side efficiently, and expected very little from her in return. He was just happy to be part of her life, and he was her biggest fan. Her mother scolded her sometimes for not spending more time with her children, but Olivia did the best she could. She loved them unquestionably, but she found business more exciting than motherhood. Joe filled in whenever he could. He and Maribelle took care of the children whenever Olivia was busy, which was most of the time. She traveled constantly. But whenever she was home, she spent her evenings with Joe and the children. She had no hunger for a racy social life, or to show off their wealth. She just enjoyed building their business into an empire, and as a result of her genius in business, their fortune grew exponentially. She talked about their children working with them one day. And never having known her own father, she valued the father that Joe was to their kids. He never missed a Little League game or a school play. He was as solid as a rock for all of them. He was someone she knew she could always depend on. He had never let her down, and she knew he never would.

Olivia thought they had the perfect family. Three children were more than she had ever dreamed of. When Phillip was twelve, Liz ten, and John seven, and Olivia was thinking about opening a store in Australia, she was startled and none too pleased to discover that she was pregnant again. She was just too busy to have a baby, and couldn't imagine how it had happened. But Joe was ecstatic when she told him, and he said he wanted another little girl. Olivia was thirty-six by then, and Maribelle was sixty-one, but said she was willing to take care of another baby. She was totally devoted to her grandchildren, and at times more of a mother to them than Olivia was herself. She was away so much of the time, and constantly visiting their stores.

Cassandra was born seven months later. This time it was a difficult birth, she was born by cesarean section, and Olivia's recovery took longer, and she chafed to get back to work. But the baby was exquisite and Joe was thrilled. Olivia had a harder time bonding with her than she had with the others. The pregnancy hadn't been as easy, it had slowed her down more, and the birth had been much harder. Without even realizing it, she resented the time and energy it had taken from her dedication to her business. And she was no longer geared to having a baby. Her first three had been born within five years of each other and were all young together. Cassandra, or Cassie as they called her, had come along later in their lives and didn't fit in as easily as the others. And right from the beginning, she was different. All three of the Grayson children were blonds, and looked like Olivia and Joe. Cassie had jet-black hair and big green eyes and looked like no one anyone could remember. And from the moment she could talk, her first word was 'No!' Maribelle whispered to her son-in-law more than once that Cassie was just like her mother. Olivia had had her own ideas as a child too, but she had been much easier than Cassie, who became the family dissident.

Cassie adored her father, and early on she always complained about how little time their mother spent with them. The others had noticed it too by then, but Olivia had an empire to run, she had to rely on Joe and her mother to do for the children whatever she didn't have the time to do. She tried to be at important events, at school plays and ballet recitals, but it was hard to cover the day to day, and Joe was always better at it, and he never criticized Olivia for the time she didn't spend with them. He understood perfectly what she was trying to do, and what she had done. He knew he could never have done it himself. And he filled in for her whenever, wherever, and however he could. Olivia always said he was a saint. She loved her children, but he was the perfect husband and father.

It was a terrible blow for her when Joe died at sixty, and she was widowed at fifty-five. It was impossible for her to imagine her world without him in it, after thirty-two years together. And she found that the only thing that dulled the pain of the loss was work. She worked harder than ever then. Cassie was already in college, the others were grown and gone, and married, and Liz had children of her own. They didn't need her as a daily presence anymore. And when Cass left for England, Maribelle moved into a senior residence. She was eighty years old and said that it was time. She had given Olivia a remarkable gift, which Olivia was well aware of. She had brought up her children for her, and had put in thirty years taking care of them so that Olivia could run the business that supported them all. Once Cass moved away, with her mother gone and the emptiness of her life without Joe, Olivia's life became only about work. And the years flew by.

It had been fourteen years since Joe's death, and now what Olivia looked forward to every year were the brief two weeks she spent on vacation with her children every summer. She had missed so much of their childhood that what she treasured now was the time she spent with them as adults. It was too late for her to repair the damage with Cass. Cassie wouldn't let her mother do that, and had put an unbridgeable distance between them ever since her father's death. He was still sorely missed by all. He had been such a good man, and a kind one, that Olivia's heart still ached whenever she thought of him. Olivia knew just how lucky she had been to be married to him, and she was well aware of the blessings he had bestowed upon her life.

Olivia had started their annual vacations in order to mend her bridges with her children, ever since Joe had died. It wasn't enough, she knew, to compensate for what she hadn't done before. She hadn't realized at the time that while she had been assuring their future, she had been missing so much of the present and past. She knew that no matter how hard you tried, you just couldn't do it all. Joe, until the very end, thought that Olivia could do no wrong. And Olivia knew how lucky she had been to have the love of a good man such as Joe. She had always loved him and their kids even if she was away a lot. Joe understood that. Not all her children did.

Olivia was still trying to make up to her children for the important moments she had missed when they were young. Her mother said they would forgive her one day, but she was beginning to wonder if that was possible. You couldn't give someone back the time you had taken from them early on. All she could do now was try. She had always been honest with them. She had loved them, and she loved them now as adults, probably more than they realized or could understand. And some of them were more forgiving than others. Liz had done somersaults for her approval, although she had it anyway. And John didn't seem to hold the past against her. Phillip kept her at a distance, and she knew that Cass would never forgive her for her sins, particularly for not being there when Joe died.

And in the final accounting, who was to say who was right and who was wrong? Olivia couldn't help wondering how different it might have been if she had stopped working when the children were born, if they would have been happier, or if having her mother and Joe there for them had been enough. They would never know. Their life would have been simpler certainly, but maybe the empire she had built for them mattered to them less than she hoped. You couldn't turn back the clock. She had done the best she could, and she still did, maintaining the business for them, and providing them with special moments and memorable summer trips. And she hoped that on the fabulous yacht she had chartered for them this year, it would be the best trip of all. One could only hope.

And she knew that what she would leave them one day, built on more than fifty years of her hard work, would sustain them, and their children's children, for generations to come. It was her gift to them as much as her love, whether they understood that and forgave her failings and her sins, or not. The business she had built for them had been an expression of her love. The die had been cast in the decisions she had made fifty years before. Olivia still couldn't believe how fast the time had flown.

Chapter 3

In recent years Olivia's invitations to her children for their family vacation had come by e-mail, roughly six weeks before the trip. They always knew it was coming, and that it would be in the last two weeks of July, ending with her birthday on the last night. That much was predictable. What they didn't know, and what she surprised them with every year, was the location. It was always someplace fabulous, and Olivia worked hard to come up with an unusual venue that everyone would love.

She wanted it to be a place and a trip that her children would remember for ever. At one time it had had to be suitable for small children, when her grandchildren were younger. Now they had reached a reasonable age, from late teens to mid-twenties, when they could enjoy the same type of location as the adults, but it had to be lively enough to amuse everyone, and not just a peaceful place to provide rest for the grown-ups. It also had to offer fishing for her sons, who were addicts of the sport, and Phillip was fond of playing golf whenever possible. Both he and John loved sailing, a passion shared by their father when they were boys. They had gone to sailing camp as kids. The vacation had to be in a place that the women in the group would enjoy – her daughters, daughters-in-law, and granddaughters – and she wanted to relax and have fun too, so that ruled out rigorous trips like trekking in Nepal. She always opted for luxury over adventure. Whatever their qualms about vacationing as a family, Olivia tried to come up with a trip that would incorporate everyone's needs and desires, accommodate their quirks, and still any fears they might have about spending close to two weeks under one roof together. It was an interesting challenge, and she always wanted it to be special, and an unforgettable holiday for them all. It was something she could do for them.

The first year, she had rented a château in France, fully staffed, in Périgord. It had been beautiful beyond belief, with picturesque terrain and vineyards, and excellent horseback riding nearby in Dordogne. Her grandchildren had been little then, and they had loved it too. There had

been a spectacular villa in St. Tropez complete with
speedboats and a private beach; a fabulous estate in Spain;
and a private island in Greece that had been a major hit.
There had been a famous house in St. Jean Cap Ferrat
that later sold for seventy-five million dollars, a Schloss in
Austria, a private island in the Caribbean that had been
hot but fabulous, and a Vanderbilt mansion in Newport.
Olivia never disappointed them, and she hoped not to
this year either. The location she ultimately selected, after
nearly a full year of research, was always a secret until they
got the invitation on the first of June.

As Amanda Grayson, Phillip's wife, opened the e-mail
early in the morning, she was the first to see this year's
location. It was the three-hundred-foot motor yacht *Lady
Luck*, built two years before, anchored in Monaco, and
they would be cruising the Mediterranean in Italy
and France. The boat included every imaginable luxury
and comfort, including a gym, a spa, a movie theater, and
a hair salon, complete with trainers and attendants, and a
crew of twenty-four, and all kinds of water toys, from jet
skis to sailboats to speedboats to delight the children.
Olivia had outdone herself.

Amanda sat expressionlessly, as she read down the
list of what was included on the boat. It was a trip
she resigned herself to every year. As Olivia was her

mother-in-law, and her husband's employer, Amanda viewed her invitation as a command performance. And however luxurious it was, it was still two weeks on holiday with her extremely powerful, successful mother-in-law. Amanda would have preferred a trip alone with Phillip. But Phillip liked the family vacation, especially spending time with his siblings, and even Amanda had to admit that the *Lady Luck* looked spectacular.

As she read through the e-mail, with her mother-in-law's note of invitation, Amanda started thinking about the wardrobe she would need. She knew that her sister-in-law Liz would share a trendy wardrobe with her daughters, who seemed to dress out of one suitcase, even if the clothes looked too young on Liz, but she had a good body and could get away with it. John's wife looked like the college professor she was, no matter what she wore. Her wardrobe always looked like hand-me-downs from her students. And Olivia would wear linen dresses, colorful silks, and Lilly Pulitzer. She was well dressed and age appropriate but never showy.

Olivia's interests lay in business and not fashion. She was far more avant-garde in the furniture designs she chose than in her wardrobe. Her hair would be perfectly cut before the trip, in her signature snow-white bob, and she would wear the string of pearls Joe had given her to mark the early success of their business, which she had never stopped wearing since, out of sentiment. She still wore her narrow gold wedding ring fourteen years after his death, and other than that, simple earrings, and a gold bracelet she wore every day. It was all very modest. But if Amanda was going to go on vacation in fabulous locations against her will, she was going to dress for the occasion, not the company at hand.

None of the Graysons felt a need to show off or be pretentious, which Amanda never understood. With the kind of money they had, why not spend it? It was an art she'd been teaching Phillip since they had married nineteen years before. She was forty-four years old, and they had met when Phillip was at Harvard Business School getting his MBA, and she was at Harvard Law. Amanda was unashamedly ambitious about her career. They had married when she graduated, and she immediately joined a prestigious law firm. She rose to the top quickly, and had been a partner for a dozen years. She made an excellent living on her own, but she would never make the kind of money that Phillip would inherit one day and had at his disposal now. His father had invested conservatively and brilliantly and set up trust funds for the children. Phillip's siblings lived comfortably though modestly, and their mother had a handsome house on an estate in Bedford, but they were not given to random displays of money, unless they had some purpose, like an important charitable donation.

Amanda had been working on Phillip for years to enjoy his money. They had bought a town house in the East Seventies, and she had filled it with beautiful antiques, many of which they had bought in London. And Phillip had a small but elegant sailboat that he kept at a yacht club in Southampton, where they had a small house. Their careers were the main focus of their lives, Amanda was deeply concerned with their social life, and they had no children. She had told him right from the beginning that children would distract them from their goals and sap their funds and energy. She didn't want them and had convinced Phillip he didn't either. More important, she said they didn't need them, they had each other and a wonderful life. What more could they want? Children would only be an interference.

Phillip had no regrets about not having children. His sister Cass had had none either, for the same reasons he hadn't. Their memories of their childhood were of being deprived of their mother. He had no desire to do that to someone else, and Amanda had no urge to be a mother and never had. It wasn't in her DNA, nor in his. There was an icy coolness to her that Phillip had always found enticing. Her seeming lack of emotion, on every subject except her own career, was a challenge to him. He wasn't overtly emotional or demonstrative either, but he had moments of deep affection for Amanda, which she rarely reciprocated. She was the original ice maiden, and when he'd met them, her parents were no different. They were distant, ambitious, self-centered people. Both her parents were attorneys. And they were very impressed with Phillip's fortune and the business he would one day inherit.

Amanda longed for Phillip to run everything himself, and it irked her that Olivia had no desire to step down and retire, and leave the empire to her oldest son. Olivia was still very much in control, as Amanda saw it, not only of The Factory, but of her children as well. All Amanda wanted was for Phillip to take over, and instead he was content to stand behind his mother quietly, in his role as CFO. Unlike Amanda, he had no hunger for the lime-light. Amanda accused him often of being 'owned' by his mother, which annoyed him, but he had no need or desire to prove her wrong. He was content in his life as it was, and happy to let Amanda run the show at home. She directed their social life and who they saw, and he knew how determined she was to meet important people and ultimately become a judge. Prestige and appearances were important to her, far more than they were to Phillip. He had lived in his mother's shadow for years, and in some ways it suited him. He had no desire to take over, and he didn't want all the headaches that came with being the CEO. He had seen how it had eaten up his mother's life, and how time consuming it was. Instead, he was happy to sail his boat on weekends, or play golf, and leave the office at six o'clock. He didn't want to stay in the office until midnight as his mother often did, or spend his life on planes to other cities and foreign countries, and he knew his brother, John, felt exactly the same way. They knew too well the price you paid for the life their mother led. Amanda considered his lack of hunger for power a major character flaw, and she never let him forget it. They fought about it often, and when she went on a tirade about his mother, he ignored her or went out. He liked his life as it was.

Amanda was tall and stately looking, blond with cool blue eyes and an excellent figure. She went to the gym frequently, except on weekends. She dressed well, and he was happy to pay for it. He liked having a beautiful wife on his arm. And he was well aware that as an only child, she wasn't crazy about his family, and thought both his sisters strange, and his brother negligible as an artist, and his college professor sister-in-law of no interest whatsoever. John's wife, Sarah, didn't play the social game, and was only interested in academia and intellectual pursuits. The only one in the family that Amanda truly admired was his mother, although Amanda had never warmed up to her and didn't really like her, but one had to respect her for turning a hardware store into a world-wide event. Amanda had to give her that. She wished that Phillip were more like her, but neither of Olivia's sons had her ambition. They were much more like their father, who had been content to stay in the background and be part of Olivia's support system. Joe Grayson had never wanted more than that, nor had his boys.

Olivia stood alone in her passionate attack on life, taking the world by the horns with her creative and financial genius. Amanda only wished she had had the opportunities Olivia had. But she benefited now from the name and wasn't shy about using it when it served her. And she was doing all she could to use it to get appointed to the federal bench, which she had been working on for several years. She wanted to be a judge so badly she could taste it, and she used every connection she had to that end. She was always annoyed that Phillip hadn't done more to help her achieve it, but he always insisted that he didn't know the right people to help her. Amanda was certain that her mother-in-law did, but she had never dared to ask her for her assistance, and Olivia had never volunteered. The relationship between the two women had always been civil, but there was no great warmth between them. Amanda loved every opportunity to be in the social columns and the papers. Olivia cared about none of that and was interested only in the business section, where she appeared regularly on the front page. Phillip never did, nor did he care. And it meant nothing to him when Amanda got them in the newspapers at some social event.

'What are you reading so intently?' Phillip asked as he walked into the kitchen, and saw Amanda reading an e-mail with a serious expression, as her coffee grew cold beside her. He helped himself to a cup, and sat down across from her at the kitchen table. As always, she was beautifully put together in a cream-colored linen suit. She was perfectly made up, and had her long, blond hair pulled back. She looked like a model.

'The summer invitation,' she mumbled, as she continued to read about the boat.

'To what?' Phillip asked as he helped himself to a yogurt from the fridge. Amanda didn't cook. She had other things to do with her time and she was always on a diet. She had been to the gym that day, as usual, at six A.M., but it paid off. She had a spectacular figure and, like his mother, looked nowhere near her age. Amanda could have passed for thirty, not the forty-four she was.

'Your mother's birthday trip,' Amanda explained, continuing to read the details about the yacht. She didn't look excited or pleased. She never was about that trip. And she didn't think his nieces and nephew should join them – it was tiring for the adults to have them along. She had particularly disliked it when they were younger. But even now she had nothing to say to them. They and Amanda politely ignored each other on the trip every year, although Phillip sometimes enjoyed them, and liked taking his nephew, Alex, fishing with him and John. It was Phillip's only contact with young people, and Alex was a bright kid. He was a junior in high school, and hoped to go to Stanford, instead of Princeton, where his mother taught literature.

'Where's she taking us this year?' Phillip asked with interest. He enjoyed the vacations with his siblings, in spite of Amanda's complaints about them. He had learned not to pay attention to what she said, since she went anyway. His only regret was that they had done nothing like it when their father was alive and they were young.

There had been family vacations in Maine, but his mother had spent most of the time on the phone to the office, and she and his father had spent the entire time talking business and making plans for new developments she had in mind. It was the only thing that interested her then, or that was how it had felt to Phillip. Olivia just hadn't had time for them when they were young. The mother figure in his life, and that of his siblings, had been his maternal grandmother, Maribelle – Granibelle as they called her. She lived with them and had been ever-present in their daily lives. She and their father had brought them up, Olivia had appeared between trips and when she came home, usually late, from the office. Their father had always insisted to them how much their mother loved them, and maybe she had, but as far as Phillip was concerned, there had been no evidence of it when he was a child.

Phillip was still fiercely devoted to Granibelle, and visited her whenever he could. She had finally retired to a senior residence on Long Island. It was luxurious, and she was comfortable, and seemed content. She had been a happy person all her life. It was what he remembered most about his childhood, the love and joy she had shared with them, and the affection she lavished on them. She still had a twinkle in her eye at ninety-five, and he always teased her and asked her if she had a new beau, which made her laugh. There had been a ninety-two-year-old a few years before who had been very attentive to her, and then he died. But Maribelle was not a sad person. Whatever the circumstances, she had seen the glass as more than half full, even overflowing with blessings. And her four grandchildren had been one of the great joys in her life. Phillip often tried to get Amanda to visit his grandmother with him, but she rarely had time.

She was too busy at the office, not unlike his mother when he was young. And yet Olivia was warmer than Amanda. There was a coolness to Amanda like no other woman Phillip had ever known.

'She's chartered a boat,' Amanda said with a cool expression as she looked up at him.

Phillip raised an eyebrow in surprise. 'That's going to make my sister Liz nervous. I wonder if she'll come. She gets seasick. Mom knows that. I wonder why she picked a boat this time.'

'I don't think she'll get seasick on this,' Amanda said cryptically. 'It's about the size of the *QE2*. It has stabilizers and every possible modern device to provide a smooth ride. It's all in the e-mail,' she said, as Phillip turned the computer so he could see. He glanced at the photographs, and read for a few minutes, and then whistled and looked at Amanda with a grin.

'That's some boat! A crew of twenty-four, spa, hair

salon, movie theater, two sailboats, three speedboats? My mother outdid herself this year. You're right, Liz will be fine. I guess her seventieth birthday is a bigger deal than I thought. Sounds like fun.' Amanda gave him a quelling look, but it didn't dampen his spirits. The boat was fabulous, and he was looking forward to it. And Amanda would warm up to it. She did every year, more or less, depending on the location and how much she liked it. He didn't see how she could resist this. The *Lady Luck* seemed like paradise to him. And he could fish with his brother, and try out the sailboats they carried on the yacht under the list of 'water toys.' Three hundred feet was one hell of a big boat.

'I have nothing to wear,' she said in a chilly tone.

'You never do.' He smiled at her. He heard it every year. Her wardrobe was key to her, and her appearance, and important to her sense of well-being on the trip and in life. 'Go shopping, have some fun,' he encouraged her. He never deprived Amanda of what she wanted. He had no one else to spend it on, and he liked spoiling his wife. 'You'll need a whole new boat wardrobe, I imagine,' he said, smiling at her, and this time she smiled back. In some ways it was a perfect marriage, except she wished he was more ambitious, while he was happy with the status quo.

'You know I hate that trip,' Amanda said with a sigh, as she took a sip of her cold coffee. The boat did look fabulous – she just didn't want to be trapped with his family for two weeks.

'It's never as bad as you think it will be,' he reminded her. 'It sounds like we'll be going to some fun places, and it really is a gorgeous boat. You always have a good time in the end.' She nodded, loath to admit it to him. 'Start shopping. You'll feel better when you do.'

'Thank you,' she said, and gave him a peck on the cheek, and walked past him to help herself to another cup of coffee. And she knew he was right. A boat as impressive as the *Lady Luck* would improve the trip immeasurably this year. She glanced at her watch as she heated the coffee. She had to be in court in half an hour. And maybe she'd go shopping that afternoon.

As she sat back down at the kitchen table, Phillip was reading avidly about the boat and stopped to look at her.

'So shall I accept?' he asked.

'Do I have a choice?'

'In reality? No,' he said honestly. He never lied to her, and she knew the vacation with his family was required of her every year. Olivia would have been crushed if they didn't go, and she made it as nice as possible for them, which her children appreciated. She was making up for the lost years and time.

'Then go ahead and accept,' she said in a dull voice. He pressed the reply button and wrote a quick e-mail accepting his mother's invitation, and then hit the send button and smiled at Amanda.

'Done,' he said, as she stood and picked up her briefcase and her bag. 'Have a nice day. See you tonight,' he said, watching her.

'Thanks,' she said and left the house. She didn't stop to kiss him goodbye. She never did. He went back to reading the e-mail about the yacht his mother had chartered, and thought about his wife. It was strange, but she always seemed just out of reach to him. It had kept him wanting to win her heart for nineteen years. She was the unattainable ice queen he would always love but never fully have. He knew it was perverse, but there was something about that that he liked. And not being able to have who he loved was painful but familiar to him. He had felt that way all his life, ever since he was a child.

Phillip's younger sister Liz was hunched over her computer, staring at the blank screen, when the e-mail came in. The sound of the computer voice saying 'You've got mail!' literally made her wince when she saw who it was from, and she suspected why. It was about that time, and she'd been dreading receiving the e-mail for days. She hated getting it every year, and hated going on her mother's birthday trip even more. She was always the odd man out, or at least she felt that way. At forty-four, she had felt like the family failure all her life.

She had been concentrating on the screen, with her eyes half closed, trying to write a short story. She had wanted to write since she was a kid. She had published short stories in her early twenties, and then had written a novel. She found an agent through a friend, but no publisher would touch it. They said it wasn't commercial enough, her characters were flawed, and her plot was weak. Her agent urged her to try again – not everyone published on the first shot. Her second novel was worse. The agent had urged her to rewrite it three times, and when she had, he still couldn't sell it. She went back to writing short stories and a few poems, and they were published in a literary magazine. And after that she'd been busy getting married, having babies, and trying to keep her head above water. She had been too emotionally spent to write and felt too unstable to even try.

She'd gone back to writing short stories several years before, but hadn't written any in three years. She was utterly and completely blocked. She still tried to write in spite of it but never finished anything. And since both of her girls were out of the house, she had told herself that it was now or never. She had been trying to write again seriously for several months, and for the past few weeks she had forced herself to sit down at her computer every day. Nothing came. She just sat there and cried. She was emotionally and mentally constipated, and what was worse, she was the only member of her family who had accomplished absolutely nothing in her entire life. As far as Liz was concerned, publishing a few short stories that no one read didn't count. It didn't matter that her agent had said she had talent. That was in her twenties and thirties. Now at forty-four, she had no achievements, no victories, no career, and her years as a stay-at-home mom to her two girls were over.

Her daughter Sophie was getting her master's at MIT in Boston in computer science, after getting her B.A. at Columbia. She was a math genius and was talking about going on to business school. Like her grandmother, she had a head for business, and at twenty-three, she was far better than her mother at taking care of herself. She was a bright, beautiful, very independent young woman. She had been the product of Liz's first marriage, to a French Formula 1 race car driver. Liz had fallen madly in love with him and had dropped out of college and run away to marry him at twenty-one. She got pregnant instantly, and he was killed in a race just weeks before Sophie was born. Two years later, with Sophie in tow, Liz had gone to L.A. and dated a well-known actor, Jasper Jones. She had been twenty-three, the same age Sophie was now, with none of her skills or capabilities. Sophie was a practical young woman. Liz had always been more idealistic. Liz had tried to get a job as a screenwriter and had gotten involved with Jasper instead. He was the most beautiful man she'd ever seen. They got married when she was six months pregnant, and the marriage had lasted eleven months.

Carole had been eight months old when they divorced. She was twenty now, and a dreamer like her parents. She had assorted talents and was a bright girl but seemed without direction. She talked about being an artist but wasn't serious about it. She had taken acting classes but had stage fright. She had done some modeling and talked about moving to L.A. but had no definite plan to do so and no job for when she got there. She went to California to see her father a couple of times a year. He was making movies after a checkered career, and had married a producer who was more successful than he was. He was still married to her, and they had had three more kids, all boys. Carole loved visiting them, and the atmosphere in

L.A. She loved the idea of moving out there and living with her father and his family, but she wasn't ready to leave New York.

Liz was constantly worried about her. She had turned into a mother hen, and both her daughters teased her about it. She called them three times a day to see how they were. She just wanted them to be happy. For the past twenty years, her daughters had been the main focus of Liz's life. She didn't want to be like her own mother and miss the boat on motherhood. So she had dropped everything for them, and now that they were gone, she wasn't even sure she could still write. She had promised herself she would try, but nothing came, and she dreaded being on vacation with her family again, and having to explain to them, again, why she had done nothing for the past year. How did you explain that to people like them?

As far as Liz was concerned, her brother Phillip was second only to their mother in the astounding empire she'd built on her own, with their father's silent, loving support. Phillip was the pretender to the throne. His wife was a successful attorney, a partner in an important law firm, and looked down her nose at them all. She was beautiful, sleek, well dressed, and had assured all of them she was going to be a judge. Liz's brother John was an incredible artist and a genius in design. His wife had a doctorate and was a professor of literature at Princeton. And her baby sister, Cass, never came on the summer birthday trips. She had distanced herself from all of them since their father's death but had become one of the most important music producers in the world, based in London, and for the past five years was living with a world-famous rock star ten years younger than she was, Danny Hell. Liz constantly asked herself how she could compete with people like them. All she had ever done was write a few lame short stories, have two failed marriages, and bring up two wonderful girls. Sophie and Carole were her only accomplishment, and no one in her family was impressed by that. She knew they all thought she was a total failure.

Her mother was always kind about her writing and tried to encourage her, but Liz feared she was just being polite. They felt sorry for her. Liz had been floundering and fighting to keep her head above water all her life. The only thing she'd ever been confident about was mothering her kids. It was the one thing she was sure of, where she never doubted herself, and she loved her daughters more than anyone or anything in the world. But she was also the only one in her family who had never finished college, had been married more than once, and whose marriages had failed. She had no career, lived on her trust, and had been paralyzed by her fear of failure all her life.

Liz lived in a Connecticut farmhouse she'd been meaning to remodel and rebuild since she'd bought it ten years before, and she'd never managed to do that either. She just never got around to it. Although the bones and structure of the place were beautiful, it was a mess, constantly leaking, with things breaking that she never quite knew how to fix. In some ways, her life seemed like her house to her: it had potential but was disintegrating quietly and falling apart. And now she had to go on vacation with all of them again. She didn't have the guts to do what her younger sister did every year, and turn their mother down and refuse to go. Instead, Liz always did what was expected of her, never wanted to upset anyone, so she and the girls went every year. The girls had a great time, and Sophie and her grandmother were soul mates, just as Liz and her own grandmother were, but each year, after the summer vacation, Liz swore she would never go again. It was just too stressful for her, to compare herself to them, and endure their casual comments and put-downs and supposedly helpful criticism about her life. No one could understand what she was doing with herself, and her time, particularly now that the girls were gone. It was impossible to explain to them that some days it took her all day to get out of bed.

The only person who had ever understood the extreme insecurity she felt was Granibelle, whom Liz went to visit on Long Island every week. Just as she had been for Phillip, her grandmother had been the real mother in her life. Olivia was more like a friend. She was always kind to her, and compassionate, but Liz was convinced that they were just too different to ever understand each other. Granibelle always told Liz to give her mother a chance, that she regretted the time she hadn't spent with them when they were children, but Liz was sure now it was too late. And the birthday trip reinforced that impression every year. She spent two weeks with them in gorgeous locations, feeling like a freak, and in agony in their midst. And now the invitation was sitting on her computer, and Liz didn't have the guts to open it. She sat and stared at it for a long time, and then finally clicked it open and looked at the photographs of the enormous yacht. 'Shit,' Liz said out loud, sitting in her kitchen. 'Now what am I supposed to do?' She felt seasick just looking at the photographs of the gigantic boat. She read the description of everything it had to offer, and even that didn't help. If her family was going to be on it, she knew she would feel miserable and inadequate, seasick or not. But she knew with equal certainty that both her daughters would love spending those days with the family on a fabulous boat. Hair salon, spa, movie theater, water toys – her mother had gone all out. Liz knew she couldn't deprive her daughters of a trip like the one her mother had planned. And she didn't want to miss being with her girls. She got little enough time with them now, and they were busy with their friends most of the time. As she did every year, Liz felt she had no choice. If she wanted to see her children and share a holiday with them, she'd have to put up with everyone else. It was a depressing thought.

She read through the e-mail several times, with the description of the boat, and forwarded it to both her daughters. And then she hit the reply button with a heavy heart.

'Thanks, Mom!' she typed the message to her mother. 'This looks incredible! We'll be there with bells on. The girls are going to be thrilled! Love, Liz.' She read it over several times, and then hit the send button. Her fate was sealed. All she could think was 'here we go again.' She had nothing to wear, but she knew she could borrow something from her girls. She still had the same lithe body she had had at their age. Her face looked older, but her body hadn't changed.

After she responded to her mother's invitation, she picked up a notepad and walked out into her garden.

There were two broken deck chairs with torn cushions on them, and if she sat down on them carefully, she knew they would hold her. She had a silly idea for a children's book. It wasn't the kind of writing she usually did, but maybe it would distract her and cheer her up. She had nothing else to do, and she wasn't going to write the great American novel in the next six weeks, so she might as well write something fun, for herself. No one in her family was going to be impressed by a children's book, but that didn't matter now. She was resigned to being the family screw-up who had accomplished nothing, yet again.

Sarah Grayson raced into the house between classes, to pick up some additional books she had left at home. The small, cozy house just bordering the Princeton campus was quiet, John was at work, as head of creative and design for his mother, their son, Alex, was in school, finishing his junior year in high school, and their golden Lab was sound asleep, stretched out in the sun. The dog picked up his head when he heard Sarah come in, and then dropped it again. He was too tired to move or do anything more than wag his tail and go back to sleep.

She checked her e-mail, to see if any students had written to her about homework, or help they needed, and she saw the e-mail from her mother-in-law instead. She opened it quickly, and then gasped when she saw the photograph of the *Lady Luck*.

'Oh my God!' she said, and then sat down heavily at her desk to read quickly through the rest. It was more than a little overwhelming, but she knew Alex would be thrilled, and John probably would too. Their summer trips were fun but always harder for her. Her parents had been serious liberals and activists, her father had been a professor of biology at UC Berkeley, her mother had taught women's studies when it had become popular as a subject. Her father had been one of the early supporters of the civil rights movement, and they knew that John had money, but they had never fully understood how much, or what it meant. Neither had she. Fortunately, she and John shared the same political views, and the same philosophies about life. They gave away most of John's income every year, to philanthropic causes, and they wanted their son to have good values that were not based on personal wealth or a fascination with money.

They had chosen to live in a small house and spend their time in the academic community. Alex knew that his grandmother had money, but he had no sense of how wealthy she was, or that his father would inherit a fourth of her vast fortune one day, or that he already had a great deal of money. They were careful to see that none of it showed. John drove a Toyota for his commute into the city every day. Sarah drove an ancient Honda she had bought from a student for a thousand dollars, and when Alex wanted a mountain bike, they had made him get a job after school and pay for it himself. Sarah didn't want their son corrupted by the more-than-daunting Grayson fortune. Their summer vacations were like trips to Disneyland for them, and for years Alex had been young enough not to make any connection between the rented châteaux and villas and what it cost to rent them. But the yacht Olivia had chartered and that Sarah was reading about in the e-mail was a different story. It would be hard to explain that to Alex. And as far as Sarah was concerned, Olivia should have been giving away the money to people who needed it, not spending it on them for a fancy Mediterranean vacation. The only thing that ever made her more comfortable was John's assurance that The Factory donated vast sums every year to worthwhile causes. But clearly this year's summer vacation had cost Olivia a fortune.

Sarah felt guilty just looking at the pictures of the boat and knowing they would be on it. She wished her mother-in-law had decided to do something more modest, but she knew how important these trips were to her, and that she wanted to provide only the best for her children and grandchildren. It was a well-meaning gesture, but Sarah disapproved anyway. She suspected her husband would enjoy it, and love the opportunity to go fishing and sailing with his brother. They were like two kids when they got together away from the office. And at forty-one, John still looked and acted like a boy to her.

Sarah had just turned forty. She had married right out of college. Their initial plan had been to join the Peace Corps together and go to South America, but she had gotten pregnant on their honeymoon, which changed everything. They'd gotten stuck in a small apartment in New York, and John's mother had convinced him to get a master's in design and, once he had a family to support, to join her in the business. He hadn't had the heart to turn her down. And Sarah had eventually gone back to school too, first to get her master's degree in Russian and European literature, and then her doctorate in American literature. She had been teaching at Princeton for ten years now, and the move to Princeton had been good for them, and they were happily folded back into the academic community. John still dreamed of giving up his job and becoming a full-time artist, but he said he couldn't do that to his mother. So his dreams of being an artist had been put on a shelf, probably for ever, and he had to be content with painting on weekends. He had shown his work several times at a local gallery, and in art shows at the university, where they exhibited work by professors or their spouses. He sold all his paintings every time. It validated him, but was bittersweet. His success at gallery shows always made him wish that he could give up his day job and devote all his time to painting.

Their ease at getting pregnant with Alex, earlier than planned, had led them both to hope that they would have many children. Sarah had wanted four or five, and the blessing of John's money meant that they could allow that to happen, but an ectopic pregnancy two years after Alex changed all their plans and dashed their dreams. Even with the help of in vitro fertilization, Sarah had never been able to get pregnant again. They tried IVF five times before conceding defeat. It had been a painful disappointment, but Alex was a wonderful boy and the joy of their life. They had talked about adopting a child from Central or South America, but once they finished their studies, they were both deeply involved in their jobs, and in the end they decided that one child as terrific as Alex was enough for them. And like his cousins, Sophie and Carole, Alex had a wonderful rapport with his grandmother. He looked forward to their summer vacations, and he took the train into the city to have lunch with her from time to time. She had promised him a trip to China with her when he graduated from high school, and Alex talked about it all the time. And Sarah knew, as she glanced through the e-mail, that he would be ecstatic when he saw the boat his grandmother had chartered for their summer trip.

Sarah sighed as she pressed the reply button to answer. The boat was definitely over the top, and it made her feel guilty to share in such extreme luxury with them, but she also knew that it was going to delight her husband and son. She wrote a hasty note to Olivia, thanking her and assuring her they'd be there; she hit the send button, grabbed the books she'd come home to get for her next class, rushed past the sleeping dog who wagged his tail again, and left the house. And as she walked into her class ten minutes later, the yacht she had just seen and would be traveling on in July was the farthest thing from her mind. All she cared about now was the class she was about to teach, her students, and the academic life she loved. And just as they did every year, they would tell no one about the trip, particularly this year. No one they knew would understand. The world of super yachts, and cruises in the Mediterranean, was no part of their real life. As far as Sarah was concerned, that was Olivia's life, not theirs.

*   *   *

Danielle Steel

The e-mail to Olivia's youngest daughter, Cass, reached her in London at three o'clock in the afternoon. It came through on her BlackBerry as she was sitting in a meeting, planning a concert tour for one of their biggest clients. Cassie Grayson glanced at the e-mail and knew instantly what it was. She saw the first photograph of the boat, and without reading the details, she closed the e-mail again. She wondered why her mother still bothered to send the invitation to her every year, since she had never gone. For fourteen years, she had refused. She was not going to be bought off by a vacation in a château in France, or on a fabulous yacht. She no longer cared. She had left the States at twenty, when her father died, and made her own good life in England. She had gotten into the music world, in production, made her own money, and wanted nothing from any of them, particularly her mother. As far as Cass was concerned, Olivia had missed her chance. She didn't care what her grandmother said whenever she saw her, Cass always said the relationship with her mother was over for her. Cass had no memories that included her, only her grandmother and her father. Olivia had been too busy building her empire then to spend time with her. With the others, she had still made some meager efforts to come home from the office at a decent hour. When Cass came along,

82

unexpectedly, seven years after John, it was too late. For both of them, mother and child. They had been the busiest years of her mother's life, and Cass had no need or desire to give her a second chance now.

Cass was happy with her life. She had a business she worked hard at and had built herself; she had friends, and she had lived with a man she loved for the past five years. For Cass, with the exception of her grandmother, her relationship with her family had ended when her father died. She had always blamed her mother for not being there when it happened. After a massive heart attack, he had hung on for two days. Cassie had been convinced he was waiting for his wife to come home. It took them a day to reach her in the Philippines, and two more days for her to get home and he had died just hours before she arrived. Cassie remained convinced that her mother's coming home in time would have saved him. It was the last straw for her. She never forgave her mother, and three months later she was gone. She had seen her brothers and sister only a few times since. She had nothing in common with them. She thought Phillip was a pretentious stuffed shirt. She couldn't stand his wife, who seemed like a bitch to her. She had nothing against Sarah and John, but she had nothing in common with them either, and poor Liz was so insecure and frightened to compete with their mother that she could barely breathe. It depressed Cass just thinking about them, and she did so as seldom as she could.

The only one she maintained a close tie to was her grandmother, whom she saw whenever she had business in the States, and occasionally she flew over just to spend an afternoon with her. Granibelle hadn't changed. She was still the same wonderful, loving woman she always had been, and she always begged Cassie to open her heart to her mother again. Cassie just listened and said nothing, rather than argue with her grandmother about it, or upset her.

Despite her feelings about her, and mostly to please her grandmother, Cass did see her mother once or twice a year. They had lunch sometimes when Cass was in New York, or when Olivia had business in London. The lunches were stressful and brief. Neither of them knew what to say to each other. Olivia had no idea how to make up for the past, and would have liked to. Cass shared nothing with her, and told her nothing about her life. She had never even mentioned Danny Hell. What Olivia knew about him, she heard from Liz, who had read about it in the tabloids. The only thing Olivia did know about Cass was that she had an enormously successful business, and that Cass had mentioned several times that she never wanted children. She said she was too busy to have them, and didn't want anyone to have a childhood like her own. The point had been made, many times.

And so had her refusals to join them for family vacations. As far as Cass was concerned, the Graysons weren't her family anymore. Phillip felt the same way about her, and made no effort to see her. He hadn't seen her in at least ten years. John felt sorry for her, but awkward about the position she had taken and didn't want to upset their mother by seeing her. Liz missed having a sister, and would have loved to talk to her and have her get to know her girls. But they had all begun to think there was too much water under the bridge. The only one who had never given up on Cass coming back into the fold was Maribelle. She told Olivia never to stop seeing her, and to stay in touch as best she could, and one day Cass would come home. Olivia no longer believed that, but she invited her to their summer vacations every year, and continued to have lunch with her whenever she could.

When she got back to her office, Cass sent the same response she did every year, declining her mother's invitation. Her answer was always brief and clear: 'Thank you, no. Have a nice trip. Cass.'

Olivia saw the message on her own BlackBerry after the *New York Times* interview. She read it, and closed the e-mail. It came as no surprise, but it hurt anyway. A little piece of her died every time her youngest child rejected her. She knew why she did it. She understood. She didn't blame her, but it made her heart ache anyway. And then, with a sigh, with the message sent and received, both women, whom Maribelle said were so similar in some ways, went back to work. Better than anyone, Maribelle knew them well.

Chapter 4

Amanda had four suitcases open and was filling all of them when Phillip came home from the office, the night before they were to leave. In addition, there was a hanging bag perched in a doorway, a special bag for shoes, and a Louis Vuitton hatbox sitting on the floor with several hats already in it. Phillip looked at the scene in their bedroom with dismay.

'How long did she invite us for? A year?' he asked, looking at his wife blankly. 'I just counted seven bags.'

'And one for toiletries,' she reminded him, 'now that you can't take them on the plane.'

'That's a relief,' he said with a wry look at her. 'I thought maybe you'd take ten. We're only up to eight.' She always overpacked.

'I can't just wear blue jeans and a T-shirt on a boat like that,' Amanda said with a look of annoyance, as Phillip set his own suitcase on their bed. His wardrobe needs were less complicated. All he needed were some khaki trousers, white jeans, one pair of blue jeans, some shirts, a blazer, running shoes, flip-flops, a pair of loafers, two bathing suits, and one tie, just in case. That would cover anything that came up, from dinner in a restaurant to swimming at the beach. It would all fit in one bag.

Amanda looked at him in irritation, as he tossed his clothes into the suitcase. Ten minutes later, he was finished, and she was still only halfway through the process, with silk dresses, cotton cover-ups, and half a dozen new outfits. She had no intention of wearing the same clothes every night. Nor would her mother-in-law, she knew. Liz and Sarah were another story, and in Amanda's opinion, both were always badly dressed, although Liz's daughters usually looked cute.

'This isn't a contest, you know, as to who can take the most clothes. My sister never brings more than one bag.'

'That's because she wears her children's clothes.' And looks ridiculous, she wanted to add, in things like bathing suits that only teenagers could wear. And Sarah was always a mess. She still wore the same style bathing suits she'd had when she got married eighteen years before and weighed ten pounds less. She still wore clothes she'd had since she was a student. She looked it, and she loved buying clothes in thrift shops, which seemed disgusting to Amanda. She couldn't understand why anyone married to a Grayson would do something like that. She had gone to Saks, Barney's, and Bergdorf's to buy new clothes for their trip. And she had bought three new hats. She never went out in the sun, except heavily protected, slathered with sunscreen, in a big hat. It was why she didn't look her age. At forty-four, she was on real time now, but so far so good. She went to the dermatologist regularly and had weekly facials to exfoliate her skin. And several times a week she applied a mask at home. Amanda had no intention of aging prematurely, or being badly dressed.

'Did you eat?' Phillip asked with interest. He was starving, and Amanda wasn't planning to cook dinner. She never did.

'I had a salad at the office before I left,' she said, folding another sundress into her bag. Phillip knew that if she had changed four times a day for two weeks, she still couldn't wear all the clothes she was bringing, or even the ones she'd bought. 'Do you want something to eat?' she asked with a look that said she hoped not. Her facial expression was clear. Kitchen closed. They were leaving on a trip. And they had to get up at dawn the next day.

'I'll make myself a sandwich in a minute,' he answered. 'I think John and Sarah are on our flight,' Phillip commented, and looked pleased. The two brothers got on well, although they were very different.

'With all the money your mother spends on a boat like that, you'd think she could charter a plane to get us there. Flying commercial is such a nightmare these days.' Amanda said it as though she had spent her entire life on private jets, which was not the case. She had never been on one in her life. But she would have liked to.

'That would be ridiculously expensive,' Phillip chided her. 'I'd rather spend it on the trip, not getting there,' he said sensibly, ever the financial caretaker, keeping an eye on the bottom line.

Phillip went to the kitchen to get something to eat, and when he came back, Amanda still hadn't closed her bags. It looked as though there were a method to her madness, but the key theory seemed to be 'take everything you own.' And Phillip couldn't figure out what she'd do with it once she got there, other than look overdressed on the yacht. But she did it on land too. She had had twelve bags the previous year for their vacation at the château whose name she could no longer remember.

'Your mother always likes what I wear,' she said, looking miffed.

'You can close them now,' she said, as she waved grandly at her bags. It was a reminder to Phillip of what the trip would be like: Amanda showing off, wearing her new clothes, and looking down her nose at his sister and sister-in-law, because she thought they were boring and badly dressed. Amanda had never made any effort to fit in. She thought Phillip was the prize, but the others were of no interest to her, and it showed. He didn't dare tell her to be nice to the others, which would set her off. She was usually warmer to him on the vacations, when she felt like it, but only when they were alone in their room. She didn't like public displays of affection, and neither did he, but even he had to admit that a yacht like the *Lady Luck* offered interesting romantic possibilities, even if Amanda was not a romantic person. Phillip knew that everything in life was a trade-off and he liked the fact that she had a big career. And he had always tolerated her lack of effort around his family, although all of them were pleasant and polite to her.

Amanda liked being the center of attention, and was unhappy when she wasn't, but that was Phillip's mother's role. She had chartered the boat for them in the first place, and it was her birthday at the end of the trip.

It was midnight by the time Amanda was finally fully packed, and she expected Phillip to move her bags to the front hall. When he tried to, he found they weighed a ton.

'What are you bringing? Rocks?' he asked her.

'No. Shoes,' she said innocently.

'Don't forget the brochure said that you can't wear shoes on the deck.'

'I won't,' Amanda said as she went to run a hot bath.

Phillip was so excited about the adventure of the trip and the time he would share with her that he got amorous with her when she came to bed. But Amanda wasn't interested. She said she was tired and had to get up too early the next day. His passion would have to wait until they got on the boat. Even on the eve of their departure, Amanda was as unavailable as ever. But this time it didn't excite him, it made him feel mildly depressed as he turned his back to her and went to sleep.

Predictably, all was chaos at John and Sarah's house the night before they left. John came home late from the office, and Sarah had final papers to correct, and a million e-mails from her students from a summer class she had just taught. And Alex had invited ten friends over for pizza and to use the pool. There were suitcases all over the place and nothing was packed. Sarah knew she'd be up all night washing towels after Alex's friends left. She had made him promise to at least bring them in to her, so they were dry in the morning when they left for the airport. Always frugal, she had let their weekly cleaning person off for the two weeks they'd be gone, and she didn't want to come home from Europe to mildewing towels.

She hadn't even thought about what to pack – it would be whatever came out of the closet first. And John had just gotten a letter, inviting him to participate in an art show at Princeton in October, and he was in the room he used as a studio, going through his recent work. He wanted to be sure he had enough for a solid show. The moment anything came up to do with his art, he forgot everything else.

Sarah went to the back of the house to find him, and saw him frowning at several paintings he had leaned up against the wall. He needed twelve pieces of recent work for the show. He didn't even hear Sarah walk into the room and looked up in surprise when she did.

'I just don't know,' he muttered. Sarah's hair was wild and frizzy and all over the place, she was wearing cut-off jeans as shorts, flipflops, and a tank top, and wishing she had lost the five extra pounds she'd been complaining about before the trip. Now it was too late, but she knew that John loved her just the way she was. They had been madly in love with each other since college, and married for eighteen years. 'What do you think?' John turned to her with a worried expression. 'I'm not sure this new thing I've been doing is fully developed yet. I wish they'd given me more time before the show. I'm not ready.'

'You always say that,' she reassured him as she came to stand behind him and put her arms around his waist. 'You have a fantastic talent, and you always sell all the work in every show. It may not look 'fully developed' to you yet, but it will to everyone else. And I like this new turn your work has taken. It's strong.' His palette had gotten bolder. He was a very good artist, and it had been his passion all his life. Design was what he did as a job. Painting was his love. And Sarah of course. She was the love of his life. Alex was the product of that, but Sarah was its source. They adored their boy, but John and Sarah had often admitted to each other that they felt like two people with one soul. They felt blessed to have found each other.

'And you always say you love all the work.' He looked over his shoulder and smiled at her. 'How'd I get lucky enough to find you?'

'Blind luck, I guess. I don't mean to be disrespectful of

the concerns of a great artist, but if we don't pack, we're going to be walking around naked on this fancy boat your mother chartered.' Her angst over what to take every year, and what was expected of her, kept her from packing until the last second. That and the fact that she worked hard at Princeton, was constantly available to her students, and hated thinking about clothes, particularly in the rarefied world his mother lived in. It was on another planet from their comfortable, easy life. She loved the way they lived, even if their house in Princeton was beaten up and old. It suited them. Most of all, it suited her.

Because he had grown up in it, John was able to travel in his mother's lofty circles, but was just as happy in their bohemian academic life. Sarah had never set foot in that other world until she'd married John. Her parents were academics, and so were all their friends. She couldn't remember seeing her father in a tie, and her mother wore Birkenstocks when they went out. So did Sarah usually, but she knew the kind of effort she'd have to make for Olivia. It used to traumatize her, and she'd been terrified she'd make some terrible social faux pas, or use the wrong fork at his mother's elegant dinner table. Now she knew John didn't care and loved her no matter what.

Olivia had been brought up with the niceties of life

even when they'd been poor. Her mother had inherited beautiful silver and china from her family, even though they'd lost their money. Sarah knew nothing about that world. And John was intelligent, gentle, and charming wherever he went. Sarah had fallen in love with him instantly when they met in college. She had no idea who he was, or the enormity of the wealth he came from. He was a simple, unpretentious, down-to-earth person and kind to everyone, rich or poor. Unlike his brother, Phillip, who Sarah thought was a snob. Their mother wasn't, but she was so powerful and successful that the world was at her feet. It had been heady stuff to absorb, and Sarah had to exist in that world with him only once a year, on the summer vacations, or once in a great while for dinner, at Olivia's Bedford home. But fortunately, she rarely entertained and was gone most of the time. All Sarah cared about was that John's fortune provided them with security, that they would never lose their house, and that Alex would be fine when he grew up. The rest was gravy as far as she was concerned. And she needed very little gravy in her life. She loved her husband, though not his world.

'I get neurotic every time I have to pack for these trips,' she confessed, but he knew it anyway.

'You're gorgeous and I love you,' he said, turning

around to kiss her. They held each other for a long moment, and Sarah sighed. Life with John was pure bliss. 'I don't care what you wear. And neither does my mother. She just wants us all to have fun. I think it's going to be great this year.' He and Alex were excited about the boat, even if it sounded daunting to her. At least at the châteaux her mother-in-law had rented, there was history to think about. The yacht was all about money, and a lot showier than what Sarah would have liked.

'You just want to go fishing with your brother,' she said, and John grinned and looked like a kid. He still seemed like a student to her, and not a forty-one-year-old man with an important job. He was totally unassuming and very handsome. And he thought she walked on water, and had a brilliant mind. She was an extremely intelligent woman, and she admitted to being an intellectual snob.

'That's true,' he agreed about the fishing. 'Phillip and I talked about it this morning. We're on the same plane to Nice, by the way.'

'I hope your mother put us in coach,' Sarah said with a worried expression as he put his paintings away carefully and turned off the studio lights. He would have to make the decision about which paintings to show when he got back. He didn't have time tonight. 'I hate it when she spends all that money on business.' And Sarah flatly refused to travel in first class. She said it was immoral, and she didn't want Alex to pick up bad habits or forget what really mattered in the world.

'I think it's pretty safe to assume she did business or first,' John said gently, trying to warn her. He knew his mother. She wasn't going to send them in economy to France. She wanted them to be comfortable and well cared for all along the way. And then he laughed, thinking how different his wife was from Phillip's. 'I'll bet Amanda is complaining that Mom didn't charter a plane for us. She says it every year.'

'That's insane,' Sarah said with a look of strong disapproval. But that was typical of Amanda. Sarah put up with her, but her sister-in-law managed to annoy her every year. 'I wouldn't take a private plane. Your mother should give that money to the poor.'

'Don't worry, she does.' Sarah knew it, or she wouldn't even have gone on the trip. The whole concept of spending that kind of money went totally against the grain with her. She couldn't even imagine, and didn't want to, what Olivia must have paid to charter the boat. The thought of it made her shudder.

They walked through the kitchen on the way back to their bedroom, and saw Alex and all his friends outside.

More had dropped by, it was turning into a party, and there were half a dozen kids playing water polo in the pool. She stepped outside the back door and reminded them not to play rough, and when she came back in, John was eating a slice of pizza, and she helped herself to one as well. That was going to be dinner, she still had to pack for her and Alex. She knew John would take care of himself.

'Stop worrying about them, they're good kids,' he chided her, and she looked serious.

'I don't want one of those good kids to get hurt. They play too rough. Every year some kid we know gets hurt in a pool. Not here, thank you very much.' She worried about their son, and everyone else. One of her students had become paralyzed in a pool accident the year before. It happened, and she didn't want it happening to them.

'They're just having fun.' Alex loved everything athletic and was on the swimming team at his school. He played soccer and lacrosse, had joined the basketball team, and was a natural athlete. At seventeen, he was still more into sports than girls, which in some ways was a relief to them. There had been no dramas, failed romances, or broken hearts. He just loved hanging out with his friends, and brought them home as often as he could. Sometimes there were a dozen of his friends, and half a dozen of her students, in their kitchen, sprawled across their living room, or barbecuing in the backyard. They ran a kid-friendly house. This was the life they chose to live.

When they got back to their bedroom, Sarah looked at the empty suitcases in dismay. She had no idea what to put in them – she never did. John laughed at her and pulled her down on the bed. He slid a hand under her T-shirt and fondled her full breasts. He loved her body and everything about her, and he gently started pulling off her jeans. She stopped him immediately and leaped off the bed to close and lock the door.

'There are kids in the house,' she reminded him, and he laughed.

'When aren't there around here?' They had only managed to have one child, but other people's children were underfoot all the time. John never came home to an empty house. It was full of life and laughter, and young people everywhere. It was the home he wished he'd had as a boy. Friendly and informal, with parents around most of the time.

As soon as she had locked their bedroom door, Sarah came back to the bed, and they began kissing in earnest and exploring each other's bodies. Their clothes were off in a matter of minutes, John turned off the light, and they gave in to unbridled passion. It was a long time before they lay sated and panting, and clung to each other like survivors in a storm.

'Wow!' he said in a hoarse voice.

'It's always wow with you,' Sarah said happily in the dark. 'I hope we never get too old for that.'

'I don't think we will,' he said, rolling over on his side to look at her in the moonlight. He thought she was the most beautiful woman he'd ever seen. She had been for twenty years. He had always felt that way about her, and still did. 'I think I'll be dragging you into bed when we're ninety. When Alex leaves for college, I'm going to chase you around the kitchen table naked every night.'

'I can hardly wait,' Sarah said, grinning, as she sat up and turned on the light. The suitcases were still there. They hadn't been magically filled while she and John made love. 'Shit, we still have to pack.' And she had to take the dog to the neighbor's, they had promised to dog-sit for them. She had a lot to do that night. 'Will you take Jeff next door?'

'Sure,' John said good-naturedly. 'I'll pack when I get back.'

'And don't let them give you a glass of wine. You'll be there all night,' she warned him, and he smiled as he put on a pair of jeans. He could shower when he got back. He

Danielle Steel

loved knowing her body had been part of his only moments before.

'Yes, boss,' he said, teasing her as he unlocked the door. Their bed was now unmade, and anyone who walked in could have guessed what had happened. It was a common occurrence at their house. They gave in to their passion for each other frequently, and they were both hoping to spend a lot of time together in their cabin on the boat. They were famous for taking 'naps.'

Half an hour later, when John got back, Sarah was frantically packing, and had filled half a suitcase with cut-offs, jeans, some faded hiking shorts, a stack of T-shirts with slogans on them or 'Princeton' written across them, and a few favorite flowered cotton dresses she'd had for years and had brought on other summer trips. She had packed two pairs of flip-flops and her favorite Mexican sandals, and a pair of running shoes in case they walked on rough terrain, or climbed on rocks. She knew it wasn't likely with his mother, but Liz liked to go running, and maybe they'd hike somewhere with the kids. Amanda, she knew, would be wearing gold sandals and stiletto heels.

It was nearly midnight when Sarah finished, and by then John had packed his bag with his summer khaki slacks, lightweight blue blazer, jeans, some blue shirts, and the loafers he would wear to dinner without socks.

He had the look down pat, and the wardrobe to go with it, even if he wore it nowhere else. Sarah added a couple of shawls, and looked at John with exhaustion. He was lying on the bed, watching TV, and Alex and his friends were still outside when Sarah closed her suitcase and set it down next to his.

'Well, that's done,' she said, looking as though she had climbed Everest. Packing for a trip with his mother was precisely that to her.

'What time do you think I should send the kids home?'

'Maybe one o'clock? Is Alex packed?'

'Probably not. I'll check.' She was still planning to do it for him, but when she went to his room, she found that he had. He was growing up. His suitcase, his gym bag, and his camera bag and computer case were sitting on the floor side by side. He was all set, so at least that was done. Now all she had to do was clean up the kitchen and do a load of towels when his friends left. She went back to their room, and watched TV with John for an hour, and by then Alex's friends were leaving on their own. Most of the girls had curfews and the boys had to take them home. She met Alex in the kitchen, throwing out the empty pizza boxes just after one o'clock.

'Thanks, Mom. We had fun,' he said, kissing her cheek. 'Do you want help with the towels?'

'Sure,' she said, smiling at him. She knew she was a lucky woman. She had a wonderful husband she adored, and a terrific son she loved just as much. Alex looked like John, but he had wild frizzy hair just like hers. And hers was always worse in the warm New Jersey summer weather. She looked like she had stuck her finger in a socket. Alex's was slightly more tame, and it looked cute on him.

They loaded the washing machine together, and she checked for empty plates and glasses outside. There were none, just a few empty soda cans in the trash, which she brought in. Alex went to bed then, and by two o'clock, the towels were done, and all was silent in the house. They all had to get up at four, to leave for the airport at five and get there at six to check in for their eight A.M. flight. Fortunately, they could sleep on the plane. It was a six-hour flight to Nice, which would bring them in at eight P.M. local time, and they were hoping to be at the boat by ten. It was going to be a very short night.

Sarah slipped into bed next to John, and he smiled the moment he felt her, and put a hand between her legs. He was too sleepy to do anything more, and she cuddled up next to him, as he put an arm around her and went back to sleep. He was dreaming of making love to Sarah on the boat.

* * *

When her brothers were getting up in New Jersey and New York to catch their flight, it was still dark, and in the farmhouse in Connecticut, Liz was already awake. She was catching the red-eye to France that night with Sophie and Carole, and she was working on her book in the meantime. It had been the strangest thing. The idea for it had come to her in a flash, it was unlike anything she had ever done, part fantasy and part real. She had started it the day her mother's invitation came for the summer trip. It was the story of a little girl and her imaginary friends: a lonely child and the world she creates and populates around her. It was allegorical and the child was her. As a child, Liz had had an imaginary friend, who had gotten her through some lonely and confusing times, and she felt as though she were solving some of the mysteries of her life as she wrote the book. It wasn't a big book, but it was deep, and she wasn't sure if it was the worst thing she had ever written, or the best. She'd been working on it night and day for six weeks. She was almost finished but wanted to do some more polishing before she left that night. No one had read a word of what she'd written, she hadn't told anyone about it, and as usual, Liz was scared. Maybe this book was the final sign that she had no talent, and was losing her mind. It wasn't a novel, it wasn't a children's book. It was a fantasy that had leaped straight out of her head onto the page. And she worked furiously as the sun came up, the day she was leaving on the trip.

Sophie and Carole had come out from the city the weekend before, packed their clothes for the boat, and left their suitcases with her. Liz had packed her own bags then too. Six suitcases were standing ready by the door. She was meeting the girls at the airport at ten that night, with all their bags, for a midnight flight. She had to leave the house in Connecticut at eight. And much to her own amazement, she had worked for fifteen hours straight when she stopped at seven. It had been like that for six weeks. She was being driven by the book. She had thought about asking Sarah to read it on the trip, but what if she hated it? Liz couldn't stand the thought of another failure.

Sarah had been writing literary novellas and short stories for years. They were of a high intellectual caliber, and were published by an academic press. No one had ever heard of them, but Liz had read them and they were good. Her style was reminiscent of Joyce Carol Oates, who also taught at Princeton and was Sarah's literary idol. It would be hard for Liz to show her little fantasy book to Sarah, but she didn't know what to do with it, and she hadn't had the guts to call her agent, and maybe never would. But when she stopped writing at seven o'clock that night, she knew that she had done all she could. She printed it out and stuck the manuscript in her hand luggage with her laptop and then went upstairs to take a shower. She had an hour to get ready and leave the house. An airport shuttle was picking her up.

As she stood in the shower, she thought about what she'd written and prayed that it was good. It probably wasn't, but she knew that she had done her very best. That was something at least. In her dreams, she wrote a book that people cared about and understood, that was as meaningful to them as it was to her. Maybe this was it. The terrifying part would be showing it to someone else. She hadn't even told the girls what she'd been doing. She'd had too many false starts, stories that went nowhere, outlines she never followed, half manuscripts and unfinished poems that lay in drawers. This time at least she'd finished it, and in a mere six weeks. The story had poured out of her like falling pearls, scattered everywhere and then gathered up in her hands like gems.

The girls had helped her pick her clothes for the boat, and shared some of their own with her, since all three of them wore the same size. She had two old bikinis she always wore, and her girls went topless in Europe, like everyone else their age. Liz could have too, and had the body for it, even at forty-four, but she didn't think her mother would approve. Having two babies at a young age had left no mark on her. But at her age, she knew she was expected to be respectable, no matter how fit and trim her body was. And there would be lots of crew around. For the rest of what she'd brought, they were either old summer clothes of her own, or things she'd borrowed from her girls. She had nothing fabulous with her and didn't really care. As usual, Amanda would be their fashion plate, which seemed like too much trouble to Liz. But she knew that her brother liked having a wife he could show off.

Liz was ready right on time, and then realized she had forgotten to leave an outfit out for the plane. She looked in her own closet and found nothing, and then headed to Sophie's, and looked through the things she still kept at home and hadn't packed. She found a pair of old white shorts, a white cotton shirt in her own closet, and an old pair of sandals she'd forgotten that laced up her leg. Her long blond hair was still wet from the shower, and she left it damp down her back, didn't bother to put on makeup, for a midnight flight where all she'd do was sleep anyway, and when the shuttle came, she flew out the door, and took out all their bags. While the driver loaded them, she made sure that all the lights were turned off and set the alarm, looked in her carry-on again to make sure the manuscript was there, and then double-locked the front door.

She was in the van when her cell phone rang and it was Sophie, checking on her. She was the organizer in the family, the responsible one. Carole was less efficient, always distracted and a little vague. And Liz always forgot things, like her handbag, her keys, or setting the alarm. But this time she had everything in control.

'Did you remember to set the alarm?' Sophie asked her in a motherly tone, almost certain she hadn't, and was surprised when Liz said yes. 'Turn off the lights? Do you have your passport?'

'Of course.' Liz would have been annoyed, but she knew her questions were well intentioned, and she had been known to forget important things over the years.

'Did you bring our bags?'

'No, just mine,' Liz said innocently, teasing her as Sophie gasped, and then her mother laughed. 'I think I got it all.' Including her precious manuscript, Liz thought, as Sophie said she would meet her at the airport. She and Carole were sharing a cab from the city to meet her there. And for once Liz felt as though she had done everything she should. For six weeks while the book rolled out of her, she had felt better than she had in years.

She almost felt ready to spend two weeks with her mother, though not quite. She had spent her whole life desperate for her mother's approval, and never felt like she had earned it, not because Olivia was critical of her, but mostly because Liz always felt as though she had been a failure. Her path had been strewn with broken dreams, failed relationships, disappointing outcomes, and promises to herself she'd never kept. The only thing she'd ever done right, or well, was be a mother to her girls. She had all the maternal instincts Olivia had never had. But Olivia had built an empire, and Liz knew she never could. So far, she couldn't even write a successful book. Maybe this time would be different, but Liz found it hard to believe it would.

Her mother was impossible to compete with, and equally so to live up to. Liz saw her as some kind of goddess at the top of a mountain with no roads leading upward and no way to reach her. As a child, she had dreamed of pleasing her and making her happy and proud of her, and she had wanted it so badly, she had never even tried. How did you impress a goddess when you were a mere mortal? These summer trips were torture for her, they tantalized her with all the wishes of her childhood that had never come to pass and never would. She didn't blame her mother, unlike her younger sister and oldest brother. She knew Olivia had been busy, but she had left Liz with an aching hunger in her soul that nothing could satisfy or fill, except the love of her children and hers for them. Both of them had been accidents, but had turned out to be the greatest blessings of her life, far more than their fathers had been.

The marriage to Sophie's father would never have lasted, even if he hadn't died, and Jasper, Carole's father, was a handsome, narcissistic flake. He was harmless and incompetent, and had spent a lifetime having beautiful children in his image and doing nothing for them. There was no one there, and never had been. And the men Liz had been involved with since, albeit briefly, had been no better. She was the first to admit she had terrible taste in men. She always fell for their words and their looks, not their actions. All of them had been handsome, and none of them had been capable of real relationships and loving her. She always seemed to pick people who were unable to love, or people who were unavailable like her mother had been. What she needed was a man like her father, but she was never drawn to men like him, and was destined for a life of loneliness and frustration as a result. And in recent years, she had given up, and decided it was too late. At forty-four, she no longer expected to find the love of her life, and when she bothered, she settled for brief affairs. They were good enough.

The girls were waiting for her at the airport when she arrived. The three of them checked in, and were in high spirits, and then Sophie noticed her mother's long legs. They were three beautiful women standing at the check-in counter, and were drawing appreciative stares from men.

'Mom, where did you get those shorts?' Sophie asked her with a look of suspicion.

'From your closet. I forgot to leave out something to wear on the flight. I can give them back to you on the boat.' She looked apologetic, and Sophie grinned. Carole was on her cell phone with a friend and paying no attention to them.

'I left them there because they're too short. You look pretty sexy, Mom,' Sophie said with a mild look of dis-approval. They were in fact very short to be wearing them in a public place.

'Believe me, at my age no one looks,' Liz reassured her daughter.

Her hair was dry by then, and fell in gentle waves and curls, framing her face.

'That's what you think. About ten guys just checked you out.'

'No worries. I'll cover myself with a blanket on the

plane.' Sophie had worn a short white linen dress, and Carole was wearing a flowered miniskirt with a white T-shirt and sexy gladiator sandals. As usual, she looked incredible, she was a gorgeous girl, like both her parents. Sophie was beautiful too, she looked like Liz, but with dark hair.

They boarded the plane in first class. Olivia had sent the others in first class too. She wanted their trip to start out right – comfortable, fun, and easy for them. It was a small gift to give to them, and Liz and the girls were thrilled as they settled into their seats on the plane. The girls wanted to watch a movie, and Liz said she wanted to sleep. And instead she took the manuscript out of her bag after takeoff, and started editing it again. She had been doing that for weeks. The girls didn't even notice what she was reading. They were sitting together and chattering excitedly about the trip. They both loved their grandmother and always had fun with her. She was far more attentive to her grandchildren than she had been with her own children. Now she had more time, and they were more interested in her and what she'd done, and the business that was her world.

After takeoff, a stewardess offered them champagne. Both girls helped themselves to a glass and Liz asked for a Bloody Mary. She sipped it slowly, as she quietly worked on her book, and then set it down next to her and forgot about it, until they hit some turbulence half an hour later, and the glass toppled into her lap. The stewardess was quick to bring damp towels and help her clean up the mess. Liz managed to save her manuscript from the accident, but Sophie's shorts and her own white shirt were a mess, and she had nothing else to change into. She looked at the girls, laughed, and shrugged. It didn't really matter, she could change her clothes when she got to the boat.

By the time the plane headed out over the ocean two hours later, all three of them had turned their seats into beds with pillows and comforters, and they were sound asleep. In spite of Liz's usual trepidation about spending time with her family, they all knew it was going to be a fabulous two weeks. And other than the minor mishap with the Bloody Mary, they were off to a great start.

Chapter 5

When Olivia reached the port in Monaco, the day before her children were scheduled to arrive, it took her breath away to see the yacht she had chartered for them. It was three hundred feet of pure luxury, and an exquisite sight. All twenty-four crew members were lined up on deck in uniform, waiting for her to arrive. The captain stood on the dock, ready to escort her on board and introduce her to the crew. It was evenly divided between women and men, and impossible to remember all of their names. There was an enormous outdoor bar, with a spectacular arrangement of orchids in a crystal vase, and a stewardess offered her champagne, which she declined. She was tired from the long trip, and rarely drank.

There was beautiful deck furniture in seating arrange-

Danielle Steel

ments, and a helipad on the upper deck, along with a
large sunbathing area. The purser escorted her around the
boat, showed her into the movie theater, the gym, and the
spa. Crew members were stationed at each location, and in
the hair salon, three young women waited at attention. She
glimpsed the main dining salon and an outdoor dining area,
peeked into the sumptuous bedrooms her children would
occupy, and was finally led to her own, which they referred
to as the Owner's Suite, filled with beautiful furniture and
impressive art. And there was a huge, inviting king-size bed,
with impeccably pressed linen sheets. She could hardly wait
to get into it. She was tired after the flight, but it was too
exciting to be here. They asked if she would be dining
aboard tonight or in town, and she said she would be staying in. She wanted to get some rest before they all arrived.
They would be constantly busy after that. And Olivia
couldn't help thinking, as she looked around her suite, how
blessed she was to be able to provide something like this for
her children and grandchildren. It had been well worth
all those years of hard work, even if she had missed some
time with them when they were young. How fortunate
they all were now, and so was she. She never took for
granted what she and Joe had built, and the fruits of it.

When the stewardess left her in the cabin, after
unpacking for her, Olivia took a long, luxurious bath. She

came back upstairs afterward wearing a long white linen caftan, and they served her dinner in an outdoor dining area, with a beautiful table setting of French china, with flowers in small vases, and silver seashells scattered around the table. They had given her precisely what she ordered, an omelet and salad, with fresh fruit for dessert. She was relaxing quietly, enjoying watching the comings and goings from other yachts in the port, when a steward came to tell her there was a call for her, and brought her a phone. She hoped it wasn't one of her children canceling at the last minute because something untoward had happened. And when she answered, she was surprised to hear Peter Williams's voice. She was instantly worried about a legal crisis at work.

'I had such a crazy week, I never got to say goodbye to you before you left,' he apologized, and Olivia smiled when she heard him. She was instantly relieved that it was a purely social call. 'How's the boat?'

'Absolutely incredible,' she said, smiling broadly, and he could already hear the more relaxed tone of her voice. 'It's the most beautiful thing I've ever seen. I'm going to refuse to leave when our two weeks are up.'

'That sounds like an excellent decision. You're going to have a wonderful time with the kids,' he said. He always enjoyed talking to her, and they hadn't had time to chat in a while. They were too busy solving and avoiding problems involving her business. He was happy that she had taken time off. He knew what these vacations with her children meant to her, and they did her a world of good. She always came back looking years younger, and full of new ideas and happy tales of the trip. 'I think my grandchildren will enjoy it too. This looks more like a ship than a yacht. I want to try the water toys with them. I want to learn to jet ski before I come home.'

'Be careful, Olivia,' he said with a tone of concern, and she laughed.

'I've always wanted to learn to ride a motorcycle too, but it's too late for that.'

'I'm glad you think so. It's not too late for anything with the energy you have.'

'Yes, it is,' she said sobering for a moment. 'I'm having a dreadful birthday on this trip.'

'There are no dreadful birthdays, looking as you do. I forget which one it is, but whatever it is, you don't look your age.'

'Oh yes I do,' she said stubbornly. 'I was thinking about it tonight. I don't know where the years go. One day you're young, and the next thing you know, it's all over. Except my mother, who is still fantastic at her age, and she looks great.'

'So do you. You haven't changed in twenty years, since we met.'

'Your eyes are going, Peter, but thank you. When are you leaving on vacation, by the way?' She knew he went to Maine with his family every year. He had a very pretty house that she had been to once, when she'd been in the area, checking out a new location for a store, and Peter had taken her there for lunch. It was a beautiful old family home, full of Early American antiques, with a big old-fashioned porch. 'I'm leaving next week. Emily's there already with our daughter. Eric and I are going up next week.' She knew that both of his children were married and had young children. He would be spending time with his family too. It did them all good to get away from the stress of their daily pace. They worked hard all year. 'We'll do some sailing and fishing. I want to play some golf. I haven't had time to play in months.'

'Thanks to me,' she said, sounding apologetic, as she relaxed and looked around her. 'You wouldn't believe how lovely this is. I'm sitting here in the port of Monaco, with the castle right above me, on this unbelievably beautiful boat. Sometimes I can't believe how lucky I am.' He always admired the fact that she didn't take it for granted, was never blasé, and had a healthy respect for how fortunate she'd been.

119

'You deserve it. You've earned it all. I hope you have a wonderful time.' Wishing her a good trip had been the only reason for his call.

'Thank you, Peter, you too. It was nice of you to call.'

'I'll see you when you get back. Take care, Olivia. And happy birthday, by the way.'

'Let's forget that, shall we?' she said, and laughed. Compared to her mother, she was a youngster, but seventy sounded very old to her. 'Have a wonderful time in Maine.'

'Thank you,' he said warmly, and a moment later they hung up, and she sat looking out over the water, thinking about him, and the business she had left in New York. She and her sons would meet on the deck every morning, to go over faxes and e-mails she would continue to receive while on the trip. They kept her abreast of everything, even when she was away. She couldn't neglect the business for two weeks, nor could Phillip and John. Too much went on there every day for them to remain out of touch. And she knew how to reach Peter if a legal crisis occurred. Hopefully, none would.

She went back to her cabin a few minutes later, and got into bed early with one of the books she'd brought with her. She read for a few minutes and turned out the light. She had left a wake-up call with the main stewardess so she didn't oversleep. She wanted to look around Monaco the next day and do some shopping, and get to know the boat before the others arrived. Phillip and John were coming on the same flight that night, and Liz several hours later the next morning, and they would set sail right after that. She could hardly wait to get under way, for her children to arrive, and the trip to begin. She reminded herself, as she fell asleep, to call her mother the next day. She had visited her the day before she left. And then her eyes closed, and she drifted off to sleep. She slept like a baby in the dark cabin, with the shades drawn, and she didn't hear a sound all night. Her last thought before she fell asleep was that it was going to be an amazing trip on the *Lady Luck*, for almost two glorious weeks.

Olivia had a relaxing, easy time in Monaco the day her children were to arrive. She did some shopping at the local stores, all branches of the fanciest shops in Paris – Dior, Chanel, Yves Saint Laurent, Lanvin, Hermès, Louis Vuitton. She bought very little, but she had a fun time looking. She never had time to shop when she was working, and she usually had more important things on her mind, like running her business, and the kind of problems that surfaced in trouble spots around the world. She had a personal shopper who knew what she liked and sent things to her home in Bedford for approval, and browsing now was a luxury. The only time she had to go through the boxes the personal shopper sent her was late at night.

The captain had sent a crew member to accompany her and carry her packages, and a car and driver to bring her back to the boat. It was a lazy day she thoroughly enjoyed, and when she got back, they had lunch waiting for her. And she spent the afternoon reading a novel, which was a luxury for her. She checked for e-mails from her office, and they were all about minor matters. She responded to them quickly and went back to her book. It was rare for her to have so much free time on vacation.

At six o'clock, after a massage and a shower, Olivia changed for dinner. She wore a pale lavender silk caftan, and indulged in a glass of champagne, while sitting on the deck. She had explored the boat so she could show her grandchildren when they arrived. And she knew how excited they would be about the water toys, especially Alex. She could hardly wait to see the kids. She was excited about their first stop, Portofino. She hadn't been there since a weekend she had spent at the Hotel Splendido with Joe, after they opened their store near Milan. It was a charming port town, with quaint restaurants and a string of tiny shops. She was sure they'd all enjoy it.

And it was spectacular at night, with an ancient church and a castle, beautifully lit up on the hills above.

The captain had told her that the boat was too big to get into port, and they would be tying up at some rocks just outside. It would be an easy trip into town by tender, and would only take a few minutes, and he said they could swim at night, while they were at anchor, if they chose. She was sure all the young people would love that. The trip she planned every summer was designed entirely for them, and she enjoyed it too.

Olivia had dinner in the outdoor dining area at eight o'clock, and by nine she was impatient for her children to arrive. The purser came to tell her that the flight had been on time, and then advised her when they were in the car. And then at last, just after ten, she saw John and Phillip's car pull up with a luggage van behind it, and the five of them got out. They looked tired and a little rumpled, and then they broke into broad smiles and excited chatter when they saw the boat. And then they saw her leaning over the rail, and she waved with a happy smile. Amanda was wearing an enormous white hat, and Olivia couldn't see her face. Alex bounded up the gangway, and both her sons followed, and her daughters-in-law brought up the rear. Amanda was wearing a dress, and looked impeccable despite the flight. Sarah was wearing cut-off denim shorts, a Princeton T-shirt, and sandals, with her wild frizzy hair and a nervous smile. She looked as though she felt shy, and Olivia knew that after a night on board, she'd relax. She always did. Amanda came on board looking as though she owned the yacht. And a moment later they were all around her, chattering animatedly, and her grandson gave her a huge hug, which she reciprocated with delight. Olivia always remembered how important her own mother had been to her children, and how powerful the bond between them was. She tried to emulate her as best she could, although she didn't live with them, as Maribelle had. But she had a good relationship with her grandchildren, and always had.

'Wow! Grandma! This is some boat,' Alex said with a look of awe.

'Wait till I show you around!' Olivia promised, and put an arm around his shoulders. 'They have lots and lots of water toys. We can take them out tomorrow.'

She had asked the chef to set out a buffet for them, and he had done a masterful job. There was sushi of all kinds, which she knew they loved, hot meats and cold ones, sliced chicken, many salads, assorted pastas, and an entire table of elegant desserts. It was a feast! The stewardess poured them champagne, and a few minutes after they had arrived, they were dining and talking, and totally revived after the trip. Even Sarah was more at ease once she started eating, and Alex had taken the chair next to his grandmother, and was telling her all the things he wanted to do. It all sounded like fun to her.

The newcomers stayed on deck until almost midnight, and then both couples went to their cabins. She saw a conspiratorial look pass between John and Sarah, and smiled to herself, knowing what it meant. The two of them could never keep their hands off each other, and it pleased her to see them so happy and their marriage solid. She and Joe had felt that way about each other for all their years together too. In fact, they had gotten closer over the years, and more in love. Their children and the business they had built together, and their profound respect for each other had been a powerful bond. In John and Sarah's case, they were still like two college kids deeply in love. Olivia noticed Alex watching them as they went downstairs. He stayed to chat with his grandmother, and helped himself to some more dessert. The pastries were delicious, and there were a dozen flavors of sorbet. He had slept on the flight and said he wasn't tired. It was six hours earlier for him, and he was in no hurry to go to bed. Olivia asked him what he'd been doing recently, and he told her about all the sports he was involved in, and he was hoping for early admission to Stanford in the coming months. She promised to visit him whenever she was on the West Coast, if he got in, and she went out there often to check their stores. Visiting their stores personally was a practice she had started thirty years before, and her travel schedule had never slowed.

When Alex finished eating, she took him to see the movie theater, which he loved, and the gym, and she had a crew member show them the rafts, floats, small sailboats, speedboats, and jet skis. They checked out the inflatable toys that they could ride on, which were all full of air and ready. There was one that looked like a giant banana and half a dozen people could ride it at the same time, if they could stay on it, as a crew member explained. That was the trick! There were three lovely small sailboats, half a dozen jet skis, and several speedboats. The family that owned the boat had everything they could have wanted. Alex could hardly wait to try it all. His eyes were huge as he took it all in, and then she laughed and asked him if he would take her on a jet ski with him.

'I'd love that, Grandma,' he said, grinning at her. 'Tomorrow,' he promised. They both laughed, and he hugged her to seal the deal.

'I'm going to hold you to it,' she warned him. 'I've always wanted to do that, and I'm scared to go by myself.'

'You've got it, Grandma.'

They went back on deck afterward, and at two o'clock Alex finally left to find his cabin. Olivia went with him and saw that his bags had been unpacked. There was an enormous TV screen in his room and a whole library of movies.

'Now don't stay up all night. You don't want to be exhausted tomorrow. You can sleep in, in the morning, but we're going to leave at lunchtime, as soon as Liz and the girls get here. We'll stop somewhere to swim and have lunch on the way to Portofino.'

'I want to try the banana thing with the girls. I saw that in a movie once, and it was really funny. Everyone kept falling off.'

'I don't think I'll volunteer for that one,' Olivia said, laughing with him, and a few minutes later, after hugging and kissing him again, Olivia left him in his cabin. He was already turning on the TV, to put in a movie, and she walked back to her own cabin with a happy smile. This was the perfect trip and boat for them, especially for Alex, who loved water sports so much. She didn't know why, but she thought he looked worried while she was talking to him, or lonely. Something felt off to her, or maybe she had imagined it, and he was just nervous about applying to college. She felt sorry for him. Kids today had so much pressure to deal with. She had never talked to him about it, but she wondered if one day he would want to come into the business. At seventeen, it was too soon for him to know, and for her to ask. Sophie, on the other hand, at twenty-three, was dying to come to work for her, and had talked about it since she was a child. And Olivia was excited to have that happen. Her dream was that one day all of her grandchildren would work there, but she knew Carole never would. She wanted either to be an artist, or to work for her father and stepmother in film production. She had no interest whatsoever in business, unlike her sister, Sophie. And Alex was too young to know. She felt fortunate as it was to have her sons in the business. She and Joe had always wanted that to happen, and it had. She was happy that he had seen their dream come true before he died. Both boys had already been working for them when their father passed away. It had made them even more responsible at an early age, and she counted on them a great deal now, even though she still ran the show, and hoped to for a long time. But the three of them worked well together. It had brought them closer to her now as adults. They had The Factory in common.

When Olivia got back to her cabin, and went to bed, she lay thinking about her children and grandchildren for a long time. She was looking forward to spending time with them, and pleased that they had this fabulous vacation to look forward to.

In the morning, Olivia went on deck. Amanda was already presiding at the breakfast table. She was wearing pale blue silk shorts with a matching blouse, and a very pretty pale blue hat to match. Olivia was wearing white cotton slacks and a starched white blouse, her white hair was impeccably done, and she had had a manicure in the salon on the boat the day before. Amanda looked ready for anything. Sarah looked sleepy and disheveled when she came up. She said she had slept like a baby, and all three of the men in the family were still asleep. Olivia suspected that Alex had stayed up late watching movies in his room.

'I thought you might like to go shopping this morning,' Olivia said pleasantly to Amanda. 'The stores are pretty fabulous in Monte Carlo. Liz won't be here till about one o'clock, we'll leave then, so you have all morning.'

'I'd love it.' Amanda beamed from ear to ear.

'I think I'll stay here. I have some reading I want to do,' Sarah said quietly, which was no surprise either. Sarah had no interest in shopping, and it showed.

'Maybe you'd like a massage in the spa,' Olivia

suggested. She was an excellent cruise director, and her whole goal was for each of them to have fun, in the way they wanted to. There were no forced activities here. She wanted it to be paradise for them, not boot camp. 'Maybe I will,' Sarah said with a dreamy look, as she ordered an omelet for breakfast. There was something sinfully luxurious about being waited on hand and foot. She felt guilty about it, and had been genuinely upset by the first-class air tickets Olivia had bought for them, but sooner or later the pampering was very seductive. Olivia was enjoying it herself, although she rarely took time for self-indulgence in real life. But this was sheer heaven, even for her.

Olivia organized a driver and crew member to take Amanda shopping, and half an hour later both of her sons appeared, looking sleepy and relaxed. They were already talking about fishing, as they ordered eggs Benedict, and the steward handed each of them a copy of the *Herald Tribune*. Amanda was just leaving. Gold sandals and a gold beach bag had appeared to complete her outfit, and she was wearing small diamond earrings. She looked absolutely perfect leaving the yacht.

Alex was the last to join them, and admitted that he had watched two movies back to back and fallen asleep at five A.M. before the second one was over, but he was in good spirits. He could hardly wait for his cousins to arrive, and he and Olivia played gin rummy after break-fast. He beat her fair and square three times.

When Amanda came back from her shopping trip, she was carrying four shopping bags and wore a blissful expression. Phillip was waiting for her on deck, since John and Sarah had gone back to their room for a nap after breakfast. No one ever commented on their frequent disappearances, although Olivia always found them secretly amusing. Alex had glanced at her for a moment when they left, and said nothing. And Phillip was happy to see his wife – he'd been bored without her.

As they sat chatting, a car pulled up with a luggage van following it. And out stepped three spectacular-looking young women, as Alex gave a whoop of delight. It was Liz, Sophie, and Carole. The girls looked pretty and fresh, and as Liz joined them on deck, she was laughing. Her hair was a tangled mess, and she looked as though someone had been murdered in her lap.

'What happened to you?' Olivia looked at her in amazement and then kissed her. She was happy to see her.

'We hit turbulence and I spilled my Bloody Mary.' Amanda looked at her with obvious disapproval, and Olivia laughed. The mishap was so typical of her daughter. As a child, she always had something spilled all over her, and if anyone knocked over a glass at dinner, it was Liz. She was absentminded and clumsy, but lovable nonetheless.

'This is some boat, Mom!' Liz said, looking at the extraordinary elegance all around them.

'They have wristbands for you to wear, so you don't get seasick,' her mother told her. 'Apparently, they're very effective. I asked them.' And with that, a stewardess handed some to Liz, and offered them to the others. No one else wanted them, but Liz put them on. 'Why don't you let them show you and the girls to your cabins, and then you can come back on deck? We're going to leave in a few minutes. We're going to have lunch somewhere where we can swim.' Olivia had worked it all out with the captain that morning. And a few minutes later, Liz and the girls went downstairs. Alex offered to show them around. Olivia could hear the motor come on, and the deckhands were untying the ropes from the dock, and adjusting the fenders. Everyone was busy, as John and Sarah came back on deck, looking relaxed, with an arm around each other.

As they pulled out of port, everyone was on deck. Liz had changed her shorts and put a clean pair on, with a white T-shirt. The girls were talking excitedly with Alex, who was telling them about the inflatable banana they could ride on, and Amanda was telling Phillip how great the shops in Monaco were, and about the pretty things she'd bought. Olivia listened to the chatter all around her, and smiled to herself. This was precisely what she had wanted. They were all having a good time.

The captain gave them a brief safety demonstration in case of fire, or 'man overboard.' He told them where the life jackets were in their cabins, and where the lifeboats were. And after that, they were ready to leave.

They all went to sit on the sundeck at the bow of the boat as the *Lady Luck* slipped gracefully out of port and headed toward Italy. They cruised for an hour, then they stopped and set anchor. The crew took the water toys out so anyone who wanted to could swim. And Olivia quietly reminded her grandson of his promise.

'Don't forget my ride with you on the jet ski,' she said in a whisper, and he giggled like a little kid.

'Of course not, Grandma.'

Olivia went below to put on a bathing suit, and by the time she came back, the toys were ready, and there were crew members standing by in tenders to help them, or follow them on the jet skis. Someone had put on music, and her granddaughters were wearing the bottoms of their bikinis and nothing else and seemed completely unconcerned. Liz was wearing the top of hers, and her body looked spectacular as she dove into the water, and moments later everyone else followed suit. And by then Alex was sitting firmly astride the jet ski and held out a hand to his grandmother. She got on behind him with ease, as both her sons looked at her in horror. By then Liz and the girls were swimming toward a narrow beach, Sarah was sitting on the platform behind the boat, dangling her feet, and Amanda was debating about whether to get in.

'What are you doing?' Phillip called to his mother, as Alex started the engine of the jet ski.

'Taking a ride with Alex,' Olivia said with a broad grin as they took off at full speed, with a tender and a crew member following them. They kept a close watch on charter guests to make sure no one got hurt, and Alex had had to show a jet ski license to use the jet ski. Fortunately, he had had one since he was sixteen. He flew through the water with his grandmother behind him, holding tightly with her arms around his waist. She was loving every minute of it, and so was he, as Phillip and John looked at each other and shook their heads.

'If anyone had told me I'd see that one day, I wouldn't have believed it. Why didn't she do things like that with us when we were kids?' Phillip sounded wistful as he said it. This was not the mother he knew and remembered. This was someone else entirely.

'She was too busy,' John said simply, and then he went to convince Sarah to get in the water with him, while she took photographs of the scene. She and John were the family photographers, and the results were terrific. It was always fun looking at the pictures after the trip. She was a little overwhelmed by his family at first. They were a fairly overpowering group and this was a far cry from their familiar life in Princeton. But she was happy to see Alex having so much fun. And it helped her relax to take photographs of everyone. They were all in a great mood.

When Liz and the girls swam back from the beach, the three young people tried riding on the banana, pulled by one of the tenders, and they all fell off immediately, amid squeals of delighted laughter. The adults watched them from the deck, laughing too. It looked like fun to all of them. The three kids had all the exuberance and resilience of youth.

'We ought to try that sometime,' John said to his older brother, who grinned.

Amanda commented instantly, 'Don't count on me.' She had already changed to a dry bathing suit, and an enormous pink hat to shield her from the sun. Olivia was delighted by her ride on the jet ski, and Alex had promised to take her on it again.

They all had an enormous lunch, after which the crew

pulled up anchor and they took off again, this time to head straight for Portofino. The plan was to arrive in time for dinner and go to a restaurant in the port. And they'd been told the shops would be open till midnight. There was something for all of them to look forward to.

As the *Lady Luck* cruised toward Italy at full speed, John and Sarah played Scrabble, the rest of them read or slept, and the kids went to watch a movie in the theater. Amanda decided to have a manicure, as Olivia had suggested, and they all looked happy and at ease. And after they played Scrabble, John did a few quick pencil sketches of Sarah's face. He always returned with several sketchbooks full after their summer trips.

It was eight-thirty at night when they got to Portofino, and the crew tied up the enormous boat to the rocks, and dropped anchor. The tiny little port town was sparkling at them, and they all went to dress and get ready for dinner. They had a dinner reservation at nine-thirty at a restaurant the captain assured them was excellent.

They reassembled on the deck half an hour later, nibbled delicious hors d'oeuvres, and could hardly wait to get ashore and explore Portofino. A large tender took them in, and only a few minutes later they reached the dock, and three crew members accompanied them to the restaurant.

'I feel like visiting royalty,' Olivia giggled, and each of her granddaughters put an arm around her waist as they walked along. Alex walked along beside them, and Olivia's three children followed at a distance, watching her with her grandchildren, and talking among themselves.

'Sometimes I wonder if we even know who she is. She's so different than she used to be . . . with them . . . ,' Phillip said as he watched his mother with her grandchildren. She was laughing and talking, and she looked happy and relaxed. He had no memories of her looking that way in his youth.

'I think she really enjoys the kids,' Liz said kindly. She was happy to see her daughters having fun with their grandmother. Her own relationship with her grandmother had always been so important to her – she was glad to see that her daughters could share something like that too.

'Why?' Phillip said, looking sour for a minute. 'She never enjoyed us.'

'She probably did, it was just different. She was younger, so were we. It's easier when they're not your kids,' Liz answered.

'Maybe,' Phillip conceded, but he looked unconvinced. This was not the mother he had known. This was someone entirely different, riding on jet skis, laughing and playing. He couldn't recall a single instance of seeing her this way when he was a boy. Although she'd been around more when they were younger, as they got older, she had been either tired, busy, or away. All he remembered was his own grandmother, and his father, and a mother he now realized he had never known. He had felt cheated all his life, and seeing her this way made him feel more so. If she had had this to give, why hadn't she given it to them?

Only Liz seemed to realize that maybe she had been different then, and more pressured by what she was trying to build. Liz recognized too that maybe some part of her had grown in the meantime. Too late for them, but not too late for her grandchildren at least. And as far as Liz was concerned, Granibelle had given them all the mothering they needed. But Phillip had wanted it from his own mother, and still resented her for what she hadn't been able to give, or hadn't had time to.

'I think she's mellowing as she gets older,' John added, and Phillip shook his head again.

'I haven't seen that in the office.'

But at least they were seeing it now. That was something.

They looked into the shops briefly, and Amanda

wandered into a shoe store, and then Hermès, and then they all went to dinner at a small, friendly restaurant, with strolling guitarists serenading the guests. They were given a table on the terrace, and took their places randomly. The grandchildren seated themselves around Olivia, and she chatted animatedly with them until they ordered dinner. The pasta was delicious, and it was after midnight when they stopped for a gelato and wandered back to the dock, where the tender was waiting for them. The castle and the church were lit up high on twin hills, just as Olivia had remembered, and a few minutes later they were taken back to the boat. As soon as they reached it, they saw that the crew had set out hundreds of floating candles on the water. They looked like they were floating in chrysanthemums, and they had done it so that they could swim at night. The young people squealed with delight as soon as they saw it, and went to their cabins to change, and the adults waited on deck. It was a beautiful sight, and Phillip and John ordered cognac, while Amanda and Sarah drank champagne. Liz had gone below to change with her girls. And Olivia settled happily in a chair to watch the action.

As soon as the kids appeared, they dove into the water off the loading deck, and swam between the candles in the warm water. Liz was in the water with them, looking like a kid herself, and for an instant Olivia was tempted to join them. Being with them was like drinking from the fountain of youth. She hadn't had this much fun in years. And the two couples sat happily on deck nearby, chatting quietly and enjoying the romantic scene. They could still see the church and the castle in the distance, and the candles on the water were magical.

Sarah and John were the first to go below to their cabin, even before the young people came out of the water, and Phillip and Amanda followed a few minutes later. And when Liz and the kids came out of the water, Olivia was waiting for them.

'That was so much fun,' Liz said, breathless.

'It looked like it,' her mother said, smiling at her, and a moment later all the kids were around them, dripping water on the deck. They had decided to change and watch a movie. Their time together was one long party. Olivia loved being on the fringes of it, and so did Liz.

'Are you tired, Mom?' she asked her. It had been a long day for all of them, and she and her girls had only arrived that morning. The others had benefited from a good night's sleep.

'Not in the least,' Olivia said, looking relaxed. 'I think I'll go to bed now, though,' she said as she stood up. She'd had a wonderful day with her children and grandchildren. It was the whole purpose of the trip, and their first day together had certainly been a great success. She hoped the rest of the vacation would be too. Even Sarah had finally relaxed, and been lively and outspoken at dinner, and more like herself. The only one who never really changed or warmed up was Amanda, but they were all used to that, year after year. 'Are you going to watch the movie with the kids?' Olivia asked Liz.

'No, I think I'll work on my—' She stopped herself before she said 'book,' and looked panicked as she glanced at her mother. She didn't want to tell her about it. What was the point? What if, like everything else she'd ever done, it was no good? 'Work on my beauty sleep,' she filled in. 'The kids stay up way too late for me.'

'Me too,' Olivia said as they walked down to their cabins together. Olivia gently kissed her cheek, and wondered what she was really working on. She knew her older daughter better than that. She was sure she did not intend to work on her beauty sleep. She wondered if Liz was working on a new book. But she was wise enough not to ask questions. She kissed her goodnight, and walked on to her own cabin, pleased at how well everything had gone. It had been a very good first day indeed.

Chapter 6

Amanda went back into Portofino with a crew member and the tender the next day. She was itching to get back to the shops and see what she could find. There were several fancy little stores strung along the port, some Italian, some French, a fun jewelry store, and she came back to the boat laden with her purchases. The crew member she'd taken with her looked like a beast of burden, carrying six or seven shopping bags, and Amanda wore a look of victory. She had worn a short pink strapless sundress with a matching hat for her trip into town, and she came back looking like the consummate shopper. Phillip always said that Amanda shopped as a form of relaxation, so he never complained about it. And Olivia suspected it was true. And as a side benefit, Amanda always looked like a page in *Vogue*. And she knew that her son liked that.

Amanda was beautiful, without a doubt, but even at her best, she was never warm. It worried Olivia for Phillip. And oddly, although he had suffered from how busy she had been when he was a child, he had picked a woman to marry who was just as intent on her career, or even more so. To the point that she hadn't wanted children, and it always struck Olivia that she wasn't much fun to be around. She was so intense about everything she did, and so determined to become a judge. She wanted to know the right people, be seen at the 'right' events. There was nothing spontaneous about her. Even her shopping seemed calculated and determined. It was hard to imagine her with messy hair, or laughing herself silly. She seemed humorless and cold to all of them, although they never said so to Phillip. He wasn't a particularly spontaneous person either, and he was serious by nature, but Olivia couldn't help thinking that a more easygoing woman might have softened him, and done him a world of good. But he never commented on Amanda's coolness, so maybe he didn't mind it, and liked her the way she was.

Olivia had far more fun with Liz, whose humility was touching in many ways. She was bright and funny and beautiful, and never seemed to know it. She was quick to laugh at herself, which was endearing. And Olivia enjoyed talking to Sarah, who was intense but extremely intelligent, and madly in love with John, which pleased Olivia no end. It touched her heart to see her so loving to her son.

Olivia had come to know her children better as adults than she had as children. She was far more aware now of their sensitive points, their fears and weaknesses, and she worried about them more in recent years than she had when they were young. In the early days, they had had their father and grandmother to protect them, and Olivia had been around as much as she could. In those days all they had had to do was keep them healthy, safe, and warm, and keep them out of harm's way, or from doing something foolish in their teen years. But now the stakes were so much higher, the risks greater, and the price of mistakes they made potentially enormous. A wrong spouse, a bad decision, a serious health problem – in their early forties they seemed so much more vulnerable to her than they had been when they were small. And there was almost nothing she could do to protect them. She had to respect them as adults, remember not to pry, and pretend not to notice when they looked unhappy. She seriously wondered if Phillip was really happy with Amanda, if she was enough for him, if all he wanted was a clothes horse obsessed with their social status and her job. It was hard to know, and she couldn't ask him, although she was tempted to at times.

When the rest of them got up, the crew slipped the yacht free of its moorings on the rocks, and they went out to find a good place to swim, and for the young people to play. It was nearly lunchtime by then, but they had all agreed to eat late. And Phillip and John wanted to go fishing. Once they had anchored at a good swimming spot across from a beach, the boys took off in one of the tenders with a crew member, and their fishing equipment. John promised to come home with dinner, and as they motored off, Olivia couldn't help thinking how much like their father they were in many ways. They were both good, quiet, solid men, who were kind to their children in John's case, and loving and supportive of their wives. And a day of fishing was a slice of heaven to them. It made her smile thinking of Joe, and knowing how pleased he would have been with how they turned out, and how devoted to the family business. He would have been very, very proud, just as she was.

The kids tried the banana again before lunch, with the same results as the day before. Everyone fell off in less than a minute, with squeals of laughter. Sarah tried to take their picture, but they fell off too quickly. Olivia was laughing just looking at them, and so was everyone else. The top of Liz's bathing suit fell off twice when she tried it with them, and Alex nearly lost his swimming trunks. It looked like a lot of fun. The only one who wasn't amused was Amanda, who was slathering sunscreen on her long, graceful arms, then decided to sit in the shade. She paid no attention whatsoever to the merriment caused by the banana. She was oblivious to all of them.

It was three o'clock when everyone came back on board for lunch. Phillip had caught a tiny fish and thrown it back, and both men were determined to do some serious fishing at their next stop. They had decided this wasn't the right place. And once again the lunch the chef had prepared for them was plentiful and delicious. There were two long buffet tables, and a round table in the middle of the deck, all laden with food they all helped themselves to generously. Sarah said she'd never seen Alex eat so much, but everyone was hungry, and the food was too good to resist, so no one even tried.

Liz, Sarah, and Amanda made a date to meet in the gym late that afternoon, and to try the hair salon after that. And after lunch, they all went water-skiing. Everyone but Sarah and Olivia got up and had a good run around the boat, and everyone was in great spirits when they finally came back on board.

They were planning to have dinner anchored to the rocks, and then take off for a night sail to Elba. And the captain promised that in the quiet waters around Elba, the fishing would be excellent. Phillip and John were looking forward to it.

And that afternoon, after their water-skiing adventure, everyone lay on the sundeck, except Amanda had gone downstairs to take a nap. She clearly needed a break from having that many people around. And Phillip seemed more gregarious after two days of hanging out with his siblings. Olivia thought it was good for him to loosen up. He was so serious, and older than his years at times. He was very sedate and respectable, but was becoming more irreverent as the days went by. He was telling John funny stories about a hunting trip he'd been on, when Liz quietly confided to Sarah about her book.

'To be honest, I just can't tell if it's terrific or awful. It's different from anything I've ever done. It's mostly allegorical, about the fantasy life of a child, but it's very philosophical in some ways. I'm afraid to send it to my agent – he might think I've lost my mind. I haven't called him in years.'

'Do you want me to take a look at it?' Sarah offered, as the sun went down, and they all relaxed together. They felt like a real family, during these holidays together, instead of separate, unrelated individuals. Maintaining that bond to one another, and to her, was why Olivia got them together every year, and so far it was working. Even the in-laws got along better, and the cousins had a ball.

'I'd love you to,' Liz said with a shiver of fear running down her spine. 'Christ, Sarah, what if it's awful?'

'Then you'll write something else. You have to try different things sometimes.' She knew Liz had been stuck for a long time. She was happy to hear that she was writing again, and intrigued to see what she'd written. 'I'd love to read it,' she said, sounding enthusiastic, and neither of them had realized that Olivia was sitting right behind them, soaking up the last of the sun.

'So would I,' she said gently. 'Can I read it after Sarah?' Liz jumped when she heard her mother's voice, and turned to see her with a look of panic.

'Mom, it's really not ready, I need to work on it some more.' Olivia nodded, but looked disappointed. She wanted to share in what they were doing, and learn more about them now, but sometimes it was hard to open those doors, and she could only enter the inner sanctum of their lives if she was invited. And apparently, in this case, she wasn't.

'I'd love to see it whenever you're ready,' Olivia said,

and Liz nodded, thinking that would probably be never. The last person she wanted to share her failures with was her mother. Olivia had succeeded at everything she'd ever done, as far as Liz was concerned, and she herself had never done anything of importance or merit. What she didn't realize was that Olivia thought Liz was an extraordinary mother, and felt like a failure in that area herself. They each had their talents and their strengths. Olivia's had come out in business, and Liz's had blossomed at home with her children. But Liz's sense of herself was always as a failure. And if her new manuscript was another example of that, she had no desire to show it to her mother.

Liz changed the subject then, and a little while later the three women went off to the gym. Olivia played Scrabble with her grandchildren when they came back from their last swim, and Phillip and John were talking about the business. They had each gotten several e-mails from the office that morning, and had already discussed them with their mother. There had been a threatened strike at their Cleveland store, but the dispute had been settled, and Olivia wasn't concerned. She had reminded them to send a copy of the e-mails to Peter Williams, to keep him informed. But work was the last thing on her mind as she played the game with her grandchildren. Sophie put down a seven-letter word, and then Alex managed two of them and beat them all soundly.

Olivia had a massage after the game, and they all dressed casually that night for dinner. They were going to make it an early night, so they could get under way to Elba. It would be an eight or nine-hour cruise, so they could arrive by morning. Elba was a sleepy spot with good swimming, and excellent fishing for the boys, and it was a good halfway spot between Portofino and Sardinia, where they were planning to spend several days.

They had dinner at nine o'clock, and by ten-thirty they were under way toward Elba. The kids had decided to spend the rest of the evening in the movie theater, and the adults all wanted to go to bed early. None of them was used to the amount of sports they were doing, and they were genuinely tired after a long day in and out of the water. But all of them felt healthier and more relaxed than they had when they arrived.

Sarah and John were the first to leave the others. Sarah had Liz's manuscript with her. She was very curious about it. Amanda went to get a massage before she went to bed. Phillip and Olivia were the only ones left on deck. He was nursing a glass of wine, and he looked pensive as they watched the yacht's broad wake behind them. The sky was full of stars, and it was a magnificent night.

Olivia was enjoying the silence and the peace, and she watched her son's face grow serious as he looked out to sea and drank his wine. For the first time in a long time, Olivia felt as though she could reach out to him. There was something so sad in his eyes, she just couldn't resist it. Whatever their differences in the past, or their respective regrets about his childhood, she was his mother after all.

'Is everything okay?' she asked him gently. He didn't answer for a long time, and then he nodded, but he didn't meet her eyes as he took another long sip of his wine. 'Phillip, are you happy?'

He looked at her then, and seemed surprised, as though he had never asked himself that question. 'That's an odd thing to say,' he commented, but he didn't seem angry that she had. 'I think so. Why did you ask me?'

It was an opening that she had hoped for, for a long time. His marriage was a mystery to her. It was so different from the warmth she had shared with Joe, no matter how busy they both were. Phillip's choice of spouse had not been what she wished for her children. She much preferred John and Sarah's cozy lovefest, but her two sons were very different, and Sarah wouldn't have suited him at all.

'My marriage to your father was very different. You

and Amanda are much cooler with each other. Is that all right for you?'

'It suits us,' he said simply.

'Is it enough?' For a moment, he looked angry, and she was afraid she had gone too far. It was a delicate thing asking adult children about their private lives, and the history of his resentments stood like a wall between them. She had just dared to come over that wall, and he looked like he was about to react severely. She had trespassed on his life.

'By what right are you asking me something like that? You were never there when I was a kid, Mom. Dad and Granibelle were, you never were. Was that enough? No, it wasn't, if you really want to know. You were wonderful when you were there, but you weren't around very often. And now you question if my wife gives me enough?'

'She's almost as busy as I was,' Olivia said gently but bluntly. 'My success was an accident. I never planned it, I never hungered for it. It hit me like a tidal wave, and I started swimming as fast as I could to keep up with it. But I never made a decision to go after it. Amanda is a very ambitious woman. She *wants* it. I worry sometimes that you'll miss out on the same things with her that you did with me – enough time together, someone to be there for you when you need them, someone to rub your back or hold your hand when you're scared or lonely. Your father did that for me. I can't see Amanda doing that for you. She's too busy trying to get where she wants to go.' They both knew that Amanda was an ice queen, but Olivia didn't say it. 'And you don't have Granibelle and your father around now to make up for it. I'm sad for you that you decided not to have children. I may have made mistakes, and I made many, but all of you are the best thing in my life now. You always were. I'd be miserable without you.'

'That's nice of you to say,' he said, looking unconvinced. 'It works better for us this way. I don't think people should have children who don't have the time to spend with them. Amanda is smart enough to know that, and so am I. Maybe we're just very selfish people.' She would have agreed that Amanda was, but Phillip had a warm side that a good woman could have developed and Amanda had no interest in doing that. She was far more interested in herself, what he could do for her, and how he could serve her ambitions. And Olivia couldn't help wondering what he was getting out of it. And like her, he was all business. Even at her busiest, she and Joe had never lost the tenderness they shared. She could see none between Amanda and Phillip.

'I don't think you're selfish,' Olivia said generously, still slightly amazed that they were having this conversation and that he had allowed it to happen. She had taken him by surprise, and the wine had helped. She knew he was being honest with her, surprisingly open and very candid. 'Cass says the same thing, about why she doesn't want children. She says she's too busy, and she knows it.' It pained Olivia to realize that she had affected her children so deeply with her frequent absences during their childhood, that two of them had decided never to have children, which seemed like a terrible deprivation to her. But she knew she couldn't have managed it herself without her mother and Joe. Joe had been willing to give more than his fair share as a father, and her mother had carried the full weight of four children, day in and day out. It had been an incredible gift to her, and made her family possible in ways it wouldn't have been otherwise. Olivia was well aware of it and eternally grateful to them.

'Not everyone is cut out to have children.' Phillip looked right at his mother as he said it. 'Some of us are smart enough to know it.' He scored a direct hit with that one, and his mother felt it go straight to her gut with a dull ache.

'I may have screwed up, but I don't regret having any of you. I love you very much, and I always did.' She wondered if he needed to hear it. It felt right to say it to him.

'Well, that's good to know,' he said as he finished his wine and set down the glass, and then he stood up. They had gone as far as he was willing to, but Olivia was touched that he had let her go that far inside his inner walls. Usually Phillip was heavily guarded, and he had never let her in before. She was glad she had broached the subject. She still didn't know if he was genuinely happy with Amanda, but she had the feeling that he didn't know that himself. She suspected that he didn't ask himself a lot of questions. He just accepted the obvious and what was. She thought Amanda was a very lucky woman. From what Olivia could see, she expected a lot, and gave very little in return. She didn't like to see it, but Phillip didn't seem to mind, if he even noticed. His emotional expectations appeared to be minimal, and he set the bar for that very low.

He kissed her on the forehead then, and went downstairs to his cabin. He left Olivia alone on the deck, staring out to sea, and thinking about him.

Amanda was lying on the bed, reading a magazine, when he walked in. He smiled when he saw her. She was wearing a white satin nightgown, her hair was freshly brushed, and she had had her nails done after the massage. She loved all the luxuries offered on the boat.

'Where were you?' Amanda asked, curious about it.

'Having a drink with my mother.'

'How sweet. And she gave you permission to come to bed?'

'My mother doesn't give me "permission," Amanda. I work for her, but she doesn't own me.'

'You could have fooled me. I would have said she did,' she said in a chilly tone, and he looked at her as though for the first time. But it was not the first time she had said it. It was an old refrain.

'Why do you resent it so much that I work for her? It's a great job. I'm going to run the whole company one day, I might as well learn how.' John had no head for business, and they all knew he would never do anything more than creative and design, and he was brilliant at what he did. But it was Phillip who would step into his mother's shoes one day. It was why he had gone to Harvard and gotten an MBA.

'You already know how to run the company,' Amanda said with a grim look. 'Your mother should step down. You're like Prince Charles and the Queen of England. She's going to run the business till she's a hundred years old, and you'll be lucky if she turns it over to you when you're eighty.'

'I hope she does live to be a hundred,' he said generously. 'I'll take it over whenever she's ready. And I'm not in any hurry to take on all the worries she has on her plate.'

'That's my point,' Amanda said with an angry expression. 'If you had the balls, you would be willing to take on those headaches now. How old was she when she stepped into the business? Eighteen? How old are you? Forty-six? You should be doing it now. You and John should force her out.'

'That's a hell of a thing to say,' Phillip said, looking shocked. Amanda had never been that blunt before.

'It's embarrassing to admit that I'm only married to the CFO. It makes you sound like an accountant. It would sound a lot better if you were the CEO. You should be. Now.'

'I'm sorry if you're embarrassed, Amanda. And as a matter of fact, my father was an accountant. I don't think my mother was ever embarrassed to be married to him. In fact, I think she was very proud of him. She may have been a lousy mother, but my father thought she was a great wife.' And he was beginning to wonder if he could have said the same about his own. Some of the things his mother had said to him, and the questions she had raised, had hit home, even if he hadn't admitted it to her. He had heard every word she said. Amanda had picked a hell of a night to go after him, and humiliate him by saying that

157

Danielle Steel

his mother 'owned' him. No one owned him, and neither did she. Phillip had no desire to be owned, only loved. And sometimes it was hard to tell if Amanda did.

'I hope one of these days you grow up and take over the reins,' Amanda said with a sigh. She had been insulting to him ever since he had walked into the cabin. He didn't say another word, just walked into the bathroom. They had both said enough for one night.

When he came back into the bedroom, with his teeth brushed, in his boxers, Amanda was in bed, her long, elegant form silhouetted under the covers. He got into the bed and turned off the light, and as soon as he did, he felt her cool fingers touch his back, and move gently toward the front of his shorts. Her timing was terrible and her words had hit him hard. Maybe she was trying to make it up to him, but he gently took her hand, moved it aside, and turned on his side with his back to her.

'Not in the mood?' she asked in a silky voice in the dark, as he marveled at how insensitive she was. How could she think he wanted to make love to her now? She had basically told him he had no balls. 'Not tonight,' he said in a cold voice, and she gracefully moved away from him, and stretched out on her side of the bed. And neither of them said another word.

Chapter 7

When they woke up in the morning, they were in Elba. It was a small, sleepy island, which was famous because Napoleon had been imprisoned there. After an early night, all the adults got up early. The young people had stayed up late watching movies, and there was no sign of them yet.

Phillip and John ate a hearty breakfast and took off in the tender to go fishing. John had a sketch pad with him, just in case. Olivia had looked for signs that Phillip was angry at her, but he appeared to be in a good mood, and kissed the top of her head before he left. She was relieved. Amanda said very little and went back to her room after breakfast. She said she had a headache, and Olivia realized that she and Phillip hadn't exchanged a word, but that wasn't unusual for them. Sometimes they didn't speak to each other for hours, or pay attention to each other all day.

After breakfast Sarah waited for an opportune moment to talk to Liz. Amanda had gone to her cabin by then, to go back to bed. Olivia was reading e-mails from her office, and checking faxes, the boys had gone fishing, and the kids were still asleep. It was as good a time as any to give her sister-in-law bad news. She turned to Liz, as they sat on the lounge chairs on the deck, and she looked serious when she did.

'I read your manuscript,' she said, and then fell silent for a minute. It sounded like a drum roll to Liz. She dreaded what was coming next.

'And? What did you think?'

'Honestly?' Sarah hesitated for only a fraction of a second. 'I hate to say it, but I don't get it. It's a children's book, a fantasy. But kids don't read books like that. There's nothing real or allegorical about it. I don't think there is anything to it that anyone will want to read.' She looked apologetic as she said it, but she was very clear.

Liz nodded, trying to fight back tears. She didn't want Sarah to see how hurt she was. 'It came straight from my heart. I was hoping it was good. It just went in a whole different direction than I usually go, and I couldn't tell.' Now she knew. She had struck out again.

'You need to go back to what you did before,' Sarah said in her professor's voice. It had the sound of total authority. It was the same voice that now and then reduced a student to rubble. What she said sounded written in stone. 'Some of your early short stories are really good. This just isn't. I'd like to tell you that it is, but I really can't. You'll embarrass yourself if you try to sell it. Your agent will throw it back at you. The concept is interesting, but the story doesn't work. It's like a parody of *Alice in Wonderland*, and the reader can't tell if you're kidding or nuts.'

'Nuts, I guess,' Liz said in a flat voice as Sarah handed it back to her, and at that exact moment Olivia looked up from her computer and saw her daughter's face, and knew what had happened. She couldn't hear what Sarah had said, but Liz looked devastated as she shoved the manuscript to the bottom of her bag as though it were a garbage can, where her manuscript belonged. It made Olivia's heart ache seeing Liz's face. She wanted to take her in her arms and kiss it better. Instead, she bided her time, finished her e-mails, and waited until Liz walked past her on the way to her cabin. She was going to hide the manuscript in a drawer, and destroy it when she got home. Olivia stopped her as she walked by, and patted the seat beside her.

'Can we talk for a minute?' Olivia asked her gently, and Liz smiled, with her mouth, not her eyes. Her eyes said she was devastated, and she tried to look cheerful for her mother. She didn't want her to know how upset she was. Olivia knew her better, she was her child after all, whether she'd been an absentee mom or not. She wasn't blind to who they were or what mattered to them.

'Sure, Mom. What about? Something wrong? Grani-belle okay?'

'She's fine. I talked to her last night. Some ninety-year-old guy moved into the apartment next to hers and she thinks he's cute. You never know.' They both laughed at the report. But she was still beautiful and full of life, even at ninety-five. 'I'm not sure exactly what Sarah said to you, but I can guess. I just saw her hand your manuscript back to you, and I want you to remember something. Sarah is a major, major intellectual snob. She's steeped in academia, and whatever she's published probably sold six copies to her friends. She has absolutely no idea what would sell commercially. I don't want you to take whatever she said to heart. Show it to someone else, like your agent.'

'She said it wasn't good enough to even show him and I would embarrass myself if I did. It's just another one of my endless flops. Don't worry about it, Mom.'

'I do worry about it. This is about you. I love you, but I just have an instinct here that she's wrong. I love Louis XV furniture, and no one loves antiques more than I do. I don't sell antiques, I sell the most commercial low-priced stuff there is, and it sells like hotcakes and has for fifty years. I'm not telling you that what you wrote is Louis XV, but that's all Sarah knows. You may have written a terrific piece of commercial art that could be a major best seller. Sarah wouldn't recognize that if it bit her on the ass.' Liz burst out laughing through the tears that had sprung to her eyes. 'You need to ask someone who knows commercial fiction. She doesn't.'

'She said it's crap, in so many words.' Liz's lip trembled, and Olivia took her hand and raised it to her lips and kissed it.

'That means you would flunk her class at Princeton. But Princeton is not the world.' She kept a tight grip on Liz's hand. 'Do you see this boat? We chartered it for a fortune, and we can afford to. We could even buy it if we wanted to, and that's from selling decent commercial goods, not fine antiques. But what I sell looks great, people love it, and they come to our stores all over the world to buy it. Commercial literature is what sells, Liz, not the kind of stuff Sarah thinks you should write. Will you let me read it? I promise I'll be honest with you. But I just have a feeling it might be good. You're a smart girl, and a great writer, and I trust your instincts too, and I can tell you're excited about it.'

'I was,' she said in a dull voice, as two tears rolled down her cheeks. 'What if you tell me it's as bad as Sarah said?'

'Then you'll write something else. It's not the end of the world. Listen, some of the lines of furniture I've designed have been pretty bad. It's all about trial and error, and having the guts to try again.'

'That's what I don't have,' Liz answered honestly. 'I always fail. And I'm scared to try again.'

'Try not to be. You have so much more talent than you think.' Olivia held her hand out then, for Liz to give her the manuscript, and Liz hesitated. 'I want it now, please. If your literary snob of a sister-in-law can read it, so can I. Besides, I think what she said was mean. Maybe she's jealous because she doesn't have the imagination you do.'

'Believe me, Mom, she's not jealous. She just thinks it stinks.'

'I'm betting that she's wrong,' Olivia said firmly, but Liz still didn't move. 'Look, let me make this clear to you. I'm a powerful woman. People all over the world are terrified of me. So what's wrong with you? Why aren't you doing what I say?' Liz laughed at what her mother said.

'Because you're my mom and I love you, and I know you're not scary, you're just a big fake. You just pretend you're scary.' Olivia laughed at what she said.

'Just don't tell my competitors that. I hear they're scared to death of me. So give me your book.' And with that, Liz finally pulled it out of her bag and handed it to her mother with a look of pain.

'If you hate it, just don't tell me how much. We'll throw it overboard together, or have a ceremonial book burning or something.'

'We'll see. I'll be honest, but polite, which is more than I can say for Sarah. I'm not sure calling someone's book unreadable is considered good manners in the publishing world. Maybe we should discuss her wardrobe with her. She looks like she got it at Goodwill.' Liz laughed again. 'And I don't think she shaves her legs. She's lucky your brother is crazy in love with her. A lot of men would think hairy legs and Birkenstocks with hiking shorts are not so cute. Maybe John needs his eyes checked. I'll have to mention that to him,' Olivia said with a pensive look, and then stood up with Liz's book in her arms.

'Thank you, Mom. It's okay if you hate it. I kind of expect it now, it won't come as such a shock. I was really excited about it, until I showed it to her. I thought I had done something special and unique, but I guess not.'

'Don't be so quick to accept defeat,' Olivia scolded her. 'If you believe in this book, fight for it. Don't just lie down and give up.'

'I can't fight for it if it's no good.'

'How many bad reviews did Shakespeare have? Or Dickens? Victor Hugo, Baudelaire, Picasso? All great artists get bad reviews. Let's not give this up quite so quickly. And no matter what I think, good or bad, you should still call your agent when you get back. He's the best judge of what sells.'

'I haven't spoken to him in three years. He's probably forgotten who I am.'

'I doubt it – your short stories were great. You have talent, Liz. You just have to be persistent and keep at it.' And then Olivia lowered her voice conspiratorially. 'We'll make Sarah eat her words.' She kissed Liz on the cheek then, and took the manuscript to her cabin and put it in a drawer. She didn't want Liz changing her mind and taking it back before she had a chance to read it. She was going to read it that night, and was glad Liz had finally agreed to give it to her. Her heart ached for Liz over what Sarah had said. She had been brutal. And Olivia did wonder if she was jealous of Liz, or maybe she was such a purist that she didn't know a piece of popular fiction when she saw it. She was far too lofty in her academic ideas. In any case, Olivia intended to see for herself. Liz was so excited about it that something told Olivia it was good.

When she went back up on deck, the young people had appeared and were having breakfast. The girls wanted to go swimming, and Alex wanted to explore the area on a jet ski. As soon as he said it, his grandmother tapped him on the shoulder with a serious expression.

'Don't forget you owe me another ride.'

'Sure, Grandma, as soon as I finish eating.'

Olivia sat down and chatted with them, and they told her about the movies they watched the night before. Olivia had never heard of either of them, and she told them she'd have to start watching movies with them, if she wanted to be up to date. That sounded fine to them.

Sarah was reading a literary magazine, and Liz smiled at her mother over the young people's heads. She was grateful for what her mother had said. It may not have been true, but it was kind. She was sure that Sarah was right, and her mother would probably echo her opinion. It seemed unlikely to her now that the crazy fantasy story she'd written was any good. She'd been delusional, as usual, and had failed again. It was familiar to her. Success at anything would have come as a surprise, not the reverse.

Olivia went off on the jet ski with Alex after breakfast, and she had a ball with him again. The girls and Liz swam to a nearby beach. They had a late lunch, when Phillip and John came back from fishing. And this time they had both caught several very decent-sized fish and were very pleased. The chef cooked three of them for lunch, and everyone tasted them and approved.

Olivia suggested they go ashore and explore Elba after lunch, but no one was interested. The kids lay in the sun and went swimming. Sarah and John took one of their frequent naps, and Amanda kept to herself with a book. And Phillip went fishing with one of the crew. And when the kids came back from swimming, Olivia played Scrabble with them again. She was having a great time. And while they were playing, John came back on deck, and started sketching the landscape around them. His drawings were beautiful, and he seemed lost in his own world as he did them.

They had an early dinner that night so they could get under way again. They were night-sailing to Sardinia and planned to be in port by morning. This time all the women wanted to go shopping.

And for some reason during dinner, Phillip and John

started telling stories about their childhood, and Liz joined in. They talked about a trip to Disneyland they'd taken, when Olivia had been away. A house they'd rented during spring break in Aspen, a dog they'd found but the owners had reclaimed. An outrageous prank they'd played on a neighbor and been forced to apologize. The stories were funny, and one led into another, but what upset Olivia was that she had been there for none of the stories, vacations, jokes, or events. None of the stories included her, only Joe and Granibelle. It made her realize how much she'd been away and how much she'd missed, and by the end of dinner she looked genuinely sad. It had been the most powerful way to illustrate to her how badly she had failed them, and how little she'd been around. She felt terrible hearing about it now. Alex had noticed the look on her face and spoke to her in an undertone after dinner.

'Are you okay, Grandma?' He looked worried. He was a very sensitive kid, and he was very fond of his grandmother.

'I'm fine.' She didn't want to tell him why she was upset, and he gently put an arm around her. They put some music on then, and everyone danced for a while, and then as they began to cruise again, the girls brought out a new game Olivia had never seen and they taught her to play, while Phillip and John played liar's dice, and Sarah and Liz joined in for money. Phillip was the big winner with twenty dollars. And Olivia won a round of the new game. Amanda had gone downstairs again to read her book. John asked his brother if she was feeling well, and Phillip said she was fine, so John didn't pursue it.

It was another fun evening, and the adults went below before the kids did, and Olivia stayed to keep them company and keep an eye on them. She didn't want anyone falling overboard while they were under way. And finally Sophie and Carole went to watch a chick flick in the theater, and Alex stayed with his grandmother to chat for a while.

'Are you okay, Grandma?' he asked her again. They shared a tender bond, even more than she did with the girls.

'I'm fine.' She decided to be honest with him then. He was old enough to understand. 'I missed a lot when my children were young. I was working all the time, and I'm sad about it now. And you can't change history and fix your mistakes. That's a good thing to keep in mind. It's better to get it right the first time around, because that's the only chance you've got.'

'I think you did it all right. Everyone seems fine.'

'I hope so. But they missed having their mother around. And I missed out on a lot too. Your grandfather and great-grandmother were around more than I was.'

'Yeah, but if you hadn't done all that, we wouldn't have all this,' he said, pointing to the boat with a grin, and she laughed.

'That's true. But that's not what's important,' she reminded him.

'No,' he conceded, 'but it sure is nice. I love this boat, Grandma. Thank you for taking us on it.'

'I'm having a great time too,' she said, happy that her grandson was enjoying it. They all were, and Amanda was just being herself, and enjoying it to the degree she did anything. She was not a team player, and the Graysons were a formidable team. 'What about you?' Olivia asked Alex. 'Are you okay? Everything the way you want it in your life?' She liked keeping in touch with him, and knowing what he cared about and what was going on. She had good talks with Sophie often too. She wasn't quite as close to Carole, who was more flighty, and a little lost sometimes like Liz. She and Sophie had more in common.

'I'm okay,' Alex said, but he sounded half-hearted. 'But?' Olivia decided to pursue it. She loved the boy.

'I don't know. You said you weren't around when my

dad and Phillip and Liz were kids. My parents are around all the time. They never go anywhere, except with me. But in a way, even if they're around, they really aren't. Some of my friends say their parents hate each other. I think mine like each other too much. They're always sitting in a corner whispering, or kissing, or in their room 'taking a nap.' I know they love me, but sometimes I feel like there's no room for me in their life, just for them. They're so tight, there's no space for anyone else. Sometimes I sit around at home and I have no one to talk to. At least your kids had each other. I just have me.' It was the dilemma of the only child, but more than that, Olivia understood what he was referring to. Sarah and John's ongoing romance shut everyone else out of their world, even their son. Olivia sympathized with Alex.

'That's a hard one. You're lucky you have parents who like each other so much. But I can see that it would make you feel left out.' Even on the boat, they were constantly disappearing to their cabin, and it was easy to figure out what they were doing. Living in a house with them had to be lonely for Alex, and it sounded like it was. 'Have you ever said anything to them about it?'

'No, it's not going to change. They've always been like that, and I'm leaving for college in a year anyway. After

I'm gone, they can do whatever they want. That's why I want to go away, even though Mom wants me to stay in Princeton. I want to get out. But she'd be really upset if I told her why.' Olivia suspected that was true. 'And . . . oh I don't know . . . I'm just ready to leave and move on.' She sensed that he was going to tell her something else, but he changed his mind and didn't.

'Anything else?'

'No, that's it. And I don't want you to tell them what I said.'

'I won't. But maybe you should sometime, just so they know how you feel.'

'They only care about each other,' Alex said, sounding sad. 'I wish I had a brother or sister.' It struck Olivia then as she thought about it that life was so ironic. She had been an absentee parent much of the time, so John made a point of being at home with his son all the time, but he was so crazy about his wife that they wound up shutting out their son, who was just as lonely as he might have been if they weren't around. She realized that we're all blind to the errors we commit, no matter how glaring they are to others, or the people we hurt when we commit them. In the end, Alex's childhood was even lonelier than his father's had been – at least her children had had their father and grandmother paying attention to them. Alex had no one, except two parents who were crazy about each other, to the exclusion of all else.

Alex and his grandmother talked on deck for a long time that night, as the boat motored toward Sardinia in the moonlight. The night sails seemed peaceful and beautiful to Olivia, and when Alex went to bed, Olivia went to her cabin, got into bed, and picked up Liz's manuscript. She could hardly wait to read it.

Chapter 8

The next morning they reached the Strait of Bonifacio just after dawn. It was the stretch of open water between Corsica and Sardinia, and the captain had warned her that it might be rough, but only for a short time, and after that the sea would be smooth again. And as they hit the swells, a series of hard bumps that made the big boat shudder woke Olivia up. She didn't feel sick, but it was unnerving. She lay in bed, feeling it for a while, and then finally decided to go up on deck and look around. She couldn't sleep anyway, and it was worse lying in bed, feeling the boat come down hard after every swell. She wondered if it had woken up the others too.

When she went out on deck in her nightgown and bathrobe, she saw Liz huddled in a protected corner of the deck, and Olivia thought she looked a little green. She hadn't gotten seasick so far, but the Strait of Bonifacio made for a rough hour or two.

'Are you feeling sick?' Olivia asked her daughter with a worried look. She was still wearing the wristbands the crew had given her, and she was convinced they had worked until then. Olivia wasn't sure if it was psychological or real, but if Liz thought they worked, that was fine.

'A little,' Liz admitted with a weak smile. 'It sure got bumpy all of a sudden.'

'It'll be over soon. It's just getting between Corsica and Sardinia. The captain said it won't be more than an hour.' And the boat had stabilizers, fortunately, it would have been worse otherwise, and the *Lady Luck* was a heavy boat, with a steel hull, that helped keep them steady too.

Then Olivia shared some good news with her, hoping it might distract her from the swells. 'I read your book last night. Twice. I wanted to be sure of my reaction when I talked to you. You kept me up half the night.' She grinned. 'I love it, Liz. It's absolutely fabulous. I have no doubt someone will want to publish it. I think it's going to be a runaway best seller, one of those cult books that everyone falls in love with.'

'You're just saying that,' Liz said mournfully. 'You don't have to lie to me.'

'I never do,' Olivia said seriously, settling a cashmere throw over her daughter's shoulders. She was shivering in the early morning breeze. 'Sarah has no idea what she was looking at. And if you don't call your agent when you get home, I will.' Her eyes bored into her daughter's, and Liz grinned.

'You really think it's any good?' She looked and felt like a child as she asked.

'I sure do. It's just what I said to you yesterday. It's not Louis XV furniture, or Shakespeare, but it's what every-body wants to read, just like what I do at The Factory. I think you'll be just as successful with your book. You need a title, by the way,' she reminded her.

'I was thinking of calling it *Crap*,' Liz said, and they both laughed.

'It has kind of a catchy ring,' Olivia added, and they laughed again. She put an arm around her daughter's shoulders and looked her in the eye. 'I'm very, very, very proud of you. It's terrific! I just had a feeling it would be. Thank you for having the courage to let me read it. I'm very excited for you about this book.'

'Now what do I do?' Liz said nervously. She had been sure her mother would hate it too.

'Call your agent. He'll know which publisher to show it to.' The idea that it might actually work and someone would publish it took Liz's breath away.

'I'm scared,' she said honestly. She had been braced for failure all her life. She had never thought about what it would be like to face success. It might even be worse.

'Everybody's scared. I'm scared a lot of the time too. A lot of things can go wrong in life, like your father dying so young, and mine even younger than that. But a lot of things can go right too. I think you're due for some good luck. I really hope this will be it.'

'Thank you,' Liz said, and squeezed her mother's hand. What she had just said meant the world to her. And for some reason she had more faith in her mother than she did in Sarah. Her mother had a point about Sarah being an intellectual snob. She hadn't understood any of what Liz had tried to do. Her mother did. 'I'll call my agent when I get home.'

And then Olivia brought up something else that had haunted her all night, along with Liz's book. 'You know, all those stories you and the boys told last night about when you were kids. It really brought it home to me how much I was away. I don't remember a single one of those stories. I'm so sorry I was gone so much. If I could do it differently, I would. It's too late now, but I just want you to know that I regret it.'

'I know you do, Mom. And honestly, we were okay.

Daddy and Granibelle were great to us, and so were you when you were home. Somebody had to do what you did, and I don't think Dad could have. It had to be you.'

'I missed so much of your childhood, though. You and John seem to have made your peace with it. But Cass and Phillip never will.'

'Phillip was always a big complainer, even when he was a kid,' Liz said, and Olivia laughed. Even from what she remembered, it was true. And Cass had been angry from the day she was born. Liz had been a happy, peaceful baby, and sunny child, and so was John. It was just who they were, even as kids.

The two women sat holding hands until the swells died down, and enjoying the peaceful sunny morning. Olivia sensed that something important had happened between them, and Liz felt it too. And in some ways it had happened because of her book. But forgiveness came easily with Liz, more so than with the others. Olivia realized that not all her children would forgive her, but if even some of them did, or just Liz, it was a gift. But to Phillip and Cass, her sins had been unforgivable, or that was how it seemed to Olivia now. And no matter how much she regretted it, it didn't change the past. History couldn't be rewritten, and what mattered was how her children viewed it, no matter how good her intentions had been.

The sea was flat again as they approached Sardinia, and by the time they slid into port in Porto Cervo, and tied up at the dock, with yachts as large as theirs on either side, Liz felt fine again. She and Olivia ordered breakfast, and they were just finishing when the others came up. Amanda said she had felt the swells, and she looked a little green. Phillip and John hadn't felt a thing. Sarah didn't seem to mind it, and the kids all thought it was fun. Neither Liz nor her mother mentioned that Olivia had read the book and loved it. They decided to be diplomatic and not say anything, so as not to challenge Sarah's literary authority.

And Amanda was excited about going ashore. Sardinia was well known for its great shopping and expensive stores. It was a hangout for the rich and famous, and Amanda seemed to come alive just looking at the other yachts and sensing the kind of people who hung out there.

The crew were standing by to escort them ashore as soon as they were ready. They were going to go swimming after lunch, but until then shopping was the order of the day. And even Olivia couldn't wait to look around.

Every important Italian store was represented on the island. Gucci, Prada, Loro Piana, Bulgari, Grisogono, and an assortment of equally expensive local stores, selling everything from furs to jewels. There were several art galleries along the port, which Alex and his father and uncle explored to pass the time. Sarah went back to the boat before the others, since she didn't want to buy any of the clothes she saw. She thought it was all much too expensive, and she met up with the boys. John was studying the paintings in the art galleries with interest. The other women stayed in town until lunchtime, and returned heavily laden with the spoils of war. Olivia even bought herself a short fur jacket, and treated her daughters, granddaughters, and daughter-in-law to a shopping spree at Prada and several other stores. She was always generous with them when they traveled together, and wanted them all to have fun. She bought Liz a gorgeous black leather jacket, and Amanda had found a very elegant black wool coat. They were delighted with what they'd bought when they met up with the others on the boat. Lunch had just been set out, and the captain offered to make a reservation for them at the popular local nightclub, the Billionaire. Olivia thought it sounded like fun.

'I hate nightclubs,' Amanda said as they sat down to lunch, her good mood of the morning instantly dispelled. 'I'm staying home.'

'I hear it's a terrific place,' Olivia tried to encourage

her, to no avail, but Phillip said he'd join them. And the kids were excited to go. 'I haven't been to a nightclub in years,' Olivia admitted, but she wanted to be with them, and she liked watching the young people have fun. In her youth, she and Joe had loved to dance, but the dances had been very different then. He had been a wonderful dancer, and they'd had some terrific times.

'We'll teach you, Grandma,' Sophie insisted, and her sister and cousin chimed in. They asked for a reservation at midnight, when the captain told them nothing started until then, or even later than that.

The boat pulled out of port as soon as they finished lunch, and they found a sheltered spot to go swimming, and Olivia rode the jet ski with Alex again. She felt comfortable riding behind him now. And Phillip and John took out two of the other jet skis and raced each other in big loops around the boat. They were having as much fun as the kids.

They stayed out until almost dinnertime, used the gym and had massages, and took their time dressing for dinner. They had asked for dinner at ten that night, and afterward they would go to the Billionaire. And when they met again for dinner, everyone had made an effort and gotten dressed up. Olivia was wearing white satin pants with a pretty organza blouse. Amanda was wearing a slinky white dress, even though she wasn't coming to the nightclub. Liz was wearing a halter top she had borrowed from one of her daughters, both of whom looked fabulous in sexy little dresses, and Sarah was wearing one of her flowery print dresses and the hairdresser on the boat had done wonders with her hair. She looked less like a professor than a pretty young woman, and John beamed as soon as he saw her. And Alex was wearing black jeans and a white shirt. They were a handsome group as they sat down to dinner, and even more so when they got to the nightclub. The women had all added high heels to their outfits, and they had to get their land legs back as they walked in.

The club was half empty when they got there, and a headwaiter settled them in a private alcove that the captain of the boat had arranged. Within half an hour, the place was swarming with beautiful young women, handsome men, people from the yachts, others who owned houses. There were mostly Italians, though Olivia heard French, English, Spanish, German, and Russian spoken as well. The place was fiercely expensive, so the crowd looked fairly racy. The music was blaring, champagne was flowing, and waiters carrying sparklers threaded through the crowd, as waitresses handed out jewelry that lit up in the dark. There was a mood of celebration all around them, and after a glass of champagne, Alex and his two cousins led Olivia out onto the dance floor, and before she knew it, she was writhing with the rest of the crowd, and having a terrific time.

'Who is that woman out there?' Phillip said to his brother with a broad grin. 'That can't be our mother. I don't think I ever remember seeing her dance like that.' She looked half her age as she danced with Alex, and her children were impressed by how fast she learned all the right moves, and she managed to look both dignified and sexy in her satin pants and high heels. And a few minutes later, Phillip grabbed his sister and headed onto the dance floor too. He had been drinking straight vodka and was in a great mood. And Sarah and John sat necking at the back of the alcove, like two kids.

The champagne poured freely, and Phillip made it halfway through a bottle of vodka before he switched to beer. He had never danced as much in one night. He had even danced with a woman in a sexy cocktail dress, and then went back to dance with Liz. He had noticed some Italian playboy stalking her and decided she needed rescuing, and she looked disappointed when he did.

'Who was that guy? Do you know him?' Phillip asked her and she shrugged with a guilty grin.

'He says he's from another boat. He's from Milan and

he just invited me to spend the weekend with him.'
Twenty years earlier, he would have been just her cup of
tea, and the kind of man she always got in trouble with.
Now it was just fun flirting with him, and it was easier
staying with her own group. But it was nice having someone pay attention to her. She had never seen her older
brother be so expansive, dance so much, or possibly be
quite so drunk.

It was three-thirty in the morning, and the party was
still going strong when they left the nightclub. Olivia said
her feet hurt so much she could hardly walk, but it had
been worth it. They had all had a ball. John and Sarah
were the only relatively sober ones in the group, and they
had had a fair amount of champagne too. It was better
than New Year's Eve, and they were all rowdy and loud
when they got back to the boat. The kids put on more
music, and kept dancing, but Olivia had finally run out
of steam. She sat down on one of the couches and felt like
she couldn't move.

'I haven't had that much fun in years,' she said with a
broad grin. 'I may have had a little too much to drink,'
she added demurely, and Phillip laughed out loud.

'Join the club, Mother. You're quite a dancer.' He had
suddenly remembered his parents dancing in his youth.
He had so few memories of them together.

'So are you.' She smiled at her oldest son.

They all stayed on deck for another hour, and it was almost five in the morning when they finally all went to bed. Phillip said he wanted to go fishing, and his brother convinced him to wait until the next day.

And as Olivia walked slowly to her room, she thought about her husband and wished he could have been there. He would have loved it, but even without him she had had fun dancing with her grandchildren, and drinking a little too much champagne. It had been a wonderful evening, and they had all forgotten that Amanda hadn't come along, and how lively Phillip could be without her. It was a side of him none of them had seen in years.

It had been an unforgettable night, and they still had more than a week left of the trip. Olivia lay down on her bed, just for a minute. She was going to get up and take off her clothes but never did. She fell sound asleep in her dancing clothes, with her high-heeled sandals in her hand, and a smile on her face. She was going to call and tell her mother all about it in the morning, but first she had to get some sleep.

Chapter 9

They all looked a little shaggy when they met at the breakfast table at noon the next day. Olivia looked surprisingly
fresh, but said she could hardly walk. Phillip was wearing
dark glasses and asked for a glass of Fernet Branca, which
was what he had used for hangovers in his youth.

'I think I may have a brain tumor,' he said, and everyone laughed. Amanda was extremely quiet. She had been
on deck alone since nine A.M.

'It sounds like you all had a good time,' she said
primly. But it had been her choice not to go.

'Grandma danced her ass off,' Alex volunteered, and
everybody laughed again.

'I had a very, very good time,' Olivia confirmed,
'except for the blisters on my feet.'

'I think I agreed to spend the weekend with some Italian guy from Milan,' Liz said with a dazed look. She had brought a bottle of aspirin to the table, and they all passed it around. They were a sorry group, but none of them regretted it for a minute. The headaches they had that morning had been worth it. 'I think if I go swimming today, I'll drown,' Liz said, wondering how many glasses of champagne she had had the night before. She had lost count. Carole, Alex, and Sophie had had fun too, and they had drunk less than the adults.

In the end, they decided to take the boat out and have lunch at anchor. They took turns having massages, and by three o'clock they all started to feel better, and went swimming after that. They took it easy and laughed a lot about the night before, what they remembered of it. Even Olivia admitted that she had had far too much champagne, and she called and told Maribelle all about it, as they went back to port in the late afternoon.

Maribelle surprised her when she said that Cass had come to see her the day before. She was in New York with one of her clients, and had gone to visit her grandmother. Hearing about it made Olivia wish she was there, but she knew Cass would never join them. But it was a relief to know that she was happy and well.

'You never know,' Maribelle said, when Olivia said she

wished Cass would come on the boat. She didn't have three children, she had four. Cassie was her lost child, the one that had slipped through her fingers and she couldn't recapture. It always felt like a terrible loss to her, even if they saw each other once in a while. But there was so much damage and distance between them now, it seemed beyond repair. 'Things happen. People change. Life has a way of working things out,' Maribelle said philosophically, with the vantage point of age. But it didn't seem likely to Olivia. Her mother laughed when she told her about the night before.

'You sound like a bunch of shameless drunks,' she said as Olivia described the scene to her. The only thing more shocking than how much they drank had been the bill. But she had been anesthetized enough not to care.

'We certainly were last night, but it was fun. Your greatgrandchildren had me dancing all night.' Olivia only wished that she had done more of that when she was young, but she had hardly ever had the time. Sometimes it was easier doing things like that when you were old.

The others all talked to Maribelle for a few minutes, and told her they missed her, and they promised to call her again in a few days.

They ate on board that night, and after dinner they left the port and headed back toward Corsica. They were going to sail through the night, and Liz dreaded going through the Strait of Bonifacio again, but the weather reports were good, and the captain said he was expecting a smooth crossing. And then as though out of nowhere, halfway to Corsica, a mistral wind came up. It was sudden and strong, the sea grew frighteningly choppy, and the boat shuddered and rode the deep swells. The kids had been in the movie theater and the adults had gone to their cabins. Liz was the first to knock on her mother's door as the boat groaned under their feet.

'Are we sinking?' She looked panicked.

'No.' Olivia smiled reassuringly, but there was no denying the pitching and tossing was unpleasant, and the boat slammed hard with a frightening sound each time they fell into a deep trough after a swell. 'I guess it's just an unexpected windstorm,' her mother reassured her, but it had unnerved her a little too, although she didn't get seasick. Liz was green.

'Should I put my life jacket on?' Liz asked with wide eyes.

'I don't think so,' Olivia said calmly as Phillip walked into her cabin, looking concerned.

'Amanda's feeling pretty sick. Do you think we should go back?' They were in the middle of open water halfway from Sardinia to Corsica, and that didn't sound like a solution to Olivia, but there was no denying it was getting worse. The heavy boat was rolling like crazy.

'I'll go talk to the captain,' Olivia said, trying not to look worried. Sarah and John appeared, and then all the kids found their way to Olivia's suite as well. Crew members were walking through the halls, taking fragile objects off tables, and putting anything that might break on the floor. They looked busy, but not worried, which was reassuring.

'Shit, we're sinking,' Liz said, as she grabbed her mother's arm.

'We are?' Carole and Sophie looked at each other, and Carole started to cry.

'We're *not* sinking, and if this were an emergency, the captain would have told us,' Olivia said above their voices as the boat continued to head into the troughs, hit hard, and shudder. 'I'll talk to the captain,' Olivia said firmly, and the entire group followed her to the wheelhouse, where the captain was watching the radar screens and adjusting several dials. He looked up apologetically as they entered.

'I'm sorry. It's a mistral. I thought we would avoid it, but it came up earlier than expected.' The winds were fifty knots, and the boat was at the mercy of them now.

'Are we in danger?' Liz managed to croak out.

'Not at all. We'll be in the shelter of land in two hours, and then it will be much better, although we will have strong winds for the next two days, but better seas.'

'Like this?' Sarah asked with a worried look, standing next to John.

'No, it will be calmer than this. It is just particularly bad here in the strait.'

'Should we go back to Porto Cervo?' Phillip inquired, thinking of Amanda sheet white and sick in their cabin.

'It would be the same. It will take us two hours to go back, or longer. We'll be better off if we just move ahead. In two hours, you'll feel better,' he assured them, and a few minutes later, Olivia led her troops to a sitting area on the same deck as her suite. The purser and two stewardesses offered them food and drink and all declined, and a few minutes later Liz disappeared and returned with her life jacket on.

'Just in case,' she said, and the others laughed, but it was no fun being on the stormy seas. The kids looked nervous and John and Sarah were worried. Only Phillip and Olivia seemed calm.

They sat together in the salon for two hours, and it was three hours before they benefited from the shelter of the Corsican coast. The sea was still rough but the winds died down a little, and finally they all went to their cabins to get some rest. The boat was pitching and rolling, but less. Liz asked her mother if she could sleep in her cabin, and she lay on Olivia's bed, holding her hand, with her life jacket on.

It was morning before the winds calmed enough for the boat to stop rolling as violently. It had been quite a night! Those who could sleep woke up feeling better in Corsica the next day. The winds were strong, but the boat was much steadier than it had been the night before. They had set aside a day for swimming and fishing off Corsica, before night cruising again back to France, where they planned to spend the rest of the trip. They had been on board for a week by then and covered a lot of ground. They decided not to swim in the still turbulent sea. They spent a quiet day on board, and sailed away from Corsica that night. The others went to their cabins, tired from the night before, Alex and Carole went to watch a movie, and Sophie stayed on deck with her grandmother to chat. There was something Olivia had been wanting to talk to her about, and this seemed like a good time.

'How would you like to come and work for me after you get your master's degree? We've talked about it before, but I wanted to let you know that I'm serious about it. I think you would be a wonderful addition. And after a year or two, maybe you'd like to run one of the stores abroad.' Sophie's eyes lit up as soon as Olivia mentioned it. It had been her dream for years. She wanted to work for her grandmother, and become the third generation to enter the business. And she loved the idea of running one of the stores on her own. It was her grandmother's way of teaching her the business from the ground up.

'How soon can I start?'

'The day you graduate,' which was only six months away. 'I wanted to make you an offer, before you took a job with someone else,' Olivia said with a smile.

'This is what I've always wanted to do, Grandma.' She could hardly wait. 'And I think Carole is going to move to L.A. when we go home. She wants to work for her dad and his wife. She's been talking about it for a long time.'

'I know she has. I think it might be good for her. I think she needs to get that out of her system. She's been dreaming about being with him for a long time, although that might be hard for your mom.'

'She already told her, and Mom's okay with it. I think she'd been kind of drifting in New York, and the art scene is hard to get into. I think L.A. might be the right thing for her, although I'm going to miss her,' Sophie said wistfully.

'So am I,' Olivia said, but she was excited about Sophie coming to work for her. The next generation had finally arrived. And maybe one day Alex would join them too. Olivia had high hopes for him as well. And Sophie was a star. Once she honed her skills and learned the business, Olivia sensed she would go far. She had a terrific head for business, and she'd been interested in The Factory since she was a child, just as Olivia had when she worked at the original hardware store when she was twelve. She thought it was the most exciting place on earth, and she still did. And she knew Sophie thought so too.

They talked about Olivia's plans for her, and Sophie's dreams late into the night, and when she went to bed, Olivia felt she had taken an important step. It was time to open their doors, welcome the new generation, and bring the young people along.

The next morning when they got up, they were in St. Jean Cap Ferrat, on the coast of France. It was one of the most elite locations on the French Riviera. Olivia had rented a house there one summer, an enormous villa. And Amanda seemed to come alive at breakfast, as they sat at anchor, looking at the expensive houses and talking about the people who owned them. Amanda had a decided interest in people with colossal fortunes. It was as though she thought everyone else was a waste of time. And when

Alex heard about Olivia's offer to Sophie, he was instantly jealous of his cousin and said so over breakfast. Sarah looked extremely displeased. She wanted Alex to work for a foundation, or be a political activist of some kind. She didn't like the idea of him working for The Factory, and usually whenever Olivia spoke to him about it for the future, she tried to make sure his mother wasn't around. He had told his grandmother that as soon as he finished college, he wanted to come and work for her. Olivia loved that idea. But for now Sophie would be coming to work for her at the end of the year. And Liz was pleased. She knew it was right for Sophie and had always been her dream. And now at last it was coming true. Alex still had to finish school, and go to college, so it was too soon to include him in their plans. Sarah was relieved.

Olivia let Sophie sit in on their morning meeting with John and Phillip, and Sophie had some surprisingly good ideas to contribute. Her uncles were impressed too. It was a good meeting for her to be part of that day – for once there were no problems, and they had gotten particularly good news about the sales figures from a new line John had just introduced. Sophie could hardly wait to join the team.

After the meeting broke up, they took the boat to Cap d'Antibes at lunchtime and anchored it outside the Hotel du Cap. It was one of the many extraordinary places Olivia had been with Joe. They had spent a fabulous weekend there, at the part of the hotel called the Eden Roc. The food was exquisite, the room had been fabulous, and they had spent their days in a private cabana, where lunch was served. It had been one of the most romantic places she had ever been with Joe. And she had made a reservation to take the family there for lunch.

They went to the hotel's dock by tender, and had lunch at the restaurant near the pool. They sat on a balcony, looking out over the Mediterranean, and ate delicious food. Her grandchildren saw a number of young people their own age, and they all wished they could have stayed there, but they were having a good time on the boat. The *Lady Luck* was an impressive sight, as she lay anchored just beyond the hotel, and everyone wondered who was on it. There were a number of Americans at the hotel, as always, and many Germans, and assorted well-known French aristocrats. It was just the kind of place Amanda loved. She said to Phillip at lunch that they should come back sometime and spend a week there. Phillip had never thought of it. He was happy staying at their small house in the Hamptons, or on the sailboat he kept at the yacht club nearby. He didn't need to impress anyone by coming to the Hotel du Cap in the South of France, but he knew it was something his wife would love.

And after lunch and a walk around the grounds, they went back to the dock and took the tender back to the boat. It was beginning to seem like home to all of them, and they swam and lay on the sundeck, before cruising slowly back toward St. Jean Cap Ferrat, where they were planning to anchor for the night. Amanda had remembered that they had friends staying there. She called them and was very anxious to go ashore and have dinner with them that night. They had invited Liz to join them. And John and Sarah had said they wanted to spend a quiet night on board. Olivia was planning to spend the evening with the kids. They wanted to organize a dance party. John and Sarah went to their cabin right after dinner.

Olivia loved having the young people to herself. They danced for a while, to the CDs they'd brought with them. The four of them played Monopoly afterward, and once the girls went to bed, she and Alex sat on the deck alone. She had had the feeling for days that he had something on his mind, but she had no idea what it was. And he fell silent for a while once they were on their own.

'Alex, can I help you with anything?' Olivia decided to break the ice. She was wondering if he was upset about her offer to Sophie, but Alex understood he was still too

young. He had five years of school to get through before
he could come to work for her.

'I don't know, Grandma,' he said quietly, looking her
in the eye. He was a very forthright kid, but she sensed
that something was troubling him, and he hesitated
before he spoke. 'Sometimes things are more complicated
than they seem.'

'That's certainly true,' she said, smiling at him.
'If you've figured that out, you're way ahead of the
game.'

'If I tell you a secret, do you swear you won't tell?'

'Yes, I do.' The only reason she would have broken the
promise was if he was doing something dangerous to
himself, but she didn't say that to him. 'It sounds like you
have something on your mind.'

'Maybe,' he said cautiously. 'I don't want Mom and
Dad to know.' It didn't sound good to her.

'Why not?'

'I don't think they could handle it.' She was flattered
that he seemed to think maybe she could. But she had
seen more of life than Sarah and John. They were thirty
years younger than she was and lived an insulated life.
Olivia had experienced more in her life and seen more of
the world.

'Well, why don't you try me then?' She wanted to help

him, and he clearly wanted to speak to someone. But she wasn't prepared for what he had to say.

'Grandma, I'm gay.' Olivia stopped for a minute, looked at him, and nodded. She was surprised, but she didn't want him to think she disapproved. She didn't, although she realized that it was certainly going to complicate his life to some degree. It already was if he felt he couldn't tell his parents. And she wasn't sure why he felt they couldn't handle it. He didn't seem to have much faith in them.

'Are you sure?' she asked calmly. 'What makes you think so?' He smiled at her innocence, as though he had said he had measles, and she wanted to know what the symptoms were to make sure he was right.

'I'm attracted to other boys, not to girls.'

'Well, that certainly clears it up, doesn't it?' she said with a sheepish grin, realizing that she must have sounded foolish to him. 'How long have you known?'

'About four years, since I was thirteen.' He sounded absolutely certain. 'I used to wonder about it. And I wasn't really sure, until this year. There's a boy in my school that I really like. And I've never been attracted to a girl. I just want to be friends with them.' He was simplifying it for her, and she didn't ask him how far it had gone with the boy he liked in his school. She thought it would have been indelicate of her.

'Have you told anyone else?' she asked him quietly. 'No. Only you.'

'And why do you think your parents couldn't handle it? Your mom is a college professor. She deals with kids all the time.'

'That's not the same. They have very old-fashioned ideas. They ask me about girlfriends all the time. My mom just thinks I'm young and I like sports more than girls.'

It reminded Olivia of how blind we can be to things happening close to us, even in our own homes. Sarah and John apparently had no idea who their son really was.

They loved him, but they expected him to be just like them. She suspected that it was a fatal error many parents made – they failed to see who their children were. She had her own regrets about Cass, and given their strained relationship, it seemed ironic to Olivia that her grandson had chosen to talk to her and had so much faith in her. He had more faith in her than she did in herself.

'What can I do to help you? Do you want me to talk to them?' 'No. I just wanted someone to know who I really am.' It was a reasonable thing to want, and it touched her that he had chosen to risk exposing himself to her. 'Are you shocked?'

'No, I'm not,' she said honestly as she sat back in her chair. 'I'm a little bit sad for you, because I think that's a hard road sometimes. Not everyone will accept you. And maybe you won't have kids. That would be sad too. Or you could adopt them, or use a surrogate to have a baby, or a friend. Nothing about it is insurmountable, just maybe a little bit more complicated.' All of that was racing through her mind, but right now his problems were much simpler. He had parents who had no idea who he was or how he felt. He was a lonely boy. 'I think you should tell them and give them a chance,' she said fairly, and Alex shook his head.

'I think they'd go nuts. Especially my dad. Mom would get over it – like you said, she has gay students. I don't think Dad could accept it. Maybe he wouldn't even talk to me anymore, or kick me out.' There was fear in his eyes. He had heard horror stories before, about other gay boys and their parents' reactions, especially their fathers. He had remembered them all, and it influenced him now.

'You're forgetting one important thing,' his grand-mother reminded him. 'They love you. That changes everything. You're their only child.'

'That makes it even worse,' Alex said with a look of despair. 'If they had another son, a straight one, it wouldn't be so bad. All their dreams, about who I'm supposed to be, are resting on me.' She couldn't deny what he said.

'What if we told them together?' She was trying to be helpful, but it was obvious he wasn't ready to share the truth with them, only with her.

'Maybe one day, Grandma. Not now. I just wanted you to know.' She sensed that it was the secret he'd been hiding, and had almost shared with her a few days before. She was relieved that he had told her after all.

'I'm very honored that you trusted me, Alex,' she said solemnly. 'I promise I won't tell anyone. But I think you should one of these days. Maybe they'll figure it out on their own.'

'I don't think so. They have denial. They haven't even figured out that I'm not interested in girls. At seventeen, all my friends are. Let's face it, sports are no substitute for sex,' he said, and laughed, which answered her earlier question about the boy he liked.

'I hope you're being careful about AIDS,' she said sternly. It was a serious issue for him now, if he was sexually active, and it sounded like he was.

'Obviously,' he said with a lofty look. 'I'm gay, I'm not dumb.'

'Sorry,' she said, and smiled. She felt as though she had grown up that night. It turned out that her grandson was more sophisticated than she was about the ways of the world. 'I just want you to know that I'm here if you need me. You can talk to me anytime. All you have to do is pick up the phone.' He actually did that often, and texted her from time to time. 'Call me if you need me, Alex. I mean that. And if you ever want me to talk to them, I will. Your Aunt Liz might be able to help with your dad. He always listens to her.' She had used that conduit to him herself, from time to time. It always worked with John. His big sister had an influence on him that no one else did, except his wife.

'Thank you, Grandma,' Alex said, and put his arms around her. He looked relieved, and like a kid again. Sharing that with her had taken a huge load off his mind. And telling her had been one of the defining moments of his life. She hadn't screamed, she hadn't fainted. She still loved him. He had been trying to check out her reaction, and all was well in his world. And then he thought of something that also mattered to him. 'Would you still let me work for you one day?' He was worried.

'Of course.' This time she looked shocked. 'What difference would it make?'

'You wouldn't be embarrassed to have a gay grandson in the business?'

'Of course not. I'm proud of you, whatever you are. And by the time you graduate, I'll be prouder yet.' He seemed satisfied with her answer, and a few minutes later, they hugged and went to bed.

She lay in bed thinking about him, and all he had said. He had given her an enormous compliment by confiding in her. It was probably more than any of her own children would have done. It proved to her again how important their relationship was. And all she had to do now was figure out how to help him tell his parents. Sooner or later they had to know. And she hoped that when he told them, they would rise to the occasion. She couldn't imagine anything less of her son John. She was sure that Alex was selling them short. But only time would tell if he was right. And all she could hope was that he was wrong in his fears about them, and his parents would be loving and supportive. She would be severely disappointed in them if not. She wished she could tell her own mother about it, but she had promised. And she always kept her promises. She had taken a vow of silence, and his secret was safe with her.

Chapter 10

When they woke up in the morning, Amanda was full of stories about the people they'd met the night before. They were people she knew from New York, and she was vastly impressed by the house they had rented. Phillip seemed to have enjoyed it, and Liz said they were very nice. It was Amanda who was the most thrilled with their visit.

And after they had breakfast, they cruised slowly toward St. Tropez, relieved that the seas were calm again. They stopped and swam near St. Marguerite Island off Cannes. It was where the Man in the Iron Mask had been imprisoned, allegedly the brother of the king. Olivia shared the story with them, and her grandchildren were particularly impressed. John sat quietly nearby, sketching the island while she talked. He already had one full sketchbook of drawings and had brought several more.

They reached St. Tropez in the late afternoon, and the captain had reserved a space at the dock for them at the outer edge of the port. It was the only space in the port big enough for the boat. The girls wanted to explore the shops and local color, and as soon as they set foot on land, they were besieged by paparazzi, who took photographs of anyone coming off a big yacht, assuming they were someone famous or important. They followed them on scooters and flashed cameras in their faces. Only Amanda loved it, everyone else was annoyed. They wandered around the town, which was one of the most populated vacation spots in the South of France. Everyone wanted to see and be seen in St. Tropez. Olivia was relieved when they went back to the boat. The crew had put curtains up around the decks, so they would have privacy in the port.

Because of the paparazzi, they decided to have dinner on board. They had wanted to try a local restaurant, but it was just too much trouble to deal with the feeding frenzy of the press. And instead of dinner, they decided to go ashore for another nightclub and made reservations at La Cave du Roy. The captain warned them that it might not be quite as much fun as the Billionaire, but when they got there, they enjoyed it just as much, although they drank a little less. 'I think Mom is turning into someone we don't even know,' Phillip commented as he watched Olivia dancing with Alex. She was actually pretty good, and had learned all her moves the night they went to the Billionaire. And this time Amanda had decided to come along. She was disappointed when no one took their picture, but she actually seemed amorous with Phillip on the dance floor that night. It had taken a long time for her to warm up, and for him to forget her comment about him having no balls. There had been a noticeable chill between them for most of the trip, which concerned Olivia a great deal. But Amanda had seemed in better spirits ever since the night they had dinner with their friends in St. Jean Cap Ferrat. She felt as though she had her own identity again, and wasn't just part of a mob.

They stayed at La Cave du Roy till three o'clock and didn't get to bed till four. The next morning, Olivia was up and dressed early. The Factory had a store in Draguignan, in the interior, and Olivia wanted to see it. She had invited Alex and Sophie to come along and both her sons. Olivia was as fresh as a rose when they got into the van, the others looked a little worn. But she was like a racehorse, once she had work to do, or a store to visit. The management of the store had been notified and was waiting for them. She spent two hours touring the store, and Sophie was excited to be with them, now that she knew she would be working for The Factory in six months. And maybe this was one of the stores her grandmother would let her manage one day. It was one of their newer ones.

Afterward, Olivia had a meeting with Phillip and John about the things she had observed while visiting the store, and what she wanted changed. Sophie sat in on that too, and was impressed by how keen her grandmother's powers of observation were. She had noticed everything right down to the most minute detail. She had even checked the restrooms and the storage areas and had spoken to a number of members of the staff in French. Alex had been impressed too. And there was a special connection between them now. He gave nothing away, and neither did she, but a silent look passed between them at times that spoke volumes and was filled with her love for him.

Her children and their spouses had dinner in St. Tropez that night, and she and her grandchildren opted to stay on board. They played games for a while and afterward they watched a movie and ate popcorn the cook had sent up for them. They were still in the movie theater when the others came home. They had had a great time together, and Phillip couldn't help but comment on how different their mother was on this trip, even during their meetings about the business. She was so much more relaxed, and much more easygoing than she was at home. All she wanted was for them to have a good time. It made him even angrier that she had spent so little time with them when they were young.

'When are you going to get over that?' Liz confronted him when he said it. The three siblings sat together on deck, after Amanda, Sarah, and Olivia went to bed.

'Maybe never,' he said harshly. 'I never had a mother for my entire childhood. And neither did you. Why are you so willing to forget that now?'

'Because I think she did the best she could. And she did a lot of other things for us. She was always nice when she was home. So she went away a lot. So what? Other parents do a lot of other things that are worse. I've been home all the time for my kids. How do I know they won't be pissed off at me someday for something else? You can't get it right all the time. It's easy for you – you don't have kids. No one is ever going to be telling you what you did wrong. You get to stay a kid all your life and be pissed at her. And look how hard she tries now. She knocks her socks off every year to give us a vacation so we can all be together. She's still trying, Phillip, and you never give her a break for the past. That seems really wrong to me.'

'Well, listen to Miss Therapy,' he said angrily. 'You don't ever get back your childhood, Liz, and as far as I'm concerned she ruined mine. I never had a mother for all those years.'

'Yes, you did. She wasn't perfect – well, neither is anyone else's. And looking at her now, she seems pretty goddamned good to me.'

'That's up to you. I don't happen to see it that way.'

'That's unfortunate for you. You're never going to be able to forgive yourself, or anyone else, until you learn to forgive her. Are you so perfect? Haven't you ever screwed something up?'

'Not the childhood of four children. That's why I don't have kids.'

'I feel sorry for you,' Liz said quietly, and John stepped in and changed the subject. He didn't say it, but he thought Liz had a point. Their mother went all out to entertain them royally every year, and he had to admit, she was wonderful with their kids. It made up for a lot with him. And he had never been as unhappy as Phillip. For him, Granibelle and their father had been enough. And when their mother was home, it was icing on the cake. For Phillip, as long as she was gone, nothing else had ever been enough. But he wasn't a happy person, even now. He was always grumbling about something, and he had a wife who withheld approval and affection, which their mother never had. She had been gone, but whenever she came home, they knew that they were loved. Phillip and Cass had just refused to accept her as she was, recognize that she had tried, and forgive her her mistakes, even now. It seemed like a waste of energy to John. Forty years of anger seemed like an unfair sentence to him. John thought their mother didn't deserve the punishment she'd been given, particularly with all she'd done for them in other ways, and still did. They dropped the subject after that, but Phillip was still annoyed. He thought his brother and sister were far too easy on her, and Cass was right. If he didn't work for her, he would have taken his distance from her too.

The next day they left St. Tropez and headed back toward Antibes. They didn't stop at the Hotel du Cap again, but docked outside the old port instead, and went into town by tender, to wander around the ramparts, and Olivia took them all by cab to a little church she knew on top of a hill with a lighthouse, which overlooked the entire coast, and had a breathtaking view. The church, called Notre Dame de Bon Port, had been built in the eleventh century and had a fourth-century chapel. Miracles were said to have happened there. They wandered into the church, and Olivia lit a candle for Joe, and afterward they stood outside, eating ice cream and admiring the view.

'How did you ever find this place?' Sarah asked her with interest. She had already taken dozens of pictures of the chapel and the view.

'Joe and I found it when we stayed at the Hotel du Cap. I always wanted to come back here one day. I just never thought it wouldn't be with him.' She smiled sadly, and Sarah gently touched her arm in sympathy. They all fell silent after that, and were quiet on their way back to the port in the cab. Olivia didn't say anything, but she had lit a candle for Alex too, for the smooth transition of his coming out, whenever it occurred.

They had dinner in the port that night, then went back to the boat. In the morning, they were going back to Monaco to spend their last day of the trip and celebrate Olivia's birthday. It had really been a perfect trip, for all of them. Even Phillip and Amanda seemed on better terms. And Alex seemed a lot happier than he had at first. Sophie had the promise of a job when she graduated. And Liz was going to call her agent as soon as she got home and had her mother's endorsement of the book. Olivia had dedicated the whole time to taking care of them, and she had had a wonderful time too. Her best birthday gift to herself every year was her holiday with her family.

And the next day, thanks to Olivia's meticulous organizing, everything went according to plan. They got to Monaco in the morning, and after wishing Olivia happy birthday over breakfast, they all relaxed and talked. After lunch on deck in the port, they took the boat out again so everyone could swim. Phillip and John went off on the tender to go fishing. And Olivia got a final ride on a jet ski with Alex, and all the kids rode the banana for a last time. At the end of the day, they pulled into port and had a sumptuous birthday dinner for her with lobster and caviar, and soufflés and a birthday cake for dessert. They went to the casino afterward, while Olivia kept Alex company on the boat and played gin with him, and then they met them all at Jimmyz, and danced until three in the morning, and they stayed up till four o'clock reminiscing about the trip. The crew had packed for all of them so they were ready to leave. They would all be off the boat by noon, and Olivia thought it had been the happiest two weeks of her life, and everyone agreed with her, as they hugged each other and wished her a happy birthday again, and went to their cabins for their last night.

She and Alex had discussed his problem with his parents again that night while the others were at the casino, and she had encouraged him once more to tell them that he was gay. And he was just as adamant that they wouldn't understand, and he wasn't willing to take the risk. Olivia thought about Alex when she went to bed that night. She had so much to think of, as well as so many happy memories to take with her. And when they left the boat, the others were going home, and she was going to London to check on their store there. They had been remodeling it for six months, and she wanted to see what had been done. It had been their original flagship store in Europe, and she had a deep, personal attachment to it.

And in the morning, they all shared a last breakfast together. Phillip and Amanda were the first to leave, and she was anxious to get back to her office. John and Sarah were going to Paris for the weekend with Alex. Liz and the girls were going home to Connecticut. And then Carole would be packing up to leave for L.A., to work for her stepmother and father. She could hardly wait to get started. Her father had called and made her an offer while she was on the boat, and Carole had jumped at the chance.

At noon Olivia left the boat alone. They had arranged for a car and driver to take her to the airport, and she turned back to look at the boat that had been so wonderful for them. Her heart ached now that they were gone, and she looked at the boat longingly as they drove away. She had so many questions in her mind now after living with them for almost two weeks, about Phillip and Amanda, and Alex, and Liz and her book. She had been so much a part of their daily lives, and now she was back to her own nomadic life, heading for London on her own.

She checked in at the British Airways counter at the Nice airport, and an hour later she boarded the plane. As she sat in the first-class lounge before that, she texted all of them about how much she missed them, and how much fun she'd had with them on the trip. Alex answered her immediately. She knew that Liz and the girls were already on their plane. Phillip and Amanda were in the air too. And then she had to turn her own phone off and put it away. She was thinking about all of them as her plane took off for London. And she looked somber when they landed at Heathrow, and she was met by her driver from Claridge's. He took her to the hotel, where she checked in to her usual suite, which was decorated in bright corals and floral chintzes, and she was startled when the phone rang. She had been lost in thought, and she wanted to order something to eat before she left to see the store. She was surprised when she heard Peter Williams's voice on the phone.

'I just wanted to be sure you got to London safely. How did the trip go?' He sounded happy to talk to her, and it was nice to hear a friendly voice. She had been feeling so alone.

'It was beyond wonderful. I'm so sad it's over. I hate to wait another year to go on vacation with them again.'

'I always feel that way when my kids leave Maine too. It's just not the same when you don't live with them any-more. And it's such a gift when you can spend time with them here and there.' It was exactly what she was feeling about the trip.

'I think I'm having withdrawal,' she admitted as she looked out the window of her hotel room. She was home-sick for all of them, and she wondered if this was how they had felt when she was away when they were young, as though their hearts had been ripped out through their noses. If so, she thought it was suitable punishment for her that she felt that way now.

'Happy birthday, by the way, a day late. It must have been fun to spend it with the kids.'

'It was. We danced till three A.M. We did that several times on the trip. In Sardinia we stayed up till five A.M.'

'You must be a lot younger than I am,' he said ruefully. 'The last time I stayed up till five A.M. was when my son was born.'

'Me too. But I went dancing with my grandchildren. You have to stay on top of it for them.'

'Fortunately, mine aren't old enough to go dancing yet. And when they are, I'll be in a wheelchair in a nursing home somewhere.'

'I hope not,' she said, laughing at him.

'I don't want to be the bearer of bad tidings, but the press has been agitating about the child labor issue at the factories in Asia again.'

'I know. I got a memo about it from my office two days ago, and I told them to copy you on it. Do they know anything we don't?' She sounded concerned. She had tried not to get upset about it on the trip, but it was an issue she always wanted to keep a close watch on. And if they were going to have to make major changes, she wanted to be prepared. The interview she had done before the trip had gone well, but the press was always unpredictable, and they both knew that the tides of public favor could turn at any time.

'I don't think so. I just think they like stirring the pot, to see what bubbles to the surface. I don't think there's anything new. Those countries are always going to be a problem on human rights issues, but we have no solid proof that any of our factories are out of line.'

'I just want to be sure.'

'I know. We're as sure as we can be. If anything changes, I'll let you know. How long will you be in London?'

'Till tomorrow.'

'I'm going back to the city tomorrow too. I'll see you in the office next week. Have a safe flight home.'

'Thanks, Peter. It was nice of you to call me.' She had been feeling lonely when she got to London. Getting back to real life seemed harsh now without her kids. She was even missing Joe. It had been nice to hear a familiar voice when Peter called. 'I'm checking out the remodel of the London store.'

'I figured that was what you were doing. I hope your re-entry won't be too tough.'

'Hopefully not. Enjoy the last of your vacation too.'

'Thanks.' They hung up then, and she ordered a bowl of soup from room service. She wasn't even hungry. Nothing seemed like any fun now without her kids.

And an hour later, she was off to the London store. It tugged at her heartstrings to see the old familiar location, and she spent the afternoon looking at the remodel and meeting the new manager of the store. He was taking her to see their new warehouses outside the city the next day, and then she was catching a flight home.

When she got back to Claridge's at eight o'clock that night, she was too tired to even order dinner. She had just turned seventy, a fact she tried to ignore and which seemed hard to believe, but she felt a hundred years old that night. All she wanted was to go back to the boat and start the trip all over again. Or better yet, rewind the film all the way back to the beginning of her life, and do it differently this time. But there was no rewinding the movie. She just had to go forward, and do the best she could. The rest of how the story turned out was up to Sophie and Alex, and their children after them. She was just a link in the chain. She and Joe had started something, and their grandchildren would finish it, or their children. And for now, all she could do was move ahead, and keep building the empire for them. She had nothing else to do.

Chapter 11

When Liz got back to the house in Connecticut, it was so empty and silent that it seemed morbidly depressing. Like her mother, she had loved being with her kids, and it was painful to no longer be with them. She looked in the fridge and it was empty. She made herself a cup of instant soup, opened her suitcase, and decided to go to bed. She called Carole and Sophie, and both of them were out with their friends, respectively in New York and Boston. The lives they had come home to were far more entertaining than hers. All she had to do was two weeks of laundry, and as she lay in bed with her mug of soup, she remembered the manuscript in her bag. She took it out and looked at it again. She could see a dozen places she already wanted to change. And she found herself wondering again if Sarah was right about it. Maybe her mother had just been kind to her. She was suddenly filled with self-doubt again.

She fell asleep too early that night, because of the time difference, and she was wide awake at six o'clock the next morning, and read the manuscript again. She didn't know if she had the guts to call her agent, and by nine o'clock, she was in a state of total nerves. She decided to put it off till the next day, until she got a text message from her mother. All it said was 'Did you call your agent yet? Do it! The book is great! I love you, Mommy.' Liz smiled when she read it, and gritting her teeth, she called her agent at ten.

She waited to hear the familiar voice of her agent and was startled when a clipped British male voice answered instead.

'Is Charles Halpern there?' she asked politely, and the British voice sounded as startled as she had. There was a long pause before he answered.

'No. He died two years ago. This is Andrew Shippers, I bought the agency from him when he got sick. Is there something I can do for you?'

They kept surprising each other. 'My name is Elizabeth Grayson. He represents – er . . . used to represent me, I guess. I was calling him about a . . . well . . . uh . . . about a book.'

'You don't sound too sure of that, Ms. Grayson. Are you sure it's a book?' he said, laughing at her, and she could feel her face flush bright red. This was harder than she had expected, and she was nervous enough about it, without having her agent die and sell the agency to someone else.

'Well, actually I'm not, sure it's a book, I mean. I don't know what it is. I was going to ask him.'

'I see,' the new agent said, although he really didn't. She wasn't sure if it was a children's book, a book for adults, or a fantasy of some kind that fell through a crack somewhere between the two. 'Would you like to show it to me?' She really wouldn't, but if she backed off now it would seem rude.

'I . . . well . . . it's kind of a strange little fantasy book. My sister-in-law, who teaches literature at Princeton, hated it. And then my mother read it and she loved it. She said I should call you, so I did. But that was when I thought you were Charlie Halpern. Now that you're someone else, I don't think you represent me, do you?' She sounded utterly confused.

'I can if you want me to, if he represented you, since I bought the agency from him. Of course, if you want to take it to someone else, I understand, and you have no obligation to me.'

Danielle Steel

'Thank you.' She didn't know what she wanted to do. She felt utterly frightened and confused.

'And with all due respect to your sister-in-law who teaches literature at Princeton,' he continued, 'academics aren't usually the best judges of commercial fiction. So your mother might have the right idea.'

'That's what she said. About academics, I mean.'

'Precisely. Would you like to come in to see me? I have some free time this afternoon.'

'I . . . uh . . .' She hadn't expected him to offer her an appointment so soon. 'I just came back from Europe yesterday, and I have a lot of laundry to do.' She couldn't believe she was saying that to him. She was willing to use any excuse to escape having someone read her book who might hate it as much as Sarah had, and then she decided to screw up her courage and go into the city to see him. If she didn't, her mother would be on her back until she did. 'Okay, never mind. What time this afternoon?'

'Is four o'clock too late for you?'

'No, it's fine. I'll be there . . . oh . . . did you move?'

'No, same place. I'll look forward to seeing you at four, Ms. Grayson,' he said formally.

'Liz. Call me Liz.'

'Fine, see you this afternoon then.' She felt like a total idiot as she played the conversation over in her head, and slid under the covers with a groan. This was harder than she'd expected it to be, now that it involved someone new.

She got out of bed at one o'clock, showered and put on blue jeans and sandals, and at two-thirty she got in her car with the manuscript and drove into the city. She was at Charlie Halpern's old address ten minutes early, and she had a knot in her stomach the size of a fist. She could hardly breathe. She parked her car, waited ten minutes, and then went up in the elevator, wondering what the new agent was like. Charlie had been in his late seventies, and had always been very fatherly, which worked for her. The person who had replaced him sounded like a grown-up. The British accent made him sound formal and official, and she was convinced he was going to hate her book. He didn't sound like a man who liked fantasy, and if he had free time on this hands the day she called him, he was probably no good.

She walked into the outer office, in the small building on Madison Avenue where his offices were. Charlie had had an ancient secretary she'd always suspected he was sleeping with, but she was gone too. Liz sat down in the waiting room, and a moment later a very attractive man walked in, wearing blue jeans, an impeccably cut striped shirt, and immaculately shined shoes. He looked about her own age. And he was so handsome, she didn't know what to say. She sat mute in her chair, clutching her manuscript to her chest.

'You must be Elizabeth Grayson,' he said pleasantly. 'Liz.' And with a gesture, he invited her to come in. She couldn't move, she sat frozen in her chair with a look of fear. He realized this was going to be hard. 'And that must be the manuscript your sister-in-law hated. I'd love to have a look.' With that, Liz stood up and followed him silently into the other room. She noticed that he'd had the entire office repainted and fresh carpeting put in. There were new paintings on the walls, of hunting scenes in England, and he had a handsome antique partner's desk. There was a comfortable leather chair for her to sit in, facing him across the desk. He was much too good-looking to be an agent, she told herself. He was probably some sort of con artist or playboy who had nothing else to do. She sat looking at him with suspicion as he held out a hand for the manuscript she was still clutching. And then she realized how neurotic she must seem.

'I'm sorry. It's just strange dealing with someone new,' she said as she finally handed the manuscript to him. It was looking a little beaten up after making the round-trip to Europe in her handbag, but he didn't seem to care as he glanced through it.

'I'm sure it is. Did Charlie sell a lot of work for you?' he asked her candidly.

'Just short stories, and some poetry. I wrote two novels, but they weren't any good.'

'Did your sister-in-law tell you that too?' he asked with a look of amusement. He looked very British, and seemed to be amused by almost everything.

'No, she didn't. Charlie said it wasn't my best work, and he was right. I don't know what to think about this one. My mother was probably just being nice.'

'Possibly. I'll give it a read and tell you what I think. If you jot your number down for me, and your e-mail, I won't have to look it up in the files. My assistant is off sick.' She wrote both down for him on a piece of paper, and she wasn't sure what else to do. She realized that she was so nervous, she must have looked more than a little nuts to him. She was terrified of what he was going to say about her book. Sarah had probably been right.

'Your sister-in-law might be jealous of you too,' he suggested. 'The book may be very good.' He tried to reassure her, but he could see how unnerved she was.

'I don't know. See what you think.'

'Happy to,' he said, smiling at her, and she thought he looked like the cover of *GQ*. She couldn't imagine what he was doing as an agent. He looked as though he should be an actor in British films. He had a kind of Hugh Grant quality about him, with even better looks. 'Have you been an agent for long?' Liz asked him in a strangled voice that sounded more like a croak to her.

'I worked for Richard Morris in London for fifteen years. And then I went out on my own, and moved here. It's worked out very well. Charlie had a lot of very nice clients, and I've added a few of my own in the past two years. I'm sorry we haven't met before. But I'm very happy to be reading your book.'

'Thank you . . . thank you . . . Mr. Shippers—'

'Andrew.' He smiled his dazzling British smile at her, and she stood up out of the leather chair, ready to retreat. 'We'll talk about the book when I've read it.'

'I've done some editing on it already,' she said nervously.

He walked her back through the outer office then, and held open the door for her. She fled down the stairs, instead of waiting for the elevator, and stood on Madison Avenue with a dazed look.

She got back in her car and sent her mother a text message immediately. 'I did it. Just left the agent's office. Old one died. New one. British. I left the manuscript with him. See you soon. Love, Liz.' She took a deep breath then and called both her daughters. Carole was at a shipping company, picking up boxes to pack her things for L.A., and Sophie was in Boston getting ready for school. There was nothing left for her to do except go home.

She drove back to Connecticut and tried to tell herself that the book wasn't important to her. And if he hated it, sooner or later, she'd write something else. Besides, he was too good-looking. The last thing she needed was an agent who looked like a movie star. It would be too distracting to work with someone like him. She went home, unpacked her suitcase, and did three loads of laundry. She went out and bought groceries, and she made an omelet and big green salad for dinner. It was a far cry from all the elegant service and delicious meals on the boat. It was embarrassingly hard to get used to real life again. She felt like Cinderella after the coach had turned back into a pumpkin, and the coachmen into mice. She fell asleep on her bed at nine o'clock, fully dressed with all the lights on, and woke up at nine the next morning to the sound of the phone. For a minute, she thought she was still on the boat, and then reality hit her again. She was home.

'Good morning, I hope it's not too early to call you.' It was Andrew Shippers on the phone.

'No, not at all. I'm usually up long before this. I'm a little jetlagged. I just got up.'

'Well, I've got good news for you. Your sister-in-law doesn't know what she's talking about. Your mother does. I read your book last night, and it's a piece of sheer genius. It's one of the most whimsical, delightful pieces of brilliant writing I've read in a long time.'

'You what? . . . You did? . . . It is?' She felt like she was about to burst into tears. And she was just as tongue-tied as she'd been the day before. Only now she was smiling and there were tears of joy and relief running down her face. She hadn't realized how much she cared about it, and what he had just said to her was like getting a gift, or winning the lottery. She was so excited she wanted to scream. 'Oh my God – you *liked* it?'

'No. I loved it. And if you don't let me represent you, I'll come to your house and stalk you. I want to sell this book.'

'Oh my God,' she said again. 'Yes, of course. Sell it. I want you to represent me. Do you really think someone will want to buy it?'

'Very much so. If you e-mail it to me, I'll get it into the right hands immediately. The only thing that might slow it down a little is that people are on vacation. But in a few weeks, everyone will be back at work. I have a few editors in mind who would be just right for this book.'

'I think I'm going to faint,' she said in a choked voice.

'Please don't. Just hang on to your hat, and I'll get back to you in a few weeks.'

'Thank you, thank you very much, Mr. ... er ... Andrew ... just thank you, and good luck with it!'

He wondered if she was always that nervous, or if it was just with him, and about this book. He could tell how personal it was. It was a beautiful piece of writing that had come straight from her soul. He was sure he was going to do very well with the book. He hadn't sold anything he liked as much in months, maybe even years.

After she hung up, Liz called her mother's BlackBerry. She thought she'd been due back in New York the night before. And she was right. Olivia was in her office, going over some charts and e-mails, and she answered on the first ring.

'Oh my God, Mom, he liked it – he loved it—'

'Who did?' For a moment Olivia was confused and then she understood. 'He did? The agent? What did he say?'

'That you were right. He thinks it's "brilliant." He thinks he can sell it. He doesn't even want me to change anything.'

'I'm so pleased,' Olivia said, beaming from ear to ear. 'I'm so proud of you.'

'Thank you, Mom. How was the rest of your trip?'

'It was okay. I missed you all like crazy when you left. I came back late last night. How's everything with you?'

'Fantastic. I'm going to sell a book.' As soon as she said it, she realized that was the next thing she had to worry about. What if he was wrong and no one bought the book?

'We'll have to celebrate,' her mother said generously.

'Not until he sells it.'

They talked for a few more minutes, and then Olivia had to take a call from Europe. Their store in Madrid was in the midst of a renovation and something was going wrong. A plumber had soldered a pipe badly the day before and destroyed a new ceiling.

'I'll call you in a couple of days,' Liz promised, and after she hung up, she decided to drive to Long Island and visit Maribelle. She was going to tell her about the book. She called Sophie and Carole after that. She missed them both terribly. And she knew it would be even worse when Carole moved to L.A. She would be so far away. But whatever else happened, she had a new agent, and he loved her book. All by herself, she did a little dance around the room.

In a mood of celebration, she drove out to see her

grandmother that afternoon. Maribelle was sitting on a sunny patio when Liz got there.

She was talking to two elderly ladies, and they were laughing at something. Maribelle was regaling them with funny stories, and she looked up with surprised delight when Liz walked up. She introduced her to the other women, and then she walked away with Liz, to sit in the facility's well-appointed living room. She had her own apartment, but she liked visiting with people throughout the day in the common rooms. What she liked about living there was all the people she met, and when she wanted time to herself, she went to her own apartment. And most of the time, she took her meals in the dining room. She no longer liked to cook, and never really had. She had cooked for the children when they were young, but Olivia had very quickly gotten them a cook. She felt her mother was doing enough for her, without having to do the cooking too.

Liz's childhood memories of Granibelle were that her grandmother was a fabulous cook, which included spaghetti and meatballs, with sauce from a jar, hamburgers, meat loaf, and waffles she popped into the toaster. It was only when she grew up that she realized her grandmother's culinary skills were no better than her own, or perhaps even less stellar. Her grandmother had other, more impressive virtues. A quick mind, a warm heart, a great sense of humor, and tireless dedication to her daughter, son-in-law, and grandchildren. Liz literally could not remember her grandmother getting angry. She always had simple explanations for things, made reasonable requests of them, and the only thing she wouldn't tolerate was their being unkind to each other, or critical of their mother, whom she portrayed as a saint to her children, as did their father. At times, they'd all found it irritating.

'Lizzie!' she said as she put her arms around her and hugged her. 'You came all this way from Connecticut to see me?'

'Of course! I missed you.' Liz was sincere when she said it. She always missed her. Her grandmother had been one of the important foundations her life was built on. She had been one of three beloved parents.

'What a wonderful trip you all had! Your mother told me all about it. She called me almost every day. I wish I had been there when you all went dancing!' Her grandmother had always loved to dance, and still did, on rare occasions, although not in nightclubs like the Billionaire or Jimmyz. Her grandmother had danced all night at all their weddings. She was a happy, fun-loving person, who always saw the bright side of things. Olivia had inherited that trait from her, along with her father's dogged determination and perseverance.

Even at ninety-five, Maribelle was an elegant-looking woman. She had the same snowy white hair as her daughter – and in her case it had turned white in her twenties, like her own mother, a trait that none of her grandchildren had inherited. But it gave her a fairy god-mother look, with her sparkling blue eyes. She had flawless skin, lovely hands, gentle ways, and was always immaculately put together. She had been tireless when she was younger, climbing trees with the boys, helping all of them with homework, taking care of them when they were sick. They had never had a baby-sitter in their lives or been cared for by an outsider. Granibelle had done it all.

And somewhere in her fifties or sixties, time had simply passed her by. She had changed very little since and looked much the same as she always did. She seemed a little smaller and a little frailer, but she was still lively, agile, and energetic. She would have cleaned her own apartment if they let her. She was still totally clear-headed, and gave them sound advice when they asked her. She was practical and down to earth, and generous of spirit. She still read the newspaper every day, and every-thing she could lay her hands on, and she had taken computer classes in her eighties. There was nothing old-fashioned about her, except her ethics. Her values were very clear, but she had a sensible view of things too. She told them to follow the most reasonable course, with as little damage as possible to all concerned. She understood the gray shadings of life, and the things one had to do to compromise sometimes. She was never judgmental, and had told them all that forgiveness was always the right answer. And she applied that to her own life as well. She held no grudge against those who had disappointed or hurt her. And Granibelle was nobody's fool. It had been nearly impossible to pull the wool over her eyes when they were children.

'We had a great time, Granibelle,' Liz confirmed, sitting beside her in the living room, while tea was served from a large silver tray. 'What have you been up to?'

'I played poker with some friends yesterday, and won twenty dollars.' Her eyes sparkled as she said it and she giggled. 'I went to a wonderful Mozart concert in New York last week, but I couldn't get anyone to go with me.' Olivia provided a car and driver for her outings, whenever Maribelle wanted one. 'Most of my friends just don't like classical music.' And neither did her grandchildren, except Phillip. 'Cass came to visit me when you were all away. She looks awfully thin to me, but she seems happy.

She brought me the latest CDs of all her clients. Some of it is really very good.' She loved to play cards and gamble, and had organized a trip to Atlantic City among some of her friends at the residence. She was always busy, engaged, and up to minor mischief.

'One of these days, you're going to get thrown out of here, for turning it into a casino,' Liz warned her with a chuckle.

'They're actually very nice about it,' Maribelle reassured her. 'I play bridge on Tuesdays with the director.' She was sharp as the proverbial tack, and interested in all their lives. Liz told her about her new manuscript then, and the reaction of her new agent. 'I don't think Sarah sees beyond the kind of literature she teaches. I recommended three books to her last year, and she hated all of them. I think it's a good sign that she didn't like yours,' Granibelle said sensibly. 'Your mother told me she loved it. You'll have to e-mail me a copy. I can download it on my computer.' Liz looked at her in amazement. It was like talking to a contemporary. Maribelle loved having all the latest gadgets.

They spent two wonderful hours together, catching up, talking about the trip, and Maribelle mentioned that Olivia was coming out to see her that weekend. 'She still works too hard, but I really think it will keep her young forever. There's no point slowing down – your mind just slows down with it. And what are you going to be writing next?' she asked with interest. Liz hadn't thought about it yet. It had taken her three years to come up with this one, even if she wrote it in six weeks. Granibelle was never idle, and had never been physically or intellectually lazy. She set an example to them all, and Liz knew her mother was a great deal like her. She couldn't imagine her mother slowing down either. She had stopped expecting that years before. And at seventy, she was no different than she had been at forty or fifty, just like her own mother. None of them could believe that their mother had just turned seventy. She'd made very little fuss about it on the boat, it was a birthday like any other. Olivia said she didn't like the sound of the number, but she certainly didn't look it. And it was just as impossible to believe that Maribelle was ninety-five. They were all sure she'd easily reach a hundred. Time had stood still for her. They were good genes for all of them to inherit.

Liz had brought her a stack of new magazines and left them with her. Maribelle subscribed to some of them, like *Time*, *Newsweek*, and *Fortune*, but she loved foreign fashion magazines too, and Liz had brought some home for her. She read *The New York Times* and *The Wall Street Journal* every day. She always warned her contemporaries never to stop keeping abreast of the news, which was good advice. And she was also grateful for good health. Life was so different if you fell ill. She got regular check-ups and a clean bill of health every year. Her own grandmother had lived to a hundred and two, in surprisingly good health, and she seemed to have inherited her vitality from her.

'Give the girls my love,' she said as she walked Liz to her car. She had a sure step and a straight back. She still had the perfect posture she'd been taught as a young girl. 'I know you'll miss her, but I think L.A. will be very good for Carole. She has a lot of illusions about her father, I think it will ground her to add some reality to it, and I don't think she's happy in New York. The art scene is just too much for her.' She had analyzed the situation perfectly, and Liz agreed with her. She was sad to see Carole leave, but in some ways she was relieved. Her youngest daughter seemed a little lost, just as she herself had been. 'And don't forget to send me your book,' she reminded her.

'I won't, Granibelle, I promise. Try to behave yourself, and don't fleece your friends here out of too much money. You're a card shark,' she accused her, and they both laughed. She had taught them all card games when they were children, and now her grandchildren loved to play cards as much as she did. Cass had always been the best at games and beat them all. And Olivia was pretty good too, although she didn't love playing cards as much as her mother. She had played every day on the boat with Alex, but for Olivia it was a pastime, not a passion. For Granibelle, it was nearly a vice, except that she'd never had a gambling addiction – she just loved the game.

'Take care of yourself,' Granibelle said as she kissed her goodbye. It was warm out, and Liz told her to go back to the air-conditioned rooms. 'And get back to work on a new book,' her grandmother exhorted, wagging a finger at her. 'You've done a good job with this one. Now you need to get on to something new.' Liz saluted as she got into the car, and blew her a kiss as she drove away, and she saw Maribelle walk back into the building with a sure step through the rearview mirror. She was one of the greatest blessings in all their lives, and a strong role model for them all. The woman for whom time had stood still.

Chapter 12

Olivia's first days back after the trip were hectic beyond belief. It was to be expected. She had stayed on top of everything through faxes and e-mails, and occasional calls from the boat, but it was still different being home. There was always more to do. The boys had felt it too. She had scarcely glimpsed Phillip since she got home, and John had taken a few more days for his trip to Paris with Sarah and Alex.

There were threatened strikes in a couple of locations, construction issues, and a new line in production, and she was keeping a watch on the human rights issues. A monsoon in India had caused a flood that destroyed six of their warehouses, and a small earthquake in Mexico had caused considerable damage to their store, but fortunately no one had gotten hurt. When things like that happened in areas where they did business, they donated heavily to local relief, and sent in medical supplies where needed. Olivia had made enormous charitable donations for years, often anonymously. She wasn't seeking publicity, she wanted to provide help, particularly to children in jeopardy. She had come up with a motto years before that she tried to live by: 'Our customers are our friends.' And it wasn't friendly to cheat customers, sell second-rate goods, or exploit children to keep their prices low. Her own high moral standards were used in the business.

She was reading a report on a potential lawsuit in their Stockholm store. A woman had refused delivery service, and dragged a dining table up four flights of stairs herself. She had injured her back doing so, and was threatening to sue them, because she said the table was heavier than it should be. It was a bogus suit, and she was obviously looking for a settlement, but she was making so much fuss about it that the legal department had brought it to Olivia's attention. She wasn't sure yet what she wanted to do. She was thinking of giving her the eight chairs that went with it as a gift. It was the sort of claim that required that kind of attention. The woman was either poor or cheap if she had refused to pay for delivery. Olivia was making a note about it when Peter Williams walked into her office. She smiled when she looked up at him. She was happy to see him, and also mildly amused about the suit. The woman had written her a letter personally, and had said that using such high-quality wood made the table too heavy and dangerous for their customers to carry. Dragging it up four flights of stairs hadn't been their intention when they made it. It was from one of their Indian factories, and Olivia knew the piece. It was a good-looking table at an incredibly low price, and John had designed it.

'Bad time?' Peter asked her, ready to leave if she was too busy, but she shook her head and sat back in her chair with a grin.

'No, I was just reading about the Stockholm suit. That can't have been a lot of fun dragging that table up the stairs. I'm thinking of giving her the set of chairs to go with it. The memo said she didn't buy them.'

'If you do, be sure you have them delivered, or she'll up the ante on the suit,' he said, laughing. 'I saw it too. I don't think she'll really sue us.' But there were others who had and would. Peter always advised her well. There had been a head injury case of a bookcase that fell on someone in an earthquake. They hadn't bolted it to the wall, and it said to do so in the instructions that went with it, but Olivia paid the settlement anyway. They carried astronomical insurance to cover real claims, and when reasonable, they settled, in order to maintain goodwill. They weren't trying to hurt anyone or take advantage of them, even when their customers were foolish.

'You look terrific,' Peter said as he gazed at her admiringly. She seemed healthy and tan and relaxed. He could see that the boat trip with her children had done her a world of good. Her vacations with them always did. And he looked well after his time in Maine too. He had come home a week early. He said he had a lot to do. And they both knew that a strike at their Spanish stores was coming and probably couldn't be avoided. Local government had made the situation worse, and it would keep them busy if it happened. And there had been an arson fire in their warehouse in South Dakota. It was hard to keep on top of it all, but they both did. You had to have a clear head and think on your feet, and be able to make rapid, intelligent decisions to prevent any bad situations from getting worse.

'Thank you, Peter,' she said as he sat down across from her. 'How was Maine?' His eyes were the same color as hers, and she saw them cloud over for a moment.

'The same as always. Emily and I don't have a lot to say to each other. I left when the kids did. I enjoyed it, but

I'm happy to be home. She'll be up there for a few more weeks till Labor Day. What about you? No more travel plans for August?' He had been more expansive than he usually was about his marriage, but she knew it anyway. He had confided in her for many years. The marriage had died shortly after their children were born, when he discovered that his wife was an alcoholic. She had promised to get treatment for years and never did. Nothing had changed, and now they had the form of a marriage but not the spirit. He had gone to Al-Anon meetings for years, and finally gave up begging her to stop drinking. He had given up on the marriage then too. Olivia had met her, she was a nice woman, and intelligent, but she looked ravaged by her addiction, which still burned out of control like a forest fire. Peter no longer went out with her socially. At sixty-three, he was married, but he had been alone emotionally for years. He buried himself in his work, as Olivia did.

'I'm not going anywhere, unless we have a problem somewhere that I need to attend to or see for myself,' Olivia answered his question. 'I have too much to do here. I don't want to start traveling again until September.'

'That sounds reasonable.' Then he hesitated and looked at her as an expression of tenderness passed between them. 'Dinner Saturday?' It was a shorthand they both understood. She nodded, and they smiled at each other.

'That sounds terrific. Bedford?' He nodded too. And then she got up and quietly came around her desk. It was after hours, her assistant had gone home, the building was quiet, and she was more relaxed than usual after her vacation. She was wearing a light summer dress, and he couldn't take his eyes off her as she approached him and then gently bent to kiss him. 'I missed you. I always do,' she said softly. She wanted him to know it, although she expected nothing from him in return. She never did. She understood his situation perfectly. He would stay where he was for ever, with Emily drinking herself to death quietly.

Peter stood up then and did something they never did in the office, but they were alone. He put his arms around her and kissed her. He sighed as he did. Holding her always felt so good. 'I missed you terribly,' he admitted. They stood kissing in each other's arms for a long moment, lost in the tenderness of it, and then they both heard a sound in the room.

Their lips parted and their heads turned, and they both saw him at the same time. It was Phillip standing in the doorway with a stack of papers in his arms, and a horrified expression. He looked like he'd been shot out of a cannon. Peter and Olivia moved apart discreetly – he gave Olivia a serious look and walked away. He said nothing to her, and as he passed Phillip in the doorway, he nodded at him.

'Sorry, Phillip,' was all he said, as Phillip strode toward his mother with a vengeance. Peter didn't want to leave her with him, but he thought it best to do so. It was better for her to deal with her son alone.

'What was that moment of insanity I just witnessed?' her son asked her, as Olivia sat down quietly at her desk. In the instant it had happened, and they had been discovered, she had made a decision not to apologize to him. He was old enough to know the truth. She and Peter had been discreet lovers for ten years.

'It's not insanity, Phillip. And it's none of your business, any more than your personal life is mine. We're both adults.'

'What, you're having affairs with the employees now? What kind of bullshit is that? What if someone saw you?'

'We thought we were alone. And Peter is not an employee, he's our general counsel. And what I do personally is no concern of yours. I'm sorry if it upset you, but I can assure you, we're discreet.' She was shaking at his accusation, but she didn't let it show. She had to take a position on the situation now, and she didn't like what he had said. Not at all.

'*Discreet?* Are you crazy, or just immoral? He's married, he's ten years younger than you are, and if the press gets hold of this, you'll look ridiculous. It will invalidate all our legal positions if people find out you're sleeping with him. And he's a married man, for chrissake! Is this what you did when you were gone all the time when we were kids? Is this what it was all about? Did Dad know? And all your bullshit about morality – what a joke! How dare you moralize to us, when you're screwing around with married men, and maybe you always were.'

'Stop it!' Olivia said in a powerful tone as she stood up at her desk. She had an instant sense that Phillip was using this as a vehicle to air his grievances of the past. 'I was faithful to your father every moment of our marriage, and he knew that. I was away so that I could build this business for all of us, and he knew that too. He wanted me to. He respected what I did, even if you don't. And I respected him. Your father has been gone for fourteen years, Phillip. I've worked closely with Peter Williams for longer than that. He was kind to me when your father died, and has given us invaluable advice for all these years. It took me four years to get involved with him after your father died, if it's any of your business, which it isn't.

He's lonely, so am I, and he's seven years younger than I am, not ten. His wife is an alcoholic, and he's married to her in name only. And we've been discreet for ten years. No one ever found out about this but you. It's not going to hurt our business, I won't let it, and neither would he.

'And you're right about one thing, it's not a shining example of morality in the absolute. But we're real people, with real lives, with grown children in their thirties and forties. I'm single, and he's respectful of his wife. I don't recommend this kind of situation, but it happens. I carry a huge responsibility here, on my shoulders alone, and if the kindness of Peter Williams helps me do that, then it's a compromise I've decided to make. It took me a long time to make that decision, and I did. It's not ideal, I'll agree with you on that. But we're human beings, and the ideal isn't always possible. He's never going to leave his wife, out of respect for her, and we're not flagrant about this.

'I'm old, Phillip. I work hard, I always have. And if this gives us both some comfort in our later years, then so be it. You don't get to decide what's right for me or not. You can decide that for yourself. We all make compromises. You've decided it's enough to be married to a woman who behaves like an iceberg and gives you precious little comfort, from what I can see. And I've had an affair for ten years with a married man. I was faithful to your father to his dying day and for years after. In all the ways that matter, I still am. I loved him when he was alive and I still do. And if this is what I choose to do, it is entirely up to me, not to you. The compromises you make in your life in order to make it work are your business. This is mine. It's a compromise, but sometimes that's a decision that one makes. I owe you no explanations, and I'm not going to discuss this further with you. Don't try to cast aspersions on my behavior when I was married to your father – that won't fly. And if you don't like what I'm doing now, then I'm sorry. But that's the end of it. The discussion stops right here.'

Her son was standing across the desk from her where Peter had been a moment before, and Phillip was shaking with rage. 'I stand by what I said a few minutes ago. You're a hypocrite. I don't know if you were faithful to my father, I hope so for his sake. But you're no saint, Mother. You're the mistress of a married man. I don't care if his wife is an alcoholic, that makes no difference. He's married and you're sleeping with him. He works for us. You're sleeping with the help. So don't lecture me.' He didn't deny what she'd said about Amanda, but he was only thinking about Peter. And he was outraged that his mother was having an affair. Olivia couldn't help wondering if it really made a difference to him that Peter was married – maybe he just couldn't tolerate the idea of his mother sleeping with someone other than his father. He was very black and white in his ideas, and she always had been too, but the situation had changed over the years, and she and Peter loved each other, in a quiet way.

'I'm going to forget everything you just said. I'm not proud of what I'm doing, but I'm not ashamed of it either. It is what it is. Two people who need each other and have the weight of the world on their shoulders. We work hard, and derive a little comfort from each other. It keeps us going on the bad days, and there are a lot of those in this business, or any business. We're not hurting anyone. I'm sorry if it upsets you, but we're all grown-ups here, even you. You're forty-six years old, and no, I wasn't there every minute when you were growing up. I wish I had been, but I wasn't. There were other things I thought I had to do, and your father thought so too. Maybe we were wrong. I'll always regret what I missed. But that's over, Phillip. We can't get those years back. I can't undo it, no matter how sorry I am if it hurt you. And I have a right to some comfort in my life, whether you like it or not.'

'You're seventy years old, for chrissake. You're an old woman. What are you doing screwing around at your age?'

'I'm not "screwing around," as you put it. I'm sorry you see it that way. And it's absolutely none of your concern what I do, as long as I run this business correctly, and don't embarrass you or myself publicly, and I'm not. The rest is up to me, Phillip. There's no vote on this issue. This isn't a board meeting, it's my life, and you don't get a voice in this one.'

He stared at her in unbridled fury, and without another word, he turned on his heel and left the room. He was seething at everything she had said to him.

She was shaking when she sat down at her desk again when he had left. This wasn't the way she had wanted Phillip to discover her affair with Peter. She hadn't wanted anyone to find out at all. But he had, and she had to live with it now. It didn't change anything, and Phillip would have to get over it. It reminded her suddenly of her own feelings when she had realized that her mother was Ansel Morris's mistress. She had hated it, it seemed so wrong to her. She had thought her mother was 'a fallen woman.' But she was thirteen years old, not forty-six. She had discovered her mother's affair just as Phillip had. She had seen them kissing one day, and her mother had then admitted it to her. She said she was lonely, and he was a kind man. But she had never married him, even at the end when he was widowed, despite their obvious love for each other.

Olivia had never believed in married people having affairs. She believed in marriage and fidelity, but so had Maribelle. She had been faithful to a married man she loved and who loved her. There had never been anyone else, even after Ansel died. And Olivia had been faithful to the only two men in her life. Joe for their entire marriage, and now Peter for ten years. It was not a spotless life, but it was a good one, and a reasonable one, given the circumstances. She didn't love it, but she could justify it to herself, and had. She had never told anyone about Peter, and hadn't intended to, although she often had thought about telling her mother. Somewhere in her heart she knew she owed her mother an apology for what she had thought of her at thirteen. She hadn't understood then how Ansel had protected her mother and how much he cared about her. Maribelle had needed him, just as she needed Peter, even though he was married to someone else and always would be.

She wondered why her mother had never married Ansel, even after his wife died, but she had never dared to ask. He had died so soon after, within the year – maybe they didn't have time. But whatever her reasons, they had been her own. Maribelle was a good woman, and an honorable one. And so was she, whatever Phillip thought now. She felt sorry for him with his limited thinking, and harsh judgments, the resentments he had carried for years. He was unable to accept or believe that people did their best, even if they weren't perfect. And he had settled for a wife who Olivia believed didn't love him, and was incapable of it. It was a sad life for him. And she preferred her own compromises to his, the love of a married man who was kind to her and whom she respected. They didn't need marriage and they loved each other. Olivia wasn't going to let Phillip spoil that for her with his black-and-white ideas about what was right and what wasn't. She had a right to decide that for herself about something as personal as this.

She called Peter's cell phone with a shaking hand, and he answered immediately with a worried tone.

'Are you all right?'

'Yes, I am,' she said firmly, determined to be, despite her son's tantrum and his accusations and low opinion of her. What mattered was how she viewed herself, and she knew she had done the closest thing to right she could, for all concerned. 'He'll get over it. He's a very rigid person, and he has a loveless marriage. It makes him harsh and unreasonable about everyone else. And he has a lot of old scores to settle with me, and grudges he can't resolve. In a way, this has nothing to do with you. It's just an opportunity for him to stay angry at me.' She knew him well.

'I'm sorry I ran out on you. I felt bad leaving, but I didn't think you wanted me there while you talked to him.'

'I didn't,' she confirmed. 'You did the right thing.'

'What did he say?'

'A lot of very ugly things. He wanted to know if I cheated on his father, and of course I didn't. Maybe it was good for him to hear. And he's old enough to know what's going on with us. He's nearly fifty – at his age he ought to be able to accept human frailty in others. If he can't, he'll never be able to forgive himself for anything. Someone once said that being grown up is being able to accept your parents as they are. The trouble is that most of us don't grow up in that sense. We want our parents to be perfect and live up to our ideals. Our children want us to forgive them unconditionally for their mistakes, but they don't want to forgive us anything. At some point that no longer works. Phillip has some hard lessons ahead of him. Cass is the same way. She's never forgiven me anything, particularly not being there when her father died. I blamed myself for that too, and I spent years thinking that he might have survived if I'd been there. He wouldn't have, and there are other mistakes I've made. But this isn't one of them. We're not hurting anyone, Peter, as long as your marriage is intact, and you're not hurting Emily with this, and I don't believe you are.'

'She's been an alcoholic for more than thirty years,' he said sadly. 'We're not stealing anything from her. Our marriage was over long before you came along.' It was what he had always told her, and she believed him. But he sounded worried anyway, about Olivia, and her son's attack. It was hard being lambasted by your children, and he felt sorry for her. His own had no idea that he was involved with Olivia, although they knew their parents were married in form only. His daughter had urged him to get a divorce years before, but he felt a responsibility for Emily, and his son turned a blind eye to what was going on but he knew how sick his mother was. She had destroyed their family when the children were young, getting drunk at their school events, not showing up, or passing out when their friends were there. She had been a humiliation to them all their lives, and they respected their father for staying with her. It was easier for them in some ways. He was always there to take care of her, so they didn't have to.

'Do you want me to come by tonight?' Peter asked her gently, and Olivia smiled.

'Yes, I do,' Olivia said honestly, 'not just because of this. I missed you while I was gone.' They usually spent a night or two together every week. He had nothing to explain to Emily. She didn't know if he was there or not. They had had separate bedrooms for twenty years, and there was a housekeeper to keep an eye on her. He offered no explanations, he just left, and could be reached on his cell phone at all times.

'I missed you too. I'll come at eight.' It was six-thirty by then. They both had a few things to finish up in their offices, and it would take him an hour to get to Bedford. She'd arrive at about the same time. She had no live-in help. And no one ever knew when he spent the night. It worked perfectly for them. He always left before her daily housekeeper arrived. Olivia knew that she suspected, but had no idea who Olivia's occasional night-time visitor was. They had managed to maintain total discretion for ten years, until tonight. It was unfortunate that Phillip had discovered them, but it wasn't a tragedy. It was evidence of her humanity. Now Phillip's ability to be human, and adult, remained to be seen.

'See you at eight,' Olivia said quietly. 'Drive carefully. I love you, Peter,' she reminded him, and he smiled.

'I love you too. See you soon,' he said, and they hung up. Olivia left her unfinished files on her desk. She was tired tonight. It had been a long day. And the altercation with Phillip had worn her out. She might not look it, and everyone said she didn't, but she felt every minute of her age tonight.

A few minutes later she picked up her handbag and briefcase and turned out the lights in her office. She was looking forward to seeing Peter.

Phillip waited until he was in his car to call his brother. He had thought about what to do about what he'd discovered. He thought the others should know. He knew what a bleeding heart Liz was, and she'd probably think it was touching or romantic. He didn't. And he hadn't spoken to his sister Cass in years. But he wanted to tell John. He was sure he'd be as outraged as Phillip was. And Phillip didn't buy the story that she'd been faithful to their father. He wondered now if that was why Cass looked so different from the rest of them. Maybe that was why Olivia had never been home. Maybe she'd been screwing around for years. Who knew what had really gone on? He felt sick when he thought of finding her kissing Peter. They had looked passionate as they embraced. Phillip's stomach turned over when he remembered it. It was seven o'clock when he drove home, one in the morning in Paris. He called John at the Ritz, where he was staying with Sarah and Alex. His brother sounded sleepy when he answered. 'Something wrong?' John asked his brother quickly. Their grandmother was ninety-five, after all, and their mother was now ten years older than their father when he died. He was always afraid of something happening to them, or his wife or son. But they were in Paris with him, so he knew it wasn't them. And a business crisis was always possible too. 'Are you okay?' John asked, sitting up in bed, as he turned on the light. Sarah was sound asleep, dead to the world.

'No, I'm not. And you won't be either when I tell you what's going on.'

'Shit. Granibelle or Mom?' Phillip was hitting his worst fears, and John hadn't picked up on the anger in his voice.

'Our mother. She's having an affair with Peter Williams. She has been for ten years, or so she says. Who knows how long it's been going on, or if she cheated on Dad before that, when she was never home.' It was a lot to absorb all at once, as John tried to sort through what he was saying.

'Mom's having an affair?' It sounded unlikely to him.

'Yes, she is,' Phillip confirmed in an undertaker's voice.

'How do you know?'

'I found them wrapped around each other in her office, when I walked in on them an hour ago.'

'They were having sex in her office?' John sounded stunned.

'No, they were kissing,' Phillip said precisely. He would have had a heart attack if they'd been making love. 'She admitted the affair to me after that. He left, and she and I had a talk about it. And he's married, if you'll recall.'

'Yeah, I remember that. He's a nice guy, though. At least he's not some fortune hunter thirty years younger than she is.' He knew their mother was too sensible for that, but he was actually surprised to hear that she was romantically involved. He thought all she cared about was her work. He thought it was kind of nice to know that that wasn't the case and she was human after all. Their father had been gone for nearly fifteen years – the anniversary was coming up shortly. That was a long time to be alone. 'Is it serious?'

'Of course it's serious. He's married. How much more serious can it get than an affair with a married man? And for ten years. Imagine if the press gets hold of that.'

'The press isn't going to care who she's sleeping with,' John said sensibly. 'They don't report affairs in the business section of *The New York Times*. She has a right to do what she wants. She has a right to be happy, Phillip. She carries a hell of a lot on her shoulders. She's had no one to support her in that since Dad. He helped her a lot, and now she's all alone.'

'Bullshit. She has us,' Phillip said, sounding pompous, as John thought about it.

'Not really. We work for her, but we don't support her. When the shit hits the fan, she's the one it hits, and she works it out on her own. Did you get in a big fight with her about it?' John suspected that he had, and he was sorry for her. Phillip was always so critical of her, and so was Cass. They never forgave her anything from the past, and this was just the kind of ammo Phillip would use against her to prove all his old theories about how bad she was.

'Yes, I did,' Phillip admitted without remorse.

'Did you actually accuse her of cheating on Dad? An affair she got into four years after he died is hardly proof of infidelity in their marriage.' John sounded upset as he asked his older brother the question. Their mother didn't deserve to be beaten up for having a discreet affair. And if she'd been involved with Peter for ten years, none of them had ever known, which was proof of how discreet she was.

'As a matter of fact, I did accuse her of that. It shows she has no morals, which casts a shadow on everything.'

'That's ridiculous,' John said, annoyed at him. 'How immoral is it for two people in their sixties, and now her seventies, to have an affair? And so what if he's married?

Danielle Steel

That's unfortunate for them, but it has nothing to do with her life with Dad, Phillip. They were crazy about each other, and she was madly in love with him. We always knew that. And if she has someone in her life now, I'm happy for her. No one wants to die alone.'

'Nor in the arms of someone else's husband. She should be better than that.' He had high standards for her, more so than John.

'She's human, for chrissake. She still looks great. She looks young for her age. Why not? Why not have some comfort in her life, and a little love? He's obviously not ditching his wife if they've been involved for ten years and he's still married to her.' It was the sensible point of view, and the humane one, which Phillip didn't share.

'You sound just like her,' Phillip said angrily. 'What's wrong with all of you? Does no one in this family have any standards? I suppose you think our grandmother should be turning tricks on Long Island so she doesn't have to die alone either?' He was furious with John for not joining in the fight of outraged virtue with him. He was turning it into a crusade, but John was not signing up.

'Give it up,' John said, sounding exhausted. He had been asleep when his brother woke him. 'This is her life, not ours. We all work it out the best way we can. She has a right to make her own mistakes, if this is one, but I'm not convinced it is. The only thing I am convinced of is that it's none of our business. As long as she's not embarrassing us or herself, or screwing on her office floor with the door open, or at a board meeting, I don't need to know about it, and neither should you. You happened on it, like opening a door and seeing something you shouldn't. This has nothing to do with us. Or with Dad. Now close the door and forget about it. You're only going to cause unnecessary trouble for everyone if you make a big issue about this.'

'I can see you inherited her morality, or lack of it,' Phillip said coldly.

'It's not up to us to judge her "morality," or decide who she should have affairs with or if she should. And she isn't cramming Peter down our throats. I respect her for keeping quiet about it. And I think you need to back off. It's only going to upset you, and her, unnecessarily. Find something else to bitch about. Now I'm going back to sleep. It's nearly two o'clock in the morning. I'll be home on Sunday, but I'm not going to get on this bandwagon with you. And if she's having a hot romance or a love affair at seventy, good for her!' John said with feeling.

'You're as big a fool as she is,' Phillip said, and hung up on him without another word. He had expected his brother to share his opinion and his outrage. He hadn't expected him to support her. And as John lay in bed at the Ritz in Paris, he was smiling, thinking about it. He liked Peter Williams. And he loved his mother, and if Peter was making her happy, what the hell. He turned over in bed and put an arm around Sarah. He wasn't sure if he was going to tell her, out of respect for his mother, but he knew that if he did, she would agree with him. He thought Phillip was all wrong on this one, just as he was about a lot of things.

Chapter 13

Peter arrived in Bedford at eight-thirty instead of eight o'clock. The traffic had been heavy, it was Friday night, and people were heading out of the city for the weekend. Olivia had a platter of cold meats and a salad waiting for him with a chilled bottle of wine, and he put his arms around her and kissed her as soon as he walked through the door.

'What a day!' he said, looking worried and exhausted. He was still upset about Phillip walking in on them, and his verbal attack on his mother. 'I'm so sorry, darling. Are you all right?'

'Actually, I'm fine,' she said, looking surprised as she poured him a glass of wine. They went out on her patio, looking over the well-manicured gardens, and sat down.

It was a pretty house. It was a good size, but not enormous. She had moved there after Joe died, once the children were all grown and her mother had moved to the senior residence. It was an easy home for her, beautifully decorated with elegant antiques and paintings she and Joe had collected over the years. It suited her, and Peter was always comfortable there. His own house had the sad look now of a place where people had been unhappy and disconnected for a long time. He hated going home, but he always loved being here, with her. It was welcoming and warm, like her.

'I don't know how Phillip turned into the morality police. I think he's unhappy in his marriage. Amanda is such a social climber, and so cold. I don't think she'd ever have married him if he didn't have money and wasn't going to run the business one day. She probably can't wait for me to retire or drop dead. She wasn't a lot of fun on the trip – she never is. And she's icy cold with him. He doesn't seem to mind though.' She wanted more than that for him, but it was up to him. He had made his choice and seemed satisfied with it.

Peter didn't like his own daughter-in-law either, but he felt the same way Olivia did. It was up to his son, and if it worked for him, there was nothing for Peter to say. He never interfered. Fortunately, he liked his son-in-law much better, and spent more time with them as a result. He loved his kids, but his children were on their own, grown and gone. The joy in his life was Olivia now, although they spent less time together than he would have liked. But they were both busy and still deeply involved in their work, and she still traveled a lot. He wondered if she'd ever slow down. Probably not. And she would have been unhappy if she did. He knew her well after all these years, and he loved her the way she was. He couldn't remember a time now when he had loved Emily and had been happy with her, but he knew he had.

They had a quiet dinner in the kitchen, and talked about Phillip and other things. Peter was planning to spend the weekend, so their time together was unrushed and relaxed. He was leaving to play golf on Sunday morning, and Olivia was going to see Maribelle then, for the first time since the trip. Liz had called her mother after she saw her, and reported that her grandmother was happy and looked great. Olivia was always grateful that was the case. Her mother was one of the mainstays of her life, and Peter had become one in the last decade. He gave her good advice, privately and professionally, and he was intelligent and kind. Their interests meshed well, the time they shared was always tender and enjoyable, and they both accepted that they couldn't be together all the time. This was enough. Olivia had no desire to marry again, and Peter had made it clear from the beginning that he wouldn't get divorced. He didn't think that it would be right if he did. Emily was a sick woman, and as long as she continued to refuse treatment, which they now realized she always would, he was going to stay where he was. But he and Olivia had spent many happy times together in the past ten years. They had taken several vacations, traveled for business occasionally, and were together for some weekends and a night or two during the week, when she was in town. She wasn't asking for more than that, which made it easy for him. There was no pressure on him to change anything, and they were good company for each other. They laughed a lot, and they had a good time in bed, which surprised them both. Their love life was as lively and exciting as it had been when it all began.

They had happened into the affair by accident, when they were on a trip. They had both gone to Chicago at the last minute, to avert a strike, and it had turned into a mess. They got stuck there for three weeks while the unions refused to back down, and they negotiated for a peaceful settlement. And by the end of the first week, they wound up in bed after a particularly stressful day, and realized that they were in love. It had been wonderful being together in spite of the strike. They had already worked side by side for nearly five years by then and knew each other well. Adding sex and love to their friendship had deepened it exponentially. They had a profound respect for each other, and he thought her achievements were remarkable. He never interfered with her decisions, but helped her reach them in objective ways, and supported her after she made them, very much as Joe had done. Both men had recognized her genius and never stood in its way, but weren't afraid to tell her what they thought. She had always listened and heeded their advice. In some ways, Peter had taken up where Joe had left off, although it was different not being married to him, and not sharing children. It left them freer, and they respected each other's independence. It was the perfect arrangement for them, at this time in their lives, just as Joe had been when she was young. This was another chapter in their lives, closer to the end of the book, although Maribelle's genes gave them both hope that they would be together for a long time.

They never talked about getting married because it wasn't an option for them. Emily was sixty-two years old and might live as long as they did, or longer, particularly since she was younger than Olivia, although in poor health after abusing herself for so many years with her addiction to alcohol, and she had a heart condition as a result. But Olivia never expected to become his wife. They were content as lovers, and the secrecy of their relationship heightened the romance in a tender way.

They went to bed early that night, and made love for the first time since she'd left. It was as wonderful as always, and afterward they lay languidly in her enormous bathtub and she told him about the trip. It sounded perfect to him. The money he had made in his lifetime was only a fraction of the fortune she had amassed, but he had a good life, had made sound investments, and could afford to be generous with her. There was a gold bracelet she always wore that her children never knew was from him. She had told them she bought it herself, as well as a pair of diamond stud earrings that he had given her recently for their tenth anniversary. She loved them too. The only jewelry she wore now was from him, along with a ring from Joe and her wedding ring. The two men she had loved had been good to her in countless ways.

They bought groceries together the next day, listened to music, went for a long walk, sat quietly reading for a few hours, and then went to bed again. He admitted to her that he thought of her constantly and wanted to go to bed with her all the time, which made her laugh.

'You must have some kind of fetish for old women,'

she teased him, 'but I'm happy you do.' She was in good shape and her body was still beautiful, but seventy was not twenty-two. And at his age, he could have had any woman he wanted. Men his age were constantly marrying young women and having new families, but Peter had all he wanted in her. She was the only woman he had been with since marrying Emily thirty-six years before. They were faithful to each other, as they had been to their spouses, and they shared many of the same ideas.

And they made love again on Sunday morning before he left to play golf with friends. She had promised to have lunch with Maribelle, and after she kissed Peter goodbye, she drove to Long Island, thinking about him. It had been a lovely weekend. It always was. She wondered sometimes if it was better because they knew they couldn't have more, so they appreciated what they had. There was none of the strife that happened sometimes with couples. They never fought. They just had a good time together, and before they knew it, ten years had gone by.

When Olivia got to Maribelle's, she was just finishing a game of cards. She had been playing bridge all morning, and poker the night before.

'Mother, you're turning into a card shark,' Olivia

teased her as they went to Maribelle's apartment for a quiet lunch. Maribelle liked being alone with her, without having her friends drop by their table every five minutes in the main dining room. Everyone wanted to meet Olivia. Maribelle wanted her to herself.

'I heard all about the trip from Liz,' Maribelle said happily. 'It sounds fabulous. I looked up the yacht on the Internet. What a gorgeous boat. The owner is a very interesting person too.' When she wasn't playing cards, she was exploring the Internet on Google, and telling everyone what she learned. Olivia smiled as she listened to her. Her mother was interested in everything about life, and anything that involved young people and what they were doing. She had read Liz's book and loved it. She agreed with Liz's agent and her mother, and said it could be a huge best seller. And what Olivia valued in her mother was that she was not only full of life, and had a positive view of things, but that she was a wise woman too.

'I had an interesting week,' Olivia said to her. She had decided to tell her about Phillip and his discovery of her affair with Peter.

'You always do,' Maribelle said to her, but she could see in her daughter's eyes that there was something more she wanted to share with her.

'I had a big fight with Phillip a few days ago,' she confessed in a quiet voice.

'That's not unusual,' her mother commented. He had been the original angry young man, and had not improved with age. He hadn't mellowed much over the years.

'This was a bit unusual,' Olivia admitted with a sigh, and then plunged in. 'There's something I've never told you. I didn't think it was important. I thought "discretion was the better part of valor," as you used to say, was the right course to take.'

'My grandmother taught me that. She was a very wise woman, and lived to be very old. So what were you being discreet about?' She was curious, although she had suspected something for years and was wise enough not to ask.

'I've had an affair with Peter Williams for the past ten years. We've kept it very quiet. We see each other once or twice a week. He's a good man, and he's been very kind to me. I love him, although differently than Joe, of course. We were married forever and had kids. This is not the same.' She wanted to make sure her mother knew that, out of respect to Joe.

'I wouldn't expect it to be. You were a kid when you married Joe. And so was he. You two grew up together.

It's never the same with adult relationships, but that doesn't mean you don't love each other. Just differently. People get married here all the time. Everybody loves the idea of love, at every age. A couple got married last month, she's ninety-one and he's ninety-three, they don't expect it to last for ever, but they wanted to get married. Love is different at every age, but it's still love.'

'Well, that's the way it is with us, and has been for ten years. Joe had been gone for almost five years when we got involved. I didn't think it was a disrespect to Joe.'

'You were still young when he died. A woman of fifty-five or sixty needs love too,' Maribelle said sensibly.

'You were even younger when Ansel died,' Olivia reminded her, 'and you never had anyone else. You were forty.'

'Yes, but after that, I was too busy with all of you. I was happy that way. Sometimes love is about not being alone into your old age. I never was. I had all the companionship I needed with you and Joe and the kids. I didn't have room or time for anyone else.' She was laughing as she said it, and they both knew it was true.

'Well, anyway, I got involved with him. And to tell you the whole story, he's married, and he intends to stay that way. He told me that right from the beginning. He's always been honest with me. His wife is a severe alcoholic, and he doesn't feel he can leave her. Ten years ago he thought he might still get her into rehab and off the booze. If he had, he would have left her, but she doesn't want to stop drinking, and now he feels she's too old for him to leave, and I'm not asking him to. Our arrangement has always worked for me. I don't want to get married again either, I'm content the way I am, and I'm happy with him. It's never been an issue, morally, for me. He's respecting his wife by staying with her, no one knows about us, so we're not hurting anyone. In the absolute, it's not an ideal situation, or a moral one, but I made my peace with it a long time ago, before we even started. It is what it is.'

'So what's different now?'

'Phillip walked in on us this week. We were kissing in my office after hours, which was stupid, admittedly. We'd never done that before, but we hadn't seen each other since the trip, so we got a little carried away, and he kissed me, right when Phillip walked in. He went crazy. He called me the mistress of a married man, which is true of course, and said I have no principles. He accused me of cheating on his father when they were young, since clearly I'm a person of no morals. He went on and on and on and on. I haven't heard from him since. I told him it was none of his business, as long as I'm discreet. And he accused me of being a fraud, said that being involved with a married man is immoral, all of which is true. But Peter is a wonderful support for me, and a great comfort. And no, it's not right that he's married. But sometimes reality falls a little short of what it should be,' Olivia said, looking unhappily at her mother. She was still upset by what Phillip had said to her, but she had no intention of giving up Peter, even if he was a married man. But it was distressing having her son see her as a moral fraud. Maribelle was shaking her head as she listened, and she looked at her daughter sympathetically.

'Reality *always* falls short of what it should be. Or most of the time, anyway. There is the absolute, and what we believe in, and then there are things that fall into the gray areas, and all we can do is the best we can, given the situation at hand. I was in the same boat with Ansel Morris too. I don't know how much you knew or remember. His wife suffered from severe depression, although they didn't call it that then. They called it melancholy. She had half a dozen miscarriages, a number of still-births, and she never succeeded in having a baby, and she pretty much shut down after that. I'm sure it was disappointing for both of them, but he went on with life. She became fanatically religious, severely depressed, and involved in the supernatural. It sounded like she went a little crazy, and she stayed that way. She hardly ever left the house after that. By the time I came along, she had been that way for thirty years, and he'd been faithful to her. He was very respectful in the early years I knew him, we were strictly employer and employee.

'And then our relationship grew and changed. He knew I was struggling financially, and he kept giving me raises. I tried to give him advice about his business to justify them. I tried to help him turn things around and add a younger point of view. My suggestions were very modest, compared to what you've done, but it worked, and he was grateful. We worked very closely together for several years, and then we realized we were in love with each other. He told me he'd never leave her, he was afraid she'd kill herself if he did, and she might have. She was mentally very ill.

'At first, I felt terribly guilty for being involved with him, but we weren't hurting anyone. We were careful, and respectful and discreet. He was wonderful to you. I just couldn't find any reason to deprive myself of his love for me, just because it didn't fit with the morality I'd grown up with. And he always said he'd marry me if he lived long enough to do so, and in the end, he didn't. And no, it wasn't the ideal thing. It would have been more respectable if we'd been married. But we loved each other just as much as if we had been. He was thirty years older than I was, and in some ways he was like a father to me, and a husband. He took better care of me than anyone ever had, and look what he did for me in the end. Was that so wrong? He stayed married until his wife died of influenza. He was kind to her till the end.'

'Why didn't you marry him when his wife died? I always wondered about that.' It was the first time her mother had ever opened up with her in just that way. Olivia had had to wait until she was seventy to ask her mother the questions she had wondered all her life. It had been a long time coming, and Maribelle was forthcoming with her now.

'We were going to. But he wanted to wait until a year after his wife's death. We even set the date. He had given me a ring, and we considered ourselves engaged, although we didn't tell anyone, not even you. And then he died seven months after she did, so we never got married. But I loved him anyway.'

Olivia sat looking pensive. Her mother had just solved a mystery for her. And then as she looked down at her mother's hand, she saw the ring and realized what it was. It was a band with three small diamonds on it. Her mother had worn it for most of her life. Maribelle nodded when she saw Olivia looking at it, and she looked wistful thinking of the man who had given it to her.

'Yes, that's the ring. I never took it off again.'

'I just figured you liked things the way they were when you didn't marry him. I never had the guts to ask you.'

'Of course I didn't. It wasn't respectable being the mistress of a married man in those days, and it isn't now either. But sometimes you have no choice. If he'd had a viable marriage, it would have been an entirely different story, and I wouldn't have done it. But he didn't. His wife was certifiably insane. And it sounds like your friend has a similar situation. Would I have preferred to be married to Ansel? Of course. But I accepted the situation, just as you do. You'd probably rather be married too,' she said simply, but Olivia shook her head.

'Actually, no, I wouldn't. At least I don't think so. I like it like this. I'd like it better if he weren't married. But I had marriage with Joe. I'm not sure I need that again at my age.'

'Well, I certainly don't at mine,' Maribelle said, laughing, 'although the oldest person to get married here was ninety-six. He married a youngster of eighty-two. I think he lived another three years, but I'll bet they were happy years. And if they hadn't gotten married, would they have been "immoral"? Was I? Technically, yes, and so are you. But technicalities are not real life. Life is about people, the decisions they make, and what they feel they have to do. As long as no one is getting hurt, the immorality is fine with me.' Her mother had just let her off the hook.

'I feel the same way,' Olivia said with a rueful expression, 'but my son doesn't. He's dealing in the absolute. The technical.'

'Phillip has led a sheltered life. It's time for him to grow up, and stop judging you. He's been angry at you for too many years. He needs to try and understand what you were doing and why, and realize that you're quietly involved with a married man who won't leave his alcoholic wife. It would be a great deal more immoral if you dragged him away. For me the criterion is always if someone is getting hurt. We all have our moral compass, and we all make compromises, but that's where the buck stops for me. Phillip needs to have more compassion. How does he know he wouldn't do the same thing in your shoes? That's the reality here. We all get angry at our parents. I think you were angry at me for a while because of Ansel, and now look, the dial turns, the years march on, Joe is gone, and you've found a man who makes you happy who happens to be married to an alcoholic. How different is that from what I did with Ansel?

'Sooner or later we all do the same things our parents

did, no matter how much we criticized them, because in the end we're all human beings, and subject to the same frailties. We all make the same mistakes, or similar ones in the end. And what it teaches us is to be forgiving, and not so quick to judge. Every one of your children will wind up making some of your mistakes. It's human nature. So who are they to judge you harshly? "There but for the grace of God go I" is true in the end. Who's to say that Phillip won't do the same thing one day? It's a long life. At sixty, you did something similar to what I did, when I was younger. And maybe one day Phillip will understand that you're not immoral, you're human, and so is he.' As she listened to her, Olivia felt a huge wave of relief wash over her. She had thought more or less the same things, but having Maribelle express it so succinctly, from the vantage point of another generation, made it even clearer for her.

'Thank you, Mom,' she said, as she leaned over and kissed her. 'I'm glad we talked about it.' She had answered the questions of a lifetime and clarified some important things. She had thought her mother didn't care about marriage and was some kind of libertine, but as it turned out, they had been engaged and hoping to get married, and he had died before they could. She was as conventional as anyone else, just struggling to make morality and reality meet, which wasn't always an easy task.

'I'm glad you brought it up,' Maribelle said peacefully, fingering Ansel's ring again. He had been a good man. And so had Olivia's father, although they had been married for such a short time before he was killed in the war. Maribelle had been with Ansel Morris for many, many years. Just as Olivia had been with Peter now. Ten years was a long time. Maribelle repeated then what she had said earlier. 'Phillip needs to grow up. Life has a way of making us do that, whether we want to or not. It did for both of us,' she said, smiling at her daughter. 'And he needs to stop whining about your being gone when he was a boy. He was fine. And if you hadn't built the business you did, he wouldn't have the job he has now. You can't have everything in life. And you were there for him, part of the time, and the rest of the time, he had me and Joe. Liz and John have understood that. Phillip will have to come to it in time.'

'I wish Cass would get there too,' Olivia said wistfully. Her relationship with her youngest child was so badly damaged and such a loss.

'She will. The biggest problem you two have is that she's so much like you. She fights it all the time. She's young. She's a wonderful woman, just like you.'

'I hardly know her anymore. At least she comes to see you.'

'Whenever she can,' Maribelle said, smiling, and with that Olivia stood up. She had been there for a long time and didn't want to wear her mother out, although that was hard to do. She was probably keeping her from playing cards.

'Thank you, Mother,' Olivia said, and gave her a warm hug. It was heartfelt.

'Just let Phillip simmer down and stew in his own juices. He'll figure it out. And sooner or later, life will give him a swift kick in the pants and speed it along.'

'I hope so. I hate seeing him with Amanda. She's so cold.'

'It's what he wanted,' Maribelle reminded her. 'Now he needs to figure out that he deserves better than that.'

'I wonder if he ever will.'

'Maybe so,' Maribelle said, and walked her out. The two women hugged again, and as Olivia drove away, she waved, and her mother smiled broadly. She looked like a woman who was at peace with herself, and now Olivia was too. She was smiling as she drove home.

Chapter 14

The night after Olivia visited her mother, she found herself thinking about Cass, more than ever. She was less concerned about Phillip now, and his reaction to her affair with Peter. And as her mother said, Phillip needed to grow up and develop some empathy and compassion.

But Cass was heavily on her mind. And at seven o'clock she decided to send her an e-mail, telling her how much they had missed her on the boat. It was true, Olivia always did, and always wished she was there.

The e-mail was only a few lines, just to tell her that she was thinking about her, missed her, had seen Maribelle that day and she was fine. She hit the send button, and didn't expect a response. She was amazed when an answer came back a few minutes later, even though it was midnight in London. Cass said that she was coming to New York on business the following week, and was amenable to seeing her mother for lunch. They managed to do that once or twice a year. It was no substitute for a real relationship, but it allowed them to keep some kind of link to each other, which Cass had never dared sever entirely. Olivia was grateful for that.

Olivia responded immediately that she would be happy to see her, whenever and wherever convenient.

Cass suggested a restaurant in SoHo, and named the time and day, and her mother answered instantly. 'I'll be there. All my love, Mom.' It was the best they could do for now.

The place Cass had suggested was a French brasserie with bistro food. It was trendy and popular and jammed when Olivia walked in, but she saw her daughter immediately, at a table in the rear, wearing a black leather jacket. She had a thin, angular face, she had porcelain skin and enormous green eyes, and she had long since darkened her already dark brown hair into nearly jet black with a navy blue sheen, and it was short and spiked with gel. She looked like one of the rock stars she represented. She was wearing a slash of bright red lipstick and she looked very modern and chic. She stood up as her mother approached the table. She was wearing a miniskirt and high heels, and there was no denying she was a beautiful girl. Several people turned to stare. As Olivia did in her world, Cass exuded self-confidence and power. She was one of the most successful music producers in the world, and highly respected in her field. She was cool as she met her mother's gaze but allowed her to kiss her cheek. 'Thank you for meeting me for lunch. You must be busy,' Olivia said, feeling her heart pound and wanting to put her arms around her youngest child, but she forced herself to be restrained. Cass was never affectionate with her.

'You're busy too,' Cass said respectfully. 'Thank you for coming downtown. All my meetings are down here. I never get uptown anymore. I'm leaving for L.A. to-morrow. Danny's starting a tour there, at the Rose Bowl. He's going to Vegas after that.' She spoke about him as though he were any normal partner, despite the fact that he was twenty-four years old and one of the hottest rock stars in the business. Cass had made his career, and moved in with him five years before. Or, actually, he had moved in with her. She had a house in Mayfair that Olivia had never seen. When they met in London, Cass suggested restaurants there too, instead of inviting her, to the house. It was her way of keeping her mother at a distance. And Olivia had never met Danny Hell. From what she had seen of him in the press, he was a handsome boy, and they made a striking couple.

'It must be hectic for you when he's on tour. I can't even imagine what organizing something like that is like.' And Cass did several a year, for other clients. As Olivia looked at her, she realized that Maribelle was right. They had both started mammoth businesses at a young age, and been extraordinarily successful, just in different fields. But few women could have done it. The only difference between them was that Cass wasn't married and didn't have children. At her age, Olivia had had three, and a husband, which had added even more responsibility to her shoulders.

'It's crazy, but I love it,' Cass said with a smile, referring to the tour, and then ordered an omelet of egg whites and several health food options from the menu. She had been a vegetarian for years. And she had an incredible figure. Olivia ordered a salad, more interested in her daughter than food.

Cass asked about her business then, and the boat trip. She didn't ask about her siblings. She had distanced herself from them too, and always told her grandmother they were all her mother's puppets, which Maribelle denied. Olivia mentioned Liz's book to her, and Cass was pleased for her. She knew her older sister had been floundering for years. And she always thought that it was sad that John had given up his dreams of being an artist to work in their mother's business. She had the least respect of all for Phillip, who she thought was pompous and a snob, and she hated Amanda. They had all been married when she left home. She hadn't seen her nephew and nieces since then, and had no desire to. She always said she didn't like children. They reminded her of her childhood, which wasn't a pleasant memory for her.

They talked mostly about external things at lunch, and politics. Cass still got money from the trust Olivia had set up for them, but she was entirely financially independent, and didn't need her mother's money. She had made her own. Liz was entirely dependent on her trust, and hadn't been able to fully support herself yet at forty-four, which Cass thought was pathetic. And she considered the fact that the boys worked for their mother disgusting. She was critical of them all, which she shared liberally with her grandmother, not her mother. And they talked about Maribelle for a while, which was a safe subject.

Their lunches were always stressful because so much was left unsaid, and Cass's anger at her mother was always felt, even if unspoken. She didn't need to say it anymore, she had said it often enough in the past, and nothing had changed. You couldn't change the past.

Olivia finally dared to ask a personal question just before the end of lunch. 'Are you happy?' Cass hesitated before she answered, which worried her mother.

'I think so. I don't know. I'm not sure I'm a happy person. I have a lot of angst, which probably makes me good at what I do.' She was a perfectionist like her mother. 'I never assume anything, or take anything for granted. I check it all out.'

Olivia smiled when she said it. 'So do I. I'm a fanatic for details.' It was one of the rare times they had talked about themselves and how they worked. Now that Cass ran a booming business, she had more in common with her mother, and they had more to say to each other.

'I micromanage everything,' Cass confessed. 'But there's a lot of detail work to what I do.'

Her admission made Olivia brave, and she ventured another question. Maybe it was time. 'What's Danny like?'

'Crazy, young, incredibly talented, noisy, nuts, spoiled, beautiful.' She spoke of him like a child, as though he were her baby, not her man. Olivia suspected he was both. 'He's fun to be with, when he's not having a tantrum or driving me nuts. It's hard for rock stars to behave like real people. They're expected to act out, so they do. He does. A lot.'

Danielle Steel

'And that doesn't bother you?' Olivia was fascinated by her life, it was so different from her own experience.

'Sometimes. I manage. I give him shit when he gets too bad. He's my alternative to having children.' Cass smiled. And Olivia sensed that she loved him from the way she looked when she talked about him. They had been together since he was nineteen and Cass was twenty-nine. Not having family around her, and being on her own, had made her more mature. It struck Olivia that she was more so than her brothers, who were much older.

'You're still happy not having kids?' Olivia asked sadly. She felt as though she had damaged her, and Phillip, irretrievably, for them to not want children. It seemed like a huge loss to her. Cass didn't tell her mother that she'd had many abortions, and always would, if her birth control failed or she made a mistake.

'Very.' They both knew why and didn't go there. It was dangerous territory for them, a minefield. All of Cass's old resentments were buried there, close to the surface.

Olivia paid the check then, when she saw Cass look at her watch. They left the restaurant, and Cass thanked her for lunch.

'Good luck with the tour,' Olivia said, and kissed her, and Cass looked at her hard for a moment, as though still trying to figure out who she was. 'Thank you for seeing me,' Olivia said sadly. Cass nodded, and then hurried away, as Olivia got into her car and was driven uptown. She felt as though she were hanging on to her youngest child by the thinnest of threads, but thank God it was holding and hadn't broken yet.

And when she got back to her office, Olivia called Alex. She'd been wanting to check on him. He was at home with friends, and his parents were out.

'I miss you,' she said to him. 'How's it going?'

'Okay. I have three more weeks before school starts.' His senior year in high school. He was looking forward to it, although stressed about his college applications. They had talked about it on the boat, and she had tried to reassure him, but the competition was fierce.

'Let me know if you want to come into town and have dinner,' she suggested. He liked the idea but was too lazy to do it.

'I will,' he said vaguely.

It was harder to maintain the connection when they didn't see each other every day, which was why being on the boat was so wonderful. For those days, she had been able to strengthen her bond with him.

'What about telling your parents what we talked about, before you go back to school? It might make this year easier for you – one less thing to worry about.'

'Or one more big thing when they go nuts.' Alex was still convinced they would.

'I think you need to have more faith in them than that.'

'I know them. My father is homophobic, and my mother is in denial.' They were damning statements about his parents, and Olivia hoped he was wrong.

'I can talk to them with you, if you want,' she offered again, as she had on the boat.

'Thanks anyway, Grandma.'

'You'll do it when you're ready.'

'Yeah, like when I'm ninety.' He laughed, and Olivia felt sad for him. He promised to call her soon, and then they hung up. She didn't want to lose touch with him now. There was so much to worry about, about all of them.

And she thought about Cass on her way home. Olivia realized that she could reach her by e-mail or on her BlackBerry, but she didn't even know where her daughter was staying in New York, and she had forgotten to ask her. Probably downtown. There was so much she didn't know about her, it nearly broke her heart. But at least they'd had a nice lunch. It was all they had for now.

Olivia hated the feeling that she lost touch with all of them to some degree once they went their separate ways after the summer vacation. They each had their own lives, problems, and joys. And so did she. It was only when they came together for an extended time that it all inter-twined and meshed, and when they left, the threads fell loose again, and she had no idea what they were doing. It was so much easier when they were all under one roof, like when they were small. But those days were over for ever. Even her grandchildren had their own lives.

Carole had left for California a few days before. She had called her grandmother to say goodbye. Sophie was in Boston and going to the Cape with friends until school started. And Olivia realized then that she hadn't heard from Phillip since their big blowout the week before. She wondered when she would if at all. She hadn't seen him at work either. She had been swamped since she got back. She hoped he was all right, despite his harsh words to her. Her mother had soothed those wounds. She was planning to see Peter that night. He was the bright spot in her life. She had much to tell him, and about her lunch with Cass. She wasn't going to tell him about Alex – she had made a sacred vow. But at least she could share with him her concerns about the others, her victories and private griefs. Her life would have been much harder without him. It was what Phillip didn't understand, and her mother did.

Chapter 15

Phillip had been in a terrible mood ever since his fight with his mother over Peter. He had talked to John about it again when he got home, and they got in a huge argument. So currently, he was at odds with his mother and his brother. He still felt the same way about it. John said he was crazy and owed their mother an apology. Phillip had no intention of apologizing to her, now or ever.

And he had hardly seen his wife since their holiday on the boat. She had been swamped at her office, had three new clients, and was preparing for a trial. She had been in the office till all hours every night, and he had gone to dinner with suppliers who were in from out of town. He was hoping to catch up with Amanda that night.

He poured himself a drink when he got home, and sat

down on the couch to relax. He was thinking about his mother again and how angry he was with her. He was relieved he hadn't had to see her in meetings all week. He wasn't sure he could have sat through it, particularly if Peter was there.

He hadn't said anything about it to Amanda yet, because he hadn't spent enough time with her. They were meeting like ships passing in the night. And he knew Amanda didn't like his mother. He didn't want to give her more ammunition for their next fight, when she would tell him he was his mother's puppet and had no balls, or now, that his mother was the mistress of a married man. It was bad enough knowing it himself, and too humiliating sharing it with someone else, even his wife.

He was going over papers from work when Amanda walked through the door. She threw down her briefcase, answered her cell phone, opened a bottle of white wine, and barely said hello. She had the glass in her hand when she finally did.

'How was your day?' she asked him in a supercilious tone, as though his days were insignificant compared to hers, since he was only his mother's slave, and she was a partner in a major law firm. It was all over her face and in her voice.

'My day was fine,' he said in a neutral tone, not taking

the bait. 'How was yours?' There was no visible affection between them. They were like two business partners meeting up after a long week and comparing notes.

'Pretty damned good actually,' she said with a sudden grin. 'I got the appointment today.' She had been lobbying for it for more than two years. 'You're looking at the next federal judge on the bench!' she said victoriously, as he smiled, and got up to kiss her.

'Congratulations!' He was happy for her. She had wanted it so badly, it had been all she could talk about for months.

'Thank you. I'll admit, it's pretty impressive, if I do say so myself.' There was nothing humble about Amanda, but it was one of the things he had always liked about her. She was a strong woman and made no apology for it. 'I think we'll need to make some changes around here. I want to start doing some entertaining, of the right people, of course. I think we need to redo the living room, the house in the Hamptons needs work, I need a new wardrobe, and you need a bigger boat.' She had it all planned. She was not going to be some two-bit federal judge. She was going to make a big splash, and she wanted to become one of the most powerful women on the bench. She had fantasies about becoming an appellate judge one day. 'And I think you need to make some very major donations to important charitable and political causes, Phillip.' She had his work cut out for him too.

'Take it easy there, Your Honor,' he said as he set down his glass. 'What you're talking about takes a lot of money. Let's not spend a fortune because you got appointed to the bench. Why not just enjoy it for a minute?' And he had no intention of buying a bigger boat. He loved the one he had.

'This is only the beginning, Phillip. It's going to be a long, slow ride to the top.' Or a fast one, judging by what she was suggesting, he thought.

'Well, I'm very proud of you. When is your induction?'

'In six weeks. I want to give a fabulous party,' she said. She had a million plans, and all of them out of his wallet. She made a very decent income but never used it. He had a great deal more, and she had always felt he should pay all her bills. And Phillip was willing.

'And what do you need a new wardrobe for, by the way? You'll be wearing a black robe over it.' He was only half-teasing since it was true.

'We're going to be going out a lot more than we do now.' She was going to milk all the connections she had. And the Grayson name was pure gold. She wasn't unaware of that. 'I think you need to speak to your mother immediately. She should think about stepping aside. As a federal judge, it's a lot more impressive if I'm married to a CEO, not a CFO. Maybe she'd give up the title, let you run the company, and just be chairman. You can at least ask her,' she said pointedly, as he looked at her, stunned. He'd heard it before, but he could see Amanda was deadly earnest.

'I don't think my mother is going to want to give up being CEO of her own company as a career move for you,' he said, hoping she was kidding, but he could see she wasn't. 'I think we're a little over the top here.' She was out of control.

'You can't just be some kind of pencil pusher, Phillip, if you're married to a federal judge.' She was drunk on her own importance, and Phillip was sobering up rapidly. Who was she? She was turning into a monster. Or had she always been as power hungry as this? He was no longer sure.

'Is that how you see me? As a pencil pusher? A numbers guy, an accountant?' She had said the same thing to him on the boat. She was castrating him with her words.

'That's what you are, as a CFO,' she said bluntly.

'I may be just a CFO, Amanda. But it's one of the biggest privately held companies in the world. That counts for something.'

'Privately held by your mother,' she said nastily, 'like your balls, Phillip. It's up to you to change that.'

'And hand them to you?' he asked, as he strode to the door. 'Where are you going?' she asked, looking angry.

'Out. While I still have my balls, no thanks to you,' he said, and slammed the door behind him. He had no idea where he was going. He just wanted to get as far away from her as he could.

Phillip walked for miles before he slowed down and came to his senses. He was so angry, he couldn't even think at first. He was shocked to realize he had gotten all the way to Thirteenth Street before he felt sane again. He had covered almost four miles since he left their house. It was a warm, balmy night, and he kept walking and stopped at Washington Square and sat on a bench for a while, looking at the houses, and listening to the NYU students swirling around him. He got up and walked some more then. He had no desire to go home, but he was hungry and wanted something to eat. He walked over to Bleecker Street and stopped at a coffeehouse that had tables outside. They served sandwiches, burgers, and pizza, and he sat down at a table among students and artists, and the eddying crowd on the street. He felt old compared to most of them, but he didn't care.

He glanced at a girl at a table next to him, intently

reading a book. She was drinking a cappuccino, and there was a half-eaten salad next to it. She kept her nose in the book. He noticed that she was pretty, with shining dark hair that hung to her shoulders and a clean-cut look. She had big brown eyes and an innocent face. There was a wholesome air about her, and then she looked up and smiled at him and went back to her reading. Phillip ordered a hamburger and a cup of coffee, and he devoured the burger when it came. He was starving after the long walk. The girl next to him looked up from her book again then, and smiled at him. She looked like a kid, and he suspected she probably went to NYU. Everyone around them did. They were on the edge of the campus. But she looked more put together than the students. He couldn't resist saying something to her when she looked up.

'Must be a good book,' he said with a shy grin. He didn't want her to think he was hitting on her. He was just being friendly. Everyone around them seemed casual and relaxed.

'It is.' She smiled even more broadly this time, and he could see how pretty she really was. She looked like an ad for something beautiful, young, and healthy. She was wearing white jeans and a T-shirt, with sandals, and her dark hair shone, it was so clean. She laughed then, and showed him what she was reading. 'It's a teacher's guide, but it's a pretty good one. I teach fourth grade.' She looked perfect for it. 'I start my first job in two weeks. I got here from Wisconsin yesterday.' She was too good to be true. She looked like an angel fallen from the sky to him. Fresh out of school, an elementary school teacher, and right out of the Midwest the day before. It didn't get purer than that. He hoped she wouldn't be devoured by the big city. 'I just found an apartment today,' she added, and he wanted to warn her not to talk to strangers. 'I have four roommates. I found it on craigslist.' She was so innocent, she was like a poster child of some kind, and he wanted to adopt her immediately.

'Did you check them out?' he asked cautiously, feeling instantly protective.

'They're all students,' she said, laughing. 'My brother said the same thing. They don't look like ax murderers to me. The apartment is really pretty, I have my own room the size of a broom closet, and it's cheap.'

'Your brother's right,' Phillip warned her. 'You should do a criminal check on them.' It made him suddenly grateful he didn't have a daughter who looked like her. He was old enough to be her father, which was embarrassing. He probably seemed like a dirty old man to her, and he was disheveled after storming out of the apartment and

Danielle Steel

walking at full speed for several hours to calm his rage, after what Amanda had said. It was no worse than anything else she'd ever said to him, but it had suddenly seemed worse to him.

'I think they're fine. They're younger than I am, they're all undergrads, and they're all girls. How bad can nineteen-year-old girls be?'

'Pretty bad, maybe,' he said suspiciously, but he was relieved to hear they were all girls. That sounded less dangerous to him. He didn't know why, but he was suddenly concerned about this perfect stranger. But she seemed so innocent and sweet.

The waitress refilled his cup of coffee, and the girl took a bite of her salad. Since they were talking, she had closed her book. 'Where are you going to be teaching?' he asked suddenly.

'I got assigned to a school in Harlem,' she said, smiling at him again. 'I know, I know, it's dangerous. But I'll be fine. I did my student teaching at an inner-city school in Detroit, which was probably a lot tougher than this.' He stared at her in horror. She was an accident waiting to happen.

'How could your parents let you come here?' he asked her, and she laughed.

'My parents died when I was eight. I live with my married sister. She trusts me.'

'New York is a tough city.'

'So was Detroit. I was fine.'

'You're very brave,' he said, looking hard at her, wondering how old she was. Maybe she was older than she looked, or a black belt in karate. He hoped so for her sake. He wanted to add, 'or very foolish,' but he didn't. 'How old are you?'

'Twenty-eight. I just finished my student teaching after my master's. I've always wanted to live in New York. I wanted to be an actress, but I wound up teaching instead. I like it. I like the kids. I was in the Peace Corps for two years, in South America.' There was more to her than met the eye. She was just a very open person, and she was clearly very independent, and not afraid to try new things. 'I was thinking about working in India for a year, but I came here instead. My sister was nervous about my going to New Delhi. She thought I'd get sick.'

'That makes sense.' And then he asked her an odd question. 'Are you always this friendly to strangers?' She laughed and shook her head.

'No. But you seem like an honest person. There are lots of people around. I don't think you're going to try and kill me at an open-air café.'

'I could be dangerous,' he said, and they both laughed. 'Are you?'

303

'No.'

'What do you do?' She was curious about him too. He had looked upset when he sat down, but he seemed more relaxed now, and appeared friendlier. And he was interesting to talk to.

'I work for The Factory,' he said simply. He didn't say he was the CFO, or that his mother owned it.

'They have great stuff,' she commented. 'My sister and brother bought all their furniture there. Do you sell furniture?'

'No, I work in the main office. In finance.'

'That figures. I guessed you were a lawyer or a banker.'

'Do I look that stuffy?'

'No.' She laughed. 'But you're wearing nice shoes and a suit. You probably have a tie in your pocket.' He laughed and pulled it out. It was a dark blue Hermès. Maybe she wasn't such a bad judge of character after all. And she had traveled the world.

They talked for a while, about her experiences in the Peace Corps, and he admitted that he'd gone to Harvard, when she said she had gone to Duke. She was a bright girl and interesting to talk to, and it sounded crazy, but he wanted to see her again. He didn't volunteer the fact that he was married and she didn't ask. She thought maybe he was divorced, and he had admitted he was forty-six when he mentioned business and Harvard. He didn't want to date her, he just wanted to talk to her again. It was midnight, and he thought he should get home, and he handed her his business card before he stood up.

'This probably sounds silly, and I'm sure you can take care of yourself, but if I can do anything to help you, give me a call.' He handed her the card that said he was the CFO. She didn't look at it and slipped it into her book, like a bookmark.

'Thank you, that's very nice of you. I appreciate it,' she said, with her big smile and beautiful teeth.

'Could I call you sometime?' he asked, and couldn't believe what he had just said. He was a married man. What would he call her about? But she nodded and smiled and wrote her cell number down on a piece of paper and handed it to him. It was as simple as that. For one totally unusual evening, he had felt like a kid again, and a free man. He was acting as though he had no attachments in the world, when in fact he had a wife at home who was about to become a federal judge and thought he had no balls. And then he realized he didn't know one important detail. 'What's your name?'

They both laughed then. They had been talking so much, they had forgotten to introduce themselves. His name was on his card, but she hadn't looked at it.

'I'm Taylor Dean,' she said, holding a hand out to him. When he shook it, her grip was firm but not too strong, and he noticed that her hands were beautiful.

'I'm Phillip Grayson.' He hoped she wouldn't recognize the Grayson name, or Google him. He was sure that knowing who he was would be too overwhelming for her. But there was no reason to suspect she would discover it.

'Thanks, Phillip,' she said, as she signaled for her check, but he had already taken care of it when he went to the men's room a short time before. It had cost him ten dollars, which was probably a big deal to her. When she realized what he'd done, she thanked him profusely, and they both stood up. She was tall, he realized, and had a beautiful figure. She looked perfect to him.

They left the restaurant together, and she headed in the direction of the apartment she had just rented. He wished he could go with her, but he had a wife at home. And she was a young girl. He was eighteen years older than she was, which was a lot, and he was married, which made the whole scenario impossible. He knew he'd probably never see her again, and eventually he'd throw her number out. He had put it in his suit pocket, like a lock of hair, or a secret code. It felt magic, and so did she.

'Take care, Taylor,' he said to her, and then he hailed a cab. 'Good luck,' he added and meant it, which told her she would never hear from him. She waved as the cab pulled away, and Phillip wanted to jump out and follow her.

He thought about her all the way uptown, wishing he were young again and free. Taylor had appeared in his life twenty years too late. He had been married for nineteen. And twenty years before, she had been eight years old. It was a cruel twist of fate. And when he walked into the house, all the lights were turned off. Amanda was in bed, and sound asleep. There was no note, she didn't stir, there was no apology, and she hadn't waited up for him.

Phillip took his clothes off and carefully put the slip of paper with Taylor's number in his wallet. He knew he wouldn't call her, but just seeing it there would remind him of the sweet girl he had talked to that night, the fourth-grade teacher from Milwaukee who was going to work in Harlem in two weeks. He felt a lump in his throat as he took off his clothes and got into bed next to Amanda. She no longer felt like a woman to him, just a judge and the person he lived with who thought he had no balls. He tried to push Taylor from his mind, and finally went to sleep.

Chapter 16

The next morning when they got up, Amanda acted as though nothing had happened. She didn't ask Phillip where he'd gone, or what he'd done. She appeared as though everything was normal, and talked endlessly about the party she wanted to give for her induction. And before that, she wanted to give a Labor Day party in the Hamptons for some important people. It was obvious that she was shifting gears and preparing to enter a whole new world. Clearly, she felt truly important and she expected him to go along with her and do the things she thought necessary to showcase her new status. She told him there would be a printed notice of her appointment in *The New York Times* on Sunday.

'And don't forget to buy a new suit for my induction,'

she reminded him as they both left for work. She had a lot to do at the office. She had to hand off all her cases to her partners before she left. She acted now as though Phillip's life were insignificant and the only one that counted was hers. 'You should let your mother know,' she said as they left the house. 'She may want to give me a party too.' Amanda expected to be celebrated by everyone she knew, and although she wasn't fond of her mother-in-law, she thought that a party hosted by her would be fitting and attract some important people. Amanda was now the new homecoming queen, and Phillip was her slave. As far as she was concerned, she had one-upped the Graysons in a major way. Phillip found her arrogance unattractive and didn't tell her that he and his mother weren't on speaking terms at the moment. The last thing he wanted to do, given her affair with Peter Williams and how he felt about it, was ask her to give Amanda a party. It would just have to wait.

When he got to his office, he went through his messages and e-mails, and he could feel his wallet burning a hole in his back pocket. He knew what was in there and how he felt about it. He finally took it out and looked at the slip of paper Taylor had given him. Her handwriting was bold and clear, and it was easy to read the number. He had no intention of calling her, and didn't know what he would have said if he did, but he couldn't help himself. It was an impulse that was stronger than he was. He called her number and heard it ringing. He wanted to hang up but couldn't. And he had no idea what to say. She answered on the third ring.

'Taylor?' His voice was barely more than a whisper.

'Yes?' She obviously had no idea who it was, but she sounded as innocent and open as the night before. He could still see her smiling at the table next to his at the café downtown. She looked as bright and new as spring.

'Hi. It's Phillip Grayson,' he said, feeling stupid. Then what? Now what was he going to do? 'I just wanted to tell you how much I enjoyed meeting you last night.' He hadn't done this in twenty years. 'I just thought I'd say hello.'

'Well, hello,' she said, with a smile in her voice. 'I enjoyed it too. I was just opening all my boxes. I've got books stacked up to the ceiling. I think I'm going to have to go to The Factory and buy a bookcase.' She was laughing, and he could just see her, surrounded by books.

'Maybe we could go together,' he suggested, and then felt stupid again. That was all he needed, to show up at one of their stores with a pretty young woman. Everyone there knew who he was. 'Actually, I was wondering if you'd like to have lunch with me today. Does that work for you?' She didn't hesitate for an instant, which told him that she didn't mind how old he was. But she still didn't know he was married.

'That sounds great. Where would you like to meet?'

He suggested a restaurant in the West Village, and they agreed to meet at one o'clock. She sounded bouncy and young and alive, and he felt like an idiot when he hung up. What in God's name was he doing? He had no idea. He had never done anything like it before, but he felt as though a force more powerful than he was making him do it. He had to see her again.

After that, he asked his secretary to find him their current catalog. He wanted to take it to lunch with him. He was going to help her pick out a bookcase and have it sent to her. He felt protective of her, and he wanted to make life easier for her. She brought out his best instincts. And it was such a small thing to do. His secretary had the catalog on his desk a few minutes later. And he arrived ten minutes early for lunch.

She was wearing a pink cotton skirt when she walked into the restaurant, with a white blouse, and her shining hair cascaded past her shoulders. She looked like a shampoo ad, and she was wearing the same sandals she'd worn the night before. It was hot outside, and she looked crisp and immaculate as she walked across the restaurant toward him with a smile.

'Thank you for coming,' he said as he stood up, and she sat across from him in the booth.

'I'm happy to get out of the mess in my house,' she said brightly, and he remembered the catalog then and handed it to her.

'I thought we could pick a bookcase for you, if you know what size you want. It's a lot easier than going to the store. I can have it delivered to you.' She looked first surprised and then pleased. He was being so nice to her, and she looked up at him with a shy smile.

'Will you get in trouble for this?' she asked him kindly, and he laughed. She was so innocent and young and looked so concerned. 'I want to pay for it, of course.' She didn't want to take advantage of him.

'No, I won't get in trouble. It's not a big deal, I promise. And I get a big discount. I'd like to give it to you as a gift, if you'll let me.' She felt awkward about it, but she didn't want to hurt his feelings.

'Well, it's a big gift to me,' she said gratefully, as she looked through the catalog and found one that was exactly the right size and showed him. It cost ninety-nine dollars, and he was sure he could have it for her by that afternoon. They marked the page, and then they ordered lunch. She asked for a salad again, and this time so did he. And when it came, he couldn't eat. He just wanted to talk to her. He was nervous. His palms were sweating, and by the end of lunch, he knew he had to level with her.

'Taylor,' he said, when the waitress poured them both iced coffee, 'I want to be honest with you. I think you're the most amazing young woman I've ever met. And I have no idea what I'm doing here. I just knew I had to see you today. You knocked me flat on my ass last night.' It was the most honest he'd ever been, and she looked touched.

'I did? I don't know how, I didn't do anything.'

'Yes, you did. You're like a breath of fresh air in my life. I'm old enough to be your father, but I feel like a kid with you. Everything about you is so decent and wholesome and alive. I suddenly realize I've been dead for twenty years. But there's something I have to tell you. I have no idea what it means to us, if anything. Or where we go from here, if we do. I'm married. I have been for nineteen years. We have no kids. My wife didn't want any. She's an attorney. She's an extremely bright woman, I've always respected her. I've never cheated on her, and I don't think I've been honest with myself about our relationship until recently.

'I don't love her, I don't even like her. I hate to admit

it, but it's true, and I'm not sure she's in love with me. I can't live that way. I haven't said anything to her, or done anything about it, and I don't know if I will. And then you walked into my life yesterday. I saw you at the café, and all I want to do now is see you again. But I don't want to get either of us tangled up in a bad situation. Do you suppose we could just meet for lunch for a while or have coffee until I figure out what I'm doing? I promise you, if I'm going to stay where I am, I won't see you again. I just don't know. It's as honest as I can be with you right now.'

Taylor thought about it for a long moment and nodded. She didn't want to get into a bad situation either. She had never dated a married man, and she didn't want to start now. She liked him, but she had thought he was free. At least he had told her the truth. She respected him for it, and she knew it couldn't have been easy to say.

'I guess that would be okay, if we just do lunch and dinner. I like you,' she said sincerely, 'I think you're a nice man. And no one should be with someone who doesn't love them. You deserve as much happiness as anyone else.'

'So do you,' he said gently and took her hand in his own. 'I promise I'll figure this out as soon as I can. Maybe nothing will ever happen with us, but I'm grateful just to know you.'

She beamed when he said it. 'Me too. And maybe we

can just be friends.' Phillip didn't say it, but that wasn't how he felt about her. He wanted to make love to her and hold her in his arms. He had never felt about Amanda as he did about this girl. He felt as though he'd been hit by a bolt of lightning the night before.

'I give you my word, Taylor, I'm not going to drag you into a mess. If it's going to be a mess, I'll disappear.' She looked sad when he said it, and he brought her fingers to his lips then. 'I'm not going anywhere,' he reassured her, 'except with you.' He had the strange feeling that Providence had dropped an enormous gift in his lap, and he didn't want to lose it. He felt like this was meant to be. He paid the check when they were finished, and then looked at her with deep affection. 'When am I going to see you again?'

'I don't know.' She was feeling a little overwhelmed. He was a powerful person, and this was a lot to digest. She would have liked to tell her sister about it, but she wouldn't approve. A married man? No way. Even just as friends. But she could tell that Phillip wanted to be more than just friends with her, and she was attracted to him. He was a very handsome man, even if he was a little square. But she liked men who looked like him. Her brother was cut from the same cloth, and was a banker in Milwaukee, with a wife and three kids, and he was ten years younger than Phillip. Her sister was forty-three, and had four kids.

'How about lunch tomorrow?' Phillip asked her as they left the restaurant, and she looked up at him with a rueful expression. 'Is that too soon?'

'Yes . . . no,' she corrected. 'I don't know.' He was so comfortable to be with, and so protective, that she was already falling for him, and they had only just met. This was crazy, for both of them. And even more so for him. He had a wife. He didn't seem married to her, but he was. At least he didn't have kids. She didn't want to be a home wrecker, but in a way she was anyway. She felt guilty and happy and excited all at once. And it was hard to resist the attention he lavished on her. He had sworn to her he had never done this before, and neither had she. She had had a boyfriend for four years in college and grad school, and they had broken up the year before. She hadn't met anyone she cared about since.

And then he remembered something else. 'What's your address?'

'You're coming to my house?' she asked, looking nervous, and he laughed as he put an arm around her shoulders. He would have liked to, but he knew it would be the end of his good intentions, if he did.

'No, silly. I want to send you the bookcase.' She

laughed too and jotted it down for him. 'I'll see what I can do, if we have it in stock.' If they did, he was going to get a private delivery van to bring it to her. It was all he could do, a small gesture, to give her something she needed, to make her happy.

'Thank you,' she said simply.

He looked at his watch then and realized he was half an hour late for a meeting. 'Lunch tomorrow?'

'I – uh – yes!' she blurted out. She wanted to see him too.

'Café Cluny,' he said quickly before she could change her mind, and kissed her lightly on the lips. He hailed a cab, which came to a screeching halt beside them, and he opened the door and got in. He was smiling at her, and she looked dazed. 'See you tomorrow, one o'clock,' he called out the window, and she waved. He called the warehouse on the drive uptown. They had the bookcase. Then he called his secretary, told her to get a delivery truck, and gave her Taylor's address. It was all taken care of in less than five minutes, and then he called her and told her about the delivery, so she could be there. 'I'm sorry I was so rushed. I was late for a meeting. Thank you for meeting me for lunch. I don't know what I'm doing, but I think you're the most wonderful woman I've ever met.'

'You don't even know me yet,' she said, sounding confused.

'I hope I will,' he said, and meant it. 'See you to-morrow, Taylor.' He rushed into the building, and slid into the meeting nearly an hour late. His brother, John, was at the conference table, but his mother wasn't. It was a finance and design meeting, about production costs, and she wasn't expected to attend. When they left, his brother looked at him strangely. 'Are you okay? You look weird.'

'I am weird,' he said vaguely. 'Amanda got appointed to the federal bench yesterday. She's reorganizing the world.'

'Have you calmed down about Mom?'

'Maybe. I don't know. I haven't thought about it.' But in light of what he was doing with Taylor, or might be doing, or could do, and wanted to do, his objections to Peter Williams seemed strange even to him. Maybe this was how those things happened. He hadn't allowed himself to think about it yet. But at least he hadn't slept with her. And he wasn't going to until he worked this out in his head.

And when he got home that night, Amanda was making lists. For parties, for social events she wanted to attend, committees she thought she should join, things she wanted him to do.

'Did you tell your mother?' she asked as she looked up from what she was writing.

He shook his head. 'I didn't see her today.'

'You could have called her.' As far as Amanda was concerned, this was big news, and the whole world was supposed to celebrate her. She had told her partners and everyone she knew with an e-mail blast.

'I have no idea where she was,' Phillip said honestly. And with that, she handed him a list of everything he was supposed to buy, sign up for, and do. It was quite a list. He felt like he had enlisted in the marines.

He opened a bottle of champagne for her then, because he felt guilty about his lunch with Taylor. Amanda didn't know, but he did. He handed her a glass of champagne, and she looked pleased.

'Thank you, Phillip.' He toasted her, and tried to force Taylor from his head. The image of her refused to move.

'So where did you go last night?' she finally asked him. She didn't apologize for her comments. All she wanted to know was where he went.

'I walked all the way down to the Village, had a burger, and took a cab back.' It was true. What he didn't tell her was that he had met the most enchanting girl he'd ever seen.

'Sorry if I pissed you off,' Amanda conceded, 'but it's

true. It would look a lot better for me, and my status, if your mother made you CEO. I'd like you to ask her to do that,' Amanda said simply. She saw no reason why Olivia wouldn't step down in order to further her daughter-in-law's career. She saw it less as an important step for Phillip than as an accessory for her, but of course it would benefit him too. It was a win-win for them, and Olivia was of retirement age after all.

'Why don't you ask her yourself?' he said coolly. 'I'm sure she'd be interested to hear your ideas.'

'I think the pressure should come from you. Maybe you should threaten to quit.'

'And then what? What if she lets me? We turn the whole company upside down so you can say you're married to a CEO? What if she fires me? Then your husband would be unemployed. That might look worse.' He was only half-joking.

'She's not going to let you quit, Phillip. You're her son.'

'And my mother is not going to relinquish her seat as CEO, even for you. And I've told you, I don't want her job. Mine is tough enough. Hers is a lot worse. I'm in no hurry to step into her shoes, even if you think that means I have no balls. She carries more responsibility than anyone I know, in any corporation, and she does it pretty damned well. I'm not sure I could do her job. In fact, I'm sure I can't. So that's a problem for you. If you stick with me, all you get is a CFO. I guess that's bad news for you.' He was being a lot tougher than he had been with her before, and he knew it was time. She had been insulting enough.

'I didn't realize you were giving me an option clause. "If I stick with you." Is that a message, Phillip?' Amanda's eyes narrowed as she asked.

'You always have that choice,' he said clearly.

'Is that a threat?'

'No, but I'm not going to have my life, wardrobe, and career remodeled to suit you, because you just became a judge.'

'It's a pretty big deal,' she reminded him with a surly tone.

'Yes, it is. And I'm proud of you. But I'm not going to pay for your induction with my balls, as you put it. They belong to me, not to you. They're not part of the deal.'

'Then what is? Are you willing to use some of the Grayson money to make contributions for me, that would help my career? That's the least you could do, if you're not willing to ask your mother for a better job.'

'I don't know how much "Grayson money" I could commit. My mother makes those decisions, and the board. And if they don't like the sound of it, they don't do it. It's not up to me.'

'That's what I mean, Phillip. You have no clout there at all.' She looked disgusted by what she was hearing from him.

'I have some clout, but not much. I never said I did. One day, but not now. You're a little premature. My mother is still very much in charge.' It occurred to him as he said it that he hardly knew Taylor, but he couldn't imagine her asking him how much 'Grayson money he was willing to commit.' Even twenty years down the road he couldn't imagine Taylor having that kind of toughness. He was astounded at Amanda's nerve to ask.

'I think we'll need to talk about this again,' Amanda said, with a very chilly tone in her voice.

'We can, and I'm certainly willing to, but it's not going to get you far.' Amanda said nothing to him after that. She finished her glass of champagne and went upstairs and took a bath. They were having dinner with one of her partners that night. And when they got to the restaurant, she made him feel like a nobody. She made it clear to everyone at the table that she was the star. And Amanda referred to him several times as 'only the CFO.' She was having a good time, but he was seething when they got home.

'Is that what I have to look forward to now? Humiliation whenever we go out, because you're now a federal judge, or about to be? It's going to be a little wearing if that's the case.'

'Then ask your mother for a better job,' she said coldly. This was war. It was Amanda after his mother, using him as the weapon of choice. It was a miserable situation for him to be in. She was trying to pressure him into demanding the job of CEO, by humiliating him until he did. Phillip had no desire to enlist for that. Amanda didn't know it, but she was signing her death warrant with him.

And he realized that night, when they went to bed, that they hadn't made love since they had been on the boat. Her attitude wasn't conducive to his wanting to make love to her. He was examining everything now, scrutinizing it under a microscope, because he had met a girl at a café the night before, but also because Amanda had been out of line for too long, and now she was worse. His mother's concern, expressed on the boat, hadn't fallen on deaf ears. She had asked if Amanda was enough for him. He no longer knew. He was asking himself that question now. He just wasn't sure.

They didn't say a word to each other in bed that night. She didn't try to seduce him, nor he her. He didn't want to give her any 'rewards' for her bad behavior, and she left him so cold now he wasn't even sure he could get it up, and he didn't want to try. And Amanda seemed satisfied the way things were. She had intimated that she didn't want to sleep with him until he got a better job. And he wasn't about to be blackmailed by her. They had come to an impasse. Phillip couldn't sleep all night and left the house for work before Amanda got out of the shower.

He was looking tense when he met Taylor for lunch that day. The night before with Amanda had left him in a bad mood. But the moment he saw Taylor, it was dispelled, and within a few minutes he was laughing with her and felt like a boy again.

'You're amazing!' she said as soon as he arrived.

'So are you.' He was smiling at her and reached for her hand. 'No, I mean *really* amazing,' she said to him with wide eyes. 'The bookcase arrived at six o'clock last night. And it's perfect. The delivery guy assembled it for me, and he put it in the right place. All my books fit, and they're off the floor. Wow! You're a miracle worker,' she said gratefully, and he smiled. It was such a small thing to do for her, in the context of his life, and he was glad he had.

They talked about her childhood over lunch, and her parents dying in a head-on collision when she was eight.

Her sister had just gotten married and Taylor went to live with her, and stayed there until she went to college. Her brother had been sixteen and had lived with them too until he left for college two years later. She said her brother-in-law was a saint to put up with them all. And she mentioned that their family was very close. And then she asked about his. Listening to her had put his life somewhat in perspective. His mother had been away a lot, but she wasn't dead. They weren't orphans, they had a wonderful life, and they'd been doted on by their father and grandmother. He realized now that in contrast to her life, his had been easy. The comparison embarrassed him.

'My mom was busy a lot,' he explained, 'she traveled constantly for work, so my father and grandmother brought me up most of the time. She lived with us, and my mom was home between trips. I have two sisters and a brother, and it sounds like my oldest sister is about the same age as yours, and my youngest sister, whom I don't see anymore, is a little younger than your brother.'

'Why don't you see her anymore?' She looked sad for him, as though it were a circumstance she couldn't even imagine, since her family was so close, even without their parents, or maybe because of it. Phillip wondered.

'It's a long story, but she got very upset when my father died. She was mad that my mother wasn't there. She was away on a business trip when Dad died, so after that, my sister moved to London. She was twenty. My mother and grandmother see her when she comes to town, and my sister saw her a few years ago, I think. I haven't seen her in about ten years. She keeps her distance. We don't have much in common. And families are complicated sometimes.'

'I know,' Taylor said, looking sympathetic. 'I had to work after school to pay for college and graduate school. My parents' insurance money ran out before that, and we used it to pay for my brother's college education. But it all worked out,' she said with a sunny smile, as his heart went out to her, and he felt like a giant spoiled brat. And Amanda's demand for a 'commitment of Grayson money' for her charitable causes in order to advance socially seemed flat-out disgusting. Taylor was real, Amanda just wasn't. And Phillip had been blessed all his life. He would have been mortified now to tell her who he was and what they had, and why the bookcase he'd had delivered to her was nothing to him, all thanks to his mother. Taylor's life put his into perspective very quickly.

They talked about her time in the Peace Corps then, and he said he'd just been to Europe, to Italy and France. He didn't tell her he'd been on a three-hundred-foot yacht, he just said they'd all been on a family vacation, except for his youngest sister. She was impressed that they'd all gone together. There were so many things he couldn't tell her about his life, because if he did, she'd be shocked by the lifestyle he took for granted. He realized that as he listened to her.

And she mentioned that she was fluent in Spanish. They had almost put her in a Spanish-speaking program in Spanish Harlem. She was excited about the job she was about to start, and talked a lot about it. And he hated to leave her at the end of lunch. She said she couldn't see him the next day. She had to go to a teacher's orientation meeting at her new school, but she was free over the weekend. He was dying to see her, but thought he had to spend time with Amanda. He didn't know her plans, although she was very busy right now, getting ready to leave her office, and handing off her cases to others.

'What about dinner on Monday?' Phillip asked her, and Taylor said that would be fine. 'I'll call you over the weekend if I can get away.' She grew quiet then, and he looked at her. She looked sad, and it cut through him like a knife.

'Sometimes I forget you're married,' she said quietly.

'So do I. We have a very strange marriage. I let it get that way, and now I don't know whether to end it or fix it.'

'You should probably fix it if you can,' she said fairly. She didn't want to destroy his marriage, and had told him that the first day.

'I don't know if I want to,' he was honest with her.

'Because of me or other reasons?' she asked softly.

'Both. I think I married the wrong person. I think everyone knew except me. I thought her coldness was a challenge. Now I realize it's impossible to live with. It's like living in an igloo.' And in the face of Taylor's warmth, he didn't want to try. 'I'll figure it out soon. I swear.' He needed to anyway. He couldn't go on like this forever, and Amanda's demands were becoming increasingly outrageous. Taylor was just making the situation more acute. She was the catalyst he hadn't expected. But all the problems with Amanda were there, and had been for a long time, even if he hadn't wanted to see them.

When he left Taylor, he kissed her gently on the cheek, and promised to call her over the weekend, just to say hello. And as it turned out, Amanda had planned to stay in her office and work all weekend, and hadn't mentioned it to him. He called Taylor on Saturday afternoon, and they went for a walk in Central Park, stopped at the model boat pond, listened to several bands, and lay on the grass. She had brought a blanket with her so they could. They stayed until six o'clock, just lying there and talking, and looking up at the trees. And at one point, he rolled over on his side, propped up on his elbow and bent down to kiss her. Her lips were so soft, they seemed to melt into his. He thought he had never tasted anything so sweet in his life.

He took her back downtown then, and they had dinner at the Minetta Tavern, an old favorite of his. And then he dropped her off at her place, and went home. It was ten o'clock, and he got in five minutes before Amanda. He had just turned on the TV, and she assumed he'd been there all evening. He was in a daze after the hours he'd spent with Taylor and their kisses in the park. It suddenly made him feel crazy when he saw Amanda. His situation had become a nightmare overnight.

'Are you okay?' she asked, staring at him intently.

'I'm fine.'

'You look sick.' She could see something, but she couldn't identify it. And she wasn't wrong. His stomach had just turned over at the thought of what he was doing. And he didn't want Taylor to get hurt. She didn't deserve it. He even felt sorry for Amanda. She was being such a fool. She was playing a high-stakes game, and she was going to lose if she kept pushing.

He went to bed early that night, and fell asleep immediately, exhausted from the tension he was feeling.

And when he woke up in the morning, Amanda was gone, without leaving him a note. She was completely wrapped up in her own world these days, with total disregard for him. She had waited for her appointment to the bench for a long time, and it had gone to her head completely. Her narcissism was total. There was no one but her on her planet.

He met Taylor downtown again, and they decided to do something different and fun. They pretended to be tourists in New York, which she was. They went to the top of the Empire State Building, and he kissed her there, with the city at their feet, and then they took a ride on the Staten Island Ferry. He had never had such a good time in his own city. Everything he did with her was exciting and new. And no matter how much time he spent with her, he couldn't get enough of her. She was the drug he had become addicted to. His whole life had turned topsy-turvy in a week, and hers along with it. And she hadn't told her family either. They were both keeping it a secret. He because he had to, and she because she knew her brother and sister wouldn't approve. It was a strange situation for them both, and a dangerous one for her. She could easily be the one to get hurt, and they both knew it.

And the following week, they kept meeting whenever

they could, lunches and dinners, and stolen moments. They went back to Central Park, and sat in Washington Square with the students. They went to the café where they'd met, and the following weekend Amanda worked again, and he spent every waking moment with Taylor. Their romance had gone on for two weeks, but they were seeing each other almost every day, and Phillip still had no idea what he was doing. Amanda appeared to be oblivious to his indifference and change of mood. Part of him wanted her to stop him before this went any further and save their marriage to prove that she loved him, and part of him hoped she wouldn't. She had no idea what was going on and was totally self-involved, more so than ever. Her hour of glory had come. And everyone was making a fuss over her at her office. She seemed to have forgotten that Phillip existed. And he had filled the void with Taylor. She filled his heart like air in a balloon until he felt like he was going to explode with excitement.

On Sunday they went to a street fair in Little Italy, ate lemon gelato, and then walked back toward her apartment. She offered to show him the bookcase, and he felt a little foolish parading past her roommates who were all young students, but he agreed to go up for a few minutes. And when they got there, no one was home.

The apartment was small and sunny, and crowded

with old, fraying furniture, most of which they'd gotten at garage sales, found on the street, or bought at Goodwill. Her bookcase from The Factory looked regal compared to everything else in the apartment, and he was touched by the simplicity in which she lived. Her room was neat as a pin, and spotless. It looked like a young girl's room. Her clothes were in the closet, carefully hung on hangers, her desk was organized, her bedspread was a pink one she'd brought from home, and there were cushions on the bed that her nieces had made her. He took her in his arms and held her as soon as they walked in. Her hair smelled as fresh as it always did, and he loved nuzzling her skin and feeling her close to him. She was wearing a halter top and a denim skirt and flip-flops, and he was wearing jeans, and before he could stop himself, he was pressing her against him, and starving to hold her naked in his arms, and all she wanted was him.

He kicked the door to her room closed behind him in case her roommates came home, and seconds later, their clothes were off, and they were engulfed in passion and couldn't stop until their bodies had exploded together and they lay panting in each other's arms, breathless and unable to move. Phillip had never wanted anyone as badly as he did her, and Taylor had totally abandoned herself to him. The dam had finally broken, and the flood tides couldn't be reversed. He was so in love with her, he couldn't think straight.

'Oh God,' he said as he rolled slowly away from her and looked into her eyes. They were the eyes of a woman surfacing slowly from the depths of passion. 'I'm so sorry . . . I didn't want to do that.' But they had had no choice, and they both knew it.

'I'm not sorry,' she said softly, and meant it, slowly catching her breath again. 'I love you . . . even if you never leave Amanda. At least we'll have had this.' And then he worried about something else.

'Are you on the Pill?' She nodded, but they had both been trusting to have unprotected sex, and neither of them was worried. Everything about this felt right. And then he realized something else as he held her close to him again. 'I want babies with you,' he whispered into her neck. He had never said that to any other woman, nor wanted to. Children were the one thing he had known he didn't want, until now with Taylor. He felt as though he had waited for her all his life. And what he had just said told him what he had to do. 'I'm not going to let this thing go on like this for long. I'm going to straighten it out soon.' And she believed him. She somehow thought that he would. She trusted him completely, which was what every woman involved with a married man had thought before her, but she knew that this would be different. Phillip loved her. She was sure of it. And she loved him.

They made love again that afternoon, and he hated to leave her after he did. He went home feeling as though he had a stone in his chest, consumed with guilt. He hadn't wanted to make love to her until he was free. And now everything was more complicated, and he had no idea what to say to Amanda or when. He took a sleeping pill before she came home that night so he didn't have to see her.

But she was there in the morning, looking bright-eyed and excited about everything she was doing, and talking about her induction as usual. He had a headache and a hangover from the sleeping pill he'd taken the night before.

'What do you want for breakfast?' she asked him as she made toast for herself. She never made breakfast for him, and he almost said 'a divorce,' but he didn't have the guts. He had to think about what he was going to do first. He had known Taylor for two weeks, and he was about to end his marriage of nineteen years. Was he insane? Was he wrong? Was this what he had been waiting for? He no longer knew. He wasn't in love with Amanda, but he no longer felt sane either. He felt as though he had gone crazy in the last two weeks.

'I'll eat something at the office,' he said, and walked out of the kitchen. She was humming something when he left, and the first person he saw in the hall when he got to work was his mother. He was so distracted he walked right past her and didn't see her. And when she called out to him, he turned around looking glazed.

'Are you all right?' Olivia asked him with a look of concern. She had never seen him look like that, and they hadn't spoken since their argument over Peter. 'Are you sick?' She was genuinely worried, and he just shook his head.

'No ... no ... I'm fine ... a summer cold ... it's nothing.' And then he remembered. If it hadn't been for Taylor, he wouldn't have said anything or understood, but who was he to cast stones now? And his mother was single – he wasn't. 'I'm sorry,' he muttered darkly.

'What about?'

'About Peter ... I didn't know ... I'm sure you know what you're doing.' She was even more worried about him after that. Phillip, the Great Carrier of Grudges for All Time, had given in far too easily. She wondered suddenly if there was trouble between him and Amanda.

'Is Amanda all right?'

'She got her appointment to the federal bench. She's over the moon about it.'

'Congratulate her for me,' Olivia said, still searching her son's eyes for some explanation of why he looked so ragged, but there was none, and he hurried away to his office a few minutes later, as though he were afraid to talk to his mother.

She was so worried about him that she mentioned it to Peter that night. He was sure there was some simple explanation, and he was happy to hear that he had apologized. He didn't find that strange at all. He owed it to her.

'Maybe he's in love,' Peter said, only half-joking. Stranger things had happened.

'Phillip?' His mother laughed at the suggestion. 'It's the one thing he's most afraid of. He'd rather have his heart ripped out with a tweezer. I'm not sure Phillip could tolerate being loved. That's why he married Amanda. The human iceberg. I think Phillip is afraid of feelings. He doesn't want to be hurt or disappointed, so he stays with her and feels nothing. It's incredibly depressing.'

'You never know, things change. Maybe one day he'll find the right woman and leave Amanda.'

'She's far more likely to leave him,' Olivia said bitterly, which was unusual for her, but she didn't like Amanda, 'if she finds someone with more money.' It was an ugly thing to say, but she was convinced it was true.

She continued to worry about Phillip, but she was busy. A strike at one of their Texas stores had turned ugly, and there was the threat of looting. They had had to hire security guards and close the store temporarily and she wasn't pleased. Peter had convinced her not to go there herself, he didn't want her to get hurt, and for once she agreed.

She stopped at a bookstore a few days later, to pick up some books Peter said he wanted, and she was reading the flap copy of a novel for herself when she glanced up and saw Phillip walk into the store with a pretty young woman. She looked half his age and was gazing at him adoringly. And Phillip looked besotted. Olivia stared at them in disbelief, and then darted behind a bookshelf so they wouldn't see her. And then he kissed her. Olivia suddenly understood why he had backed down about Peter. She wondered if this was serious or just a fling. She had no way of knowing, and she didn't want to ask him. She waited until they left, paid for her books, and called Peter as soon as she left the store and told him what she'd seen.

'I told you he was in love,' Peter said, chuckling.

'I don't know if he's in love or having an affair, but I hardly recognized him. He looks crazy about her. She looks very young and she's very pretty.' But now she was even more worried about him. If his wife found out, it was liable to get ugly. And expensive.

'He's a big boy, Olivia,' Peter reminded her. 'He'll figure this one out for himself.'

'I suppose so, but he certainly wasn't being discreet. He kissed her right in the bookstore. Anyone could have seen them,' just as she did. Even Amanda, if she had walked in.

'Maybe he's serious about her,' Peter suggested.

'I don't know what I wish,' Olivia said with a sigh. 'I'd hate to see him go through a divorce, but I'd hate like hell to have him spend the rest of his life with the ice queen. He deserves so much better.'

'Then maybe he'll get it,' Peter said simply. 'He'll do whatever seems right to him. Now, when are you coming home for dinner?' He had gotten to Bedford before she did and was cooking dinner.

'As soon as I can get there. I stopped to pick up the books you wanted, which was when I saw Phillip.' She was already driving home.

'Well, never mind him, get your ass home, woman. I miss you.'

'All right, I'll be there as soon as I can,' she said, smiling. They hung up, and she got on the highway, and was home less than an hour later. As she pulled into her driveway, it was nice to see the house all lit up and know that Peter was waiting for her. She was lucky she had him, and she knew it. And all she wanted for her son was that one day he'd find the love of a good woman, one warmer and kinder than Amanda. And all she could do now was wait to see what would happen. Life was even stranger than fiction.

Chapter 17

Phillip and Taylor had been sleeping with each other for a month, and he didn't know if he was in heaven or hell, he was so confused. He had even spent a night with her at the Plaza. They had taken to meeting at hotels for a few hours in the evening because he didn't want to run into her roommates and compromise her further. She had started her new job by then, and she could only see him in the evenings. His life felt like a high-wire act with no net under it. He wanted to be with Taylor, and was madly in love with her, but he had no idea how to get out of his marriage. He had lost ten pounds, and his mother was watching him with great concern from a distance. Discreet inquiries had told her that his sister, brother, and grandmother knew nothing, and she said nothing either.

Olivia was wondering what he was going to do about the young woman she had seen him with. Peter thought it might be just a moment of passion, but it hadn't looked like it to her. And Phillip was admitting nothing. He was late for every meeting and had begun to feel desperate when one evening he came home, and found Amanda waiting for him in the living room, looking official. The moment he saw her, he felt sure that she knew what he'd been doing. He was about to admit everything, when she silently handed him a letter. It was to his mother.

'What is this?' he asked her with a stunned expression. 'I'm not a child. You don't have to report on me to my mother.'

'Read it,' she said, and he sat down and read it. She wasn't telling Olivia about his affair. She was essentially blackmailing his mother and had given her an ultimatum. Either Olivia stepped down as CEO, and relinquished the position to Phillip, or she would divorce him. She said that she had decided she was unwilling to be married to one of his mother's 'minions,' in light of her new position as federal judge. Either she was going to be married to the CEO, or she wanted a divorce. The gloves were off. He almost laughed out loud when he finished reading the letter.

'You're not serious about this?' He had been sure when

he saw her waiting for him that she knew about the affair. Now he was sure she didn't. All she wanted was to be married to a CEO. Maybe she didn't even care that he was in love with someone else. She appeared not to have noticed.

'I'm very serious. I finally realized that you're never going to confront her, so I did. Either she makes you CEO, or I'll divorce you, and it will cost you, and her, a fortune. She won't want that, and she won't want the embarrassment of a divorce in the family. So we both get what we want. I get an important husband, and you get the status she should have given you years ago.' Amanda had it all figured out, to her advantage. Either way, she got what she wanted. Status, or money. And she didn't seem to care which it was.

'I told you when you brought it up before, I don't want to be CEO yet. I don't want the headaches that go with it.'

'She's more of a man than you are,' Amanda said, looking at him with disgust.

'That's probably true, Amanda. And so are you. The trouble is, I don't want to be married to a man, I want to be married to a woman, and one who doesn't put my head on the chopping block to get what she wants, or is willing to blackmail my mother. I don't think she'll take kindly to your letter. In fact, I'll spare you the embarrassment of sending it to her.'

He knew what he wanted now. He had known all along, he just didn't know what to say or how to do it. But Amanda had just handed him his passport. And he was going to grab it. He had the woman he wanted. And Amanda wasn't it. He was sure. He had never been as sure as at that moment. He didn't love Amanda, and she didn't love him either, or she would never have written that letter. She was willing to sacrifice him to get what she wanted. He was just a pawn as far as she was concerned. Phillip looked at her just as coldly. 'Don't bother sending the letter. I pick Plan B. I want out of the marriage. My decision, not yours this time. I'm finished.' Amanda looked stunned. It wasn't the reaction she'd expected. Not by a long shot.

'It will cost you,' she said with eyes that bored into his.

'I'm sure it will. We can work it out with our lawyers. You have what you wanted. You're a judge now. And I'm not going to be your dancing dog to make you look good. I'm not going to be a CEO just so you can show off.'

'She'll keep you on the back burner for ever.'

'Maybe. Maybe I'm happy there. But this isn't how I want to take over as CEO. When I do, it will be because my mother is ready to step down, or I earned it. I'm not going to let you bludgeon her out of a job she does brilliantly after she spent fifty years building the business. She deserves to be the CEO. It's her company. I haven't earned it yet. I hope that someday I will. But that's none of your business, Amanda. I should have left you years ago. You never loved me.'

'You have me confused with your mother,' she said through clenched teeth.

'No, I don't. She actually does love me. I finally figured it out. She may have made some terrible mistakes when we were younger, but I finally realized that she loves me. I guess sometimes in life you have to make tough choices and do what you think is best at the time. That's what you're doing now. You are willing to sacrifice our marriage to enhance your status. And I'm willing to step up to the plate and get a divorce rather than to hang on to something that never existed. All I ever was to you was a stepping-stone to something else. I think if my name weren't Grayson, you'd have been out of here a long time ago. Or you'd never have married me in the first place. That's over now. You've had all you're going to get from me. You'll have to get the rest in the divorce.' Fortunately, they had a strong pre-nup, and Amanda knew it too. She wasn't going to get as much as she hoped. 'I'm done.' He felt clear-headed and sane for the first time in weeks. She had done him a huge favor.

'That's ridiculous,' she said, still holding the letter he had handed back to her. 'Maybe she'd agree to step down in a year. I might be willing to wait for that,' Amanda said, looking panicked.

'You don't understand, this isn't a negotiation. It's over. Find another horse to bet on. I'm disqualifying myself from the race.'

'I wasn't serious about a divorce. I was just trying to frighten your mother. For your sake, as well as mine.'

'Don't do me any favors. And I am serious. I want a real life, not this ridiculous farce of a marriage, while you calculate what you can get out of it and tell me I have no balls.'

'I was just trying to get you to stand up to your mother.' She was no fool, and she could tell that she had overplayed her hand and was trying to back down. He wouldn't let her. He had beaten her to the door. And he knew just who and what he wanted when he got there. And she wasn't it. Taylor was. After a month, he knew that she was the love of his life, and he wanted a life with her. And she was in it because she loved him, not for what she could get. She didn't even know who he was. She just loved him. And he loved her and didn't want her to get hurt.

Danielle Steel

He went upstairs and packed a bag then, and Amanda followed him upstairs.

'What are you doing?' She looked nervous. Phillip didn't. He felt better than he had in months. Maybe years.

'I'm packing a bag. You can stay here until we decide who gets the house, or put it on the market.' He had paid for it, but he was willing to give it up. All he wanted now was out.

'You don't have to leave, Phillip. We can work this out.'

'No, we can't.' And then he turned to her with a dead look in his eyes. 'I don't want to. I want a divorce.' Her letter had been the last straw and the impetus he needed to leave. It told him exactly who she was. She had over-negotiated her position and given him what he needed to walk out. He zipped up his bag then and headed back down the stairs. She stood looking at him from the landing, and the one thing she hadn't said to him was that she loved him. It hadn't even occurred to her. And Phillip had noticed. It cleared his conscience to leave. She didn't love him, and never had. She was incapable of it. And he had stopped loving her a long time ago. Their marriage was dead.

'Call me when you come to your senses,' Amanda called after him. She didn't run down the stairs and beg

346

him not to leave. A woman who loved him would have.

'Don't hold your breath,' he said softly, and then turned to look at her for the last time as his wife. 'Goodbye, Amanda.' And with that, he opened the front door and walked out, and closed it quietly behind him. The whole thing had taken half an hour. It had been bloodless. It didn't even hurt because their marriage no longer had living roots. Everything about it was dead.

He hailed a cab then, and gave the driver the familiar address downtown. When they got there, he handed the driver a twenty-dollar bill and asked him to wait. He left his bag in the car and ran up the stairs. One of her roommates opened the door. She said Taylor was in her room, but she was still awake. He knocked on the door and let himself in. Taylor smiled the moment she saw him. Her whole face lit up, and she jumped off her bed and put her arms around his neck.

'What are you doing here?' she asked him. She didn't even have time to get worried. He was kissing her and pulled her close.

'I left her. We're getting a divorce.' He was smiling when he said it, and Taylor's eyes flew open wide.

'Just like that? What happened? I talked to you an hour ago and everything was the same.'

'She hit me over the head one time too many. She was going to blackmail my mother and give her an ultimatum. It told me everything I needed to know. Our marriage has been dead for years.' He had told her that before, but now he was sure. 'We'll talk about it later. I have a cab waiting downstairs. Pack a bag.'

'Where are we going?' She looked stunned.

'The Plaza. I moved out of the house. We can stay there for a few days, until we figure this out. Take enough stuff for a few days.'

'Can you afford it?' She looked worried. 'You don't have to do that for me. You could stay here.'

'I love you, but I don't want to share a bathroom with five women. And I don't think they'd be too thrilled to have me.' He put her suitcase on the bed, opened it, and pointed to it. 'Pack. I'll wait for you in the cab.' He kissed her again then, and she came downstairs five minutes later, carrying the bag, and her backpack of schoolbooks. Everything had happened so fast, she didn't know what to think. And what if he went back? But he didn't look like he would. He looked calm, strong, and sure, better than she'd seen him in weeks. Ever since they met, he had been tortured about the decision. Now the decision had been made. And he knew it was the right one for him. And Taylor was the right woman.

The cab took them to the Plaza, and Phillip checked in. He took a suite, and Taylor was awestruck as she looked around the room.

'This is crazy, Phillip. What are we doing here? You'll be broke.' She knew he had a good job and wore nice suits, but this was too much.

'No, I won't.' It always amazed him that she had never looked him up on the Internet. All she knew was that he was the CFO of The Factory. She didn't want to know more than that. She loved him. 'I'll find an apartment in a few days. We can stay here till then.' He ordered room service for them, and Taylor went to run a bath. When they'd stayed there before, they had taken a room. She couldn't even imagine what a suite would cost him. She didn't want to know.

He got in the bath with her a few minutes later, and they sank into the luxurious tub. He still couldn't believe it was over with Amanda. She hadn't intended to, but she'd made it easy for him in the end. And it felt totally right to him to have left. He wasn't sad. He was relieved. He felt nothing for Amanda. The last month of loving Taylor and living with Amanda had been insane. He never wanted to go through anything like it again. And it had been hard on Taylor too, not knowing if she'd lose him or not.

'The divorce may take a while,' he warned her. Even with a prenup, it was going to be a nasty fight.

'I can wait,' Taylor said quietly. 'I'm not in a rush.'

'I am.' He smiled at her. 'I've waited a lifetime for you. What took you so long?'

'I was busy.' She smiled, and he kissed her, and they got out of the tub. Room service came up shortly after. He had ordered club sandwiches for both of them. They ate them wearing the hotel's big fluffy terry cloth robes and talked and laughed like two kids. And this was only the beginning. They had a lifetime ahead of them. And as they lay in bed that night, he held her in his arms, thinking of all the things he wanted to do with her. There was so much he wanted to share with her and show her. She was not only the love of his life, she had become his best friend. He had told her about his mother and his grandmother, his brother and sisters. He knew they were going to love her. But best of all, he did, and greatest of all was that she loved him. And as she slept beside him that night, he looked at her and knew he had been given a priceless gift.

Chapter 18

Phillip walked into his mother's office the next morning and waited until she got off the phone. She seemed busy, but he only needed a few minutes of her time. And she was relieved that he looked better than when she'd last seen him. He didn't have the wild, distracted look he'd had for the last month.

'I just wanted to tell you,' he said quietly, 'I left Amanda last night.' For a long moment, Olivia didn't comment.

'Are you all right with it?' That was all that concerned her. She wanted him to be happy. And he never had been with Amanda, or not in a long time. He had been emotionally starved and didn't know it. 'Yes, I am. I should have done it years ago,' he said, in answer to his mother's question.

'What happened?' She assumed it had something, or everything, to do with the girl she had seen him with at the bookstore.

'She wanted you to make me CEO.' He laughed when he said it.

'Now?' Olivia looked surprised.

'Now. As befitting her status as a federal judge. She feels she needs to be married to a CEO.'

'Well, you will be one day,' Olivia said calmly.

'Not for a long time, I hope,' he said, and meant it. 'It was either that or a divorce. So I picked Door Number Two. A divorce. It works for me. But it's liable to get costly.'

'As I recall, you have a good pre-nup.' Olivia was pensive.

'She'll probably try to break it. She's an attorney.'

'That won't get her far,' Olivia said, looking annoyed, and then she couldn't resist asking him what she already knew and he hadn't admitted. She wondered if he would. 'Was there any other reason?'

'Several. Our marriage was dead. She never loved me. I'm not in love with her anymore.' He took a breath. 'And I met someone else. A month ago. It happened very fast.'

Olivia was impressed that he'd been honest with her. She didn't think he would be. 'Who is she?' Olivia asked with obvious concern.

'A girl I met in a café a month ago. She's a fourth-grade teacher in Harlem. She just moved here from Milwaukee. She's wonderful and I love her, and she loves me. She's twenty-eight years old. And she has no idea who you are.' Olivia smiled.

'It sounds like a good start. She's very young.'

'She makes me feel young,' he said with a peaceful look. She had never seen him look that way before. 'I want to have children with her.' Olivia looked at him, stunned.

'She must be something. I never thought I'd hear you say that.'

'Neither did I.'

'Well, don't rush into anything. And you'll have to wait for the divorce. That's a good thing. It'll give you time to get to know each other. Am I going to meet her? Before you start having babies with her?' He laughed and his mother smiled.

'Yes, when things settle down. I don't want to over-whelm her.'

'It sounds like you already have.' Olivia smiled at her son. 'Where are you staying?'

'At the Plaza, until I figure this out.'

'You can stay with me in Bedford if you want,' she offered.

'Thank you. I think I'd rather be in the city.' He hated the commute, but appreciated the kind offer. 'But I'll keep it in mind. And Mother.' He hesitated as he looked at her. 'I'm really sorry about what I said about you and Peter. I was out of line. I think life got even with me immediately. I no sooner said all that to you about Peter being married than I fell madly in love, and I was a married man having an affair. It's funny how sometimes you wind up doing everything you said you never would. The ironies of life. And even more so, if it's something your parents did and you thought you disapproved of. Then it happens even faster.' He smiled and Olivia chuckled.

'Life has a way of doing that to all of us.' She had disapproved of her mother's affair with Ansel Morris, and forty-five years later she was doing the same thing with Peter. And now Phillip with the young girl he was in love with. 'It never pays to be too righteous. We end up eating our own words.'

'And a lot of humble pie. I'm really sorry.'

'It's all right.' She stood up and came around to hug him. 'I'm sorry about Amanda and the divorce, but I'm happy for you. You deserve a lot better than you were getting.'

'I think I've found it.'

'Let's hope so. Just give it time. Don't do anything too hasty.' But at least legally, he couldn't. It had been hasty enough as it was. In the space of a month he had fallen in love, had an affair, and left Amanda. He had definitely been in the express lane.

'I look forward to meeting her. What's her name by the way?' She didn't tell him she'd already seen her, and she didn't intend to.

'Taylor.'

'Nice name.'

He left her office then and went back to his own, and Olivia went back to work, and when she did, she was smiling. It was funny how things worked out. She had thought he would never leave Amanda. Two months ago they'd been on the boat together, and now she was history. You just never knew in life what would happen.

Chapter 19

Two days after Liz went to see her new agent in New York, Andrew Shippers, she had started working on a new outline, for another book. She wasn't sure where it was going, but she had been working on it for three weeks, when he called her, and asked if she would come to the city to see him.

'Is something wrong?' she asked him, sounding nervous. Maybe he had decided not to represent her book, and like Sarah, the publishers thought it was no good, and he didn't want to tell her that on the phone.

'Why do you assume something's wrong?' he asked, curious about her. She seemed to be an extremely nervous person. She had been so unnerved when she met him, he thought she was going to collapse in his office.

'I always expect bad things to happen,' she said simply, and she was so honest about it that he couldn't help chuckling.

'Well, why not try expecting good news instead of bad? Maybe I have something wonderful to tell you,' he said, sounding very British. She still remembered how handsome he had been when she went to his office. She hadn't been prepared for that either.

'Do you have something wonderful to tell me?'

'Come in and see me,' he said firmly.

'When?'

'Does tomorrow work for you?'

'No, I'll be a wreck by then. What about today? I'll drive in.' He smiled when she said it.

'Elizabeth, you're incredibly talented. But you're also incredibly neurotic. Have you tried acupuncture or yoga?'

'Both. I hate needles, and I sprained my neck and a muscle in my groin when I tried yoga.'

'Valium, then. Thorazine. Laughing gas. Something. Fine, come in and see me at five. Can you wait till then?'

'I'll have to. I think I can make it till five.' She didn't press him to tell her on the phone, because it was obvious he wasn't going to. He was a very stubborn man.

She decided to dress up for the occasion. She wanted to look nice. She wore a short black skirt she borrowed from Sophie's closet, and a sexy black sweater from Carole's, and her own high heels. She had a triple wardrobe at all times, thanks to the clothes the girls left with her at home. She put long, sexy earrings on, and at four o'clock she headed out the door for the drive to the city. She remembered to put gas in the car, which was rare for her, and an hour later, she was parking outside his office. She was right on time, and wondering what the good news was, if there was any. Maybe he was just kidding, and didn't want to fire her as a client over the phone, or tell her that every publisher in the city had turned her book down. But three weeks wasn't enough time for them to do that. She had no idea what he was going to say.

His secretary led her into his office, and Andrew was waiting for her. He was reading contracts at his desk and put them down when she walked in.

'You look lovely,' he said as she sat down. 'And calm. Did you take a Valium?'

'No, half a bottle of vodka while I was driving.'

He looked concerned and she laughed.

'Just kidding.' She seemed considerably calmer than she had the first time he saw her, and on the phone that morning. She was just a worried person, but not a total neurotic. He was relieved to see it. And whatever else she was, she was an incredibly talented woman. That he was sure of.

'So what's the good news?' she asked as she looked straight at him, and he tried to forget she was an attractive woman. This was business. She was telling herself the same thing about him. He was so handsome, she had to pretend to herself that he wasn't.

He got right to the point. 'Two publishers want your book. They had a bidding war. And I like one house better for you. They've offered you an advance of five hundred thousand dollars, just for rights for North America. You keep the foreign rights, which means we can sell them separately. They want your book desperately. Hardcover, massive first printing, softcover. And I took the liberty of showing it to a film agent I work with in L.A. He thinks he can sell it for a movie. He's showing it right now, to two producers. One already loves it. And I'm expecting to hear from him tomorrow. There's the good news,' he said in his clipped British way, as Liz stared at him from across the desk. Her mouth nearly fell open at what he told her.

'*Five hundred thousand dollars?* Are they crazy?'

'I assume that means yes. And you can tell your academic sister-in-law that that's what really bad books sell for these days. Commercial ones, that is, that a publisher is dead sure will be best sellers. They're hoping you're going to sell a million copies.'

'I think I'm going to faint,' she said, and almost meant it.

'Don't. I hate women with the vapors. My grandmother was always fainting when I was a child. It traumatized me deeply.'

'Then I do need Valium or vodka.'

'Fine. Then let's go up to the Carlyle and have a drink.' He stood up and picked up a linen jacket he had tossed over a chair with a silk pocket scarf in the breast pocket. It was Hermès. He was beautifully dressed. 'I think we have good reason to celebrate. This is why I didn't want to tell you on the phone. I didn't want you fainting all alone in your kitchen. You might've hit your head. Very dangerous. Head injury. All that.'

'Wait a minute. Tell me again. You're serious, right? You're not kidding.'

'I'm not kidding. You're about to become a very wealthy woman.' He didn't know that she already was anyway. He didn't know the connection to Olivia Grayson, and wouldn't have cared if he did. His own family had a great deal of money in England. He was the black sheep who had escaped and was enjoying being an agent in New York, particularly doing deals like this. It had been the easiest sale he ever made.

She followed him out of the office and down the stairs, and she offered to drive them to the Carlyle. He looked hesitant for a moment. 'Do I trust your driving? You can't have the vapors if you drive me.'

'I won't. I promise. I'm a very good driver.'

'Fine,' he said, and he got in when she unlocked her car. And he told her some more details about the deal on the way. It all sounded fabulous to her.

'We should have the contracts in about a week,' he said as she found a parking space on Madison Avenue, and they got out at the Carlyle, and walked into the Bemelmans Bar. She hadn't been there in years, and it was a nice, civilized place for a drink.

He ordered scotch and soda, and she ordered a glass of champagne. 'Thank you,' she said sincerely. 'Thank you for getting me this wonderful deal. I really didn't think you could sell it. I thought you were firing me as a client, and didn't want to do it over the phone.'

'That's what I like,' he said, raising his glass to her. He was pleased with the deal too, and he loved the book. 'A cheerful, optimistic woman. Tell me, how did you become so unsure of yourself? Kidnapped by gypsies as a child and soundly beaten?' She laughed at the idea.

'No, just naturally insecure. I come from a family of

very successful overachievers, and I've been terrified of failure all my life. I've actually never succeeded at much of anything until this.'

'That's not true,' he reminded her. 'Your short stories are excellent. I read all of them last week.'

'Thank you for doing that. I wrote two terrible novels, though, that Charlie couldn't sell.'

'Thank you for reminding me. And your poems are also very good.' He had actually read her work. She was amazed. 'So tell me about your overachieving family. Mine makes me feel insecure too, by the way. So I escaped to America and became an agent. It annoyed them completely.'

'Well, let's see, my mother is very successful in business. Brilliant actually.'

'In what field?'

'She turned a hardware store that my grandmother inherited from her boyfriend into a very successful business. My older brother is a Harvard MBA and works for her. My other brother is a very talented artist and also works for her. His wife is the one who teaches at Princeton and hates my book. My baby sister is a very successful music producer in London. Both my marriages failed, and I have two wonderful daughters. That's the whole story. It's hard to compete with all that.'

'You just did,' he reminded her. 'That's the biggest advance I've ever gotten for a first novel. And I'm sure the book is going to be a great success. That ought to put them all in their place. Why did your marriages fail? In ten words or less?'

'I married a French race car driver when I was twenty-one. He got killed in a race before our daughter was born. That's my daughter Sophie. Then I married a moderately famous actor, Jasper Jones, and we got divorced in less than a year. He had an affair with one of his leading ladies. We had my youngest daughter, Carole. That's it.'

'At least you married interesting people. I married a very dull woman I met at school. She ran off with my best friend. She's gotten fat, and now he's bald, and un-fortunately they're very happy, which proves that bad-looking people deserve each other. And I've never married again. I was cured. I lived with a woman for about six years, but we never married. She then became a nun, so I can say that I've driven at least one woman into the convent. I thought it was a bit rude, but she was a nice girl. I've sought out atheists ever since. Are you religious?'

'Sometimes.' Something occurred to her then. 'Is this a date? Or are you taking me out as my agent?'

'I'm not sure. What do you think? Which would you

prefer? You're a very beautiful woman, even if you are a bit neurotic and very insecure, so either one would work for me.'

'Are you married?'

'No. Never again.'

'Living with anyone?'

'Unfortunately not. I'm very messy so no one wants to live with me, and I have a dog that snores.'

'Dating anyone?'

'Not lately. Dry spell actually.'

'Okay, then maybe it's a date.'

'I agree. Now that we've gotten that out of the way, we can get off on the right foot. Would you like to have dinner?'

'Tonight?' Liz looked startled.

'Or another time, if you have other plans.'

'I don't. I just wasn't expecting to have dinner.' Nor a date. But she liked him. A lot. And he was gorgeous.

'Sometimes the element of surprise is good. Sushi?' 'That sounds good. What kind of dog?'

'English bulldog. His name is Rupert. After my uncle. He looks like him.'

'And let me guess.' She had picked up on the fact that he was more than likely an aristocrat, and she had noticed he was wearing a crest on a ring. 'Eton and Cambridge.'

'Eton, Oxford, Cambridge. Right, you've got that down. And I hated Eton. Very un-English of me. I got beaten up all the time. I was small as a child, only got tall later. They sent me when I was seven.'

'How awful. I hate the English system.'

'So do I. That's why I never had children. One of many reasons. Why have them if you're going to send them away when they're practically in diapers?'

'I agree.'

'My brothers all loved it.'

'What are the other reasons why you never had children?'

'They remember everything you do wrong, blame you forever for all your mistakes, and hate you for everything you do.'

'Sounds like my older brother,' Liz said, laughing. 'He's still mad at my mother for not being around enough when he was a child, and she was always working.'

'And do you hate her too?'

'No, I love her. She did her best, and my grandmother took care of us, and she was terrific.'

'Women are much more forgiving. One must always have daughters if one has children. I come from a family of five boys. What do your daughters do?'

'One is finishing a master's in computer science at MIT, and then she's going to work for my mother. And my youngest daughter just moved to L.A. to work for her father and stepmother, who produce movies.'

'The actor is now producing?' He remembered, he was paying attention.

'Yes, he is. Or his wife is. He works for her.'

'And your mother seems to be employing the entire family. Good thing she didn't give you a job, or you wouldn't have had time to write the book.'

'I'm working on another one now, but it's just in the early stages.' He looked pleased to hear it, paid for their drinks then, and took her to a small sushi restaurant where the meal was delicious. And they talked for several hours about the book business, how he'd gotten into it, and his boyhood in England. He told her about his allegedly very eccentric family and made her laugh. They had a very good time together, and she dropped him off at his apartment after dinner. He lived at the Dakota, on Central Park West, which was a famous old building, full of well-known people and beautiful apartments. And she knew he wasn't relying on his work as an agent to buy something there.

'I had a very good time,' he said to her before he left. 'I'm glad we decided it was a date. It would be a shame to waste an evening like that on just an agent.'

She smiled at him. She really liked him. 'Thank you for selling my book.'

'Happy to do it. Any time. Keep working on the new one. I'll sell that one too. I'll do anything for a commission.'

He walked into the building then with a wave, looking very elegant and very British. She'd had a wonderful time.

She turned on the radio then and drove home in a great mood. And first thing the next morning, she called her mother and told her about the book.

'Ohmygod, Mom, he sold it for five hundred thousand dollars! They loved it! And he's trying to sell it as a movie.'

'I told you it was good. I loved it too. Let Sarah put that in her pipe and smoke it.'

'I thought she knew.'

'She only knows academic books. I'm very, very proud of you.'

'Thank you, Mom. I have to tell Granibelle. She loved it too. I had dinner with my agent last night, by the way.'

'The new one?'

'Yes. He's British, and very nice. He took me for a drink at the Carlyle, and out for sushi.'

'As a date?'

'We decided it was. We took a vote on it.'

'Well, that's interesting.'

'And I'm working on a new book.'

'You're full of good news,' her mother said, pleased for her. 'Do you think you'll go out with him again?'

'I hope so. Maybe he won't ask me.'

'I'll bet he will.'

'He lives at the Dakota.'

'He must be very successful, or have money.'

'I think it's the latter. He's very aristocratic, and very British. He went to Eton, Cambridge, and Oxford.'

'Well, see what happens. And congratulations about the book.'

'Thank you, Mom, for your faith in me.'

'You deserve it. You're just a late bloomer.' Liz liked that. She was a late bloomer, not a failure. It put a whole different spin on things and her view of herself.

Andrew called her himself later that morning and told her what a good time he'd had with her. He told her to call him the next time she came to the city, and he'd take her to dinner again.

'Why don't you come out here? It's only forty-five minutes on the train. Or you can drive, if you prefer.'

'I'd like that. What are you doing this weekend?'

'Nothing,' she said honestly. 'What about Saturday?'

'Why don't you come out in the afternoon? We can sit in the sun, and then go out to dinner.'

'Sounds great. E-mail me the directions, and I'll drive.'

'You can bring Rupert if you like.'

'He doesn't like the heat, and he gets carsick. I'll introduce you next time.'

She was looking forward to seeing him again. Her book had sold for an exorbitant amount of money. She was working on another one. And she had a date with a very handsome man. Things were definitely looking up in her life.

Their date on Saturday went well too. He arrived at three o'clock and they sat on her patio drinking iced tea and talking. There was no news about the movie deal, but he said it was really too soon. Those things usually took longer than books to materialize. She told him about her new book idea, and he said he liked it very much. And they went to a small, cozy Italian restaurant for dinner. He told her funny stories and had her laughing all night. He didn't head back to the city until nearly midnight, and when he walked her to her door, he kissed her. She hadn't expected it, and he was handsome and sexy, and it was a memorable kiss.

'I'm glad we decided these were dates,' he said

afterward, and kissed her again. 'This could be habit forming,' he warned her, and he finally got in his car, and she waved as he left. It had been a very, very nice evening. Andrew Shippers was definitely a wonderful addition to her life.

Chapter 20

Olivia was enjoying a peaceful Sunday afternoon in Bedford after Peter left to play golf as he always did, when she got a call from Alex. He sounded as though he'd been crying.

'Well, I was right.'

'What about?'

'I told them. Dad went nuts. And Mom couldn't stop crying. He called me a fag.' And by then Alex was crying too, and Olivia was shocked.

'Oh my God, I'm so sorry.'

'I'm leaving. I just wanted to call you and tell you what happened.'

'Where are they now?'

'They're out. They went to lunch with friends.'

'Where are you going, Alex?' She was desperately worried about him, and sorely disappointed in her son.

'Maybe a friend's house.'

'Why don't you come here? You can stay with me for a few days.'

But she knew he'd already started school. 'Can you take a couple of days off school?'

'I'm dropping out.' This was serious.

'Don't do anything stupid. They'll calm down.'

'I don't care. I hate them. And they hate me.'

'They don't hate you. They don't understand.'

'They don't want to understand. Dad says he's ashamed of me. Of my being gay. He says there's something wrong with me.'

'How could he say something so stupid?' Alex was crying again. 'Take the train to New York. I'll meet you there. I'll drive you back here.'

'You don't have to do that, Grandma.' He sounded so lost and broken. She wanted to strangle John, or give him a good shaking, and Sarah too.

'I want to. Just call and tell me what train you'll be on.' He called her an hour later, and she told him to leave a note for his parents that he'd be with her, and he promised he would. And as soon as they hung up, she picked up her handbag and car keys and ran out the door to meet him in New York.

He came off the train looking beaten. And he threw his arms around her and burst into tears. She held him for a long time while he cried, and she did too, and then they went to her car and she drove him back to Bedford. When they got there, he sat slumped in a chair looking sad, and they talked all afternoon. He said he hated his parents and his school, and he didn't want to go to college, and the boy he liked liked someone else, and maybe wasn't gay after all, he wasn't sure. It was all so complicated and so much weight to carry for a boy of seventeen. She wanted to call John and Sarah, but since they knew where Alex was, she was waiting to hear from them. They never called.

She cooked dinner for Alex that night, and put him to bed in her guest room. All she could do was tell him how much she loved him, and be there for him.

And at midnight, she got a call from Liz.

'I don't want to worry you,' she said, sounding serious. 'But I got a call from John and Sarah. Alex ran away. They had some kind of fight about something, and when they got home, he had left. You haven't heard from him, have you?' She knew how close the boy was to her. 'They didn't want me to call you, but I thought I should.'

'He's here,' Olivia said quietly. 'Did they tell you what the fight was about?'

'No, something about school, I think.' Liz sounded surprised. 'He's usually such an easy kid.'

'It's a lot more serious than that.' Olivia didn't want to violate Alex's confidence, but since he had told his parents, she decided to tell Liz. 'It's my fault, actually. I told him to be open with them. He's gay. And apparently, John went berserk and called him names and told him he was ashamed of him. I told him to leave a note when he left. He said he did, but I guess he lied to me about that. He says he doesn't want to go back.'

'Shit. How could John be so stupid? And they lied to me about it, but they sounded scared. They wanted to know if he had called Sophie. I called her, but he hadn't. So I figured I'd call you. I'm glad he's with you. I'll tell John and Sarah.'

'Tell them not to come out here. I want to talk to them first myself. He wants to drop out of school.'

'He can't,' Liz said, sounding worried. 'He'll screw up everything for college.'

'But they could screw up his life if they handle this badly. It will mark him for ever. Maybe it already has. He was a mess when I picked him up in New York.'

'You picked him up in New York? That was nice of you, Mom.'

'He's my grandson, and I love him. I don't care if he's gay or not. And John better figure that out too, and fast.'

'Maybe I'll go talk to them tomorrow.'

'I wish you would. He always listens to you,' her mother said, sounding sad. She felt so sorry for Alex.

'I'll let them know he's with you now.' John called her ten minutes later. 'How did he wind up with you?'

'He called me, and I invited him out. I told him to leave you a note. I'm sorry he didn't.' But that was all she was sorry about, she was furious with her son. 'You and Sarah have some serious fence mending to do, and you'd better start thinking about what you said. He has a right to be treated like a human being, by both of you, and with respect.'

'Did he tell you what happened?' John said in a trembling voice. 'I caught him kissing some kid at the pool, a boy. So he told me he's gay.'

'Would you have been mad if you caught him kissing a girl? No, you wouldn't. He doesn't like girls. He's attracted to men. That's who he is.'

'He doesn't know who he is at this age.'

'Yes, he does. Just like you did at his age. What if I told you that I was ashamed of you because you're attracted to women? Could you change that? Would you want to?'

'He's not gay.'

'Yes, he is,' Olivia said firmly, in the voice that made strong men quake. She meant business. She was a lioness defending her grandson. 'What right do you have to tell him what he is? He knows better.'

'How did you get into this, Mother?'

'He told me this summer. And I encouraged him to tell you and Sarah. I told him you'd understand. He didn't think you would. And I'm ashamed of you that he was right. If I'd had any idea you would behave this way, I'd have told him not to tell you. I love you, but I'm very disappointed in you. Alex needs our support, all of us. If his family doesn't support him, who will?'

'I'm not going to support his carrying on with boys in my house.'

'Then he shouldn't live with you, because he's gay, and he has a right to do that.'

'What are people going to think?'

'Come out of the dark ages, for God's sake. They're going to think you're a total jerk if you don't, and they'll be right. What about Sarah? Is she as backward about this as you are?'

'She's heartbroken. She hasn't stopped crying since he told us.'

'Neither has he, and he has more reason to than you

do. His father is an idiot. And what does Sarah have to be heartbroken about?'

'First, she couldn't have more kids, now she'll never have grandchildren. She's devastated.'

'She might. Lots of gay men have children now, of their own or they adopt them. And that's beside the point. This is about Alex, not about her. You all need counseling so you can deal with this decently for Alex's sake.'

'When did you get so modern?'

'When he told me. And I'm telling you right now, I'm not letting him come home to you until the two of you get your act together and can treat him right.' John was shocked. 'And you can take me to court if you don't like it. I'm not sending him home with your attitude and Sarah's. You'll damage him for ever.'

'He's already damaged.'

'Then he needs your help more than ever.'

'What's he going to do about school if he's in Bedford? He never should have left.'

'Tell them he's sick. He wants to drop out.'

'He can't do that.' John was outraged.

'That's what I told him. But I'm not sending him home until you shape up. So for now, he stays here.'

'I'll talk to you tomorrow,' John said and hung up. But at least they knew he was safe, and not lost.

Alex still looked depressed when he got up the next day and his grandmother cooked him breakfast. Olivia told her office she would work from home that day. And Liz went to see John and Sarah. She told her mother afterward that all they did was cry. Both of them had stayed home from work. She had suggested counseling to them too. And Sarah had called someone at the university before Liz left. They were going to see the counselor the next day.

That evening Olivia took Alex to a movie, and out to dinner in Bedford. It did him good, and he looked better when he got home. But he hadn't heard a word from his parents. They called him the next day. They had been to see the counselor, and he had set up sessions for them for the next month, with Alex if he was willing, or without him if he wasn't. He told them the attitude adjustment was theirs to make, and he was very clear about it. John sounded like someone had died. His fantasy son. The real one was alive and well and still needed his father and mother.

Olivia stayed home with Alex for another day, and then she invited him to come to the office with her. She had some meetings she had to attend. She knew John had taken the week off, so Alex wouldn't run into him. Once he heard that, Alex went into town with her. And Phillip was surprised to see him in the office.

'How's your dad? He's been out all week.' Phillip had been told he was sick.

'I don't know. I haven't seen him,' Alex said bluntly. 'I'm staying with Grandma.' That came as a surprise too. They were all full of surprises these days. He told Alex he had just left Amanda. Alex then told him he was gay and his father couldn't deal with it, so he was staying at his grandmother's, who was fine with it. Phillip looked shocked, and called his brother to discuss it. Basically, Phillip agreed with his mother and Liz. John had to find a way to accept it. He took Alex out to lunch after that. And by the end of the day, Alex was in decent spirits, and he was chatty all the way home to Bedford. And he went into town with Olivia the next day too. John called her in the office and said he and Sarah wanted to come out to Bedford on Saturday, and Olivia told him not to come unless he could be supportive of his son. The counselor had told him the same thing.

Sarah and John looked mournful when they arrived, but they were civil to their son. There were tears and recriminations and questions, but in the end John put his arms around him and told Alex he loved him. It was a major adjustment for them. And on Sunday, Olivia drove Alex back to Princeton. He said he would try going home and see how it worked out. But Olivia could see that John was trying. His acceptance wasn't going to come overnight, but Alex had learned that his uncle and aunt and grandmother accepted him as he was, and his parents would have to get there in their own time. Alex was willing to live with that. He went back to school on Monday, and he called his grandmother every day. He told her that after two days in her office, he was more certain than ever that he wanted to work there one day.

'Then you'd better stay in school and go to college,' she told him, and he laughed. She hadn't, but the business was far more sophisticated and complicated now.

'Yeah, I know,' he said. And he reported to her that his parents were doing better. They were trying. It was all she could ask for, and they'd gotten through it. It had strengthened her bond with her grandson. She was his defender, protector, and ally.

'Thanks, Grandma,' he said before he hung up. 'For everything. I love you.'

'I love you too.' And she loved her son too, even if he had a long way to go to understand Alex and accept him as he was. It had been a lesson for all of them. And for John most of all, that things don't always turn out as we expect or even hope. The only thing that mattered in the end was that he loved his son, and that Alex knew it.

Chapter 21

Phillip's lawyer had very sensibly advised him that Taylor could spend nights with him, but it was smarter if she didn't actually move in. With the benefits of no-fault divorce, Amanda couldn't sue him for adultery, but there was no point annoying her unduly. Sooner or later she was going to find out about Taylor, and it was easy to guess that her fury over it, and jealousy, were going to cost him. The fact that he was moving on with his life so quickly, and that Taylor was sixteen years younger than Amanda, was bound to cause some pretty severe waves. So Taylor kept her room at the apartment in the Village, but she spent almost every night with him.

He found a furnished apartment on Upper Park Avenue, which was sunny and pleasant, and by mid-October he had moved most of his clothes from his house to the apartment. As he had suspected she would, Amanda wanted him to give her the New York house in the divorce, and she also wanted the house in the Hamptons. Her lawyer said he could keep the boat. Their pre-nup said she could have neither since he had bought both homes, and their lawyers were battling it out. He didn't go to her induction, but sent her flowers and a note. He had no battle with her personally, he just wanted out. Despite the more modest but reasonable terms of their pre-nup, she wanted a million dollars for each of the nineteen years they'd been married. Phillip wasn't surprised, and Olivia was livid. She told her mother that the woman's greed was beyond measure.

As always, Maribelle was very supportive of her grandson when he came to visit. She told him she was sorry about the divorce, and asked him about the new woman in his life. He had told all of them about her, but none of them had met her yet. Phillip wanted to let the dust settle. All they knew was that she taught school, was very young, and they had been together for two months. It had been a whirlwind romance, which they all realized had toppled his chilly marriage to Amanda. They could hardly wait to meet her. Their passionate love affair was astoundingly unlike him. In two short months, he seemed to have mellowed, and was being much nicer to their mother. Liz and Olivia had talked about it a lot. John and Sarah were less interested, they were still trying to adjust to Alex's announcement. And Maribelle had told Cass about Phillip when she called from the tour with Danny. They were in Dallas.

Phillip was at the Southampton house with Taylor, by prearrangement with Amanda, when he finally told her about his mother. The small house was filled with beautiful contemporary furniture and expensive art. Taylor didn't recognize all the artists, but the overall impression was one of exquisite taste and valuable objects. It was a peaceful place, and they spent a quiet weekend there, walking on the beach, and cooking together. It was a beautiful Indian summer weekend.

'Do you think you'd have gotten divorced anyway, if we hadn't met?' she asked him. She felt guilty at times for how quickly his house of cards had come down, and although he didn't complain about it, she sensed that they were battling hard over real estate and money.

'Maybe,' he said honestly, 'probably. I was too lazy, and maybe too scared to deal with what I wasn't getting. I got used to the way things were. I think everyone else saw what I didn't, or didn't want to, how cold she was, and how greedy. She's not a happy woman and she's very ambitious. I thought her coolness was a challenge and at first I liked it, but we'd drifted apart more than I knew. She's driven by her ambitions, socially, professionally, and financially. And the stunt she pulled about my job would have done us in anyway. She'd gotten very insulting about it for the last few years. Once she went after the federal judgeship, she wanted me to be more ambitious too.'

'What's wrong with your job?' Taylor asked with a look of surprise, lying on the beach next to him, and looking at the expression in his eyes. There was a deep hurt there that he never explained and that she sensed was about him and not the divorce. They were still getting to know each other, although he felt as though she'd been part of his life forever, but there were things he had not yet shared, and she always felt them. She didn't want to pry, but he peeled off his layers and revealed himself like an onion. She had told him all the things that mattered most to her and that she cared about, along with her old griefs and sorrows, like the loss of her parents, but she was younger and less complicated, and despite her parents' death, she had already understood that her home life had been happier than his. He talked a great deal about his memories of his grandmother and father, but very little about his mother, and she knew that his parents hadn't been divorced.

'Amanda thought my job wasn't important enough,' he explained as they lay on the sand. His eyes were gentle, and he looked happy, more so than he had in years, possibly in his entire life. He had a profound, peaceful sense that all the decisions he had made recently were right. It was wonderful to feel that way. 'She wanted me to be CEO, so she could say she was married to a CEO.' He had mentioned it before, but Taylor didn't know just how far she had gone to try and force his hand. He hadn't wanted to share all the details, and tried to keep his battles with Amanda separate from her. It seemed cleaner to him that way.

'CFO sounds great to me,' Taylor said generously, and it was obvious that he had done well if he had a house in the city, the one they were staying in in the Hamptons, and a boat. She hadn't lacked for anything with him. She was in love with him, not what he had. And he was young enough to make back whatever he lost, if that was what he wanted. She didn't really care. She was used to living on a great deal less and was happy as she was. 'Besides, you can't just walk into your boss's office and say, 'Hello, I want to be CEO.' You have to get there over time. That sounds pretty crazy and not very reasonable to me.' Phillip smiled as she said it.

'In theory, that's true. I had kind of a leg up, though,

Danielle Steel

and Amanda wanted me to use it. I didn't. She was furious about that.'

'What kind of leg up?' Taylor asked casually, she couldn't imagine what it was. And then he laughed.

'My mother is my boss. I work for her.' It was the first time he had admitted it to her, but he couldn't put it off any longer. She had to know.

'You do?' Taylor looked surprised. She was a bright girl, but she had no experience with the lofty circles he had access to, or the kind of money. 'She works for The Factory too?' she asked innocently, and he kissed her.

'No, she owns it. She started it, out of a hardware store my grandmother inherited. My mother started working there when she was twelve, and turned it into what it is now, with stores around the world.' He almost sounded proud when he said it, but not quite.

'She did? That's fantastic!' Taylor said with a look of amazement. 'She must be an amazing woman.'

'So I'm told,' he said quietly, and then conceded, 'She is, but I was upset as a kid that she was always away working. You don't build an empire like that overnight.'

'I'll bet you don't. So your brother works for her too?' She knew they worked together. He nodded. 'Does the whole family work at The Factory?' She was curious about it now. It sounded intriguing, and so did his mother. She had to be an unusual woman with an incredible amount of vision and drive. Taylor was impressed, which only made Phillip mildly uncomfortable. He wasn't afraid she was after the money, but he wasn't looking for allies for his mother, or fans, he wanted his own. He always had, even if it meant condemning her.

'No, just my brother and me,' Phillip answered her question. 'He's head of creative and design. He designs all the furniture you like so much, like your bookcase, and figures out all the new trends with my mother. I told you about my sister Cass in London. And my other sister, Liz, has been trying to be a writer all her life. She just sold some kind of fantasy book a few weeks ago. My grandmother got out of the business early and left running it to my mother. She took care of us, and my father was the CFO, like me. He was an accountant and he helped my mother manage the business end of it. I basically have his job now, although he was a lot smarter and more creative than I am. I just keep the boat steady, but everything is already all set up. That's what Amanda was upset about, she wanted me to have a bigger job. I guess I'm like my father. He was always the behind-the-scenes man, and he liked it. My mother was the star.

'She does a good job. She just turned seventy, and I

don't think she'll ever retire. I hope she doesn't. I'm not sure I could run the business. It's a mammoth undertaking now, and it's entirely family owned and run. My mom will never sell it, and she shouldn't. But I guess she's got the genes to be around for a long time. My grandmother is ninety-five and going strong.' He looked pleased as he said it, and his voice softened even when he talked about his mother. In some ways, he was proud of her, and it was all new to Taylor. 'Amanda wrote her an ultimatum, demanding that she step down. She accused me of not having the balls to confront her, so she did it herself. It wouldn't have gotten her anywhere, but that's pretty much why the house of cards came down. That, and meeting you, of course. It all happened at the same time. And to tell you the truth, I like my job. I dread the day I'll be in charge. It scares the hell out of me. What if I screw everything up? I don't have her creative genius or her vision. I'm a numbers man, like my father. A pencil pusher, as Amanda said.' With no balls, he added silently.

'I'm sure you'll be great at whatever you do,' she said confidently. 'You don't have to worry about it yet. But wow, that's quite a story about your mom, and even your dad. It sounds like they did it together, even if she was the front man. You have to have the numbers guys to back up the creative, like you and your brother.' It was a lot to wrap her mind around.

He nodded again. 'She's been grooming us to run it since we were kids. She wants to get the grandchildren into it one day. I think two of them might do it. My sister Liz's daughter Sophie, she's going to work there when she gets her master's from MIT this winter. And my brother's kid, Alex, but he's still in high school, so who knows. He just knocked his parents on their asses by announcing that he's gay. My mom was fine with it; my brother, who's thirty years younger than she is and supposed to be so free thinking, with his college professor wife, nearly had a stroke.'

'It sounds like you're related to some very interesting people,' she said with admiration, and then asked him an important question. 'Are you still mad at your mother for not being around more when you were a kid, even though you know now what it takes to run the business?'

'She was *never* around,' he said for emphasis, and then corrected himself. 'Well, she was, but not enough. My sister Cass never forgave her for being in the Philippines ordering furniture when my dad died of a heart attack. It took us a day to find her and two days for her to get back.'

'She must have felt pretty bad about that herself,'

Taylor said sensibly, with a degree of sensitivity and intuition. 'Does she feel guilty about you guys as kids?'

'I think she does now. But it's a little late. You don't get the years back. She makes a lot of effort now to be there for us as adults, and she's good with the grandchildren, better than she was when we were kids. She's older, and she has more time, although she still travels constantly. She has lots of energy. She just turned seventy in July. That was the trip I took on the boat.' He had told her about it when they met, in a more modest version than going into detail about the *Lady Luck*. 'We do a trip with her every year, on her birthday. This was a big one, the birthday and the trip.'

'At least she makes that effort,' she said quietly. 'Do you all get along?'

'Pretty much. Except my sister Cass, who never comes. I haven't seen her in years. She pretty much divorced herself from all of us, except Granibelle, whom she visits, and she sees my mother a couple of times a year for lunch. I don't think any of them ever really liked Amanda, although they were polite to her, and she hated them. She just came on the trip because she knew she had to. Our summer trips are a command performance. My mother would go through the roof if we didn't show up,' or be very hurt, he thought and didn't say it. Taylor got the picture. They were a strong family, and she could guess easily that their mother was a powerful woman, a force to be reckoned with. He made her sound even tougher than she was. And Taylor couldn't help wondering if Olivia Grayson was power hungry like Amanda, or actually human. The fact that she'd had four kids and loved her husband was an interesting detail. It sounded like they'd had a solid marriage, and the business kept them all together, in one way or another.

'So why didn't you tell me about all this before?' Taylor asked him quietly.

'I don't like to show off,' he said honestly.

'Were you afraid I'd be after the money?'

'No,' he said quickly, too quickly, and then tempered it a little. 'Yes . . . maybe . . . I don't know. It's a lot to hit someone with right away. It's a very, very big business. We have more than a hundred stores worldwide, factories, production outlets, hundreds of thousands of employees. You add it all up, and it's pretty impressive. I wanted you to see me, and not The Factory or my mother.'

'That makes sense,' she said pensively. 'It must be fun to have all that money,' she said, looking childlike for a minute, and he laughed. 'I guess it is. None of us goes wild with it, although Amanda would have liked to. We live better than the others. John and Sarah live in a little house in Princeton, he drives a six-year-old car, and they love their lifestyle. And Liz lives in an old farmhouse that's going to come down around her ears one of these days. She never gets around to fixing it up and probably never will. And I don't know how Cass lives, but she's made her own money, kind of like my mother. She's a big success in the music business. She lives with some rock star called Danny Devil or something.' He was not part of Phillip's world, and Taylor laughed out loud when he said it.

'Danny Hell? Are you kidding? He's the biggest rock star on the planet.'

'Yeah, if you're under twenty maybe. Apparently my sister discovered him. She's good at what she does. I read an article about her last year. I think she has my mother's head for business, although that's a pretty crazy world. So this guy Danny is a big deal?' he asked her, with renewed curiosity about his sister. He hardly ever thought of her now. She was no longer on the screen of his life and hadn't been for a decade, and she wanted it that way.

'The biggest. He'll be as big as Mick Jagger one day. He's still just starting out. He's only been around since I was in college and that's not very long ago.'

'Don't remind me,' he said, looking sheepish and then worried. 'And you don't mind being with an old guy like me?' It was never lost on him that he was old enough to be her father. They were eighteen years apart, but she didn't seem to mind.

'You're not an old guy, and I love you. You're young too, Phillip.' He was only in his mid-forties – she just happened to be a lot younger, but she never thought about the age difference when they were together. And he seemed younger every day as he got used to her and relaxed. She gave him a whole new perspective on life. She was the polar opposite of Amanda.

'Taylor, I want to marry you when this is all over, but it may take a while,' he warned her. The financial arrangements with Amanda were going to take time to work out. He had told Taylor that before, and for the moment, the situation was getting worse. It would be a while before it got better, and she settled for something more reasonable than what she was asking for now. She was threatening to try and overturn their pre-nup, which he knew was an empty threat, she was a lawyer, but she was greedy in the extreme, and this was her big chance.

'I'm not in any hurry. I'm not going anywhere,' Taylor said gently, and then she kissed him. 'I'm glad you didn't tell me about all this stuff before. I never want you to think I'm here because of that. I don't care if we live in a rat hole somewhere. I just want to be with you.'

Phillip knew that without a question of a doubt, he wasn't worried. 'I know that. So do I. I want to have babies with you,' he said softly.

It was the second time he had said it to her, and he meant it. 'I never wanted kids before, because I was so unhappy as a child. I didn't want to make someone else unhappy, and I guess I didn't see it, but Amanda is like my mother, the bad side of her, the busy business side. I think my mom actually liked having kids and she loved us. Amanda is all about her work and her ambitions, and I don't think she'd be capable of loving a child.' Taylor would be the perfect mother to his children, she was just the right woman for him. Destiny had given him a great gift the day he met her, and another chance. 'How many kids would you want, by the way?' He had never thought to ask her, but it was obvious that she would want children. She was that kind of girl, and she loved kids, or she wouldn't be an elementary school teacher.

'I've always wanted four,' she said, looking dreamy for a minute. And with him, they could afford them. She had always thought that in real life she'd have to settle for one or two. Phillip looked startled.

'Could we start with one, and see how it goes?' he said, looking strangled, and she laughed at him and kissed him again.

'They usually come one at a time.'

'Not always. And I'm getting a late start.'

'We'll make up for lost time. Maybe two sets of twins would do it,' she teased him.

'I think I'm going to faint,' he said, and pretended to collapse on the sand. It was utterly amazing to him that a little over two months before he had been living with Amanda, and now he was here with this remarkable young girl, talking about having four children, and planning their future as though it were the most natural thing in the world. 'It's amazing how life changes, isn't it?' he said to her seriously. 'One minute you think you know exactly what you're doing and where you're going, and the next you're ass over teakettle, and everything has turned around. It's kind of nice, if you don't mind the bumps.' He was happier than he'd ever been in his life.

'My brother said strange things happen in New York,' she said, laughing, 'and he was right.' She had told her family about Phillip by then. She had explained that he had a good job, was a wonderful man, was forty-six years old and getting a divorce. They were nervous about his age but willing to give him a chance if he was good to her. And they had no idea about his relationship to The Factory because she had known nothing about it, and now that she knew, she didn't want to tell them yet. She wanted them to be impressed by him, not by what he had, and the magnitude of that would be hard for them to ignore.

They walked down the beach together on Sunday, hand in hand. He said he wanted to take her somewhere for a vacation, maybe the Caribbean that winter for Christmas, and he wanted to introduce her to his grandmother before anyone else. She was the essence of the family for him, and what he loved most about it. He described her to Taylor as this adorable sparkling little old lady who loved to play cards. She had taught him to play poker and liar's dice. And Taylor said she was dying to meet her. He suggested they go out to Long Island to visit the following weekend. They had nothing but time ahead of them now, and wonderful plans.

They had just walked back into the house on Sunday afternoon, and were talking about packing to go back to New York, when his cell phone rang. It was his mother, and she sounded strange to him. Distant, frozen, shocked. He knew something terrible had happened the minute he heard her voice.

'What's wrong?' he said, and sat down as Taylor watched his face. She knew what those calls were like. She still remembered what her sister's face had looked like when they got the call that their parents had been killed.

Without knowing it, she held her breath, and so did he. He listened for a long time, and she saw tears spring into his eyes and roll down his cheeks. She went to rub his shoulders, and laid her face against his back, so he would feel her love for him, and her support.

The conversation with his mother was brief. All Taylor heard him say was that he would go back to the city immediately, and he'd come right out to Bedford as soon as he could, and then he hung up. He turned to look at Taylor then, and he was crying openly. His voice caught on a sob.

'My grandmother,' he explained in two words. 'She was playing cards this afternoon, and she went to take a nap. They came to check on her two hours later, and she was gone. She died in her sleep. You're never going to meet her now,' he said, sounding like a brokenhearted child, and for now he was. She was the grandmother he had adored all his life and she had adored him too. Taylor put her arms around him making gentle sounds as she cried too, and Phillip sobbed in her arms. He sounded like his heart was torn in half, and for now it was. Granibelle was gone.

Chapter 22

They packed quickly and closed the house, and Taylor offered to drive them back to the city. Phillip let her, which was unlike him, but he was distraught. He said almost nothing on the way back, and whenever she looked at him, she saw that he was crying, and she reached over and touched his face or his hand. She didn't know what else to do. She was glad that she was with him when he heard the news. She remembered as though it was yesterday how devastated she had been when her parents died. And his grandmother had been like a third parent to him. He was crying all the tears of his childhood, and for all the times he had been brave. Forty years of pain and disappointment were flowing out of him like a flood that engulfed everything as Taylor drove.

'I can't imagine life without her,' he said miserably. 'I was going to visit her this week, but I didn't have time.' But Taylor was aware that he had seen her two weeks before. One always regrets the last time one missed, but she knew how attentive he was to her. He went out to see her at least twice a month, sometimes more.

'You're lucky you had her for so long,' Taylor said quietly, 'and that she enjoyed her life right to the end. It's hard for all of you now, but it's a nice way for her to go.' She reminded him, 'She didn't suffer, she was happy. She played cards with her friends and she went to sleep.' It was a perfect death, but it had shocked them all. They had all believed Granibelle would live forever because they loved her so much. 'How was your mom?' Granibelle was her mother after all.

'I think she was in shock. She always does everything with us by order of age. I was probably the first one she called. I'm sorry to leave you, baby, but I've got to go to Bedford when we get back. My mom said something about making arrangements. I don't even know what that means. I guess the funeral will be in a few days.'

'Don't worry about it,' she said with a loving tone in her voice. 'I'm here for you. I'll do whatever you want. I just don't want to intrude.' She hadn't met any of them yet, and although they knew about her, this wasn't the time for her to suddenly appear. She totally understood that, and was a gentle, caring person.

'I'm glad I was with you when my mother called,' he said as they reached the city.

'So am I,' she said, and asked him if he wanted to stop at his apartment first. He said he had to get some decent clothes so she drove him there, and said she'd take a cab home after he left. She didn't want to delay him, she knew he was anxious to get to Bedford as soon as he could. The others would be gathering there, and were probably already on their way.

'You don't mind getting home on your own?' He looked worried about her, but he was concerned about his mother too. She wasn't young either, and this would be a huge shock for her. He had thought about it on the way back. At first he had thought only of the loss to him, and now he realized what it meant to her too.

'I'm fine,' Taylor said quietly. 'Don't worry about me. Just take care of yourself. Are you going to be okay driving? Do you want to call a car service?'

'I'm okay. Thanks for driving us in, though.' She helped him pack his clothes, and remembered underwear and socks, shoes and a belt. He had been about to leave for Bedford with only two suits and three shirts and nothing else. He didn't know how long he'd be there. He suspected they might all stay out for the week, until after the funeral, and told Taylor he'd let her know. 'I'll miss you,' he said sadly, and then started to cry again. 'I'm sorry I'm such a baby, but I just loved her so much.'

'I know you did.' She understood.

He wondered if he should call Amanda, but he didn't want to. He'd text her about the funeral, but he didn't want her there sooner. He wished he could take Taylor with him, but it wasn't right to introduce her to all of them when they were dealing with their grief and the shock of losing Granibelle. He wanted her to meet them at a happier time, when they could appreciate her. He was just sorry she would never meet his grandmother now. It was a huge, huge loss to all of them.

He kissed her goodbye when he left, and the doorman hailed a cab to take her to the Village, and she watched Phillip's car disappear up Park Avenue and hoped he'd be all right.

He called her from the road, and reached Bedford an hour later. He was the first to arrive, his mother said the others were on their way. Her housekeeper had come in to help. All of Olivia's children and grandchildren would be staying at the house, crowded into every room.

Olivia looked dry-eyed and strong, but she was shaken, and Phillip could see her hands tremble, whenever she picked up the phone. It was a terrible shock for her too. She had been close to her mother all her life, and Phillip didn't remember a single disagreement or argument between the two of them. He just hadn't heard them – there had been some, but not many. The two women had been inordinately close for all seventy years of Olivia's life.

'At least they're together now,' Olivia said sadly, thinking of her late husband, and her mother's sudden death that afternoon. 'Apparently she was fine,' she explained to Phillip over a cup of tea. She sounded as though she were trying to explain it to herself and just didn't understand how this could happen, although her mother was ninety-five. 'She wasn't sick, she didn't say anything to anyone about feeling ill. She was playing bridge with a group of ladies, and afterward she said she was going to lie down before dinner, and that was it. The doctor said she never woke up. Her heart just stopped, just like that.'

'I hope she won some money,' Phillip said, trying to lighten the moment, and his mother smiled. 'She taught me everything I know about cards.'

'She taught me everything I know about life,' Olivia said, looking stricken. 'She was always so wonderful to me. Even when we were poor, she made sure that I had everything I wanted or needed. She forgave me everything, all my stupid mistakes.' She looked at Phillip as she said it and he looked pained. He realized now what a tough time he had given his mother over the years. It seemed so much less important now, in the face of this enormous grief, and it reminded them all of their own mortality and how brief life could be, as in the case of Phillip's father. At least for Maribelle it had been a long, full life, although they had all hoped she would make it to a hundred and often talked about the celebration they would have for her hundredth birthday. She had almost made it to ninety-six, in remarkably good shape.

Liz arrived shortly after Phillip and she said the girls were on their way. Sophie was driving down from Boston, and Carole was catching the red-eye from L.A. and would be there the next morning at dawn. And John and Sarah had left Princeton with Alex half an hour before. The family was coming together, as they always did in good and bad times. More than an empire, Olivia had built a dynasty. It was at moments like this that they all understood it, and relied on each other to get through hard times. The last funeral they had experienced together was Joe's. That had been far more shocking, and Cass's misplaced anger at her mother had made it even worse. Phillip suddenly understood that now. Maribelle's death was much more peaceful. No one was angry. There was no one to blame. She had just slipped away the way she herself would have wanted, peacefully, after an afternoon of playing cards.

'Did you call Cass?' Phillip asked her quietly after Liz arrived.

She nodded. 'Of course. She's flying in from Dallas. She's on tour there with Danny Hell.'

'I hear he's a big deal,' Phillip said, trying to distract his mother, and she smiled.

'So I'm told.' They were both acutely aware that it would be the first time Cass had come back into the fold in fourteen years. And it took Granibelle to do it. Olivia knew she would have been pleased. She couldn't imagine a life without her, and neither could anyone else.

An hour later Sarah and John arrived, and Alex looked as devastated as they all felt. He went out to the kitchen with Liz, and they talked for a while. He said things were going better with his parents. They were still getting therapy, and he had gone with them once, to explain the way he felt. He said they were being more accepting, and trying hard, although his father had asked him if he thought he might change his mind one day about being gay, as though it were a choice, and they both smiled.

'Your father always was a little obtuse, even as a kid. I think it's the artist in him. He just doesn't get what goes on in the real world. He's got his head up in the clouds, or up his ass,' Liz said, and Alex laughed. He always liked how outspoken she was, and how honest with her girls. His parents weren't dishonest with him as much as they were with themselves. They saw the world as they wanted to perceive it, and as though everyone were like them. Liz had had some hard knocks, and was more realistic about the world and honest with herself. Alex wished his parents were more like her, but at least she was his aunt. And Olivia was his hero. She had handled his recent crisis perfectly, and he had loved staying with her. He was glad to be back in Bedford, but not about the reason why. Everyone was sad to lose Granibelle, no matter how old she was.

Phillip ordered dinner for all of them from a nearby take-out restaurant. The three siblings and Sarah, Olivia, and Alex sat down to dinner in the dining room. The housekeeper set the table and stayed to clean up. They talked about Maribelle all through dinner, and they told funny stories about her, and some of the outrageous things she'd done when they were kids. And this time Olivia added some stories of her own, which made them all laugh. It was a relief to remember the happy times. They all knew about Ansel Morris too, because of the hardware store he had left her. They thought he was a devoted beau she had never married, out of deference to her late husband, Olivia's father. What they didn't know was that he had been married for most of the time they were together. She had never told them, they didn't need to know, and Olivia didn't tell them now. It was a racy side to their grandmother that they were unaware of, that she had been the mistress of a married man. Olivia found herself thinking that maybe that kind of relationship was genetic, since she was now in the same situation herself, after being critical of her mother for it for a lifetime, until their recent conversation, which had cleared it up for her. She liked knowing that her mother had planned to marry him in the end, and that he had died before he could. It seemed more respectable to her, although she had no intention of marrying Peter.

When she called him to tell him the news, he expressed his deep sorrow for her loss and offered to drive out from the city, but she didn't think he should be there. The children knew about him now, but he was still her lover and a married man, and the children weren't close enough to him to warrant his being with them, and he understood. She didn't need to explain.

Sophie arrived from Boston at ten o'clock, and they all sat around till midnight and decided to play cards, in honor of their grandmother. It had been Phillip's suggestion, and they liked it. Even Olivia joined in. They played for money, as she would have, and the table got rowdy and loud. It was the perfect way to spend the night, thinking about her. She would have approved. And Phillip called Taylor between two rounds of cards. She could hear the screaming and hooting in the background and was surprised.

'What's going on?'

'We're playing cards in honor of my grandma. I just won twenty dollars from my sister, and she's mad as hell. And my nephew won ten from her. She's lousy at cards,' he said, sounding better than he had when he left. Taylor was glad that he was with them.

'That sounds like the perfect way to spend tonight. She would have loved it.' It sounded like a good Irish wake to her, although they weren't Irish, but it was the right idea. She couldn't wait to meet them all and hoped they liked her. Phillip said that after everything calmed down and everyone had done their mourning, he was going to introduce her, maybe on Thanksgiving. And for now, Phillip had a lot to do to help his mother. Taylor was grateful that he'd called. She told him that her heart was with him and all her thoughts, and he told her that he loved her.

* * *

Liz walked her mother to her room that night when Olivia was ready to go to bed. She looked tired and more her age than she did normally. This had been very hard for her. It was the end of an era.

'I was lucky to have her this long,' she said to her daughter, and put her arms around her. They were both wondering what it would be like to have Cass home, but neither said it, and Liz stayed with her until she undressed and got into bed. And then Liz went back to the others, and had a drink with her brothers and Sarah. Alex had gone to bed by then too, after hanging out with Sophie for a while, and bringing her up to date on everything that had happened with him in the last month. She told him that she'd always known he was gay, even when he was a little kid. She said his parents would probably adjust eventually. Alex was beginning to think so too, after a very bumpy start.

The three siblings sat drinking wine after Sarah went to bed. It was comforting to be together, and Liz asked Phillip about his divorce.

'It's going to be a mess,' he said, resigned to the reality of it. 'I'm beginning to think it was always about money with her.' Their mother had long thought so, although she had never said it to him. It would have been too wounding and would have caused yet more problems between them, but she had always said it to Maribelle. And Liz always thought so too.

'What's with the new woman in your life?' Liz was curious to hear about her, and hoped she was better than the last one. But she had done no better than he in the marriage market.

'She's wonderful. You'll love her. I didn't think she should come here now. But you'll meet her soon,' he promised. Eventually they all went to bed, sad, but grateful to be together, to give each other strength.

Liz got up when Carole arrived from California. It was early, but she heard her come in and went to greet her, and Sophie joined them a few minutes later. They went out to the kitchen for coffee, since the housekeeper hadn't come in yet, and then Olivia came in, looking tired but with a clean face and freshly brushed hair, in a satin dressing gown. And within half an hour the whole family was there. They were up early, and talking animatedly at the breakfast table, when the doorbell rang. Liz went to get it, and Cass walked in. The two sisters looked at each other and put their arms around each other. Liz hadn't seen her in years.

'Wow! Are you beautiful!' she said, and Cass laughed. She was wearing tight black leather pants, a tank top, a leather jacket, and high heels, with her hair short and spiked. 'You are *hot*!' Liz said, and Cass laughed again. They were happy to see each other, and walked into the kitchen together, and for a moment everything stopped as they all stared at her. Olivia was the first one on her feet, hugged her, and then the conversation exploded at the table again as everyone got up to greet her, and looked happy to see her. The prodigal daughter had returned.

She sat down at the table with them, ate a piece of toast, and told them about the tour with Danny Hell. They had a thousand minor problems, but it was going well, until this bad news about Granibelle. She looked as devastated as they all did, but by the end of breakfast it felt as though she had never left. She didn't seem angry anymore, just sad about her grandmother. Granibelle was the focus of it all.

And that afternoon was hard for all of them. Olivia had made the arrangements, with Liz and Phillip's help. Her mother's body had been taken to a funeral parlor in Bedford, and there would be a viewing for the family, if they wished it. But Olivia requested a closed casket, and they were going to the funeral parlor that afternoon to pay their respects. Phillip had offered to pick up the clothes Olivia had requested for her. They wouldn't see her in them, but Olivia wanted her mother properly dressed. And Phillip, to lighten the moment, said he was going to throw in a deck of cards.

But the moment was painful for them all. They all cried as they stood around the casket, in the small chapel. There were white roses and orchids all around that Olivia had ordered, and a heavy scent of flowers in the air. And Olivia broke down in Liz's arms at the enormous sorrow of losing her wonderful mother. And then she knelt and said a few moments of prayers, as they fell silent, heavily impacted by the sudden awareness that this was all too real. Granibelle was gone.

They were somber and silent when they got back to the house, and discussed what to do next. The funeral was in two days and they decided to stay in Bedford together, before they disbanded. Phillip, John, and Olivia had a phone meeting with the office, and everything was in control. This was a family time and none of them wanted to leave until after Maribelle's funeral.

And Peter came out to visit Olivia that evening after work.

'How are you holding up?' He was worried about her. He knew it was a terrible shock and an enormous loss, and there had been no preparation since Maribelle hadn't been ill or failing.

'I'm all right,' she said with a sad look, and he put an

arm around her and held her gently. 'It's nice having Cass home. My mother would love that. I just wish she hadn't died to make it happen.' Olivia smiled through her tears, as Peter held her hand with an arm still firmly around her shoulders.

'I'm so sorry, Olivia.'

'I know you are.' He patted her hand. He stayed long enough to see all the others and extend his condolences to them. Everyone was pleasant with him, and Phillip was polite, and then Peter left. And that night they had dinner together again. As much as a wake for her mother, Olivia felt as though it was a celebration to welcome Cassie home. She seemed surprisingly comfortable with her siblings, and even her mother, after being away for so long, and she was catching up on all the family news, and telling them a little about her life, which was very different from theirs. Her nieces and nephew were in awe of her and thought she was very cool. She hadn't seen them since they were children, and she was impressed by how grown up they were.

The next day they received visitors at the funeral home who came to pay their respects. And the following day was the funeral, which was beautiful and elegant and deeply sad. Olivia had selected the music she knew her mother would have wanted, including Beethoven's 'Ode to Joy,' which was the essence of her – light and beautiful and happy and effervescent. And after the minister, each of Olivia's children spoke about Maribelle from the pulpit. Phillip went first and told wonderful stories about his grandmother, remembered from his youth, and how she had taught him to play poker when he had his tonsils out when he was six. Liz threaded beautiful stories about her grandmother, and John explained how she had loved art and encouraged him to be an artist and be himself. And then Cass went up to the front of the church solemnly, in a plain black dress, black stockings, high heels, and a hat with a small black veil. She looked striking as she stood there and told stories that reduced them all to tears. She was a powerful speaker and a beautiful woman, and her love of her grandmother and how important she had been to her were evident in every word she said. As Olivia listened to her, she realized that her baby was all grown up, and had turned into a remarkable person who had tremendous powers of drawing people to her and focusing their attention. And what was evident to her too, as she listened to each of her children speak, was how much of a mother Maribelle had been to each of them when Olivia couldn't be herself. She had filled in for her and given them something Olivia never could have, and she felt guilty and grateful all at once. It

Danielle Steel

made her feel very small and insignificant and brought the point home to her all over again of what a remarkable person her mother had been and what an enormous loss for them all. As the family filed out behind the casket in the recessional, to the sounds of Beethoven, there wasn't a dry eye in the house.

They went to the family plot afterward and had a small service with only the family present, and then they went home to the two hundred people who had gathered there to mingle and lend their support. Peter stood close to Olivia most of the time, without intruding, and she was grateful for his comforting presence. Her children saw people they hadn't seen in years, and Cass was welcomed back by all who knew her. Amanda had been at the funeral in a serious black Chanel suit, but had had the good taste not to come to the house. Phillip thanked her for coming on the way out, and she looked moved by the service too. She was human after all.

And when everybody finally left, the family collapsed into chairs. They looked exhausted. It had been an emotional few days, and a beautiful funeral for the mother, grandmother, and great-grandmother they all loved so much. There had been a lovely photograph of her on the funeral program, she was laughing and looked as joyous and mischievous as she had been. They all looked worn out. And Liz was organizing a big pasta dinner, left for them by the caterer for that night. They had served champagne and hors d'oeuvres after the funeral, but Phillip admitted that he was starving now.

'Let's get out of our black clothes,' Olivia suggested. 'We need to lighten up a little. Granibelle wouldn't like us being so sad.' Peter had left with the others, and Phillip had spoken to Taylor dozens of times in the past few days. He couldn't wait to see her now. They were all leaving in the morning, after one last night together, and the next day, Olivia, Phillip, and John were going back to work, and Cass, Sophie, and Carole were leaving to go back to the cities they had arrived from. It had been an intense family time.

And dinner that night had all the exuberance and excited chatter that had been so typical of Maribelle herself. The pasta was delicious and the wine and conversation flowed.

They all toasted Maribelle, and then Phillip tapped his glass with a spoon and said he had an announcement to make. All heads turned toward him, wondering what it was. He was a little tipsy from the wine, but they all were. It had been an intense few days and they needed relief from it now.

'I'm in love with a wonderful woman and I'm going to

marry her when I get divorced.' A cheer rose from the crowd, and Liz said loudly, 'Goodbye, Amanda!' and they all laughed, and then she went next. It reminded Olivia suddenly of when they were children and made outrageous announcements at the table. She had an instant sense that her mother would have loved this and would have joined in with some outrageous announcement of her own. They were a lively group and carried away in the moment, with love for each other.

'I sold my book for a fortune,' Liz announced, and Sarah managed not to roll her eyes although she looked momentarily pained, 'and I think I'm dating my agent, although I'm not entirely sure. He's British and very handsome and aristocratic. But I am sure I sold the book!' she said, and they all laughed. Her not being certain if she was dating Andrew was so typical of her.

'Tell us when you know,' Phillip shouted across the table, and they all laughed again, with her but not at her. Liz was rarely sure of anything, for most of her life.

Alex got in the spirit of it then, looked around at his family, and spoke up in a clear voice. 'And I'm gay. And I am sure,' he said, laughing, as even his mother smiled, and everyone else chuckled, and both his cousins, seated on either side of him, patted him on the back for being so brave and coming out. No one at the table looked upset, not even his parents, and Alex looked pleased.

And then Cass stunned them all. Her return to the fold had been heartwarming and surprising enough. She could have flown in for the funeral, kept to herself, and left right afterward. Instead she had been with them for three days, like everyone else. And she seemed to have enjoyed it too. She had spent hours talking to her sister and mother, and trying to get to know her nieces and nephew, and had been a good sport about her two older brothers teasing her, as they always had.

Cass's announcement topped them all.

'I'm having a baby. I'm pregnant. I just found out. And I'm keeping it. And I'm not marrying Danny Hell. He's the father. I'm having it in June. And I'm sure too.' They all stared at her openmouthed for a minute, and then the conversation at the table exploded again as they all congratulated her, and her mother looked at her with a long, slow smile of approval. She didn't care that she wasn't getting married, she had come that far into modern times. She was just happy that her daughter had healed enough from the wounds of her childhood to want a child of her own.

'I'm thrilled,' Olivia said in a clear, strong voice, raised her glass to her daughter, and blew her a kiss.

'And as the oldest of the grandchildren,' Sophie said, taking over the floor, 'we love you, but we think you're all a little nuts. You're supposed to be our role models, Uncle Phillip is getting divorced and remarried five minutes later, Mom can't figure out if she's dating her agent or not, which is pretty typical of her, and means she probably is. And Aunt Cassie is having a baby and not getting married, and it will probably be born with a tattoo. You're terrific, guys, and we love you. Thank you for being our family.' They laughed uproariously, and everyone talked at once to Cass about her baby and congratulated her again. Olivia wondered what had changed her mind and made her decide to have a baby, but whatever it was, it seemed like a good thing to her, and she knew her mother would have been thrilled.

And as a final tribute to Maribelle, they all played cards until three o'clock in the morning, drank a lot of wine, and reluctantly went to bed.

They were a sober group the next morning at breakfast, ready to go back to their own lives, but in the bittersweet way of real life, the three days they had spent together had been wonderful and beautiful, happy and sad. And before they disbanded, Olivia invited them all to return for Thanksgiving. It would be sad for all of them this year without Maribelle, but Olivia wanted them to be together.

'And that means your significant others too,' Olivia said precisely. 'Phillip, you're welcome to bring Taylor. Liz, if you decide you're dating your agent, you can bring him. And Cassie darling, I would be honored if you bring Danny. He's the father of my next grandchild, after all.' There were tears in her eyes when she said it, and Cass hugged her mother before she left.

'Thank you, Mom, for everything.'

'Thank *you*, and take care of yourself and the baby.'

'I will. I just hope I don't screw up his or her life. I'm as busy as you were.'

'You won't make the same mistakes I did,' she said gently. 'You're going to be a wonderful mother.' Cassie hugged her again, and then went out to the limo that was waiting to take her to the airport. The tour had moved on to Houston, and she was meeting Danny there.

They had all agreed to come back for Thanksgiving, and it was only six weeks away. When everyone had left, Olivia rode into the city, to go to her office. She felt as though she'd been away for a year. And she already missed her mother. She had so much to tell her. So much had happened in the past few days, but somehow she had the feeling that her mother knew it already, and wouldn't have been surprised. They were the children she had brought up to be their own people, and follow their hearts, use their heads, and always be honest and brave. They were the same lessons she had taught Olivia, and they had served her well.

Chapter 23

The weeks before Thanksgiving were full for all of them. Phillip was in constant contact with his lawyers over Amanda's increasingly unreasonable demands. She was still threatening to try and overturn their pre-nup, although his lawyers insisted she didn't have a chance. She was using the threat to try and increase the settlement and alimony he gave her, and he finally gave her the city house just to move things ahead. He didn't want to live there with Taylor anyway, but he was keeping the cottage in the Hamptons. His lawyers were telling him the divorce would take about a year. And he and Taylor were happy in the meantime. All was going well with them.

John had his art show shortly after Maribelle's funeral and Liz, Phillip, and Olivia went. He had chosen some of his best work, and by the end of the evening, everything had sold.

And after she got back from her grandmother's funeral, Liz had had dinner with Andrew Shippers several times. They alternated her coming into the city for dinner, with his coming out to the farmhouse in Connecticut, which he was slowly helping her to fix up. He enjoyed working on it with her when he spent weekends with her. They were sliding into a relationship that worked well for both of them. And news of her girls was good. Sophie was excited about getting her degree and moving back to the city, and Carole was working on her father's latest movie and had decided to stay in L.A. She had finally found herself, and was a total West Coast girl. She had discovered her niche, and sounded as though she had grown up a lot in the past three months.

The relationship Liz was building with Andrew was exciting and fun for both of them. They were exactly the same age and had the same birthday, which he insisted was a sign that they were meant to be together, and for once in her life she felt confident and sure, and didn't feel she was making a mistake. The sale of her book had given her new faith in herself as a writer, and being with Andrew gave her self-confidence as a woman. And the week before Thanksgiving, the dramatic agent he'd been talking to for months finally came through. They wanted to make a movie of her book. He waited until the weekend to tell her, and she screamed when he told her. She was hard at work on her new book, and now she was selling a movie. And as soon as he told her, they went straight to bed and made love, which they usually did as soon as he arrived. The sex between them was extremely good, but she had fallen in love with him too.

He lay propped up on one elbow afterward, looking at her and loving what he saw. He had never been as happy with anyone, and they had a lot in common, and enjoyed sharing the literary world.

'Tell me something. Are you sleeping with me because I sold your book, and now a movie, and you're going to be very, very rich and famous because of me? Or because you find me irresistible?' he asked, teasing her as he always did. She loved that about him too.

'Both,' she said with a grin. 'Today, probably because of the movie, usually because of the book and the money. *And*,' she added for good measure, 'you're a terrific handyman, and you're going to keep my house from falling down around my ears.'

'That's a good point. I'll admit, my carpentry is excellent. I hadn't thought of that, although I'm not sure

I love the idea of your sleeping with the handyman. Have you ever done that before?'

'Never,' she said with a grin, 'but you're really good.'

'True, I am. So tell me, how much is your family going to hate me when I meet them at Thanksgiving? How much interrogation will I have to endure? Quite a bit, I imagine. For all they know, I'm just out of prison, which might be a bit unsettling for them.' They had been dating for three months, and he had met Sophie, but not Carole, when she came home for a weekend. Sophie loved him, and Carole was sure she would from everything she'd heard.

'My family is going to love you,' Liz reassured him. Andrew was never insecure, but he was nervous about them. He knew all about The Factory and its remarkable history, and he was curious to meet her mother. He thought she should write a book about her life, although Liz said she would never do it. Olivia was much too discreet and modest to write about her own life. He told Liz that she should do it in that case, but she didn't think her mother would like that either. 'Besides, my sister's boyfriend is going to upstage you,' she said about Thanksgiving, 'He's twenty-four years old, a rock star, and they're having a baby in June.'

'What a fascinating group of people you are,' he said,

intrigued by her, and the stories she had told him about her life and youth. 'I can hardly wait to meet them, although it's disappointing that the rock star will upstage me. Maybe I should get a tattoo,' he said, musing, and then he pulled her toward him, and suddenly they were both laughing, and he was kissing her and they made love again. She always laughed a lot with him, and she loved his sense of humor.

And when they all assembled for the Thanksgiving weekend, it was like Maribelle's funeral without the sadness. They were happy to be together and they missed her, but they chattered constantly, and the house was bulging at the seams. It was the first time anyone had met Taylor, and they were all interested in her. She was a little overwhelmed at first, but she was genuinely nice to everyone, and obviously madly in love with Phillip. She stayed close to him, and they held hands most of the time. And after talking to her for a while and walking with her in the garden, Olivia came back beaming and it was obvious that she approved. She was everything Amanda wasn't and everything Olivia had always wanted for him.

Liz and Andrew were the next arrivals from the city, and he charmed everyone with his quick wit and very dry sense of humor. He regaled them with stories about allegedly ghastly hunting weekends in England, and his misspent youth. And he assured them all that Liz was a very, very talented writer, and he was sure that she would be famous one day. It was music to Olivia's ears.

And the hit of the weekend was Danny Hell. He was funny, irreverent, and outrageous, he had a cockney accent an inch thick that Andrew imitated to perfection, and the two of them bantered endlessly in slang no one else could understand. He was young, talented, and hip, and it was obvious he was crazy about Cass, and he said he was thrilled about their baby, and played guitar with the kids while the adults stared in amazement. It was an utterly perfect time, as Cass watched Danny like a mother hen. Cass and her mother got a little quiet time together, and she stunned Olivia by asking her if she'd come to the birth.

'To be honest, Mom, I'm scared to death. Of the delivery and everything else. Danny keeps saying everything's going to be fine, but what does he know? He's twelve years old,' she said with damp eyes, and her mother was deeply touched. She gave her a warm hug. 'He's right, it will be fine. And I'd be honored to be there.' She couldn't believe that, after all this time, Cass wanted her at her child's birth. It didn't get better than that. And Maribelle had been right. It had all worked out in the end. 'I'll come and see you before then. There's a château in Provence I want to check out this spring, for next summer's vacation. We're going to need a very, very big place this year, with all of these new faces.' Olivia was expecting Liz to bring Andrew, if he was willing. Taylor would be with Phillip instead of Amanda, and Cass was finally joining them, with Danny, the baby, and a nanny.

'I'll be in New York a few more times before the baby,' Cass told her, and they went back to the others, excited about their plans. Cass felt much better about the delivery knowing her mother would be there. But she was still terrified she'd never learn how to be a mother. Labor and delivery seemed like the easy part to her.

Olivia told Peter all about it when he called to wish her a happy Thanksgiving. She was full of news about her family and described the newcomers to him, including the exuberant and exotic Danny Hell, who was basically just a lovable child. She could see why Cass had fallen in love with him, although it was hard to imagine him as a father. Cass would have to be adult enough for them both, which scared Cass even more.

Peter was with his own family for the weekend, as he always was for holidays, which was the downside of dating a married man. Holidays were not included, but she was busy and happy with her own clan.

'I'd like to come and see you on Monday,' Peter said before they hung up, sounding unusually official.

'Is something wrong?' She was instantly worried.

'No, I just want to have a quiet evening with you, after everybody leaves. I miss you.'

'I miss you too,' Olivia said softly. He was always the unseen person in the room. They all knew he existed, but he was never there when they were.

'See you Monday,' he said, and they hung up, and she went back to her children and grandchildren. Danny and Andrew were singing a cockney song that Olivia suspected was profoundly rude if they could have understood it. It amused her to see the aristocrat and the wildly successful cockney boy arm in arm, and all the others laughing with them. It made her miss her mother all over again, and before they knew it, it was the end of the weekend. It had been a huge success, and as they left, they agreed that the new additions had made it even better. Everyone was happy for Phillip and loved Taylor as they got to know her, and Andrew and Danny were a huge hit with old and young alike. And Andrew had enjoyed finally meeting Carole. They had spent a good two hours talking about the movie business, about which she was learning a great deal. She had found her niche at last.

Olivia stood waving at the door as they all left, more excited than ever now about their summer plans, and the baby who would be born six weeks before that, if it arrived on time. Unfortunately, all of them had separate Christmas plans, so Olivia wouldn't see any of them for Christmas. Liz and Andrew had agreed to rent a house in Stowe with John and Sarah, and Alex and Sophie were going with them. Carole was staying in California with her father. Phillip was taking Taylor to St. Bart's. And Cass and Danny were staying in England for Christmas – they hadn't been home in months, and Cass wanted to take it easy. But at least the following summer they'd all be together, and Olivia knew she'd see them individually between now and then.

'So how was it?' Phillip asked Taylor as they drove back to the city on Sunday night.

'Incredible. You have an amazing family,' she said, and he could see that she meant it.

'A little crazy maybe, but we all seem to get along. And now that my sister Cass is back, my mother looks really happy.' He was just sorry his grandmother hadn't lived to see her come home. But he also realized that her death had brought Cass back, that and her baby with Danny. 'I really like her boyfriend,' he admitted.

'So do I. And Andrew is nice too. Your sister really seems to like him.'

'I think this time she found a good one.' Then he turned to Taylor with a grateful look. 'And so did I.' He leaned over and kissed her, and they drove home reviewing the high points of the weekend.

In her bed that night, Olivia did the same, thinking about all of them and missing them. The house was like a tomb without them. She was glad she'd be seeing Peter the next day.

Chapter 24

As promised, Peter arrived shortly after Olivia got home from work, but he looked unusually somber, and Olivia was instantly worried. She had sensed it on the phone two days before and he had denied it. With the recent loss of her mother, reminding them of their mortality, she was suddenly afraid he might be sick.

They chatted for a few minutes about a worrisome situation that had come up in the office, a fire in their warehouse in New Zealand, and then Olivia couldn't stand it any longer.

'Peter, are you all right?'

'Yes, I am,' he said smiling at her, 'very much so.'

'You seem so serious,' she said, and he smiled at her and took her hand in his own.

'Something unexpected came up this weekend, and I want to talk to you about it, but I didn't want to do it on the phone.'

'Is something wrong?'

'Not at all,' he reassured her. He was still a little stunned himself. 'Emily has decided to go into rehab. I think the children talked her into it. It's long overdue, and it would be wonderful for her if she can finally stop drinking. I can honestly say it's ruined her life, and ours, and impacted on the children. We talked about it after the children left on Thanksgiving. She's very determined. She has the place all picked out, and it's supposed to be very good. They have a very good success rate, and she's prepared to stay there as long as it takes.'

'I'm happy for her,' Olivia said quietly. She knew what an agony his wife's drinking had been for him. And she was silently wondering what that change was going to do to them. Maybe if his wife got sober, he would want to end their affair. If so, she had no right to object, and she wouldn't. Emily was his wife after all, and Olivia had no claims on him. He was a married man. She accepted the fact that she had no right to him at all.

'As it turns out,' Peter went on, 'she wants to make a clean slate of it. She's convinced that one cause of her drinking was her unhappiness in our marriage, and I think she's right. It's an addiction, but we were never happy, right from the beginning. We were never suited to each other. She feels now that she wants to cut our losses. She's filing for divorce. And I agreed. I think it will be a huge blessing for us both.'

'My lord,' Olivia said, stunned. She had never expected that in a million years. 'Well, that is a surprise. Do you really think she's serious?'

'Completely. She had already called her lawyer when she told me. And we're in complete agreement about the divorce and the division of property. I think it will all be taken care of very quickly. And what that means,' he said, looking deep into Olivia's bright blue eyes, 'is that I'm about to be a free man.' And before she could stop him, he was in front of her, down on one knee. She hadn't seen that since Joe had proposed to her forty-seven years before.

'Peter, what are you doing?' she asked with a look of astonishment. She hadn't been prepared for this at all.

'I'm proposing to you, Olivia,' he said with his deep love for her in his eyes. For the second time in her life, a worthy man was asking for her hand in marriage. 'Will you marry me? I would be deeply honored, and I will try to make you happy for the rest of my days.'

'I'm sure you would,' she said with a lump in her

throat. 'But Peter, I'm seventy years old. I'm too old to get married.' She had never considered it a remote possibility for them, and she still didn't now. They had always had their own lives, and there had been no hope of their getting married as long as Emily was alive.

'As the French say very intelligently, love has no age. Olivia, will you marry me?' he asked again, and she dropped her face into her hands and then looked at him.

'Peter, I truly love you, but I can't. I've never considered getting married again. I never thought you'd get divorced.'

'Neither did I,' he said sincerely. And he had never held that hope out to her. He was an honest man. 'Emily is giving me a great gift now. We haven't been in love with each other in years. She knows it as well as I do. And with the hope of being sober, she wants to be free as much as I do. We don't belong together, we never did. But you and I do. I think we'd be happy together and a very good match.'

'So do I. But why do we have to get married? Why can't we just date, and do what we do now? Spend the night together when we can?' He was sitting in a chair, looking at her by then, and had come up off his knees. It hadn't gone as smoothly as he thought it might. He had expected her to throw herself into his arms, or hoped she would, after all these years of loving each other in secret. She suddenly wondered if her mother had felt this way when Ansel's wife died, but her mother had said they'd gotten engaged. She didn't even want to do that. She loved Peter. But she would have felt unfaithful to Joe if she married someone else. And she really didn't want to be married. She was comfortable with the way things were. He looked infinitely surprised, and sorely disappointed by her answer.

And he laughed ruefully at what she had just said. 'You feel too old to get married. I feel too old to date. I want to be at home in my own bed, with the woman I love. Dating may be exciting, but it's not for me. It never was.'

Olivia knew that he and Emily had married very young, and made a colossal mistake. She didn't want to make one herself. And she thought getting married would be, for her in any case, although maybe not for Peter. She wondered if he would look for someone else, and the prospect of that hurt, but not enough to force her into marriage.

'So now what do we do?' Olivia said sadly.

'I guess we go on as we are,' he said with a look of resignation. 'I'm not going to lose you, and I'm not going anywhere. I love you. But I don't consider this dating. You're the woman I love. I'll stay with you as often as you let me. I'll look for an apartment in the city. Emily thinks we should sell the apartment. I think she's right – it's a depressing place, it's seen too many unhappy times. I'll get something small, for me. You can stay with me if you like, if you want to spend a night in the city, and I'll stay here with you whenever you'll have me.' He was a very reasonable man, and he loved her very much.

'Peter, I don't deserve you,' Olivia said beaming at him. 'I truly love you. I just don't want to get married. But if I did, it would be you. I promise you that.' He believed her, and he had the hope that eventually she might change her mind. Olivia knew she wouldn't. She was sure.

They talked about his divorce for a few more minutes. It was an amazing development in their lives. And things were going to be so much simpler. They could go out in public, he could escort her places, they might travel together, and they could spend holidays together at last. He was a free man.

And then, after they had sorted it all out, they wandered into her bedroom. He still couldn't keep his hands off her after all these years, and they made love, to celebrate not their engagement, as he had hoped, but the freedom of their love.

Afterward she lay looking at him and gently touched

his face, trying to find an explanation for herself for why she didn't want to marry him, even though she loved him.

'Maybe I just like living in sin better,' she said, and he laughed and pulled her closer to him.

'You're an evil woman, Olivia Grayson,' he teased her, and she giggled mischievously, feeling young after making love with him.

'Yes,' Olivia said happily, 'I suppose I am.' It was the only explanation she could come up with for not marrying him. And she found herself wondering if Maribelle would approve of what she'd done. One thing was certain, the world was upside down. Her oldest son was getting divorced and married again, which she was pleased about, Liz 'thought' she was having an affair but wasn't sure, Cass was having a baby out of wedlock with a rock star, and her grandson was gay. And she had just opted to continue living in sin after loving a married man for ten years. The world had certainly changed.

Chapter 25

Since all of Olivia's children and grandchildren had plans for Christmas, and both of Peter's were going to their in-laws, they agreed to be together for Christmas, quietly in Bedford. They had never before spent a holiday together, and they were looking forward to it. And Olivia knew it would take some of the ache out of missing Maribelle. She still felt her mother's absence every day, and reached for the phone at least once a day to call her, and then remembered she wasn't there. She knew she would miss her wisdom and her love for ever, and her gentle, sunny ways. Hers had been the legacy they would all cherish for their entire lives. She had given so much to so many.

But spending Christmas and New Year with Peter seemed like a good idea to Olivia, and Peter was thrilled.

He had spent morbidly depressing holidays for years, trying to compensate for an alcoholic wife. She was already in rehab and supposedly doing well, and the divorce was under way.

Olivia had her Christmas shopping finished early, as she always did, for each of them. She was planning to have dinner with all of her children, before they left for Vermont, and Phillip for the Caribbean, to give them their gifts, and now that Peter was free, she was planning to invite him. She had everything organized.

And in the first week of December, she had her annual mammogram. She always dreaded it, and feared that at her age, lightning could strike at any time. The Russian roulette of life. Her assistant Margaret reminded her of it the day before, and Olivia told herself the morning she went that she had nothing to worry about. Maribelle had never had any problems of the sort – why should she?

She recognized the technician from previous years, and everything went smoothly. It was never pleasant, but it wasn't agonizing, and she was reminding herself of how foolish she was to worry about it every year, as she got dressed and the technician came back in the room.

'Could you come into the office for a few minutes, Mrs. Grayson?' she asked, still holding Olivia's chart with films from previous years. She went diligently every year.

'Something wrong?' Olivia felt a chill run down her spine.

The woman didn't say yes or no. She just smiled brightly, and said that the doctor wanted to see her for a minute. Olivia's blood ran cold at the words. This was too much. First she lost her mother, now her health was going to start falling apart. And Maribelle had been in good health for her entire life. Olivia wanted to believe that that was some kind of safe passage for her, but suddenly she wasn't sure.

She walked into the doctor's office, fully dressed as though her clothes were a form of armor to protect her, but she felt vulnerable and scared. He had several films in a light box up on the wall, which showed her left breast frontally and in profile. It just looked like a mass of gray to her. He pointed to a spot she couldn't see at first, a little darker than the rest.

'I'm not liking this spot a lot,' he said with a frown. 'It could be the beginnings of a small mass. I'd like to do a biopsy.'

'Now?' She looked horrified and felt like she wanted to run out of the room, but her legs had turned to Jell-O and she wanted to scream, while pretending to be perfectly calm. But she was anything but calm. She was panicked.

'You could come back tomorrow if you like. But I think we should do it right away.'

'Do you think it's cancer?' she asked in a hoarse voice.

'It could be a small malignancy.' He confirmed her worst fears. Olivia knew that one in eight women got breast cancer, and she was suddenly petrified. What if she was that one?

'And if it is?'

'That will depend on what we find. Often with something very early, we can handle it with a lumpectomy and no further treatment. If it's at a more advanced stage we can talk about chemo and radiation, or hormone therapy. You have no family history of breast cancer from what I see, so hopefully this is very early and a lumpectomy would do it.'

'You're sure it's cancer?' For a woman who ran an empire, she suddenly felt helpless and small.

'No. That's why we want the biopsy,' he said firmly. 'Does tomorrow work for you?' No, never works for me, she wanted to say, but she knew she had to be responsible, and she was suddenly terrified of facing this alone. She didn't want to frighten her children, and she thought of calling Peter, but she had just turned down his proposal, she had no right to burden him with the threat of cancer if she didn't want to be his wife. This wasn't his problem, it was hers. She nodded at the time the doctor suggested, and left the room in a daze. The technician was waiting for her outside with her sunny smile.

'You'll be fine,' she said. Easy for her to say, Olivia thought, it wasn't her breast. She explained that they would make a small incision under local anesthetic, take out a small section, analyze it, and if necessary, after the results, operate to remove the lump. And she'd be fine. Easy peasy, scary as shit, she thought.

Olivia went back to her office, feeling as though she'd been hit by a bus. Margaret looked at her when she walked in and thought Olivia looked a little gray.

'Everything go all right?' she asked her.

'Perfect.' Olivia smiled a wide, fraudulent smile. She had decided on the way back to the office that she would tell no one, and if she had to have a lumpectomy, she would do it alone. Her children didn't need a cancer scare after just losing their grandmother. It would be too much for them, she decided, which meant she had to face it alone. She refused to tell Peter, and take advantage of a man she loved but didn't want to marry.

She spent a terrible night, wide awake, waiting to go in for the biopsy, and it was not quite as 'piece of cake' as the technician had promised. It was terrifying and painful, the anesthetic didn't work perfectly, and the incision was bigger than she thought. They told her they wanted to get a good sample so they didn't miss anything. And afterward her breast hurt terribly. She had planned to go to the office, but went home instead, and told her assistant she had stomach flu. She stayed in bed for the rest of the day and felt lousy, and when Peter called and said he wanted to come over that night, she told him she had stomach flu and didn't want to give it to him. She had never felt so alone in her life. Liz called her, and she listened to all her excitement about Andrew and her book. Olivia felt as though she were hearing her from another planet. She felt distant from everyone and very, very frightened. For the first time, she was aware of her own mortality. Her mother's death had brought that home to her. And what if she had cancer now? What if she died? Her children would be devastated, but she knew she had to die someday, just not yet. She suddenly wondered if she had made the right decision about Peter, which seemed pathetic. She didn't want to be with him out of fear or need. She felt weak and small and scared. She almost called him and asked him to be with her, but she didn't. She forced herself to be brave. They had told her they would call her with the results of the biopsy in five to seven days.

Olivia was back in the office the day after the biopsy,

and it was the longest week of her life. She told Peter she was still sick over the weekend and avoided him, and she spent the days alone, in terror. It was the following Tuesday when the doctor called. He announced it was 'good news,' which sounded debatable to Olivia. It was an early-stage cancer, and if no lymph nodes were involved, and it was contained with clean margins, he was sure that they could get it with a small incision, and get by with a lumpectomy, which he suggested doing as soon as possible. And they would have the results from it in a week, to determine if she needed chemo or radiation, or possibly get by without it. It all sounded like bad news to her. Merry Christmas.

She agreed to do the surgery on Friday, so she could recover from the procedure over the weekend. And she was seeing the children for their early Christmas dinner a week from Monday, so she had to be in decent shape. The doctor said she would be fine by then, with ten days to recover.

To make matters worse, Peter wandered into her office and told her he was hoping to spend the weekend with her. He looked elated when he said it. He was so happy about his new freedom, and what it meant to them. He could be with her as often as they wanted.

'I can't. I have to work,' she said tersely, not looking up

from her desk. She was afraid to look into his eyes, for fear that he would see the terror there. When she finally did look up, she saw that he looked hurt.

'Are you angry at me?' he asked gently.

'No, of course not,' she said, forcing herself to smile at him. 'I'm sorry. I was distracted. I just haven't been feeling well. This silly stomach bug I picked up, and now I have a mountain of work to do this weekend. End-of-year sales reports to go over.'

'Are you sure?' She could see that he didn't believe her and he was right.

'Positive. I promise, we'll play next weekend. I'm sorry to be such a bore.' This would be the second weekend she'd be avoiding him. He didn't look suspicious, he looked hurt.

'I could come out and read while you work,' he suggested with a hopeful look.

'I'd feel too guilty,' she said, feeling like a monster. She didn't want him to see her hurting, or know that she had cancer, even if it was 'only' stage one. It was her own dirty little secret. And she didn't want him to see her weak. She wanted him to see her strong, the epitome of the independent woman she thought she was, until the biopsy. He left her office looking sad.

The days until the surgery seemed endless, the night before a nightmare. Peter called and she didn't pick up her phone. She didn't trust herself not to beg him to come over and go to the hospital with her for the surgery.

She was at the hospital at six A.M. as they had told her. They ran tests, put in an IV, and at seven-thirty she was being rolled into surgery, with a feeling of total panic. She had never been so terrified in her life. And minutes later she was unconscious.

She woke up in the recovery room, feeling sick to her stomach. She was woozy, and by the time they wheeled her to a room, the pain in her breast was excruciating. They gave her a shot for the pain and the surgeon came in and told her how well it had gone. It had been very small, well contained, and if her lymph nodes proved to be clear in the pathology report, there would be no need for further treatment. All she had to do was get checked every six months to make sure it hadn't returned. Mammograms would be sufficient.

And then he told her she wouldn't be able to use her left arm for the next two weeks while it was healing. He had forgotten to mention that before, but fortunately she was right-handed. She stayed in bed at the hospital all day, dizzy from the pain and the medication, and at six o'clock they discharged her. She had arranged for a car and driver to take her back to Bedford. The house was empty when she got home.

And Peter called almost the minute she got in. She had to sit down in a chair she was so dizzy, and she realized she was foolish to be alone in the house. She planned to go straight to bed without dinner. She wasn't hungry. She felt sick from the pain meds, her breast was aching miserably, and she had a headache.

'Where were you all day?' he asked, sounding anxious. 'I've been calling you and you didn't return my calls. Margaret said you didn't come in.'

'It's that stupid stomach flu again, I'm feeling rotten.' She sounded it.

'Ohmigod, you sound awful. I'll come over and take care of you.'

'No, don't. You'll catch it. It's miserable.'

'Why do I get the feeling that you've been avoiding me all week?' It had actually been almost two weeks since they found the shadow on her mammogram, and she had been avoiding him since then.

'Because you're paranoid, and I love you.'

'I love you too. I want to see you.' He sounded worried and insistent, and she wasn't up to reassuring him.

'I promise, I'll be fine in a few days. And you're coming to dinner with the children a week from Monday.'

'I'm not waiting to see you till then.' He sounded horrified at the thought, but the truth was she wanted to give the breast time to heal, and have the pathology report before she spent time with him. 'I'll stay over this week if you want,' he offered. She didn't have the courage to tell him he couldn't. Then he would know something was seriously wrong, but she would still have the bandages on, on Monday, and even the following week. She'd have to tell him something. And the doctor said her breast would be tender for several weeks after that, and there would be a small indentation where they had removed the lump. Sooner or later she'd have to explain it to Peter, even if it was benign. But not yet. Not when she felt so sick and hurt so much, and felt so small. This wasn't the side of her she wanted him or anyone to see. The frail, human side. She was used to showing the world her strength, not her weakness. 'Let me know if you want me to come by over the weekend,' he said hopefully when they hung up, and she practically crawled into bed, took another pain pill, and passed out.

It was a long, lonely weekend. She did a lot of soul searching as she lay there hurting. She had done everything she wanted to with her life. She had created a successful business to leave to her children. She had provided security for them. She had lived to see her grandchildren, and she would see Cass's baby born in June. She had brought up her own children as best she could. She had loved two wonderful men. But suddenly, as she examined all of it, it didn't seem like enough. She hadn't taken time to play, to relax and have fun. She had been so busy working that it had taken precedence over all else for most of her adult life, if not all of it. The only time she took off was two weeks every summer for her children. She realized that she wanted to slow down a little now, not a lot, but enough to enjoy herself, and spend time with Peter. He meant more to her than she had admitted to herself. And she didn't have to marry him, but they could be with each other more. She didn't want to die alone in an empty, silent house. She'd realized that over the weekend, as she listened to the silence. She had never felt lonelier in her life.

She called all of her children over the weekend, and finally Peter. She felt a little better, but not enough. It had been depressing, but a revelation of sorts too. She had realized she wasn't going to live forever. She didn't have another hundred years to play with. She would have whatever she got, and she wanted to make it good, better than she had been, more fun, and gentler, and bask in the love of the good man who loved her.

'I miss you,' she said to him when she called him. This time she was the first to say it.

'I miss you too. I've been lonely for you all weekend.'
It was good to hear.

'So have I.'

'Are you feeling better?' He sounded concerned. He
had been for days.

'A little,' she said honestly. Her breast didn't hurt quite
as much, but it had been a jolt to her system. And she
realized she would have to tell him something at least,
she hadn't figured out what yet. The truth, or only some
of it. She hadn't decided. She wanted to tell him about
the epiphany she'd had too, but not until she was feeling
better. She had managed to get through this alone, but
she wasn't sure she wanted to do that again, or why she
had to. She had realized that it was okay to share her
burden with someone else, particularly if he loved
her. She would have done it for him.

She thought of him that night, and wished he had
been there for the weekend, near her, while she slept. She
wished she had allowed it, or felt that she could. There
was always a voice in her, telling her to be strong, and she
had been. But suddenly she wondered if it was so important to always be strong, to never let her guard down,
to run the empire with an iron hand. For the first time in
her life, all she wanted was to be a woman. It was enough.

Chapter 26

The week she waited for the pathology report was agonizing, and she got the results on Friday. It was the best she could have hoped for. Clean margins, no involvement in her lymph nodes, and the earliest stage of cancer. She needed no further treatment. It was an enormous relief. All she had to worry about now was a recurrence, which hopefully wouldn't happen.

And that week, Peter couldn't spend the weekend with her. He was going to Boston for his daughter's birthday. She was off the hook until he came to the early Christmas dinner for her children on Monday. She had been dodging him for days and he sounded discouraged. And she was lonely for him. He called her often during the weekend.

'I can't wait to see you tomorrow,' she said, and meant it. She knew he was planning to stay over after dinner. Maybe she would tell him then. It was the first time he was going to be at a family event with her children, which was important to her and to Peter. It was a turning point in the relationship. She had told Phillip after Thanksgiving that Peter was getting divorced, and he was pleased for her, even if she said she didn't want to get married. It was still cleaner if he was free. And now they could spend holidays together. Christmas would be their first.

'Well, get better by tomorrow,' Peter told her, with a little romantic lilt in his voice, and she almost groaned. She still couldn't pick her arm up, and then she laughed. Maybe he was right and they were too old for dating, particularly if her body was going to betray her and fall apart. This time the road to repair had been a little rough. She envied her mother's perfect health until ninety-five. She hadn't been as lucky, after her first brush with cancer. She knew that she was luckier than most, but it had scared her nonetheless. It had been humbling.

And when Monday night came at last, the table was beautifully set, the house was filled with flowers, the Christmas tree was up, and Olivia was feeling better. She wore a red satin jacket, and black tuxedo pants with a white silk blouse. Everyone looked very festive. Taylor had come with Phillip, and Andrew with Liz, Peter was there and seated at her right at the table. Everyone had understood by then what his role in her life was. For years, they had never suspected, but now they knew. And Phillip had passed the word that Peter was getting divorced. It was entirely respectable.

Taylor looked like a young girl in a pretty white wool dress with her long coltish legs, and dark brown hair cascading down her back. Sarah had found some strange macramé creation in a vintage shop that she was very proud of, and Liz looked beautiful. Andrew had worn a dark suit and looked dashing and aristocratic. And Olivia gave out their gifts before dinner. They were all saving them until Christmas, but each one had a pile of several presents that she had carefully chosen herself. As she handed them to each person, she saw Peter watching her with a questioning glance. He looked at her even more intently as she accepted their gifts with one hand.

'Did you hurt your arm?' He had seen her operating awkwardly, using only her right arm. No one else had noticed.

'No, I'm fine,' she lied, but she did feel better. And everyone was in good spirits. Taylor was wildly excited to be going to St. Bart's with Phillip, and the others were happy with the house they had rented in Stowe, and to be going skiing together. Liz had warned Andrew that she was a terrible skier, and he said he didn't care, and preferred après-ski activities to the icy slopes himself. Alex was planning to enter some ski races, and was a fabulous skier. And John was planning to paint while Sarah skied.

They had a delicious turkey dinner, with traditional plum pudding and hard sauce for dessert, which reminded Olivia of their Christmas dinners when they were young, with everyone around the table, and Maribelle cooking the turkey. In recent years, Olivia had a caterer do it, and it was exquisite.

She looked tired by the time her children and grandchildren left, laden with their presents. And she was saving their gifts to her to open on Christmas Day. She and Peter planned to exchange gifts then. He put an arm around her after everyone had left, and suggested they go to bed, and she knew the moment of truth was coming. She couldn't fob him off in bed, and he would see the bandage.

She came back into the bedroom in her dressing gown, and stretched out on the bed with a sigh. It had been a stressful three weeks for her, and she was still feeling shaken by it. Peter was already in bed and she could see from the look in his eye that he was about to get amorous with her. She looked at him with a serious expression and reached for his hand.

'There's something I have to tell you.'

'You're pregnant? Fine, I'll marry you. We'll have a shotgun wedding,' he said with a smile and she laughed.

'Not exactly. No, actually I've had a hell of a few weeks.'

'I had a feeling that you did.' He didn't look surprised. 'You sounded awful.'

'When I had my annual mammogram, they found a small lump. It was malignant, stage one cancer. They think they got it all, so I'm fine. I didn't want to worry you. I had the lumpectomy last Friday, and I was a mess all week, to be honest. It scared the hell out of me, and it kind of woke me up. I'm not ready to retire, and I probably never will be. At least I hope not. But I don't want to push quite so hard. I want to take a little more time to smell the roses, as they say. With you, if that's okay with you. And I thought of something else. I still don't want to get married. And you don't want to date. But I think I'd like to try living with you, if that appeals to you. You could move in here, if you'd like to.' She looked at him tenderly. He was stunned.

'Why didn't you tell me any of this, about the lumpectomy?' He looked angry, and she was shocked.

'I knew something was wrong, dammit. You wouldn't even take my calls. What do you think I am, some kind of fair-weather boyfriend? I love you. I want to be here for you, in good times and bad. I don't want you going through something like that alone. You don't have to be so brave, Olivia. You get to be human too. I'm here because I love you, not just for a good time. And I warn you, I am going to be very, very angry at you, if you ever do something like that again, and go through all that, and don't call me. In fact, I want to be here, as part of the furniture, so you don't have to call me.'

'I felt stupid that I didn't. I was miserable. And scared. I was so shocked at first, I didn't know what to do. And then I was in the middle of it, and I just kept going. I promise I won't do anything like it again. And what do you think about my other idea, about living together?'

He leaned over and kissed her then. 'I think I may have to, otherwise I'll never know what you're up to. I don't trust you.' He still hadn't gotten over what she'd told him, and he was upset about it. 'I can't believe you'd go through all that and not call me.'

'I know. It was stupid,' she admitted readily, and she regretted it.

'Yes, it was. And I would love to live with you, Olivia. And I suppose we don't have to be married. I just thought it would be nicer. I'm old-fashioned, I guess. But if you prefer living like a couple of libertines, and that won't upset your children, then I'm signing up. Where do I enlist?' He was smiling as he leaned down and kissed her. And then he remembered and looked concerned. 'Does your arm hurt?'

'I can't use it for a couple of weeks.' She opened her robe then and showed him the bandage. It was bigger than he'd expected.

'My poor baby,' he said, as he put an arm around her and held her close to him, and a few minutes later they slid into bed and turned off the lights.

'So when are you moving in?' she asked him in the dark with a giggle.

'Is tomorrow too soon? I thought you'd never ask me,' he said, and turned to kiss her in the dark. 'Olivia, you are a terror, but I love you.'

'I love you too,' she said, snuggling up to him, and feeling safe again for the first time in weeks. They had come up with the perfect solution. And she loved the idea of their living together, and so did he.

They spent the following weekend moving some of his things in and arranging them around the house. They blended in nicely, and she had cleared two closets for him. Peter seemed to fit right in as though he'd always been there. It was just like their romantic weekends together, only better. He loved to cook, and sometimes he had dinner for her when she came home from work. They had gone to two Christmas parties together in New York. She had dinner with him and his children, who were warm and welcoming to her. She had called her own children once they made the decision and told them he was moving in, and no one objected. She hadn't told her children about the lumpectomy and didn't intend to, only about Peter moving in. And Liz had news of her own.

'Andrew is moving in with me after we get back from Stowe.' They had only been dating for four months, but it felt right to both of them, and he assured her that she needed a handyman in residence, which sounded good to her too.

'I'm happy for you, sweetheart,' her mother said.

'I think Peter is good for you, Mom,' Liz said thoughtfully. 'Maybe he'll make you slow down a little.'

'I've been thinking that myself. Just enough to have some fun and not work *all* the time.'

'You've earned it.' She had been working at jet speed and then some since she was eighteen.

'We're going to Provence in March or April to check

out a place for next summer. And I want to see Cassie before she has the baby. She says it's already started to show.'

'I doubt it,' Liz said. 'She's such a string bean. She's going to look funny pregnant.' Olivia was grateful that the baby had happened and she would get to see it born.

'I must say, we've turned into a very modern family,' Olivia commented. 'We're both living with men without being married, and Cass is having a baby without marrying its father. I never would have thought it. Do you think you and Andrew will get married?'

'Who knows?' Liz said honestly. 'It's too early to think about it. What about you and Peter?' She was surprised her mother didn't want the respectability of marriage, but she had gotten too independent.

'We don't need to. Maybe I'll change my mind later. But this is fine for now.'

'That's how I feel with Andrew.' They chatted for a few more minutes and hung up. Olivia talked to them all before they left for Stowe, and she checked in with Alex. He said things were going well, and he was planning to finish his college applications over Christmas. Stanford was still his first choice.

She talked to Cass in London too, and she said she was

fine and getting bigger. Talking to her made Olivia miss Maribelle more than ever.

She had opened her gifts from the children on Christmas Eve, and they were lovely. They were all things she loved and would have picked for herself. Even Taylor had given her a gift, a pretty scented candle, and Alex had given her a locket with his picture in it. She put it on immediately, and called him afterward to thank him. He told her he had picked it out himself and bought it with his allowance.

She and Peter had exchanged gifts with each other on Christmas morning. She had bought him some sweaters she knew he needed, and a beautiful Patek Philippe watch. He loved it and put it on as soon as he opened it. And then she opened the box from him. It took her breath away when she saw it. It was a beautiful sapphire ring from Tiffany, and he slipped it on her finger.

'It's not an engagement ring,' he said carefully, 'unless you want it to be. It's a living together ring for now, but any time you change your mind, I'll say a magic word over it, and presto magic, instantly it will become an engagement ring.' He kissed her, and she smiled.

'I love it.' She thought of the ring Ansel had given her mother that she had worn ever after and that was in Olivia's jewelry box now. 'I'll never take it off.' She admired it all day, every time she saw it on her finger. It was gorgeous and meant the world to her.

Phillip had also bought Taylor a ring, and gave it to her in St. Bart's. He had sneaked it down with him, in his pocket, and put it on her finger on Christmas morning. In their case, it was an engagement ring, and Taylor was stunned when she saw it. It looked like a headlight. He slipped it on her finger and asked her to marry him. She accepted, and would have even without the ring. They were now officially engaged, and he called his mother and told her. She congratulated them, and Phillip said he hoped the wedding would be next Christmas, after the divorce.

And in London, Danny had had a tiny red electric guitar made for their baby. It was adorable and actually worked. Cass laughed when she saw it and hung it in the nursery. And she told Danny it was exactly what she had wanted. He was thrilled, and said he thought so.

They all had a wonderful Christmas in their various locations.

And after Christmas, John had a surprise for his mother. It wasn't one she had wanted, and it came as a shock to her initially. He and Sarah had been discussing it for months. He walked into her office with a nervous expression.

'How was Stowe?'

'It was fantastic. Mom, I have something to tell you,' he said, as he looked across the desk at her. He had told no one yet, except Sarah, not even Phillip. He wanted to tell his mother first. 'I'm leaving,' he said, with a sad expression. He didn't want to let her down. But he had realized that he had to follow the path that was right for him, and The Factory had never been it. It was her dream, and one day Phillip's, and his son's, but it had never been his. He had gone to work for her to please her and his father and because it was expected of him. Now that was no longer enough. He had realized it during his counseling sessions about Alex. His son was true to himself and had set them all a good example. Now he had to be too. 'I want to paint full time.'

She was quiet for a long moment, thinking about it as she looked at him, and then she nodded. She had learned that lesson too, that you had to follow the path that was right for you. She tried to think of what Maribelle would have said, in all her wisdom, and listened to her mother's voice in her head.

'I respect what you're doing, and I want you to be happy,' she said, smiling at him, and he got up and hugged her with a look of relief.

'You're not angry?'

'How could I be? You've worked here for eighteen years. You've done your bit. If you want to be an artist, you should be. Just give me time to find someone who can take over creative and design, and then you're free.'

'Of course,' he said reasonably. 'I already have some ideas.' He'd been thinking about it for weeks.

'Have you told Phillip?'

'Not yet. I wanted to tell you first. Only Sarah knows, not even Alex.'

'Thank you,' she said gratefully, 'for everything you've done.' She walked him out of her office and then went back and sat down, thinking about it. It would be sad losing him at work, but he had to do what he believed was right. She looked out the window then and saw that it was snowing. There was a thick layer of snow on the ground. It looked beautiful. She wanted to go for a walk in it with Peter, and maybe they would when they got home to Bedford that afternoon. She wanted to take time to do things like that now. To walk in the snow, to spend weekends with Peter, to go to London to see Cass. She walked to her desk with a smile and went back to work, and she had the strong impression that her mother would have been proud of her. She could feel it.

Chapter 27

In March, Olivia and Peter took the trip she'd been talking about for months. She combined it with business, as
usual, and spent two days at their store outside Paris, and
another day in Bordeaux, and then they traveled to
Provence to look at the château. It was incredible and
enormous, in beautiful condition, fully staffed, and there
was room for everyone. The gardens had been designed
by Le Nôtre, who had done the gardens at Versailles, with
arbors, miles of rose gardens, and a maze. It had been the
summer palace of one of the mistresses of Louis XV, and
had miraculously escaped being destroyed during the
Revolution. Its current owner had fully restored it to even
more than it had once been. Olivia was planning to stay
there for a month with Peter, and the children were

coming for two weeks, unless they wanted to stay longer. It was the longest vacation she'd ever taken.

She and Peter spent the nights as guests there, and they agreed that her family was going to love it. She had invited Peter's children to join them. There was room for them all, with some twenty or twenty-five bedrooms lining the long halls.

They explored the area over the weekend, and were delighted with their decision, and from there they went to London to see Cassie. She was six months pregnant by then and looked enormous, and they knew it was a boy. Danny was beside himself with excitement and wanted his band to play at the birth, which Cass had vetoed. She promised to let them play for the baby the minute they got home.

Olivia was happy to see her, and they went shopping for the baby, and bought stacks of tiny clothes, and furniture for the nursery. Danny had had a tiny piano made to match the guitar.

'I'm not sure I can keep him calm until the birth,' Cass said to her mother. 'He wants to see the baby, especially now that he knows it's a boy.'

'It won't be long,' Olivia said, enjoying her daughter. 'Only three more months.'

'It's so scary, Mom. I wonder if I'll ever feel ready, I'm so afraid I'll do something wrong.'

Danielle Steel

'You won't.' Cass had just turned thirty-five, and they had just hired their nanny. Olivia told her about the château in Provence then. It seemed like the perfect place for them that summer. They had loved the boat the year before, but it seemed too complicated with a baby. He would only be six weeks old when they gathered in Provence.

She spent two days with Cass, wandering and shopping and helping her get the nursery ready, and then she spent two days in their London stores. Peter had friends in London, so he was busy, and at home John was training his replacement so he could leave in May. All of them were busy, and Alex called her while they were still in London. He had gotten into Stanford and was over-joyed, and she told him how proud of him she was.

Sophie was working in the New York store by then, in a training program for management. Olivia was thinking of sending her to London in a few months, and Cass had offered to have her stay with them until she found an apartment. Everyone was busy and had plans of their own.

Peter and Olivia went from London to Milan and then to Paris again for work. Olivia found everything in order, and then they went back to New York.

The next three months flew by, and Olivia had her

follow-up mammogram before she went back to London and everything was fine. This time she was going to London alone to wait for Cass's baby. And Peter was going to join her once it came.

When she got to London and saw her daughter, she almost burst out laughing. She had never seen anyone so huge. It was all in her belly. Danny could hardly contain himself – he put his mouth to her enormous belly and talked to the baby all the time. Sometimes he sang to it or played music, and he swore his son was going to be a musical genius. Cassie seemed amused by his antics, and he spent an afternoon taking Olivia around in his bright red Rolls, and she had a ball.

The baby was two days late when Cass had her first labor pains. She was calm and peaceful about it, told her mother what had happened, and shortly after, her waters broke, and they took her to the hospital. And Danny sang to her all the way.

'I love you, but I think you'd better shut up now. The pains are getting bad,' she told him between contractions, and he stopped singing and held her hand.

'It's going to be all right, you know,' he told her in a gentle voice. He was a child at times, but when she needed him to be, he was a man. Olivia watched them quietly, and then helped her into the wheelchair at the hospital. Olivia and Danny were given hospital pajamas to change into while the midwife examined Cassie, and Danny turned to Olivia in the room where they were putting on the pajamas.

'You know how much I love her, don't you?' he said to Olivia, and the person talking to her was no child. As playful as he had been before to distract Cassie, he was entirely serious now.

'Yes, I do.'

'And the baby. I would die for them, I would. I love your daughter more than life. There's nothing I wouldn't do for her. She's a fantastic woman. I'd be nothing without her.'

'Just be good to each other,' Olivia said gently. 'That's all you have to do.' She was thinking of Joe when she said it, and all the children they had had, who had turned out to be wonderful people, and now even Cassie was back in the fold.

'I will, I promise,' Danny said solemnly, and then he kissed Olivia, and she smiled.

'I know you will, Danny. Now let's go and meet your son.'

'Right on, Grandma. Off we go,' he said, and propelled her out the door, and when they found Cassie in the labor room, the pains had gotten bad. The nurse had told her she was dilated to four. But with a first baby, she had a long way to go. Many hours.

For the next eight hours, Olivia watched Danny massage her back, hold her hand, rub her neck, croon softly to her, and dry her tears when she was crying and saying she couldn't take it anymore. She had wanted to have it naturally and then changed her mind and wanted an epidural, and by then it was too late. Danny stood on one side of her and Olivia on the other, urging her on, and Danny held her aching shoulders when they told her she could start to push. She was exhausted by then and looked at her mother in despair.

'I can't, Mom, I can't . . . it hurts too much.' She was crying, and Danny looked beside himself. His eyes implored Olivia to help them, and there was nothing she could do except hold Cassie's hand. Cassie got a minute's respite and started pushing again, as the midwife told her she could see the baby's hair, which suddenly gave Cass a second wind. She worked harder than Olivia had ever seen any woman work, while tears streamed down her cheeks and Danny's, and then they heard a powerful cry and a long, thin wail. The baby was out, and he was a big, beautiful, bouncing little boy, as Danny clung to Cass and told her how much he loved her. She looked around with amazement to see her baby, and Olivia cried watching all three of them. The midwife let Danny cut the cord and hand his baby to Cassie, and then they handed it to Olivia, and all she could think of was Maribelle and how much her own children had meant to her. Olivia was carried away on a tidal wave of joy.

'You were fantastic!' Danny said to Cass, as their son nursed at her breast. Olivia bent down to kiss her daughter's cheek, and Cass smiled at her mother.

'Thank you for being here, Mom. I couldn't have done it without you and Danny.' And she meant it. Olivia knew at that moment that she had her daughter back for ever and her sins had been forgiven her. It was the most beautiful moment of her life since her own children were born.

'What are you going to call him?' Olivia asked them. She felt closer to Danny than she ever knew she could. They had a bond they would share for ever, this precious child, who was sleeping peacefully in his mother's arms and weighed just over ten pounds.

'Harry. Harry Hell,' Danny answered, and Cass nodded, looking pleased.

'That'll work,' Olivia said, smiling at them with an enormous sense of peace. It didn't matter to her at all that they weren't married. All the same ties were there as if they were, and she knew how much Danny cared about

Cass. He was young, but he was a man. And his son would help him grow.

'I want to have four more,' Danny said, as Cass groaned loudly. 'Could we wait a while?'

'Sure, I'll give you a week, then I'll have you knocked up again,' he said in his strongest cockney accent, and they all laughed, even the midwife who was sewing Cass up where she had torn. But she was so happy holding her baby, she couldn't feel a thing.

Olivia left them for a few minutes and went to call Peter then. 'We have a big, beautiful baby boy,' Olivia said proudly. 'Ten pounds.'

'How's Cass?' he asked, sounding concerned.

'I've never seen her happier, and Danny was great.'

'I'll be there tomorrow,' he said. 'I'll catch the first plane out.'

'I can't wait to see you,' she said, sounding excited. Watching her grandson's birth had been a miracle she knew she'd never forget. It was the final healing for her and Cass, and she was so grateful to have been asked.

When she walked back into the room, Cass and Danny were beaming at each other, and the midwife had gone. 'We're getting married,' Cass told her mother.

'I just proposed,' Danny explained.

'Well, it's about goddamned time,' Olivia teased them,

happy for them. 'Peter will be here tomorrow.' But she was planning to stay another week until Cass got settled at home, and she'd be back in a month to get organized at the château before everyone arrived.

'Can we get married in Provence when everyone is together?' Cass asked her mother. Olivia loved the idea, and so did Danny.

'I'll get everything organized.' Olivia beamed at her. She'd just seen a birth, now she was going to organize a wedding. She loved being part of Cass's life again, in ways she never had been before. They shared an intimacy now that they had never had. 'All you have to do is pick the day.'

She stayed with them for another hour until they took Cass to a room, and then she went back to the hotel. She wanted to leave them alone to enjoy the moment between them, and it had been a long day for her too. But she was so excited, she couldn't sleep. After Cass had called to tell her the news, Liz called her mother to see how it went, and they went over all the details. Liz was thrilled for her baby sister and excited about the wedding.

And Olivia was still flying high from all the excitement when Peter arrived the next day, at six o'clock at night. She'd been with Cass all afternoon, holding the baby and talking about the wedding. Harry was a gorgeous child.

And Danny was pouring the champagne like water. He was ecstatic.

She told Peter all about the wedding when he walked in.

'That sounds like a fine idea,' Peter said as he sat down in their suite. 'It's a beautiful place to get married.' And then he looked at her tenderly. They had been through a lot together over the years, and in the last six months, her brush with cancer, her reconciliation with Cass, the birth of the baby. He wondered if she would be more open to the idea and hoped she would. 'Any chance we could get married there too? Maybe a double wedding?'

She didn't answer for a minute, and smiled at him.

'It's possible. I'll have to ask the caterer, and get back to you,' she teased him, and he came to put his arms around her.

'I'll do whatever you want. I'm not pushing you.' He wanted to be sure she knew that, but she sounded more open to it and less adamant.

'Let's think about it and see how we feel.'

He nodded and kissed her again, and as she touched his face, the sapphire he had given to her sparkled on her hand. He was well aware that it was not yet an engagement ring, but he still hoped it would be one day.

Chapter 28

The day they all arrived at the château in Provence was like a three-ring circus multiplied by ten. Cass and Danny arrived with the baby and the nanny first, and Olivia got them settled into two adjoining rooms, with a spectacular view of the gardens, close to Olivia and Peter's suite. Phillip and Taylor flew in from New York with Sarah and John as they had the year before. Alex came with Sophie this year – they had taken a flight together – and Carole came from California. Liz and Andrew were the last to arrive, and they were planning to visit his family in England afterward. Peter's children and their children were coming for the second week, which gave the Graysons a little time alone before they arrived.

Dinner the first night was exquisite chaos and music to

Olivia's ears, they were laughing and talking, the kids were playing cards. John and Phillip played liar's dice before dinner, Cass and Danny showed the baby off to everyone, and to add to the general confusion, the wedding was the next day, because Danny said it was his lucky day. It was the anniversary of the first concert Cass had arranged for him. But Olivia had it all in control. She tried to convince everyone to go to bed early, to no avail. They stayed up half the night, playing cards and laughing and drinking, while Cassie nursed the baby, and Danny played a song he'd written for him called 'Oh Harry.' And Peter laughed watching all of them.

'Well, they're certainly not a quiet group. You've got a very lively bunch here.' It reminded her of vacations when they were young. Maribelle would join in the merriment, shouting and laughing and playing and even jumping on the beds with the children. But this was the best year of all. Cass was with them, Harry had been born, all her children had partners who made them happy and whom they loved and so did she.

She managed to convince them to go to their rooms at three o'clock in the morning, so they wouldn't be totally exhausted the next day, and she and Peter finally went to their room too. The château was working out perfectly for them so far, and she and Peter had walked through the gardens peacefully before everyone arrived. As always, Olivia had arrived the night before, this time with Peter. She warned him that it was the last peaceful night they'd have, and he seemed game. His life had been quiet for too long. And they were planning to spend two weeks alone after everyone left. So for now, he was ready for the fun.

The next day dawned spectacularly beautiful, sunny and hot. The florist arrived with everything Olivia had ordered. She'd hired a local band to play soft music in the background, and then dancing music later. The chef had the menu Cass wanted, they had beautiful linens to put on the table, and there was a canopy set up over the table to shade them from the sun. The wedding was set for seven that night, and Olivia planned to spend the day checking all the details. She wanted it to be perfect for Cass.

By six o'clock everything was in place. The minister and local judge were due to arrive any minute, since they needed to make it both legal and religious.

Danny had asked Andrew to be his best man since they were fellow countrymen, and he said Andrew spoke fluent cockney and would understand him if he got nervous. Cass had asked her mother to be her witness, and Phillip was walking his sister down the aisle. She had bought a wedding dress in London by a famous designer, two sizes larger than she would have worn normally, but she looked exquisite in it.

Everything was all set, as Olivia went to put her dress on. It was a champagne-colored lace, trimmed in ivory satin, which looked beautiful on her and was the right color for the mother of the bride, but pretty enough to look romantic.

Cass appeared at the top of the stairs with her older brother, and came regally down the château staircase and into the garden, with her mother walking solemnly behind her on Alex's arm. Cass held an enormous bouquet of lily of the valley, and Olivia a smaller one of pale beige orchids the same color as her dress. She knew Cass was wearing a blue garter, and she had lent her Maribelle's ring from Ansel as her something borrowed, and Danny had bought her a huge diamond wedding band at Graff's. And right before Cass went down the stairs, Olivia hugged her close and they exchanged a conspiratorial smile.

'You okay, Mom?' Cass whispered.

'I'm fine,' Olivia whispered back. Cass was the only one who knew what was about to happen. Olivia looked beautiful and hesitated for only an instant as she looked for Peter, and saw him waiting for her at the altar. And as she took her place beside him, the others understood. It was a total surprise.

Olivia's something blue was the sapphire ring Peter had given her, and she had borrowed a hairpin with a pearl on it from Liz that she had tucked into her upswept hair. Peter was standing at the altar with Danny and Andrew, and the ceremony began as both couples stood in front of the group, exchanging their vows in turn. Peter had told his children what they were planning to do, and they felt too awkward to be there, in deference to their mother, but had sent congratulations and would join them in a week to celebrate.

Danny and Cass were declared husband and wife first, and Peter and Olivia immediately after. The grooms kissed their brides at precisely the same time as the assembled company sent up a mighty cheer and the judge and minister shook hands.

'We did it!' Olivia said breathlessly to Peter after he kissed her.

'Yes, we did,' Peter said, beaming at her, and then all the Graysons swarmed around them, hugged each other and congratulated the two brides and grooms as Cass and Olivia looked at each other, and both of them thought of Maribelle at the same moment, and Cassie touched her ring. They knew she was with them in spirit and they were all together now.

Olivia thanked Alex for walking her down the aisle and doing such a good job of it. She was wearing the locket he had given her under her dress. And she and Cass both tossed their bouquets to Taylor later on. It was everything a family should be, and that theirs had always been: joyous, exuberant, loving, and strong. They held together in the hard times, and celebrated in the good ones. They had forgiven one another their mistakes, and learned from one another. The family Olivia had created was her greatest achievement, and as each of them looked at her that night, they knew that they were like her and at the same time different, unique, separate, and woven together. They were part of a tapestry with Olivia at its center. She was irrevocably a part of them, just as they were a part of her, and together they were whole.

Winners

Danielle Steel

Lily Thomas is an aspiring young ski champion training for the Olympics, a young woman with her heart set on winning the gold. But in one moment, Lily's future is changed forever, her hopes for the Olympics swept away in a tragic accident. Her father Bill has pinned all his hopes on his only daughter, and his dreams are now shattered.

Dr Jessie Matthews, the neurosurgeon who operates on Lily that night, endures a tragedy of her own, and other brave survivors also fight to alter the course of destiny and refuse to be defeated. When Bill builds a remarkable rehab facility for his daughter, countless lives are forever altered, and each becomes a winner.

Winners is about more than surviving – it is about courage, victory, and triumph.

AVAILABLE NOW